BENEATH THE WESTERN SKY

The Cowboy's Dream

Book 6
Home on the Range Series

BENEATH THE WESTERN SKY

The Cowboy's Dream

Rosie Bosse

POST ROCK
PUBLISHING

Beneath the Western Sky
Copyright © 2022 by Rosie Bosse

ISBN: Soft Cover – 978-1-64318-107-3
ISBN: eBook – 978-1-64318-109-7

**POST ROCK
PUBLISHING**

Post Rock Publishing
17055 Day Rd.
Onaga, KS 66521

www.rosiebosse.com

I would like to thank my veterinarian sister, Dr. Mary DeBey, for her advice given me throughout this book. All information related to wounds and treatment, both of horses and humans, was a result of her knowledge.

Thanks, Dr. Mary.

My Western Home

Oh! Give me a home where the buffalo roam
Where the deer and the antelope play.
Where seldom is heard a discouraging word,
And the skies are not cloudy all day.

Chorus:

A home! A home!
Where the deer and the antelope play.
Where seldom is heard a discouraging word
And the skies are not cloudy all day.

Oh! Give me a land where the bright diamond sand
Throws its light from the glittering streams.
Where glideth along the graceful white swan,
Like the maid in her heavenly dreams.

Oh! Give me a gale of the Solomon vale
Where the life streams with buoyancy flow.
On the banks of the Beaver, where seldom if ever,
Any poisonous herbage doth grow.

How often at night, when the heavens were bright
With the light of the twinkling stars,
Have I stood there amazed and asked as I gazed
If their glory exceed that of ours?

I love the wild flowers in this bright land of ours
I love the wild curlew's shrill scream.
The bluffs and white rocks, and antelope flocks
That graze on the mountain so green.

The air is so pure and the breezes so fine,
The zephyrs so balmy and light.
That I would not exchange my home here to range
Forever in azures so bright.

Dr. Brewster M. Higley, 1871
Smith County, Kansas

PROLOGUE

Thank you for choosing to read the sixth novel in my Home on the Range series, *Beneath the Western Sky, The Cowboy's Dream*. You will see the history in this prologue wound through the fiction of the story. May reading never be boring and may my "friends" draw you in!

The Texas Trails

The Texas Trail was not as clearly defined as we think of roads today. In some places, it spanned over twenty miles wide. Finding water was the foremost concern of the trail boss while crossing northern Kansas and southwestern Nebraska. Only a few major rivers could be counted on to provide consistent water. Smaller streams often dried up, and the last forty miles before reaching the South Platte were the longest, driest stretch of the journey.

Texas fever quarantines in 1873 affected Abilene, Ellsworth, and Wichita as shipping points in Kansas along with Schuyler and Kearney in Nebraska. As the Kansas quarantine line was pushed further west, the cattle trails followed. In 1874, John Lytle forged the Western trail from Bandera, Texas to Dodge City, Kansas. By 1876, most Texas cattle drives had abandoned the Chisholm Trail and were following the Western Trail, some continuing even further north to the higher markets in the northwest. Once the Western Trail was extended north to Ogallala, it was more commonly known as the Texas Trail. It entered Wyoming in the southeast corner by Pine Bluffs and continued north along the Wyoming Territory's eastern border, ending near Miles City in the Montana Territory (the borders of Wyoming as a territory were the same as Wyoming's borders today).

Demand caused the higher livestock prices in the north. Many new cattleman jumped into ranching to cash in on the cattle boom. In addition, the Indian agencies required around twenty-five thousand head of cattle per year. Combine those factors with the gold rush of 1876 in the Dakota Territory and the demand for cattle was on.

Shipping costs were also a factor. Many Texas cattlemen were frustrated with the Kansas Pacific Railroad and began to look for a less expensive shipping option to Chicago. The Union Pacific was happy to oblige but first that railroad had to establish shipping points along its line. As more settlers encroached on the grazing lands of Nebraska, the shipping point continued to move west. In 1873, it reached Ogallala and the small town was established as the terminus. It remained a major shipping point for the next ten years.

In 1884, the Kansas legislature passed a law that moved the quarantine line west of Dodge City. An outbreak of Texas Fever in western Nebraska that same year resulted in large cattle losses among local ranchers since domestic breeds were susceptible to the illness carried by the ticks. The longhorns were immune to the devasting disease. The following year, the entire state of Kansas was closed to Texas cattle from December through March. Nebraska livestock producers also asked for laws to ban Texas cattle. A few more drives followed the Texas Trail in the late 1880s, but the cattle drive era ended in 1886, twenty years after it began.

South Platte River

The South Platte River flows from its headwaters in the Mosquito Range west of South Park in Colorado across the northeastern side of that state. It is one of the two main tributaries of the Platte River. The South Platte joins the North Platte in western Nebraska to form the Platte River. The Platte dips through Nebraska and flows east until it joins the Missouri River at Plattsmouth on Nebraska's eastern border. Most of the way through Nebraska, the river is wide, boggy, and shallow. The everchanging mud bars make it difficult for even canoe travel, and the many islands are constantly changing. An 1849 traveler wrote, "Tis hardly possible to guess the width of the river as we seldom see the whole at once, on account of the numerous islands that are scattered shore to shore." Pioneers often described the Platte River as a mile wide and an inch deep.

A river of many names, the South Platte was first named by the Arapaho who lived on its banks. They called it Niinéniiniicíihéhe which can be translated loosely to Tallow River. Since tallow is animal fat, we can assume they meant Fat River. The early Spanish explorers gave it the name of Rio Chato or Calm River. In 1702, it was named Rio Jesus Maria. Finally, French trappers called it the Platte, the French word for flat. That is the name that remains today.

Ogallala, Nebraska—
The Town Too Tough For Texas

Ogallala began as a Union Pacific water stop in 1867. It consisted of a water tower and a section house. The name came from the Ogala Sioux Indians. They pronounced it Oklada. Ogala means "scatter" or "to scatter one's own."

The town of Ogallala is located three hundred miles north of Dodge City, Kansas. Although it was a logical choice as a terminus because of the improved/settled lands to the east and the lack of water to the west, Ogallala didn't become a railhead until the Union Pacific Railroad built cattle pens and loading chutes just west of the town in 1874. Cowboys drove the herds north and loaded them onto the Union Pacific trains headed east. Additional cattle went to the surrounding ranches and reservations. While some herds did continue on, for many cowhands, Ogallala was the end of the drive.

Once the herds arrived at Ogallala, they were pushed across the South Platte to graze on the open range north of the river. There were often ten to twelve herds of two thousand five hundred plus head of cattle each grazing there, waiting to be loaded onto the trains. Additional cattle were often waiting on the south side of the river as well. The horses were sold as soon as the cattle were delivered, and the cowboys were paid off. Card sharks, gamblers, saloons keepers, and soiled doves were always ready to help the drovers part with their money. Some cowboys didn't have enough wages left to buy a train ticket home to Texas. They were compelled to remain in the north country or had to mortgage their wages to get back home.

Life in Ogallala changed with the seasons. During the winter and early spring, the town was quiet and fairly peaceful. The herds began to arrive in June, and cattle filled the loading pens through August. During those summer months, Ogallala earned its name as the most dangerous town in Nebraska. This was saying something for a town whose permanent population was around one hundred. One Texas trail boss told his men to avoid the town all together. That became a point of pride and Ogallala soon called itself "The Town Too Tough for Texas." Andy Adams in his book, *Log of a Cowboy*, called Ogallala the "the Gomorrah of the cattle trail."

Conflicts between the cowboys who were often from the south and the northern soldiers were also common. The Civil War was still fresh on people's minds, and disagreements often led to fights.

The town did quiet down after the herds passed in August. It remained relatively calm until October when area cattlemen brought in their own cattle for shipment east.

Ogallala's boom time was from 1874-1884 when the large herds moved north. During that time, it became "The Gateway to the Northern Plains." The town was unique because most of the businesses were south of the tracks facing Railroad Street, and the town was only a block long. The two most notorious saloons were the Crystal Palace and the Cowboy's Rest. They were on Railroad Street which ran parallel to the rails. In addition, there were two houses of ill repute. Also on Railroad Street was the Ogallala House. It was a fine hotel known for its food. Two supply houses, the courthouse, and a shoe store completed the business district.

In 1875, a large jail was completed, second only to the jail in the much larger town of Omaha. The Spofford House was opened in 1875 as well, but it was built north of the tracks. It was an upscale hotel known for its luxury. In 1876, a small school was added.

In 1874, the first year that Ogallala became the railroad terminus, fifty thousand head of cattle arrived. By 1877, that number was eighty thousand and in 1878, it rose to one hundred twenty thousand. The younger cattle herds were sold to Nebraska and Wyoming ranchers for winter pasturing. A year or two later, those same herds were rounded up and shipped east. Longhorns usually went to market at four years of age and by then weighed well over a thousand pounds.

A large bronze sculpture known as "The Trail Boss" overlooks the Boot Hill Cemetery. The treeless hill that became the cemetery was originally called Mount Calvary but was later renamed Boot Hill. Most men who died violently were buried with their boots on which is how the cemetery received its name. Many of the graves there are believed to be those of cowboys and cattle thieves. However, Civil War veterans and some early citizens of Ogallala rest there as well, including a few women and children.

The dead were placed in canvas sacks, lowered into shallow graves, and marked with a wooden headboard. The cemetery was used from 1874-1884 although it is not known exactly when the first burial took place.

Boot Hill Cemetery was later abandoned and some of the original graves were moved. The graves of those remaining were neglected. No valid records were kept so it is unknown where people are actually buried or even who for certain is buried there. The community, with a grant from the Union Pacific Railroad, is now working to research and upgrade Boot Hill.

The loss of the big herds ended Ogallala's heyday. By the early 1900s, Ogallala had calmed down. Still, the cattle industry is a vital part of both the city's and surrounding Keith County's commerce.

Nathaniel Kimball Boswell

N.K. Boswell was a peace officer in the new Wyoming Territory. During his long law career, he served as county sheriff, Deputy United States Marshal, city marshal, penitentiary warden, and chief of the Wyoming Stock Growers Association Detective Bureau. According to history, he handled more outlaws than Hickok, Masterson and Earp combined, and he did it without ever killing a man.

Boswell moved to Cheyenne in 1867 before Wyoming was even a territory. He liked the new town of Cheyenne and sent for his wife. He quickly traded a claim he held in a Colorado Territory mine for a stock of drugs. With that, he opened the first drugstore in Cheyenne. Although he knew nothing of the pharmaceutical business, he was not concerned. He claimed there were plenty of unemployed druggists he could hire to run his store. That proved to be true and Boswell opened a second store in Laramie, fifty miles west of Cheyenne.

Lawlessness was a problem in both new communities and Boswell soon joined the local Citizen's Committee, just one of many vigilante groups formed to fight crime. The actions of the vigilantes proved effective, and many outlaw members were caught.

In 1869, Albany County was organized in the Wyoming Territory. This huge county stretched north from the Colorado Territory border to the Montana Territory border, encompassing four hundred miles. Boswell was appointed the new county's first sheriff. In 1870, he won his first election.

Woman's suffrage was adopted by Wyoming in 1869 and Sheriff Boswell summoned a woman to serve on the jury for a trial in Laramie in 1870, surprising many of the local residents. He then appointed a woman of "large proportions and commanding presence" as a court bailiff.

Although Boswell never killed a man, he was known to be deadly accurate with his six-shooter. He was said to have once brought down a running fugitive with a pistol shot at two hundred twenty yards. This took place in Red Oak, Iowa in 1870.

In 1873, a new territorial penitentiary opened outside of Laramie. In addition to his duties as county sheriff and Deputy United States Marshal, Nathaniel Boswell took on the position of the prison's first warden.

Tax collecting was a duty that came with the job of sheriff and Boswell despised it. He declined to run for re-election in 1872, serving instead as city marshal of Laramie. In 1878, the Albany County Commissioners asked him to run for sheriff once again, promising that tax collection would not be part of his job. He ran and was easily re-elected.

Boswell had no problem with giving prisoners a little incentive to share the information they held. He once hoisted an outlaw by the neck and lowered him continuously until the man gave Boswell the information he wanted about the leaders of the gang the outlaw was part of. The technique was effective and the two fugitives were soon captured.

Using this information, I made Sheriff Boswell the no-nonsense sheriff in this novel. As a man who had little tolerance for unnecessary actions, I doubt he would have been too excited to serve warrants on trumped-up charges, especially one against a woman where self-defense was a factor.

Old Shawneetown Bank

The salt works on Salt Creek were the most important contributing factor in the development of the first pioneer settlement at Shawneetown, Illinois in 1800. That salt was sold to the settlers of the area as well as to those passing through. The location of a federal land office there in 1812 was also important. The jail was erected in 1810 and a courthouse in 1815.

The land the town was built on originally belonged to the United States. In 1814, lots were auctioned off to the residents. The bidding was brisk and the lots sold for premium prices. Two years later, the city was flooded, and flooding continued to be a problem. Even so, by 1818, thirty log houses made up the settlement. Shawneetown and Washington, D.C. are the only towns in the United States chartered by the United States Government.

Old Shawneetown was the location of the first bank in the state of Illinois in 1813. Local legend says that the Shawneetown Bank refused to buy the first bonds issued by the city of Chicago on the grounds that no city located that far from Shawneetown could survive!

The first bank was built of logs. That was followed by a new four-story Greek Revival building of stone and masonry in 1839. Greek Revival was a popular style for banks of that period because it was believed the structure expressed the American ideals of liberty and freedom. It's style gave the impression of strength, solidness, and dignity. This was important since many banks and bankers at that time were viewed with great distrust.

Soon after the new building opened in 1841, another financial depression set in. The Bank of Illinois at Shawneetown suspended operations until 1842. Two years later, the building again stood empty and remained so for a decade until the State Bank of Illinois opened there in 1854. Other banking businesses occupied the building until 1942 when it was deeded to the state of Illinois. The Shawneetown Bank, located in Old Shawneetown, is the oldest structure in Illinois built specifically as a bank. It is now managed by the Illinois Historic Preservation Agency as Shawneetown Bank Historic Site.

Note: In 1937 a great flood hit southeastern Illinois. It forced an evacuation of Shawneetown. Much of the original town was destroyed and the federal government relocated what was left to higher ground three miles west of the original location. The new site became Shawneetown while the old village is called Old Shawneetown.

William Sturgis

A New York native and a Civil War veteran, William Sturgis moved to Cheyenne in 1873. He and his brother, Thomas, were two of Wyoming's early cattle barons. They founded the Northwestern Cattle Company as well as the Union Cattle Company. The latter was one of the largest ranching operations in Wyoming at that time.

They were also founding members of the Wyoming Stock Growers Association. Thomas was Secretary and William was Assistant Secretary for several years. Besides that position, William was also in charge of editing the Association's brand book.

William was deeply invested in the development of the new city of Cheyenne. He was director of the Stock Grower's National Bank in Cheyenne and was involved in the creation of the Cheyenne Electric

Light Company. In addition, he had extensive iron and copper mine holdings. When the famed Cheyenne Club was formed, he was one of its first officers.

William Sturgis built his historic Sturgis house in 1884 at the height of his wealth and power. However, he sold it two years later as a result of the heavy losses he suffered after the Union Cattle Company failed in the "Big Freeze" winter of 1886-1887. The house has survived through the years nearly intact. It still stands in Cheyenne today, an excellent example of the Shingle Style home popular in Wyoming's cattle baron days. The house was listed on the National Register of Historic Places in 1982.

William Sturgis was a mover and a shaker in Cheyenne history and I decided to make his story part of this novel. However, nowhere in the information that I read was a wife or a son mentioned. Those parts of this story are fictional.

Wyoming Brand History

Imagine holding in your hands a book that contains over one hundred years of Wyoming branding records. That book exists in the office of the Wyoming Livestock Board. The old, ragged, one-of-a-kind volume contains the first known collection of brands ever compiled in the state. It was published in 1899, ten years before the state of Wyoming took control of brand management from the counties.

Today, there are hundreds of thousands of cattle brands in the United States. About thirty thousand of them are registered in Wyoming. Of those thirty thousand, only about twenty thousand are actively used. Some people keep brands registered because of emotional or historical attachments even though they never intend to use the brand on livestock again.

America adopted its branding tradition from Mexico, but according to an article by David Dary on the Texas State Historical Association website, the practice may have started long before then. Egyptian tomb paintings estimated to be over four thousand years old depict roundups and cattle branding. Nevertheless, branding spread from Mexico to present-day Texas and from there it followed the flow of cattle and horses across the country. However, the brands used in the United States are simpler and much easier to read then the old Spanish brands.

Records do not show which brand was first registered in Wyoming. However, the oldest brand in continuous use would be the M Hook. The Yoke 9 was first used in 1857 by John Walker Myers. It was suggested to Myers by a friend that the M hook used in Pittman shorthand would be a good design. He embellished it and in 1942, it was being used by the third generation.

Mrs. Eliza A. Kuykendall, wife of Judge William L. Kuykendall, recorded her "rolling M" as the first brand in Laramie County in the Wyoming Territory on December 3, 1870. She had used that brand on her cattle before the family moved to Cheyenne in the winter of 1867. The M brand was later transferred to the Wyoming Stock Growers Association to be used in branding mavericks during roundups. It eventually became the official maverick brand of the Territory.

Some brands are humorous such as S. Omar Barkers brand of the lazy SOB or the infamous 2lazy2P. To be legally binding, the brand must have at least two characters and be at least three inches in diameter.

Wyoming Stock Growers Association

The Stock Association of Laramie County was organized in 1872 to combat cattle rustling. Five cattlemen met in a livery stable in Cheyenne to organize a vigilante committee to cope with cattle rustlers in the area. By 1879, it had been renamed the Wyoming Stock Growers Association (WSGA). Its purpose covered a wide range of activities including managing roundups, tracking cattle shipments, and verifying cattle brands as well as cattle health and public domain issues. By the late 1800s, before Wyoming became a state, the WSGA was one of a few large organizations that wielded any type of authority in the region.

In its early years, the WSGA was especially effective in eliminating cattle rustlers. Stock detectives were hired and paid with the assistance of the Laramie County Commissioners. Of course, right and wrong never stay on one side. Innocent people were caught along with the rustlers.

One of the more controversial laws enforced by the WSGA was the branding of "maverick" calves. According to WSGA laws, only members of the association could brand those calves. This rule obviously created contention and conflict between the large and the small cattlemen. It was one of the direct causes of the Johnson County War in Wyoming in 1892. The museum in Kaycee, Wyoming has some wonderful history on this conflict including the death of Tom Horn.

The WSGA still exists today. To become a voting member, one must raise cattle, horses, mules, or sheep.

Cowboy Music

In 1871, Dr. Brewster M. Higley, an ear, nose, and throat doctor, moved from Indiana to his new homestead in Smith County, Kansas. There in 1871, he wrote what he called, "My Western Home" while sitting in his little cabin. The song was published in *The Kirwin Chief* newspaper on March 21, 1874.

Higley's friend, Daniel E. Kelley, a Civil War veteran and musician, set the poem to music and created a waltz. Kelley played the fiddle and was a founding member of the Harlan Orchestra. The orchestra frequently performed the waltz at dances.

The song, with its lilting music and nostalgic words, was popular. It was shared by travelers as they crossed the country via stagecoach and train. Cowboys also sang it on trail drives, and the song spread quickly across the country. It gained huge popularity in 1932 when the newly elected President Roosevelt declared it his favorite song. That brought forth people who wanted to claim the song as their own and a legal battle ensued. However, there was enough proof that the song had been sung all over the west long before the would-be music thieves claimed that they wrote and copyrighted it in 1905.

"Home on the Range" as Higley's poem became known has been recorded by many artists and is the official state song of Kansas. The little cabin east of Smith Center, Kansas where Dr. Higley wrote his poem and raised his family has been refurbished. It is quiet and peaceful there as one looks out the door of the cabin and across the valley. It is easy to see how Higley would have been inspired to write the song that he did. "Home on the Range" is now one of the most loved and best-known songs of the American west.

"Streets of Laredo" or "Cowboy's Lament" as it is also called has long been one of my favorite songs. The song is a story of a young cowboy who is cut down in the prime of his life with a bullet to the chest. He knows he is dying and he wants to talk about the send-off that he will receive. The song is a ballad. That means it is a song that tells a story through a series of short stanzas. This type of song is easy to learn. It would have been easily repeated around campfires throughout the west, and especially on cattle drives.

An interesting sidenote is that the song may have its origins in an older Irish ballad known as "The Unfortunate Rake." That song is said to have been written in 1740. However, the earliest written version of the Irish song is from the late 1700s to early 1800s. It is called "The Buck's Elegy." This version of the song is about a young man dying of a venereal disease. The song is set in Covent Gardens in London, England which was then considered a popular location for acquiring the services of prostitutes. The young man laments the fact that he didn't know his condition in time to take mercury, a common treatment for syphilis at the time. If fact, one version begins with the line, "As I was walking down by the Lock Hospital." This is a reference to a hospital for the treatment of venereal disease. Other versions change it from Rake to

Cowboy to Soldier to Sailor. Some versions even change genders and make it about a dying woman.

Frank Maynard (1853-1926) claimed to be the author of the earliest Western adaptation of the song. Maynard told a journalist in 1924 that he was the first to make a cowboy the primary subject when he altered the words in the winter of 1876. In 1911, he self-published a poetry book that contains his version. However, his version differs from the most common cowboy lyrics sung with the song. Ah, the history of cowboy music!

Bear Sign

Bear sign or doughnuts have been around for a long time. The original doughnuts were not like we know them today. They did not have a hole in the middle. Instead, they were more like a pile of batter or dough that was fried in hot oil. In fact, one of the first names they were called was oilycakes.

Several theories are suggested on how the hole came to be in the center of doughnuts. Interestingly, those theories are attributed to seafaring men. After frying, the center of the dough ball was rarely cooked all the way through. The consumption of too much raw dough (which contains yeast) can cause digestive problems and even instability if too much is consumed since yeast plus sugar makes alcohol! A sea captain by the name of Captain Hanson Gregory claimed to have been the first to decide to punch a hole in the center of the dough before cooking. He did this with the lid of a pepper can. He stated that it was done in 1847 during a long voyage. Since he was sixteen at the time, I doubt that he was the captain. Perhaps he was helping the cook in the galley. Other seafaring men have claimed it was their invention as well so I guess we will never know.

That brings us to the name of bear sign. This was a western name that developed during the 1800s. When the dough was dropped into the hot oil, it formed a variety of sizes and shapes. Men who worked in the outdoors were quite observant and many believed the cakes resembled bear scat that was common at the time. Hence, the name bear sign. Even after holes were cut in the doughnuts, the tasty treat continued to be a favorite among cowboys. Riders quickly learned who made bear sign and they often rode many miles to get a handful of the crunchy cakes coated in sugar or rolled in glaze.

I did include a recipe for bear sign in this novel. That recipe was taken from inside the front cover of an old *Larkin Housewives' Cook Book*, copyrighted 1917. The recipe was written in the original owners handwriting and labeled "Doughnuts."

The Larkin Company was established in 1875 and many of the recipes in this little book mention Larkin flour, baking soda and other dry Larkin ingredients. Women from all over the United States were asked to submit recipes. According to an excerpt from inside the cookbook, over three thousand recipes were submitted. Of those recipes, five hundred forty-eight were selected to appear in print.

Since Martha, Laurel, and Grace were unavailable to submit their recipes personally, several of my friends copied those recipes in their original form from this cookbook. Thank you, Debbie Berges, Dianna Younger, and Rose Bernasek.

Historic Texas Ranches Mentioned in This Novel

The ranches discussed here were chosen for their location and the fact that they were early Texas ranches. You will see their names mentioned in this novel as well as in other novels in my Home on the Range series.

The Waggoner Ranch is a historic ranch located thirteen miles south of Vernon, Texas and is one of oldest continually operated ranches in Texas. Established in 1850 by Daniel Waggoner, it was and is still known for being the largest ranch under one fence. At five hundred fifty thousand acres, it spans six counties and is half the size of Rhode Island.

There is a more extensive description of the Waggoner Ranch in the prologue of my fifth novel, *Up the Western Trail, Point the Tongue North.*

The King Ranch was founded in 1853 in Corpus Christi, only eight years after Texas was admitted to the Union. Richard King, an Irish immigrant and then New Yorker, came to Texas as a riverboat captain on the Rio Grande River. There he met Texas Ranger Gideon K. "Legs" Lewis. They were the founding partners of what would become the King Ranch. That partnership worked well and probably would have continued had Lewis not expressed so much interest in a married woman. Her husband ended Lewis's life with a shotgun. Lewis had no heirs and when his share went up for auction, King was able to purchase it. King led some of the first cattle drives and worked hard to make livestock marketing easier for Texans.

Today, the ranch's eight hundred twenty-five thousand acres lay in four South Texas counties. Its Running W brand is well-recognized, not only on livestock but also on the Ford Super Duty King Ranch edition truck. The King Ranch is now a successful, multi-faceted agribusiness corporation. It is still owned by descendants of Richard King and his wife, Henrietta.

The 6666 or the Four Sixes Ranch is a two hundred seventy-five-thousand-acre ranch founded by Captain Samuel "Burk" Burnett in 1868. Burnett began his ranch at age nineteen by purchasing one hundred head of cattle wearing the 6666 brand from Frank Crowley of Denton, Texas. He also received the brand with that purchase. (Sorry, no card game story here!) Burnett drove longhorns up the Chisholm Trail from South Texas. He leased land before buying the acreage in King County that would become the 6666 Ranch. The ranch currently has three locations across west Texas.

The Hashknife Ranch was begun in 1875 by J.R. Couts and John N. Simpson when they drove a herd of longhorns from Weatherford, Texas to what is now Abilene, Texas. A dugout on a creek bank became the ranch headquarters. Their brand was unusual because it resembled a hash knife—a common kitchen tool at the time used to chop meat and vegetables. The brand would have been nearly impossible to alter so was effective against rustlers. In 1881, Simpson and two new partners purchased the Miller Creek Ranch from the Millett brothers. The Hashknife was known as a tough, no-nonsense outfit.

The Miller Ranch was owned by the Millett brothers. Eugene C., Alonzo, and Hiram Millett came from Guadalupe County in South Texas to Baylor County to begin ranching in 1879. They were rough and armed their riders for the purpose of intimidating settlers to move off the open range, including the citizens of the new town of Seymour. I did use them as part of this novel although I tweaked the years just a bit.

The Thume family is fictional. However, their characters fit what the bad element of society could have been like in the 1870s.

* * *

Be sure to ask for all my books at your local libraries and bookstores!

Rosie Bosse
17055 Day Rd. Onaga, KS 66521
www.rosiebosse.com

Special Shared Recipes

Bear Sign

1 egg   1 cup sour milk
1 cup sugar 1 tablespoon
butter   1 teaspoon baking
powder ½ teaspoon soda
flour to make dough
flavoring if wanted.

Martha McCune

Griddle - Cakes

Stir together two cups flour, one-half
teaspoon salt and two teaspoons baking
powder. Add gradually one cup
water or milk. Drop by spoonfuls
on a hot greased pan when full of
bubbles, turn and cook on the
other side.

Laura O'Brien

Spice Cookies

1 cup molasses, one-half cup sugar, one-half cup each lard and butter, four cups flour, one teaspoon each ginger, salt, soda and cinnamon, one-half teaspoon nutmeg, two eggs. Heat molasses to boiling point, add sugar and shortening. Mix and sift dry ingredients, add to first mixture with the eggs lightly beaten. Chill in the ice house or well and roll out when cool. In warm weather, prepare the mixture over night or some hours before using so that it may be easily rolled. Raisins or finely chopped dried apples may be added if desired.

Grace Hallagher

Southwest Nebraska
June 1, 1879

CHAPTER 1

A LONG, DRY DAY

MERINA STARED AHEAD AT THE BARREN LAND. They had been following the Western Trail or as some called it, the Texas Trail from Dodge City, Kansas toward Ogallala, Nebraska for nearly forty days.

The early days of the trip had been enjoyable. John Kirkham had purchased one thousand head of steers from Gabe Hawkins, the trail boss, and he knew the route well. The water had been adequate and the weather fair. Even the river crossings had been relatively easy. However, the last three days had been difficult. The wind blew from the northwest and was blowing the dust from the livestock back in their faces. Following a herd was always dirty but with a strong wind, it was even more difficult. The cattle didn't want to walk into the wind either, so the riders were fighting to keep the cattle headed north. Only Emilia didn't seem to be affected.

The small girl's eyes sparkled as she looked over at her sister. "Isn't this fun, Nina? Even Hawk is smiling!" Emilia had named her pony Hawk after their trail boss. She seemed to love the big man and he treated her with affection as well. Emilia leaned down over Hawk's neck as she whispered to him, "We are having fun, aren't we, Hawk? When we get to the big town, I will ride you down the street and you can prance like a fine horse."

Hawk flicked his ears back and forth and switched his tail. He was a small, buckskin-colored Shetland. His hair was fluffy, and he wasn't the prettiest horse around. He was proud though and Emilia was correct—he would prance down the street.

Emilia was a beautiful little girl and was a smaller, younger version of her older sister. Both had black hair that gleamed in the sun. Merina kept her long hair in a braid and most of the time, it was tucked inside her hat. Emilia's curly hair wouldn't stay in her braid and was usually loose by the end of the day.

Merina shook her head as she watched her sister. She murmured, "Your hair will be tangled again tonight, and you will cry when I brush it out. Maybe I should just cut it off." Merina frowned as she thought of what her brothers would say. Neither Angel nor Miguel would agree to that and her frown deepened. "Perhaps we will have Angel brush your hair tonight," she told her little sister.

Emilia glared at her sister. "I will ask Señor Hawkins to brush my hair. He will not chase the rats so much and make them bite me."

Merina stared at Emilia in surprise. "You cannot ask Señor Hawkins to brush your hair! He is our boss and has no wife or children of his own. He would have no idea how to brush a small girl's tangled hair."

"He is a nice man and I will ask him. When he comes back tonight, I will ask him then."

Merina sighed as she looked down into the determined little eyes of her sister and then she looked away. *Señor Hawkins will not be back before dark. He rode ahead to see how far we are from the South Platte River. Perhaps Emilia will have forgotten about this by tomorrow.*

They made camp early that evening. Tall Eagle said that they would leave earlier in the morning than usual, probably while it was still dark, and travel while it was cooler. "We have at least two days drive in front of us before we reach water."

It rained that night and even though they were sopping wet and uncomfortable, it did mean that there would be small puddles of water for the cattle to drink from. Merina arose a little after midnight and took the horses back to a small arroyo to water them. She had noticed it as they rode by and knew that it would fill briefly with water. The horses drank fully and then she moved them back to the rope corral. Shortly after she returned, she heard a rider come in.

Gabe was back. She could not hear the conversation between Tall Eagle and him, but the Indian took Gabe's horse. The big man dropped down on his saddle and was quickly asleep.

CHAPTER 2

NIGHT DRIVE

COOKIE BANGED THE TRIANGLE WELL BEFORE DAYLIGHT, and the men drug out of their blankets rubbing their eyes in confusion. Gabe had a cup of coffee in his hand. His eyes were bloodshot, and the planes of his face were drawn down in exhaustion.

"Boys, we have two hard days in front of us before we reach the Platte River. We are going to move out early this morning. I told Cookie to wait on breakfast until we stop, probably in about five or six hours. We'll push them while it's cool and then stop in the heat of the day. We will move them again tonight and hopefully reach the river tomorrow sometime.

"Let the cattle drink if you come across any puddles or buffalo wallows that have water. They are thirsty and this next day is going to be a hard one. Once they smell the water of the Platte, they may try to stampede, and we need to keep them slowed down. Grab some coffee and let's move out."

He tossed the grains of his coffee on the ground and dropped his cup in the wrecking pan. Emilia was smiling at him over the side of the wagon and he stopped beside her.

"Good morning, Emilia. You sure look pretty this morning.

"Why don't you ride with Larry for a while today? I think that Hawk is a tired pony, and we want him rested so he can prance when we reach Ogallala." He smiled at her again and chucked her under the chin.

Emilia hesitated and then nodded as she climbed up onto the seat beside Larry.

The young woman driving the wagon was nearly seven months pregnant and she gave Emilia a bright smile. "I would love to have some company this morning, Emilia. I get lonesome riding in the dark." She handed Emilia a small box as she whispered, "Besides, Cookie gave us some bear sign to eat. There isn't enough for everyone so the two youngest get to eat it." Larry pointed from her stomach to Emilia and the small girl scooted closer as she began to chatter.

Merina smiled up at Gabe. "Thank you for suggesting that Emilia ride in the wagon. She would never have agreed if I had suggested it. She falls off her horse when she is tired so this would have been a sad ride."

Gabe grinned at her and winked, "I guessed that. It's earlier than usual and is going to be a long day." He added quietly, "Thanks for watering the horses early this morning."

Merina watched him walk away in surprise. She didn't know how Gabe knew but obviously, he had heard or seen her come and go. She watched him a moment longer and then quickly pulled the pins from the rope corral as the men switched out their horses. *At least the ones they ride today will be less thirsty.*

Tall Eagle handed Gabe the reins to Watie and the trail boss led the way into the dark. John Kirkham rode with him. Tobe and Tall Eagle rode point with Rusty, Angel, Tab and Bart at flank on the sides of the herd. Miguel, Rufe and Nate were on drag. The riders on drag ate the most dust and it was going to be a dirty ride today. They pulled their bandanas up over their noses and hollered at the cattle as they pushed them up the trail.

36

Cookie pulled out after the herd and then passed them with Larry's wagon behind. He rode beside Gabe for a moment getting his instructions and then pointed his team toward the north.

The cattle moved slowly, bawling for water. The cowboys worked the herd around to take advantage of any little pools that they could. They moved the cattle until about 10:00 a.m. and then let the tired animals stop. The grass was sparse and coarse, but some of the cattle still grazed. Those riders who hadn't been on nightguard the night before took turns riding around the herd while the rest of the men moved toward the chuckwagon. Talk was quiet and once the men finished eating, they moved out to relieve those who were riding herd.

Kirkham walked up to stand beside Gabe. "I figure we came about ten miles. We should have ten to fifteen more to travel before we reach the river."

Gabe nodded. "I think it will be fifteen. I am worried though that they will stampede when they smell the water. I think we had better break them into smaller herds so that they don't pile up on each other if they start to run."

Kirkham was silent a moment and then commented quietly, "Several creeks that I was planning on were dry since the spring rains were light. I haven't had to move thirsty cattle like this. I guess you have had to do some night drives before."

Gabe took a drink of his coffee before he answered. "I have but it is never good. We are going to lose some of the weaker ones. Some will just lay down and refuse to go any further. And then some of those will get up and move when it cools off. The rain last night helped even if it wasn't comfortable for us."

His eyes moved over the herd and he studied some of the cows. "More of those cows are going to drop calves and we'll have to keep loading them up. Most trail bosses just shoot the calves, but I hate to do that. We will pack them as long as we can. You boys up here are building

herds. We should be able to sell the pairs and those pregnant cows too."
He threw out his coffee and grabbed Watie's reins.

"I am going to ride up ahead and see if there are any creeks or arroyos
that have water in them."

Kirkham nodded. "I'll come with you."

CHAPTER 3

A WORRIED TRAIL BOSS

THE TWO MEN RODE NORTH AND RUSTY WATCHED THEM GO. He commented quietly to Larry, "The boss is worried 'bout water. I think we're still too far from the river fer all these critters to make it alive."

Larry put her arm around her husband. Her hair had been cut short and was now growing out. It was a dark reddish-brown and hung in curls around her face. It was too short to pull back and long enough to blow in her eyes. She had it tied up in a bandana and Rusty thought she was beautiful.

He pulled her close and kissed her as he patted her stomach. "How's the little feller doin'? Ya ain't hurtin' anywhere are ya?"

Larry smiled up at this cowboy who had stolen her heart on the drive to Dodge City. She shook her head, "No, he's a tough little fellow. He doesn't seem to mind the wagon ride at all."

Rusty nodded. "I'll help y'all clean up an' then ya go lay down. It's goin' to be another long night tonight."

Larry washed the dishes while Rusty picketed the mules away from the herd. He saw a little water in the bottom of an arroyo and led the team down to the water. "Now ya mules drink up. This here is all the water y'all be gettin' till we reach the river." The mules sniffed the murky water and then drank thirstily. Rusty pounded their picket pins into the ground and then headed back towards the wagons.

Emilia's head was nodding. Rusty took her plate from her hands and lifted the small girl into the wagon bed. She never opened her eyes as he laid her down. He watched her for a moment. When he looked up, he saw Larry smiling at him and he winked at her.

"Mebbie that little feller 'ill be a tough little gal with curly hair an' that 'ill be all right too."

Larry's smile became larger and Rusty winked at her again as he unrolled his bed and lay down. He was next to ride herd and he wanted to catch a quick nap. He stretched out his left leg and flexed it. The break was almost healed. He still had a limp, but he could now put a little weight on it. "'Fore long, I might even be able to mount my hoss on the left side like a normal feller," he muttered to himself as he dozed off.

Cookie shooed Larry away. "Git on back to that there wagon an' lay down like Rusty told ya. We ain't a gonna eat till 'round 2:00 this afternoon so ya cin catch a quick nap. Shoot, I might even take one my own self."

Larry laughed and Cookie grinned at her. They both knew that Cookie barely slept at all and he certainly wouldn't let the men see him taking a nap.

As Larry lay down beside Emilia, she could hear the men riding herd singing to the cattle. Some could barely carry a tune while others had fine voices. Larry slept about an hour. She was helping Cookie with dinner when a fine Irish tenor echoed out over the herd punctuated now and then by a soft Spanish ballad. Larry smiled. Rusty and Angel had the best singing voices of all the men, and everyone enjoyed their music.

CHAPTER 4

LET'S TAKE THIS HERD HOME

GABE WAS BACK BY DINNER AND HE WAS QUIET. Kirkham's face looked grim and the men all knew that the trail ahead was going to be a hard one.

After everyone had grabbed their plates, Gabe walked out to where they were all sitting. "We'll move out again tonight about 8:00. That will give us a little daylight. We should have some stars tonight. We'll push them all night and we should be able to make another ten miles.

"Most of the cattle are up and grazing now. They are going to be restless and that makes them ready to stampede, so keep your eyes open. Keep the singing loud tonight. They need to know where you are, so they don't get spooked." He started to walk away and then stopped, "And if it starts to rain, watch for gullies. We need to take advantage of any water we can find."

The cattle plodded into the night. Gabe grinned through the dirt around his mouth as he watched Waggoner's two cows lead the way. "You old girls were trouble in the beginning, but you have been quite the asset on this drive. Just hang in there awhile longer—you only have a few more miles to go." Both cows were heavy with calves and Gabe hoped they wouldn't calve before they reached Ogallala. He remembered what Dan Waggoner had told him. "When they calve, you won't find those babies until it is time to gather in the fall."

Gabe frowned as he studied the cattle. *What am I going to do with those two cows?* He pondered that awhile and then nodded. *Maybe I should cut out the best cows of what I have left and take them with me to Cheyenne. I know Badger has some cows, but I don't really know how many."* He laughed softly to himself and muttered out loud, "I sure didn't think I would get attached to two old trouble-making cows when I picked the two of you up. Of course, I could sell you. Most trail bosses would like to have an old trail-broke cow to lead their herd up the trail. Shoot, Goodnight has an old mulberry steer that has made the trip with him more times than he can count." One of the cows looked over at him and snorted. Gabe grinned at her.

"Yep, and you are just cantankerous enough that if I try to split the two of you up, you'll be nothing but trouble. I reckon I will just hang onto you. I'll have the boys sort off enough of the best cows to fill a couple of train cars and you can just be my first seed stock on my new ranch." The two cows followed him as they headed north in the moonlight.

They moved the herd until a little after midnight. The cattle were dragging now and the men at the back of the herd were having a hard time keeping the stragglers moving. The cattle were strung out for over a mile.

Gabe rode back along the herd and talked to his men. "We'll stop for the night. Figure out who is going to ride herd first and the rest of you catch some sleep. When we move again, we're going to split the herd to try to keep them from stampeding over each other when they smell the water."

The men nodded dully, and herding arrangements were quickly made. Cookie was camped ahead of the herd, but he wouldn't be making breakfast until around 6:00 a.m.

Rusty unhitched the mules and once again searched for water. One barrel on the wagon was nearly full and he gave each mule about a gallon of water before he picketed them on the coarse grass.

He filled Larry's canteen. "Drink this up. You cain't afford to git dry like I cin."

She smiled wanly and sipped lightly.

Rusty shook his head, "Nope, drink it up. We'll be at the river by tomorrow an' Ogallala is jist across it. I'll limit my water, but y'all need to keep a drinkin'."

Larry's lips were cracked, and she drank gratefully.

Rusty pulled her close and whispered, "Little mommas need more water an' there ain't a feller here who wouldn't give ya a drink a his. Now ya take care a that little ol' baby."

Tears filled Larry's eyes as she looked up at Rusty. He smiled down at her and winked. "Now y'all better git over there an' git some rest. Y'all don't have to help Cookie till 'round 6:00 in the mornin', an' I cin wake ya up."

Emilia had chattered most of the ride and had fallen asleep around 10:00. Larry crawled in the wagon next to her and was soon asleep as well. When Merina checked on her sister, Emilia was curled up next to Larry with Larry's arm around her. They looked comfortable so Merina unrolled her blankets under the wagon. Then she walked over to where Gabe was lining out the next day.

"Get some sleep, boys. We'll make our last push as soon as breakfast is over. The cattle will start to smell the water around mid-morning and we'll have a hard time holding them back. I want all the babies loaded in Larry's wagon before we go so put your bedrolls in Cookie's wagon. Those calves will make quite a mess. Rusty, you'll drive Larry's wagon across. Angel, you and Tall Eagle will push the first group. When they are across, you can come back over and help guide the second bunch across.

"There is a wide band of grass on the north side of the river. Cappy, you and John will push them onto that and hold them there. The rest of you boys will need to push the last stragglers. They will be the slowest and the weakest. Tall Eagle, Angel and Miguel, you be ready to drag anything out that starts to bog down."

He looked over at Merina. "You take the horses across first thing. I want them watered well before the cattle arrive. Have one saddled for Rusty and make sure he has it so he can help us in case we need more men.

"Cookie, you follow me. We'll be moving faster once the cattle smell the water and I want you to have a good lead. Rusty, you will be right behind Cookie. I want those wagons in behind the horse herd and out of the water when the first cattle arrive."

The men listened quietly and then Gabe added, "Boys, this is the last hard days ride you will have for some time. It is going to be touchy when those cattle start to run so be alert. I don't want to lose any of you and especially, not this close to the end of the drive." He looked at each man and said quietly, "It has been my pleasure to ride with each one of you. Now sleep fast and let's take this herd home."

CHAPTER 5

DREAMS AND PLANS

RUSTY AND ANGEL TOOK THE FIRST TURN OF NIGHT HERD, and the cattle settled down as the two men sang to them.

Merina drank a cup of coffee slowly and then walked toward the wagon. Gabe touched her shoulder and she turned around.

"You have done a fine job, Merina. No man could have done it better." He paused and then added, "Be careful tomorrow. That river is full of sand. Wait for me to show you where to cross unless you see the cattle coming. Then look for the most recent tracks and push the horses in.

"Keep Emilia with you. I would like her to ride in the wagon, but she should be all right if she stays with the horses." He smiled at her and winked. "And then let's have a steak in Ogallala to celebrate."

Merina smiled up at him. "Si, Señor Gabe." Her eyes sparkled with humor as she added, "You are the boss—for one more day."

Gabe's eyes lit up and he laughed out loud. He was still smiling when he returned to the fire and rolled up in his blankets.

Miguel looked from Gabe to his sister. His bright eyes glinted with humor and she glared at him before she crawled under the wagon.

Merina pulled her blankets up and listened to the men's voices as they discussed what they would do in Ogallala and beyond.

"What will I do?" she whispered to herself. "Angel and Miguel can take riding jobs. They can live on the ranch with Señor Gabe but where will I go? I cannot live in a house with men. Emilia and I will need to stay in town and what will I do?" She could feel the panic welling up inside of her. *If only I was a man like my brothers. I too could take a riding job.*

Merina forced herself to calm down. She said a small prayer that everything would work out. *Emilia is my first responsibility. She is more important than my happiness.* Merina slowly relaxed and drifted off to sleep.

A tall man walked by in her dream. His eyes were dark blue and curly, black hair showed from under his hat. His face was somber but when he looked at her, he smiled. He looked so happy that Merina smiled too. Then she realized that he was not smiling at her. He was smiling at someone behind her. Merina frowned in her sleep and then awoke. Her frown became deeper as she turned on her side and forced herself to close her eyes. *I do not wish to dream of this man. I am not interested in any man and for sure not one who is still in love with another woman.*

Gabe was doing some thinking too. He had enjoyed seeing Merina every day even though they spent little time together. *Cattle drives are no place for courting* he thought to himself and then almost laughed out loud at the thought. *Me thinking of courting? And when am I going to have time for that? I have a ranch to buy, cattle to run, and an operation to build. I don't have time for a woman and for sure none so stubborn as Merina. Besides, she has shown no interest in me at all. Why once we reach Cheyenne, she will be so busy walking out with other men that she won't even give me a thought.* A frown creased his face and Gabe growled under his breath at the thought of other men courting Merina.

The small blond woman in his dreams was always riding away and no matter how he tried to stop her, she never turned around. Now another woman stood watching him as he called to Grace. She stood to the side and said nothing. He couldn't see her face, but she had black hair that shined in the sun. She held herself proudly. As he called to Grace, the black-haired woman turned and walked away. He stood puzzled. Gabe didn't know how to stop either one of them and then he awoke.

The sky was still dark, and Cookie was banging the triangle. The men drifted up to eat. There was a feeling of excitement and expectation in the air. The men knew that the next few hours were going to be difficult ones. They would do their best to make sure all the cattle crossed safely and that meant each man would be in danger. Still, the drive was almost over.

Gabe climbed out of his blankets. He hadn't slept well, and he almost felt surly. Cookie handed him a plate and he ate quickly. Tall Eagle led Buck up to him and dropped the reins. The horse nickered and rubbed his head against his friend. Gabe rubbed Buck's ears and then dropped his plate in the wrecking pan. He mounted and waved. "Let's move out."

Cookie stowed the wrecking pan with the dirty dishes in the wagon, the bedrolls were loaded, and the mules were hitched. He snapped the traces and followed Gabe toward the river.

Rusty lifted Larry up and then climbed quickly into the second wagon. He kissed his wife before he released the brakes. The mules were ready to go and moved out briskly. Rusty grinned down at Larry. "The best part a this day will be ridin' with my wife. Now ya jist hang onto my arm an' let's make this here ride as pleasant as we cin."

Larry was afraid of the river, but she scooted closer to Rusty and took hold of his arm. When he grinned down at her again, she laughed, and the tension began to drain out of her. Soon they were talking and making plans for their new life in Cheyenne.

The wagons had moved about a mile when the lead cows caught the scent of water. They lifted their heads as they sniffed the air. Soon they were moving at a trot and the cattle behind them began to trot as well.

Gabe hollered at Cookie and Rusty. "Push those mules! The cattle are coming!" He waved his arm at Merina and she moved the remuda toward the river at a lope.

CHAPTER 6

A Dangerous River Crossing

WHEN THE WAGONS REACHED THE RIVER, the cattle were about a half mile behind them. The mules wanted to stop and drink, but the two men snapped the lines and pushed the mules across the river. The wagons slowed a little once they reached the other side, but the cattle were charging into the water and the wagons needed to be out of the way. The mules were pushed up the riverbank and onto the flat area beyond the water.

Rusty handed Larry the lines and then grabbed the horse that Merina led toward him. He raced back into the water and around the cattle that were already in the river. The men behind the first group were hollering and popping the cattle with their ropes. The second group was coming on the run and they needed to have the cattle further across the river. Rusty pushed his horse toward the lead cattle and swung his rope. The cows buck-jumped into the deeper part of the river. It wasn't deep enough to swim but the churned sand was soft and the bottom of the riverbed was already boggy. One of the front steers tried to turn around and Rusty charged his horse toward it, swinging his rope and hollering. Longhorn cattle had no fear of a man on the ground, but they were afraid of a man on horseback. The steer turned around and lunged for the far shore. Soon, the river was full of bucking, plunging cattle.

Slowly, the cattle crossed the river and climbed up on the other side. They were still thirsty and tried to turn back into the river instead of moving out onto the grass but Cappy and Kirkham were there to push them.

Merina was sitting on top of the riverbank. She had three horses saddled and ready to go in case a horse went down.

Emilia's little pony was thirsty. He jerked his reins out of her hands and galloped back toward the creek. Merina raced her horse after Hawk, reaching for the reins when a steer charged the small horse.

Hawk tried to jump out of the way and almost went down. He staggered to his feet and buck-jumped into the water toward Gabe. Hawk was the only horse that Buck would let close to him and the little pony was running for the only safety he knew.

Buck swung his head and lunged toward the steer with his mouth open. He screamed and the steer swung away. As Hawk slipped and went down, Emilia flew over his head toward the surging cattle. Gabe swung Buck around and lunged for the back of Emilia's shirt. He jerked her up and out of the water as steers surged around Buck. The horse bit and lunged his way to the outside of the cattle. He planted himself between the surging cattle and Hawk. The little Shetland staggered to his feet and Gabe grabbed his reins. He held the sobbing Emilia in one arm and led Hawk with the other, guiding Buck with his knees.

When they reached the riverbank, Merina tried to lift Emilia out of Gabe's arms, but the little girl wouldn't let go. Gabe dropped Hawk's reins and patted her back.

"Now, now, Emilia. You are fine and Hawk is fine. I do think that you should go with Merina and get Hawk away from the cattle though." He smiled at her and patted her back as he added softly, "He's mighty scared so he needs you to be brave."

Emilia stopped sobbing and looked at Hawk. She nodded and Gabe set her on her pony's back.

He handed the reins to Merina. Her face was pale, and her hands were shaking as she took the reins.

Gabe squeezed her shoulder, and then wheeled Buck around. The last group of cattle was almost to the water. Gabe pointed upstream.

"Bring them in up there. They'll bog down here. The sand is too deep!"

The riders in the water turned the cattle to the west and the thirsty animals plunged into the water. Gabe roared, "Keep them moving! They need to drink as they cross. They'll sink down if they stay in the same place for too long!"

Once again, the river was full of bawling, bucking cattle as they pushed to cross, stopping now and then to drink. Two of the pregnant cows went down and were quickly hauled to their feet by Angel and Miguel. The two vaqueros were wizards with their long riatas. Their ropes were longer than the Texas lariats and they were able to snake them through the herd of cattle to snag the animal they wanted. They drug both cows to the edge of the water and then flipped their ropes off when the cows were almost to the riverbank. Nine head had to be pulled out of the stragglers and then the river was once again quiet as the sand started to settle. Before long, the water would clear, and the Platte would be ready again for whomever dared to take it on.

Once all the cattle had crossed, the cowboys began to bring down a few head at a time to water. Some of those even ventured into the deep sand and had to be pulled out.

Tall Eagle grabbed a pot out of the wagon and filled it with water. He and Angel headed back down the trail to see if they could coax the cattle that had gone down to get up with a drink.

Three of them lay on the trail. One had little feet protruding from her and Tall Eagle signaled to Angel to rope her. Tall Eagle pulled the calf easily and then dropped it as Angel flipped off his rope. He jumped on his horse as the cow swung around to charge him. She stopped and sniffed the calf. Soon, she began to lick it. Angel charged her and rushed her into the water while Tall Eagle grabbed the calf and dropped it over his horse with the front feet on one side and the back feet on the other. His horse lunged into the water and pushed his way across. Tall Eagle dropped the calf to the ground. The angry cow swiped her horns in the ground and then once again, sniffed her calf. It wobbled to its feet and she began to lick it.

Tall Eagle rode upstream about a quarter of a mile before he dismounted and cleaned up. He wasn't taking a chance of dismounting close to an angry momma cow. He rarely showed emotion but as he rode toward the group of happy cowboys, he grinned. He looked over at the laughing Angel. "Once again, Angel, you were right where I needed you to be."

The cowboys slapped both men on the back and the teasing began. It was after 9:00 a.m. It had taken nearly three hours to cross the South Platte River.

All It Took Was a Smile

A **SMILING JOHN KIRKHAM RODE UP TO THE GROUP OF COWBOYS.** He pulled some cash out of his vest pocket and handed each of the men $5.

"You boys did a fine job. I don't believe I have seen a smoother river crossing than I just saw. I figure you saved me quite a few head of cattle so here is a little bonus for each of you."

The men stared at him for a moment. Then each took Kirkham's money and thanked him.

He studied the riders and shook his head. "I know most of you are going on north, but I would sure hire any of you who want to stay on here and work for me. I pay $40 a month and have one of the best cooks in the country." He started to ride away and then turned back. "I have a daughter too but I won't let her fraternize with cowboys just so you know."

The men stared after him and Tab whispered, "What's he talkin' 'bout? I don't reckon I never fraternized no one before."

Kirkham winked at Gabe as he rode toward the town. Unlike most cow towns, all the Ogallala businesses were built on the south side of the tracks. A few houses were on the north side, but the commerce was on the south. The only street in town ran parallel to the railroad tracks and was rightfully called Railroad Street. The cattle pens and chutes were just to the west of town. Kirkham called back, "The cattle can graze this stretch until we get them penned. This is all open range, here and on north of town as well."

The riders were still discussing what Kirkham had told them when a pretty girl on a paint horse raced out to meet Kirkham.

"Father! I'm so glad you are home! Were you able to hire any riders? Mac said to ask you since we are so short-handed."

Bart, Tab, Rufe and Tobe stared at her. They looked at each other and then at Gabe. Gabe began to laugh, and the four men rode slowly after Kirkham. They were all discussing what needed to be said and Tobe was elected to do the talking.

Tobe nodded at the young lady and then addressed Kirkham. "Mr. Kirkham, we'd be willin' to stay on an' ride for y'all. We've talked it over an' we'll give it a try."

Kirkham's eyes twinkled as he looked the four serious young men over. They were all doing their best to keep their eyes on him and not look at his daughter. She laughed as she put out her hand.

"Oh Father, don't be so ornery. My name is Ann, Ann Kirkham. We would love to have you ride for us. Now tell me your names."

They visited awhile and then the four smiling cowboys rode back to Gabe.

Tobe's face was serious, but his eyes were twinkling as he spoke, "Well Boss, guess we won't be makin' the trip with y'all to Cheyenne. We have us a ridin' job with Kirkham."

Gabe looked from one to the other and shook his head. "Sure am glad I didn't need you fellows to trail any further. All it took was a smile from a pretty girl to drag you away from me." He grinned at the four men and shook each of their hands. "Well, let's meet at the Ogallala

House for supper tonight and I will pay you out." His smile became wider as he added, "I reckon it's a good deal that you are riding for Kirkham. These are his cattle and as soon as we get them in the pens, they are your problem."

The four cowboys stared at their trail boss a moment and then began to laugh.

Gabe waved his arm around the cattle. "Let's get them sorted. The steers are Kirkham's and the cows are mine. I want to sort off the two lead cows and then forty-eight more head of the best cows. None with calves though. That is enough for four train cars. Let's start sorting. Cookie will have dinner ready in about an hour."

CHAPTER 8

THE END OF THE DRIVE

GABE HAD THREE OFFERS ON HIS COWS BEFORE NOON. The cowboys had sorted off fifty head for him, and they were grazing away from the remaining two hundred. Gabe turned down the first offer.

He shook his head at the man. "Tell your boss he is going to have to do better than that. I won't sell them for less than what Dodge City was paying."

A second cowboy rode out about a half an hour later and said that he was repping for a brand north of Ogallala. "The Boss is prepared to pay $40 for the cows and $45 for the cow/calf pairs. Kirkham said you had about two hundred fifty head."

Gabe slowly nodded. "I do but I am planning to take fifty head on north with me."

A third cowboy rode through the herd. His hat sat at a rakish angle on his head and he had a sardonic smile on his face. He listened to the conversation and then asked, "What will it take to get all two hundred fifty?"

The other rider looked irritated and the man shrugged. He grinned at the three of them. "Just reppin' for the brand."

Gabe frowned and Rusty stepped forward as he pointed at the fifty head Gabe had saved back, "Now those there cows are the best a the lot. We is a plannin' to take them on north with us." He paused and then added, "See those two lead cows? Now those there old girls, they led this here herd all the way from Texas, through Dodge City an' clean north to here. They be kinda close to our hearts. None a them fifty are fer sale an' fer sure, not those two lead cows."

The smiling cowboy studied the cattle and then looked from Gabe to Rusty. "I don't know which of you fellers is in charge here but I'm reppin' for some gents back east. Between you an' me, they don't know their tail ends from the back side of a jackass, but they're convinced they're a goin' to get rich in the cattle business. They sent me out here to buy cattle an' I have cash money. I'll top whatever that feller offered you, but I want 'em all."

The other cowboy stuttered and then glared at the smiling man. "Dang it, Zeke. Ya know we cain't pay the kind a money yore boss is throwin' 'round. Still, I'll be durned if I'll let him git these cows cheap. I'm offerin' $100 a head fer the cows an' $115 fer the pairs. Now ya top that, ya tinhorn."

Zeke pulled out his wallet and Rusty held up his hand. "Now hold on. That might be 'nough fer the forty-eight head, but it ain't 'nough fer those two lead cows. Why they cin lead yore herd just plumb anywhere ya want to go. No sir. If ya want those two cows, they's gonna cost ya $150 each."

Zeke paused as he studied Rusty's face. "They cross rivers with no balkin'?"

Rusty nodded, "They ain't seen a river they don't like an' we crossed a plenty these last two months. Ya jist point 'em to where ya want 'em to go an' they'll march like two little ol' soldiers. Jist don't separate 'em."

Zeke grinned and shrugged. "Ain't my money. I just take orders from the Duke." He looked over at the first cowboy and grinned, "Jack here, he's just jealous cause he works for a real cowman, one that knows what he's a doin' an' don't throw his money around." His grin became bigger as he added, "Wait till I tell him that you offered $115 for a pair. Why, he'll pucker up so tight, he'll dang near explode." He paused and looked back and forth between Gabe and Rusty.

"I'll top Jack's offer. $110 for the cows and $120 for the pairs, plus $150 each for those two lead cows." He pulled out some money and held it as he waited.

Gabe pointed to Rusty. Zeke counted the money out into Rusty's hand. He shook hands with both and began to haze the cattle toward the pens.

Gabe looked around at his men and laughed as he waved, "Help him drive those cows, boys, and then head on into town. Be sure to ride the horse you want to keep though. This drive is over!"

Rusty handed Gabe the money and the trail boss shook his head. "Rusty, I'm keeping you around. I believe you could squeeze money out of a banker."

The red-haired cowboy grinned and moved toward the cattle to help Zeke drive them to the pens.

Angel and Miguel followed them. Kirkham had sent his men out earlier and now, only the horses remained from the thirty-five hundred plus head of livestock that they had brought north from Texas and Oklahoma.

Rowdy Rankin of Cheyenne had made an offer on their horses in Dodge City when he was there picking up some other horses that he had purchased. The horses they were selling to him would be loaded into the cars in the morning and would be in Cheyenne by that afternoon.

Gabe was keeping Buck and Watie. "What horse are you going to keep, Nate? You surely have a favorite by now."

Nate nodded and looked slowly over at Gabe. "Think I can keep two? I like that roan and this buckskin."

Gabe studied his little brother and smiled. Nate was taller and stronger than when he started. *My little brother is growing up.*

"That'll be fine. I'll expect you to do a man's work on our ranch so I reckon two horses will be good."

Merina was bringing the remuda in and the cowboys working around the pens stopped to watch her.

One asked, "That gal make the drive up from Kansas? Shoot, I'd go back to trailin' cows if that's how things are done now."

Gabe glared at him and the cowboy grinned good-naturedly. "No offense, Mister. It's just that I helped bring several herds north an' we never had no women on them."

Gabe held the gate as Merina drove the horses in. She gave him a bright smile and Hawk pushed up to rub on Buck. The big stallion nibbled on the Shetland and the same cowboy laughed again as he shook his head.

Emilia climbed up Gabe's leg and hung on his shoulder. He smiled at the little girl as he winked at the surprised cowboy.

"Emilia here is why I changed my rules. Why she is just about the best help around."

Emilia beamed up at him and kissed his cheek before she slid down his leg and back onto Hawk. She leaned over the pony and whispered loudly, "Today is the day, Hawk, when you prance down the street. You have to hold your head high and swish your tail."

She smiled up at Merina. "Hawk is going to prance when we ride into town."

Merina laughed at the small girl. "Well, he should prance. He did a fine job on the drive." She looked over at Gabe. "If it's all right with you, I am going to try to get us a room. I hope something is available."

The cowboy who had spoken earlier watched her ride away and slowly whistled. "Sure wish she was stayin' 'round here. I ain't seen that purty of a woman in a long time."

Gabe felt a prick of irritation, but he pushed it down and didn't answer.

Angel, Miguel and Rusty were riding toward him. Gabe pointed toward the penned horses. "You fellows pick a mount for each of you. Rusty, get one for Larry too. We are selling the rest and they will go out on the train in the morning." He hooked a lead rope onto Watie and Nate did the same with his roan.

Gabe grinned as he looked over at Nate. "Come on, little brother. Let's go take a bath and see if we can find some place to sleep. Cappy, you comin' with us?"

CHAPTER 9

OGALLALA: QUEEN OF THE COW TOWNS

THE THREE MEN RODE SLOWLY PAST THE TRACKS TO RAILROAD STREET. Cappy studied the buildings and whistled low under his breath.

"Ain't been here fer some time. This here were jist a water stop fer the railroad last time I come through. Warn't even no town here. Nothin' but a water tower an' a section house. She's a hoppin' little place now."

Gabe nodded as he looked up and down Railroad Street. The Cowboy's Rest and the Crystal Palace saloons were going full tilt even though it was barely noon. Past them, he could see two houses of ill repute, two supply houses, a shoe store and a few homes. They turned toward the livery. As they rode by the Ogallala House, they could see that it was busy. The Spofford House sitting north of the tracks was a fancier hotel and looked newer. The jail and the schoolhouse also looked new. Gabe looked around for steeples or bell towers, but he didn't see anything that looked like a church.

Cappy pointed behind them. "Fellow down ta Dodge told me that over two million cows have come up that trail since '74 an' a fifth that many hosses. That's a lot a stock ta push through this little ol' burg."

Gabe looked around and his eyes came to rest on Boot Hill. "Some of the boys who came here never left."

Cappy chuckled, "Shore 'nough. That's why it's called Boot Hill. They bury those boys with they boots on. Just wrap 'em in a sack, dig a shallow grave, an' stick up a wood marker. Shoot, won't be long an' folks won't even 'member who was buried here 'cause the markers 'ill all be gone."

Gabe was quiet. They had left markers themselves on the drive from Texas. The stampede in Oklahoma had taken eight men. He thought of Fluff who had been snake-bitten. Fluff had been Rusty's pard and he had given his horse to another rider whose mount had gone down during a stampede. The other rider was getting married when he returned to Texas. That man survived but Fluff didn't make it.

They had been lucky on the drive from Dodge City to Ogallala. They had driven all the way north through Kansas and into Nebraska. They hadn't lost any men and only a few cattle.

"I sure won't miss crossing rivers. We were darn lucky on that Platte River crossing. We could have lost a lot of cattle and some men as well."

Cappy's blue eyes were serious as he looked over at Gabe. "That's what a good trail boss does fer a drive. He limits the problems an' handles 'em quick. That there river crossin' were a good one 'cause a you."

Gabe was quiet. He wasn't used to receiving compliments and his neck turned red as he rode. Several women called to them from their windows and Gabe ignored them. "Keep your eyes straight ahead, Nate. If you look at them, that gives them permission to come into the street to talk to you."

"Are they looking for dance partners? Bart told me that there were several dance halls here. He said some of those gals might teach me how to dance."

Gabe frowned and shook his head. "You aren't going to learn to dance here."

They dismounted in front of the livery and the three riders led their mounts inside. Gabe asked, "You have any oats? These horses have come a long way."

The hostler nodded. "Just come in on the train. I ain't too busy jist yet if ya fellers want me to brush yore hosses down. Cost ya an extry two bits fer all of 'em."

Gabe nodded. "Put it on the Diamond H Ranch account. We'll be here one night, maybe two."

Cappy pulled his shotgun out of the boot on his saddle and slung it over his shoulder. He grinned at his two friends as he patted the gun. "Ol' Bertha an' me, we stick close ta each other."

The three men stopped at the Ogallala House to check on rooms. Gabe knew Rusty was behind him, so he asked for two rooms. The clerk shook his head. "Little gal came in a while ago and reserved the last three rooms. She took one and put two down for the Diamond H Ranch."

A grin filled Gabe's face. "Well, that's us. We'll take one room and a young couple will be here in a little bit. They'll take the last one.'

The clerk nodded. The three riders strolled out of the hotel lobby and stood on the street for a moment before they headed toward a supply house. Gabe chose the one that had the most women coming in and out.

He grinned and nodded towards the women. "They seem to like to shop around for the best deals. I don't like to mess around with that, so I just watch a few women who look like they like to haggle and follow them."

The men soon had their new clothes and turned toward the bath area. Gabe and Cappy each smoked a cigar as they soaked. Gabe shook his head when Nate wanted one. "Not till you are eighteen. You aren't a man grown yet."

Cappy chuckled and three of them enjoyed their baths. They all dropped their dirty clothes into their bath water and sloshed them around. It was a poor job but better than nothing. They squeezed out the wet clothes and rolled them up before they headed back to the Ogallala House.

Kirkham was waiting for them. Gabe sent Nate up to their room with the wet clothes while Cappy and he followed the man to a table in the corner. They pulled up an extra chair for Nate.

Kirkham's smile was big. "The cattle are delivered, and everyone is happy. I think we should make another run."

Gabe shook his head. "Not me. I'm done crossing rivers. This was my tenth time up the trail and I'm putting down roots. We bought a little ranch outside Cheyenne and we are going to run our own operation."

Nate looked from Gabe to Kirkham. "I might be interested in making another drive, Mr. Kirkham. I was wrangler from Texas to Dodge and a drover from Dodge on up. I think I'd like to do it again."

Gabe scowled and Kirkham nodded as he looked from one brother to the other. Nate was a younger version of Gabe. He smiled easier but both had dark blue eyes and dark curly hair. Gabe was a solid six foot three while Nate was lanky and nearly six foot. "I'll wire your brother if I decide to trail another herd. Now let's get this business taken care of so we can all enjoy our food."

CHAPTER 10

CLOSE OUT THIS DEAL

ABE AND KIRKHAM HAD AGREED ON $30 PER HEAD when Kirkham bought the herd in Dodge City plus a $20 premium for every head delivered to Ogallala. One thousand head of cattle left Dodge City and nine hundred ninety-four arrived in Ogallala.

John Kirkham pushed a bank draft across the table for $49,880. Gabe stared at it a moment. Then he folded it and shoved it into his pocket. He reached across the table and the two men shook hands. "It's been a pleasure, John. That would have been a tough drive without you knowing the rivers."

Kirkham nodded and added quietly, "And a tougher one without one of the best trail bosses I have ever worked with."

Gabe was quiet and once again, the red climbed up his neck.

"Cattle drives are good money, Gabe. Shoot, we do these another ten years, and I will own my ranch free and clear."

Gabe stared at the table and then looked up at Kirkham. "You won't be driving another ten years, John. Too many things are changing. Too many farmers breaking up the grass where we have to cross and too many fences. Shoot, those Kansas farmers don't even want us crossing their land at all with our cattle because of the ticks, and that is just going to get worse. You add in an expanding railroad and I figure we have another two, maybe four years of driving cattle north."

Kirkham was quiet a moment and then he frowned. "Things are always changing, aren't they? Just about the time you figure out how to make things pay, something changes, and you have to figure it out all over again."

The men visited a while longer and then enjoyed their food when it arrived. Once they were finished, Kirkham pushed back his plate and pulled out his wallet.

"We need to settle up on your drovers. $30 per month for each of them? $60 for your cook? How about you? What do I owe you?"

Gabe shook his head. "I had some of my own cattle, so you don't owe me anything. Larry gets a wage though. Cook's helpers get $25 per month." He paused and then added, "Both of those women were good help. They almost made me change my mind about women on a drive." He grinned up at Kirkham. "Almost."

Gabe listed his riders and the wages each should receive. When Kirkham paid him, he pocketed the money and wrote the numbers in his tally book.

Kirkham stood and extended his hand to Gabe again. "Gabe, it's been a pleasure. I'll sure recommend you as a man to work with if I have occasion to."

He looked over at Nate. "Young man, you have a fine brother. If you grow up to be the kind of man he is, you are going to be a success at whatever you do." He winked and added, "And I'll sure let you know if I decide to make another drive."

Nate grinned at him and nodded. "Thank you, sir."

"Cappy, best of luck in Wyoming. I know you were up that way when you were just a little older than Nate here. Hope you like it as much this time around."

As Kirkham walked away, Cappy chuckled. "That there man owns more cows than anyone around. He owns most a his land, too. Lots a folks jist graze but ol' John, he wants ta make sure it's his so there won't be no disagreein' down the road." He grinned at Gabe. "Good feller ta have as a friend. Knows lots a men in important places. Shoot, some folks say the president's been out an' stayed ta his ranch. I don't believe it though. Ol' Hayes be too busy back ta Washington with his own problems ta be traipsin' 'round out here."

The men laughed and then looked up as the dining room became quiet. Merina had stopped in the doorway and was looking across the room for an empty table.

CHAPTER 11

Too Tough for Texas

A **ROUGH LOOKING MAN STOOD UP AND WAVED AT HER.** He was dirty and his scruffy beard looked like it hadn't been trimmed in weeks. He grinned through broken teeth.

"Come on back here, honey. You cin sit with me. In fact, you cin sit *on* me!"

Merina stared at the man and then muttered in Spanish, "I would rather drink kerosene and spit on a campfire."

The man had no idea what Merina had said. He reached for her arm as she tried to walk by his table. Merina jerked her arm away and continued toward the table where her friends were seated.

Gabe's neck began to turn red. He stood and glared at the man before he stalked forward to take Merina's arm. Emilia smiled up at him and he lifted her up as he escorted Merina to where they were sitting. Nate and Cappy had already found two chairs and stood waiting with smiles on their faces.

The rough man cursed and spoke loudly, "So ya lousy cowboys git all the fun? Come on over here, Missy. I'll give ya a time ya won't forget."

Gabe carefully set Emilia down and handed Merina off to Cappy. He strode across the room and hit the sneering man. The man fell back, and Gabe stood over him. He ground out, "If you get up, it had better be to apologize. Otherwise, we can take this outside."

The man lunged to his feet with a roar. Gabe grabbed him by the neck of his coat and drug him to the door. He kicked him through the doorway and then stood quietly with his arms hanging loosely as he waited for the man's next move.

"We can do this with fists or with guns. Either way is fine with me."

Men began to push through the door. One hollered, "Take 'em, Daggert. Don't let no stinkin' Reb push ya 'round. Ya put the boots to 'im. We beat those yella'bellies at Gettysburg an' ya cin stomp another one today."

Gabe grabbed the man who had spoken and slammed his head into the doorjamb, barely looking around. The man dropped to the ground and the men behind him rolled him out of the doorway.

Cappy stepped up beside Gabe and pointed his shotgun at the men crowding in the doorway. "This here's a fight twix the two of 'em. The rest a ya boys stand back or I'll have ta shoot me some fellers. Now, I jist hate ta do that 'fore a good meal." He patted the shotgun. "Ol' Bertha an' me, why we been up an' down an' across this here country a fair number a years. An' unlike me, this ol' shotgun jist don't care a'tall 'bout shootin' folks, jist any time a day. She ain't so peaceable as me." Cappy grinned around at the watching men but his eyes were hard as he cocked his shotgun.

Angel and Miguel stepped out of the Cowboy's Rest and started slowly up the street. They were watching the crowd carefully. Miguel took the thongs off his guns and Angel loosened his knife inside his shirt. Soon Gabe and the man on the ground were surrounded by cowboys who rode for a variety of brands along with men and women from the saloons and businesses along the street.

One rider looked up at Angel and nodded toward the street. "That's Daggert. He stomped a cowboy to death jist yesterday. He wears lumberjack boots with studs on the bottom of 'em so's he cin do as much hurt as possible when he stomps a man. If the feller he's a fightin' is a friend a yours, ya better hope he don't go down."

Angel slipped through the group of men and nodded at Gabe.

"Señor, I see that you have offered to help clean up this town. Yes, I think this hombre could use a little...what do you say...polish?"

Daggert came off the ground with a roar and charged. Gabe stepped aside, shoved hard as the man dove for him, slamming the man's face into the dirt. Daggert shook his head and lunged to his feet. He pulled a long knife out of his coat and swung it at Gabe.

Gabe dodged the thrust and spun Daggert sideways, shoving him again.

Daggert backed up and wiped off his nose. He was bleeding but his small eyes looked deadly.

"Yore gonna die, cowboy. I'm gonna take ya apart an' put the boots to ya. An' then I'm gonna cut ya up so bad that yore ol' momma won't never know who ya are." He sneered at Gabe and added, "I'll show ya that this here town is too tough fer Texas cowhands."

A wagon with a broken wheel was sitting close by. Several spokes were missing, and the metal rim was loose. Gabe jerked one of the spokes out of the wheel and held it in his hand. He said nothing as he waited for Daggert to charge him again.

Once more, the man roared and flashed his knife. He feinted and slashed at Gabe. Gabe swung the spoke at the side of Daggert's face and the man went down. He came up on his hands and knees, shaking his head. Gabe kicked him and he fell on his face again.

Gabe leaned over him and growled, "When you get up, you get out of this town. Men like you have no cause to be anywhere close to women. And if you come for me again, I'll kill ya." He turned to walk away, dropping the spoke as he walked.

Daggert lunged off the ground and charged at Gabe's back with the knife held high in his hand. The crowd began to yell but Gabe was already spinning. He grabbed the man's outstretched arm and twisted it back, shoving the knife into Daggert's chest. Daggert fell on his face in the street and Gabe walked quietly toward the horse tank. He washed his hands and his face. He said nothing to the men as they opened their circle to let him walk through. He paused as he stepped into the doorway of the Ogallala House and growled, "I won't tolerate coarse behavior toward women."

Nate had pushed his way through the crowd of men. His eyes were big as he watched the fight from the doorway. When the fight was over and Gabe finally spoke, Nate grinned proudly. He backed out of the doorway and hurried back to the table where Merina and Emilia were eating.

Merina had ordered her food as if nothing had happened. Her heart was beating heavily but her face showed no emotion. Emilia was oblivious to everything but trying to catch the small peas that were rolling around on her plate.

"I can't catch those little balls, Nina. They are too quick for me."

Merina handed her a spoon as she cut up the meat on Emilia's plate. "Try not to make a mess, Emilia. The people who own this house work hard for us to fix a fine meal. We must always be thankful."

She looked up as Nate came back to the table. His eyes were shining, and he was smiling. Slowly, Merina relaxed, and her heart slowed down.

When Gabe walked over and sat down, she looked at him. His face looked angry, and his knuckles were skinned.

Her eyes began to sparkle, and she laughed softly. "I think it was not so much of a fight. I think, Señor Gabe, you have fought many times before." Her eyes became darker as she added, "Perhaps next time, I will let you use my knife."

Gabe looked startled and then slowly began to grin. Emilia was smiling at him and he took her fork. "Poke them, Emilia." Then he whispered, "Or just use your fingers. I won't tell Nina," and he popped one into his mouth.

The men slowly came back into the eating house. Rusty and Larry appeared and walked toward their friends.

Rusty looked around the room. He could tell from the murmur of conversation that something had happened. Finally his eyes settled on Gabe. He noticed the skinned knuckles and looked around at his friends in surprise.

"I miss a party? Looks like Gabe here was whackin' on somebody."

Gabe shrugged and Nate tried to be as nonchalant as his brother. Angel and Miguel were quiet but Cappy was grinning.

He winked at Larry and she shook her head. His ornery eyes settled on Rusty and the blue-eyed cowboy grinned when Cappy winked at him as well.

Cappy patted his gun. "Ol' Bertha here is jist disappointed. She be all ready fer some fire an' brimstone an' it jist plumb fizzled out."

He looked over at Gabe and drawled, "Yore a right sudden feller, Gabe. Jist sudden. No warnin', jist sudden like."

Gabe glared at him and Cappy laughed.

"Who wants ta do some fishin' this afternoon? I saw some ol' catfish down there in that river an' they was jist a beggin' me fer some bait. Now I found some worms a hidin' in the livery an' I'm a goin' ta go fishin'."

Emilia jumped up from the table so fast that she almost tipped her chair over.

"Me! Me! I want to go! Please, Nina? Can I go?"

Angel laughed and took her hand. "I think I would like to go fishing as well. Let's go change your clothes or Nina will smack both of us." Miguel and Nate followed the happy group out of the room and Rusty pulled out a chair for Larry before he sat down.

CHAPTER 12

A Visit to The Cemetery

RUSTY STARTED TO ASK GABE WHAT HAD HAPPENED, but he stopped when Gabe looked up at him.

"Get the wagon sold, Rusty? What poor sucker did you take advantage of this time?"

Rusty's eyes twinkled and Larry began to laugh.

"A herd is heading up to the Dakotas to move beef to the reservation. Their chuckwagon broke down. Rusty convinced them that for the time and the money it would cost to fix all the things that were wrong with it, they could buy his wagon and be out of town today. They gave him $100 for yours and left their old one out in front. The broken wheel is still on it."

Gabe's eyes began to twinkle and Rusty laughed as Gabe pulled a splinter out of his hand.

"I reckon that there wagon deal helped us twice, Boss!"

Gabe nodded soberly and when Merina laughed, he chuckled. "So what are you two going to do this afternoon?"

Rusty shrugged and Gabe stared out the window before he continued.

"The train leaves at 9:00 a.m. I want the horses fed and watered before they are loaded, and we all need tickets." He paused and looked at the young couple, "You have your tickets yet?"

Rusty shook his head. "Nope. We thought we'd wait an' get 'em with y'all." His blue eyes sparkled as he added, "Don't want to git on the wrong durn train an' have ya leave us here."

Gabe grinned and then stood. He looked down at Merina. "Want to come along? I need to send Badger a wire as well and tell him when we plan to arrive in Cheyenne. He wants to introduce us to his family."

Merina hesitated and then nodded. She stood and Gabe offered her his arm.

The two young couples walked out of the Ogallala House and up the street to the train station. Gabe bought tickets for everyone. Merina started to protest, and he shook his head. "We'll settle up tonight when I pay everyone out."

The train ride would take about seven hours, so they expected to arrive in Cheyenne the next afternoon. That would put them in town on June 13 about 4:15 p.m. Their next stop was the express office. Gabe handed the agent his messages and picked up several letters.

"You have an Angel Montero or a Merina Montero riding with you? I have letters for them too." The agent paused as he waited for an answer.

Gabe pointed at Merina. "This is Merina and Angel is her brother."

The agent handed her the letters. "I have tried to give these to every cowboy who came in here. The one for Angel was forwarded from Dodge earlier this month and the one for Miss Montero just came this week. Luck on your move." He started tapping the messages out that Gabe had handed him. One was for Rowdy telling him that his fifty-nine horses would be arriving on the 4:15 train. The other was for Badger.

Gabe could feel his stomach stating to clench and unclench. His ranch was almost a reality and he was getting excited. He looked down a Merina.

"You haven't picked out your horse yet. You need to do that today, so we know which ones go with us and which go to Rowdy."

Merina looked up at him in surprise. "I already have a horse. I want to keep Mascota."

Gabe grinned at her. "Well, that was Cole's horse, not mine. All the riders get to keep a horse so you can pick another one…unless you don't want one. Then I will be glad to sell it."

Merina frowned and Larry laughed. "Merina, take the horse. The first time that I met Gabe, I was terrified of him. He was so grumpy, and he snarled at me. Eventually, I figured out that he was just irritated at himself because he was breaking his rules. Now I know that he is an old softy. Still grumpy but he has a good heart."

Gabe looked at Larry in surprise and then slowly turned red. He glared at Rusty and frowned as he growled, "There it is again. What is so grumpy about me?"

His three companions began to laugh and Gabe slowly grinned. "Come on, Merina. Let's go look at those horses." He looked back at the grinning Rusty and his face turned red under his tan. "See you two for supper. 8:00 at the Ogallala House. They have a back room and we have it. Some big cowman has it from 5:30 to 8 and we have it for the rest of the night."

Rusty was still laughing when Gabe turned around and Merina looked up at the tall man in surprise. When she saw his blush, she almost blushed herself. *Rusty thinks that we are courting! He has no idea that we are friends only.*

The street was busy, and the saloons were loud even though it was midafternoon. Gabe tucked Merina's arm a little closer and moved faster as they walked past the saloons to the livery.

Mascota nickered at Merina when she walked in and tried to push through the stall door. She rubbed his head and whispered to him in Spanish. She studied the horses and then looked up at Gabe.

"I think I would like to wait for a mare. I want to breed Mascota. I want to breed him to an Arabian. They are a proud horse. I want to start my own herd. Maybe when we get to Cheyenne, I will do that."

Gabe was surprised and then he nodded. "I reckon that would be a good idea. You can run your horses on my ranch. Then they will be handy for you to work with every day. We can—"

Merina shook her head. "No, I cannot live on your ranch with you. It would not be good even as friends. You are a man and I am a woman. Even with my brothers there, people would talk. No, I will not live on your ranch."

Gabe stared at her in surprise. It had never occurred to him that Merina would not live on the ranch. He assumed that they would all live in the house together. He frowned. *Larry will probably feel the same way.*

Merina moved closer to Mascota and talked to him in Spanish. "Men. They understand nothing and yet, life is so easy for them. So uncomplicated."

Gabe listened to her but did not respond even though he understood what she was saying. He looked away and smiled wryly to himself. *She's right. Of course she can't stay there with single men. And what about Angel and Miguel? Will they all try to stay together, or will Angel and Miguel stay out at the ranch? And what will she do? She will need a job to make a living.*

"Any idea of what you will do in town?"

Merina's dark eyes sparkled as she smiled up at him. "The saloons are always hiring. I'm sure I will find something."

Gabe stared at her in surprise. When he realized that she was teasing, he grinned. He laughed as he took her arm, "But I don't think they allow you to carry big knives strapped under your clothes in those establishments.

"Want to find a spot and read our letters? I have no idea who mine are from. How about you?"

Merina lifted hers up. "It looks like a woman's handwriting. The one to Angel is from a Thomas Ridgway in Shawneetown, Illinois. That is where Señor Cole did his banking business. I am guessing that it has something to do with him.

"Let's go to the cemetery. They call it Boot Hill. I like cemeteries. I listen to the voices of those who have gone before. I offer prayers for them. I pray that they will have a peaceful rest."

Gabe followed her as she led the way up the hill to the cemetery. The oldest grave was dated 1867 and the most recent was just yesterday, June 11. The wooden markers were faded and rough, and the graves were untended. He stared at the marker dated June 11. *That is the cowboy who died yesterday, the one that Daggert stomped to death.* The marker said, 'Unknown Cowboy Died, June 11, 1879.' Gabe stared at it for a moment. *If that had been me, what would they have written?*

"I think these men have been forgotten. Perhaps they were cowboys or strangers who were passing through. They have no family to care for them here."

Gabe agreed as he looked around. He had never visited a cemetery before. Once folks were buried, they were just gone. He tried to remember them as they were when they were alive. To him, cemeteries were a reminder of sad times and he avoided them, but Merina saw them as a place of peace and of hope. He studied her face as she talked.

"If I lived here, I would come to visit these men and I would talk to them. They would know that someone cared about them."

Gabe turned Merina toward him. His eyes were intense as he asked, "Would you let me kiss you, Merina?"

Her eyes opened in surprise. She studied Gabe's face and then slowly shook her head. She touched his cheek and whispered, "No, I will not let you kiss me. I don't think it is me that you want to kiss. I think that you kiss a memory." There were tears in the corners of her eyes and she looked away quickly.

"This was not a good idea. We must go." She pulled away and moved quickly down the hill.

Gabe caught up with her in just a few strides and turned her around once again. Merina's eyes were full of tears and he wiped them with his thumbs. "I know very well who I want to kiss. Grace was a dream. Yes, I wanted that dream, but we were never allowed to make it something more. And then you came along with your dark eyes that laugh and cry and show love for your family. A woman who was close to me every day but one who held herself apart." He paused and added softly, "A woman with a tender heart that she hides." He tipped her face up as he talked. He pulled her close as he stared down at her.

Merina went still and then she pulled away. She hurried down the hill and almost ran back to the Ogallala house.

Gabe stared after her and then cursed under his breath. His mouth twisted in a sardonic smile. "Good job, Gabe. You are two for two. Stick to cows. You understand them better than women and that is a fact."

He heard voices coming up from the river and he strolled down to meet them. Angel looked at him in surprise.

"Merina isn't with you?"

Gabe shook his head as he looked away from his friend. "She went back to the Ogallala House. I think she is going to rest for a while."

Angel studied his friend. He could see the tenseness in Gabe's face even though the man pretended that all was okay. "Si, she is a difficult woman."

Gabe laughed dryly, "Yes, difficult and hard to understand."

He scooped up the little girl who stood beside Angel smiling up at the men. "And how about you, Emilia? Did you catch any fish today?"

Emilia nodded excitedly and began to give Gabe a complete story of the entire afternoon. He laughed and lifted her up onto his shoulders.

CHAPTER 13

MERINA'S SECRET

MERINA COULD SEE THE STREET FROM HER HOTEL WINDOW, and she watched them walk by. Her eyes were puffy from crying and her bottom lip trembled as she fought another round of tears. She whispered, "Never have I wanted to kiss a man so much as I wanted to kiss you, Gabe, but your heart still belongs to Grace. And I won't be your second choice."

She splashed water on her face and dabbed her eyes. Merina could feel another round of tears coming and she fell on the bed as she sobbed. She tried to hold her tears back but they continued to leak out of her eyes until she fell asleep.

It was evening when Merina awoke with a start. The small pocket watch that she carried showed 7:00 when she looked at it a second time. She washed her face and repinned her hair. Then she changed her mind and let it fall down her back. She tied it up in what some women called a ponytail. It was so thick and curly that it dangled in ringlets down the back of her neck. Her dress was wrinkled from sleeping in it, so she changed into her traditional full skirt and bright blouse. Sitting down on the bed, she opened the letter. She read it twice and then laid it down beside her as she smiled. Taking a deep breath, she started down the stairs.

Gabe was just loping up to change and he stepped aside for Merina to pass. She gave him a small smile and walked slowly on down the stairs. Gabe watched her go and then continued to the top of the stairs. He turned again to look down at Merina as she joined her brothers.

Merina stared at Emilia in surprise. The little girl had on clean clothes and her hair was brushed. Someone had pulled it into a high, crooked ponytail. She looked at her brothers in surprise.

"When did you change Emilia's clothes? I didn't hear anyone come in."

Emilia rushed up to Merina. "I asked Señor Gabe to brush my hair. The rats didn't bite me so much and then he put it in a horse's tail for me."

Merina smiled down at her little sister. When she looked up, Angel caught her eye and she looked away. *I do not want to answer any questions from a snoopy older brother.*

Gabe was back down the stairs quickly. He had changed into a dark red shirt and clean britches. His black vest and hat had been brushed and the bandana was new. It irritated Merina that she noticed those things and she turned her back.

Angel's eyes narrowed down as he watched his sister. He caught Gabe's eye and for a moment, he saw the loneliness in his friend's face. Angel raised his eyebrows in question, but Gabe shook his head slightly. He nodded toward the door and the two men led the Diamond H cowboys into the back room. Angel maneuvered to seat Merina by Gabe and she glared at both of them. Angel grinned but Gabe looked uncomfortable.

Gabe had ordered steaks for everyone and Emilia wanted to trade places with Merina to sit by her Señor Gabe. Merina traded quickly and Gabe even seemed more comfortable.

Once the meal was over, Gabe pulled out his tally book. He had kept an accounting of all money that had come in during their trip along with the expenses. The gift of Gallagher's cattle had come as a huge surprise.

He had a tally sheet for each hand along with their pay from him and from John Kirkham.

Rusty studied his carefully and then pointed at it. "Boss, ya forgot to put the price a the train tickets on here."

Gabe looked around the room at his friends.

"Boys...and ladies," he added with a grin, "this drive will probably be my last one. That's the plan anyway. You all gave more than 100%. We lost some good men when Cole's herd ran over the top of ours and those men are missed. But Rusty gained a wife and some of us are moving to Wyoming. We are all going to start a new life." He paused and continued more softly, "I don't know what it is going to be like there. I'd like to keep all of you on, but if you have an opportunity to buy something of your own or if you get a better offer, you need to do it. I don't want to hold any of you back out of loyalty.

"Tomorrow, we will meet with Badger and I'm guessing we'll meet his family too. We might even see the ranch. I don't know how big the house out there is, but we will fit whoever wants to stay until we get all of this figured out." His face tightened a little and he took a breath before he continued.

"Gallagher died after I met with him in Manhattan and he left me his cattle. Between his cattle and the Cole cattle, I have enough to buy Badger's ranch and stock it as well.

"So the train tickets are on me and thanks for a fine job."

The men were quiet for a moment and then they cheered. They each held more money in their hands than they had ever seen. Gabe had split the sale of the wagons and the extra horses among all the men just as he had promised. He had also given them each the $10 bonuses he had offered them at the beginning of each drive if they took the herd through without it being cut.

Merina's envelope held a promissory note for a mare, and she looked at it quietly before she slipped the envelope inside her bag.

Cappy's envelope contained his salary plus the loan repayment from the money he had given Gabe to buy cattle. He pulled out $40 and shoved the envelope back to Gabe.

"Now ya jist use that there money fer seed money an' buy us more cows. It were cow money an' that's what it needs ta be used fer. Sides, I'm a bunkin' with ya an' I ain't gonna have no livin' 'spenses!" He winked at Gabe and then grinned at the table of riders. "I'm kinda like a grandpappy to these here young'uns an' I want ta stay close to 'em." He tossed some hard candy toward Emilia and scattered more down the table. "I intend ta make my last years happy ones."

The men all laughed, and Gabe grinned at his old friend as he pushed the money back inside his shirt.

CHAPTER 14

MAKING PLANS

THE MEN BEGAN TO TRICKLE OUT. Miguel invited Nate to go with him to see Ogallala.

Gabe frowned and then nodded. "Only in the two saloons. One beer and no dance halls."

Nate's face crumpled. "But Gabe, I want to learn to dance."

Gabe shook his head. "Absolutely not. You can learn in Wyoming."

Merina laughed. "Nate, I will teach you to dance when we get to Cheyenne. I know many dances, both Texan and Mexican. I can teach you all of them."

Nate's eyes lit up. "Thanks, Miss Merina. I'm going to count on that." He left the room in a rush to catch Miguel.

Merina smiled at Gabe. "He is a good boy. Perhaps you are too hard on him?"

Gabe stared at her. "You do realize that the dance halls are not just dance halls. There are cribs behind them, and the dance is often just a prelude to what takes place after."

Merina blushed under her tan skin and then her eyes glinted with humor. "Then perhaps you are a smart brother to keep him away...but not so smart to send him with Miguel." Her bright eyes were snapping, and Gabe frowned as he looked toward the door.

"Well, I wasn't planning to go to bed right away anyway."

Merina laughed and stood as she bid them good night.

Gabe walked her to the door. "Grace, I am sorry about earlier. I didn't mean to make you cry."

Tears showed in the corners of Merina's eyes as she looked up at him. She took Emilia's hand and walked quickly toward the door. The little girl looked back at Gabe and waved. He winked at her and she came running back. She jumped up at him and as he lifted her up, she kissed his cheek. "Good night, Señor Gabe," she whispered as she held his face between her hands. Then she slid down and skipped back to her sister. Merina watched quietly and then she whisked her sister out of the room.

Gabe rubbed a big hand over his face and walked back to Angel. He shook his head and muttered under his breath.

Angel didn't hear what he said but he looked from Gabe to the empty doorway.

"Merina has never cried over a man before, my friend. And you called her Grace."

Gabe stared at Angel and then cursed softly as he sat down. He ran his fingers through his hair and said bleakly, "Heck of thing to be in love with a dream that never happened and a woman who is dead."

Angel sat down beside Gabe. His bright eyes were full of laughter as he nudged his friend.

"Ah but now you know what love is. The pain, the confusion, the worry…"

Gabe looked at the small man next to him and laughed, "I guess I do."

He pointed at the envelope that Angel held. "Have you read it yet?"

Angel stared at the envelope and then slowly shook his head. "No, I am not so good with the words on pages. They are like many turkey tracks and I have trouble chasing them. Merina is much better. We are both hoping you will read it with us."

Gabe looked up in surprise and Angel laughed. "Cappy offered to stay with Emilia while Merina comes back down. Miguel is not so interested. He said just to tell him what it says, and if he needs to shoot someone." Angel looked at Gabe seriously as his eyes sparkled. "Miguel is not so interested in business as he is in saloons…and fighting…and dance halls."

Gabe snorted. "Then we better look that over so we can find our brothers!"

Merina hurried back into the room and Gabe stood to pull out her chair. When they were all seated, Angel opened the large envelope and handed the sheaf of paper that was inside to Merina. She scanned the pages quickly and then looked up at the two men in surprise.

"I think that Señor Cole left us his ranchero."

She handed the papers to Gabe and he read over them slowly. Finally he looked up with a smile on his face. "He sure did. You are owners of a six-thousand-acre ranch north of Buffalo Gap, Texas complete with any remaining cattle, horses and improvements."

When Angel stared at him, Gabe pointed to the paper. "Improvements are the buildings, fences, wells—anything that makes the ranch operate." He flipped to the last page, which was a hand-written letter from Thomas Ridgway, First National Bank of Shawneetown, Illinois. Gabe's face drew down in a frown as he read it.

"Ridgway is handling Cole's affairs. He says here that he has been informed that squatters are moving in. They are rustling the cattle and horses. The letter says you need to get down there and register your claim or there will be nothing but empty land before long."

Merina's face became pale and Gabe put his hand over hers. "Angel, you and Miguel head back down there. Leave tomorrow. We can change your tickets to the other direction in the morning. Merina and Emilia can go on north with us." He paused and his face lost a little color as he looked from one to the other, "Unless this means that you won't be moving to Cheyenne. Maybe you would rather stay in Texas and run your ranch there."

Angel looked at Merina and she turned pale. "The bad hombre I killed has many friends. I cannot go back, and you will not be safe." Her eyes were large as she stared at Angel.

Gabe studied the papers again and then looked from brother to sister. He stated quietly, "Let's send a wire to Ridgway. He said that he will be traveling to Texas to look at rail locations. Let's see if he will meet you at Dan Waggoner's ranch. They meet often with railroad tycoons, so he is probably planning a stop there. Tell no one you are coming, not even any friends that you have down there.

"Have Merina sign this today and then you and Miguel sign it in front of a witness—hopefully, Ridgway. If not, Dan Waggoner will vouch for you. I will put my name under Merina's as her witness. Travel like you are just two vaqueros headed back home after a drive."

Gabe frowned. "I wish I could go with you. Two men might not be enough."

Angel laughed softly. "Ah, you forget, Señor, we have many friends. Perhaps the bad hombres will just desaparecer!" He waved his hands in the air. "Today they are here and tomorrow they are gone....and no one knows to where."

Gabe grinned at Angel and squeezed his shoulder. "Angel, I am sure glad that you came north with Cole, and I'm even more pleased that you will be joining me in Cheyenne." He took $200 from his money belt and handed it to his friend. Angel shook his head, but Gabe thrust it at him. "You might have some expenses and you can pay me back when you return. Take it and don't let these papers out of your sight. Put them in your saddle bags. Do you want one horse or two?"

Angel thought a moment. "We will take two so we can travel faster. How many days from where the train leaves us?"

Gabe drew out in his tally book where the train would go and what route they would take. "You are familiar with the area around Denison?"

Angel slowly shook his head. "I have been there but only one time."

"The tracks south will end at Denison. From there, it is a five-day ride to Dan Waggoner's ranch, but you can make it in three if you push. Avoid the towns and pay attention to the people around you. I think Denison will be the most dangerous. Maybe you should get off the train before it arrives there and take your horses across the Red River in the dark. The train will stop somewhere north of the river to refuel. Slip into the livestock car and unload there. Don't take the ferry. Swim your horses across."

Merina watched the two men as they studied the route. Her heart twisted again. *Gabe is such a good man. If only he would let his heart be free.*

Finally, Angel pushed the papers toward Merina to sign. Gabe signed under her name, Witness: Gabe Hawkins, Owner Diamond H Ranch, Cheyenne, Wyoming. He also added a line under where Angel and Miguel would sign that said, *Signatures only accepted if witnessed by Thomas Ridgway or Dan Waggoner.*

"Once it is signed, show it to the sheriff or marshal in Buffalo Gap. If they don't have one, you are on your own but make sure you hang onto this.

"Talk to John Simpson about buying the ranch. He has the Hashknife outfit right next to Cole's Circle C. He may even be the one who informed Ridgway about the squatters."

Angel listened closely as Gabe talked and nodded when Gabe spoke about John Simpson.

"Si, I know of him. I have worked with the Hashknife riders before gathering cattle."

Gabe nodded. "Simpson's a good man.

"You will probably have to sell the cattle and they won't bring much unless you get lucky. Look the horses over and see if any would be good enough stock to bring back up this way." He paused and then asked, "Did Cole have any Hereford or Angus cattle? Cows? Bulls?"

Angel nodded. "He had just bought some Herefords before we left on the drive. They were to be delivered after he returned."

Gabe leaned forward. "If you find them, bring them north. It would be worth the shipping to have them here and I'll buy them from you if you don't want to keep them." He grinned and added, "If they are bulls, you might have to bring a couple of girlfriends. They will behave better if there are girls along." Both men were laughing as they looked at Merina and she rolled her eyes.

"Men always think they are in charge, but in the end, they are the ones who are led," she commented as she looked at both men coolly.

Angel laughed and Gabe nodded soberly. "You have us confused most of the time and yet we just keep coming back. Mostly, we are flummoxed around women." Gabe paused as he looked at the laughing Angel. "Well, Angel might not be, but I am for sure."

Merina laughed and stood up. "You had better find your brother before our brother gets him into trouble."

The men followed Merina out of the back room and when she went upstairs, they walked outside.

Gabe looked over at his friend. "You good to go? Need anything else?"

Angel shook his head and they followed the sound of bottles breaking to the nearest saloon.

CHAPTER 15

A Night on the Town

THE TWO MEN PUSHED THEIR WAY THROUGH THE SWINGING DOORS OF THE CRYSTAL PALACE. They entered just in time to see Miguel throw a knife at a target on the wall. The man standing unsteadily beside him was a cowboy that Gabe knew, and he was drunk. Gabe stopped beside the man and grabbed his arm as he talked to him.

"Shorty, what are you doing trying to beat an expert with a knife when busting broncs is your specialty?"

The man looked up at Gabe and then grinned. "Hello, Preacher. I heard you was in town. Anytime some feller is smacked around fer bad behavior, I jist look fer y'all."

Shorty tripped as he walked forward, and Gabe caught him. He put his arm around the man's shoulders and led him to a table. "How about some coffee, Shorty? Aren't you headed north to the Dakotas tomorrow with a herd?"

Shorty frowned and nodded. "I am but I need a little cash to git a new pair a boots." He pointed at his boots which had the soles coming off them. He nodded toward Miguel. "That feller bet me I couldn't beat 'im in a knife toss an' I figgered mebbie I could."

Gabe laughed dryly. "Shorty, neither of us could beat him sober and you sure won't beat him drunk. How about I loan you $15 for a pair of boots and you go sleep off this drunk. Someday, you can pay me back or help another fellow out."

Shorty stared at Gabe out of bleary eyes and slowly nodded. "That would be fine, Preacher. I reckon I'll jist do that."

Several of Shorty's friends helped him up and walked him to the door. One came back and leaned over the table to talk to Gabe.

"Thanks, Preacher. That gambler is jist a itchin' to shoot somebody tonight an' we was afraid it would be Shorty. That was mighty square of ya. I'll see to it that ya git yore money back."

Gabe grinned and waved him away. "Shoot, Jack. You know that Shorty would do that for any of us."

Jack laughed and sauntered out of the saloon.

Gabe's eyes followed the men drinking and gambling around the saloon before they rested on the gambler. The man turned to look at Gabe and the smirk on his face became bigger.

Gabe stood. He grabbed Nate with one hand and Miguel with the other. "Come on, boys. Your fun here is over. We have an early morning tomorrow."

Nate was a little unsteady on his feet and Gabe turned him around to glare at him. Nate stared back at him and grinned loosely. "Ya said one beer, but ya didn't mention whiskey." His words were slurred and Gabe smacked Miguel on the back of the head before he spun Nate back around. "Last time you take my brother out."

Miguel grinned and shrugged. "I think maybe I am not someone you should expect to behave when so much fun is to be had."

Angel shook his head and looked mournfully at his younger brother. "You see, Señor, compared to Miguel, I am an angel."

Gabe snorted and turned Nate and Miguel into the dining room of the Ogallala House. He pointed at Angel. "Watch them." Then he walked back to the kitchen to ask for coffee.

He returned with a full pot and four cups. He filled them and stared at the two younger men. Nate grinned at him and tried to wink while Miguel laughed out loud. Gabe pointed at the coffee and then at his brother. "Drink. I want you sober."

An hour later, a subdued Nate stumbled upstairs. When he started to lay down on the bed, Gabe pointed at the floor and threw a blanket at him.

Cappy looked up from his blanket and grinned at Gabe. He said nothing as he rolled over.

Gabe jerked off his boots and stared at his little brother. Nate was already asleep with his boots still on. Gabe pulled them off and then rolled him onto the blanket. He covered him with another while he growled, "You'll have a headache tomorrow. I hope it's bad enough that you won't want to do this for a while."

He lay down on the bed, put his hands under his head and thought about the next day. *I had planned on Angel and Miguel for help. Who knows how long they will be gone? Maybe Merina will change her mind and help me till her brothers get back.*

He thought of Merina's bright eyes that always seemed to contain a secret joke and he smiled as he fell asleep.

CHAPTER 16

WEST TOWARD CHEYENNE

THE MEN WERE UP EARLY. All the horses needed to be watered and fed before they were loaded. The train ride would be at least seven hours with no delays, and they were going to have to water them along the way as well. Gabe planned to put them in seven cars. Their personal horses would need another car and the tack would be stored in the front of that one.

Cookie met them at the barn. He was in no hurry and Gabe looked at him with a question on his face. Cookie grinned at them. "Got me a job trailin' on north up to the Montana Territory. Always wanted to see that country an' now I'll get paid to do it. I'll sell my wagon up there an' see ya later this fall or mebbie in the spring if we run late an' she snows us in."

When Gabe stared at him in surprise, Cookie slapped him on the back. "Ah relax, Gabe. Ya have Larry to cook fer ya. I figger by this fall, y'all will have the sleepin' arrangements figgered out an' mebbie I'll have a real bed 'stead of bunkin' on the floor or mebbie on the ground."

Gabe shook his head in disgust. "This crew just keeps shrinking. Before long, it will only be Nate and me."

Cappy piped up, "I ain't goin' nowhere.....'course I don't 'tend ta work much neither."

Cookie chuckled. "If I leave ya fer a time, y'all 'ill appreciate me more when I come back. 'Sides, when I thought 'bout sellin' my mules, it just plumb made me sad. I reckon I cin part with the wagon, but Gert and Mary are goin' with me wherever I end up."

Gabe laughed and nodded. Cookie helped them water and feed the horses. Once they were done, he shook hands with each of them. "I'll see ya boys in a couple a months."

The men headed back to the Ogallala House and Merina met them with Emilia. The little girl was bouncing with excitement.

"Nina says we are riding on the big train and we get to ride in seats this time! Can I sit by you, Señor Gabe? Can I see out this time?"

Gabe lifted her up with a smile. "You sure can sit by me and you bet you can look out the windows. Now let's go eat and we'll see if the waitress will pack us a bait of food for the trip."

Nate was pale and Gabe's eyes twinkled with humor as they ordered food. "Better eat up, Nate. Supper is a long time from now and I don't know what Cheyenne has to offer for food houses."

Merina ordered tea and handed it to Nate. "Drink this, Nate. It will calm your stomach." She patted his arm and smiled at him.

Nate tasted the tea. It wasn't as bitter as the coffee and Merina was right. His stomach rolls did slow down.

Angel and Miguel were quiet during the meal and Gabe pulled out his tally book. He tore another page out of it and wrote, *Catch the train south at Elkhorn or Fremont, Nebraska. Take it to Manhattan, Kansas. Take the westbound train to Junction City and catch the Katy south there.*

"You can go south at Omaha but that will take you to Kansas City and then you will need to backtrack some. There is only one train south through the Indian Territory and into Denison so be sure they give you the right connections.

"Take some feed for your horses and plan to water them several times. The ride south on the Katy will be over thirteen hours long."

Angel studied the paper and then nodded as he shoved it in his pocket.

The men had the horses loaded by 8:30 a.m. The gear was stashed, and Gabe added several bags of oats as well. He covered the oats with the saddles and pulled them all together with his rope. Rusty attached his rope and the pile of gear was snug. Angel and Miguel helped Merina and Emilia onto the train and then jumped back off. Emilia stared at them for a moment and then tried to get off as she held out her arms, crying for her brothers.

Gabe scooped her up. "They will be coming later, Emilia. Now be a big girl and smile for your brothers."

They waved as the train pulled out and Emilia buried her head in Gabe's shoulder as she sobbed. Merina lifted her down and held her until the sobs were sniffles. Gabe pulled out a package from his war bag. He studied it a moment and then leaned toward Merina as he asked, "I wonder what this is. It smells like candy, but I don't buy candy. I don't even like it."

Emilia quit crying and sat up. She stared at the package in Gabe's hand and then she pulled open one end to peek in. Her eyes opened wide and she whispered, "It *is* candy! Can I have some?"

Merina scolded her for asking but Gabe was laughing as he gave her two pieces and then offered some to Merina, Cappy and Nate.

Nate shook his head and Gabe pointed at it, "Sugar is good for hangovers. Might do you some good, little brother." Nate silently popped a piece into his mouth and Gabe leaned back in his seat. He pulled his hat down over his eyes and appeared to be asleep.

Before long, he felt a little body climb on top of him and Emilia settled in for a nap as well. Gabe wrapped his long arms around her and smiled as they both relaxed.

CHAPTER 17

TELL ME ABOUT GRACE

CAPPY SLID OVER NEXT TO MERINA. "So tell me 'bout yoreself, Merina. What do ya plan to do once we reach Cheyenne? I doubt ya want to stay in a house with a bunch a smelly men. Got any plans yet?"

Merina nodded and pulled a letter out of her bag. "I have been offered a teaching job in Cheyenne. Several of the women in the community signed a letter that Martha McCune sent me. It was waiting for me in Ogallala. Martha even offered to let Emilia and me stay with Badger and her until I decide what I want to do."

Cappy's old eyes twinkled and he chuckled. "I reckon that's a good plan. Yore a smart gal an' ya like kids. I reckon ya be jist fine."

Merina was quiet for a moment and then she looked at the old man seriously.

"Cappy, tell me about Grace. Tell me what kind of a woman she was."

Cappy's old eyes watered as he leaned back in his seat.

"I reckon she was jist 'bout the sweetest little ol' gal I ever did know. She kinda reminded me a my Mary. She had a wide-eyed innocence 'bout 'er. Always saw the best in folks an' trusted ever'body.

"I reckon that's why Gabe here liked 'er so much. She was kinda opposite a him. He's a little jaded with folks. Seen too many bad ones I reckon.

"Gabe's ol' man was nothin' like Gabe. He was worthless as a turd at a dinner party. Gabe now, he's been a takin' care a his family since he was jist a squirt. He left home at fourteen an' he's been a sendin' money home ever since. That's why he ain't a ranchin' a'ready.

"His ol' man took the money an' gambled it away. When Gabe found out, he went back home. It was too late to save their little ranch though, an' his momma died shortly after. Gabe, he stepped up an' took care a Nate, jist like you's a doin' with Emilia there."

Cappy was quiet a moment and then added, "Gracey was kinda like a granddaughter ta me. I loved that little gal to pieces. Plumb broke my heart when she took sick. I sat with 'er those last days 'fore she died. We all thought she was a gettin' well an' then she jist faded away.

"I talked to 'er 'bout Gabe an' 'bout his family. I think that's when she falled in love with 'im. Oh she was a fallin' 'fore she took sick, but she ate them stories up.

"I was jist shore she'd get better an' when I seen that wouldn't happen, I wanted 'er to leave this world happy. I reckon she did.

"We talked 'bout the hereafter too but she knowed way more 'bout that than I did. Sister Rose an' her talked 'bout that.

"Gracey warn't 'fraid a dyin'. She was jist a little sad that she'd never kissed a feller. She'd wanted Gabe ta kiss 'er an' he 'most did on their hossback ride. He's a gentleman though an' he didn't do it. I reckon he regrets that too now."

He added quietly, "A nice gal like yoreself could do a lot worse than Gabe. Shoot, if I had a gurl, I'd *try* to marry her up to Gabe. He's a fine man an' I told Gracey that too."

Merina looked over at Cappy. Her eyes were full of tears, but she smiled at him.

"Thank you for sharing that with me, Cappy. I think Gabe's a fine man. I think maybe he is not over Grace yet. Maybe he never will be."

Cappy patted her hand. "Ya jist let time take its course, Merina. Gabe's big heart is broken an' he never let that happen afore. He'll heal up. He ain't had time ta do no thinkin' on hisself these last two months. He'll have some time once we finalize this here deal on his ranch. 'Sides, when ya work ta fix a place up, ya start ta think on who ya want to share it with. An' don't ya worry none that ya ain't like Gracey. The Good Lord don't make no two folks the same. The two of yous is friends an' it'll grow from there."

Merina stared at Cappy for a moment before she leaned over to kiss his gnarly cheek. "I see why Gracey loved you, Cappy. You are a wise man," she whispered softly. She smiled at him again and leaned back in her seat.

Cappy looked at Merina and Gabe, side by side and yet with distance between them. He smiled at them and leaned back in his seat. He thought to himself, *yous two kids 'ill be fine. Give 'er time an' this here deal'll have a happy endin'.*

CHAPTER 18

THE EAVESDROPPER

GABE REMAINED STILL AND LISTENED TO CAPPY TALK. He could feel his heart squeeze when he thought about Grace. He wanted to look over at Merina, but he forced himself to breathe evenly. When they finished visiting and Merina fell asleep, he gently lifted Emilia off his chest and laid her down in the seat. He quietly left the car and went to stand outside on the gangway between the cars. The morning air was cool, and the train chugged the miles away.

Before long, Rusty joined him and the two men listened to the sounds of the train in silence. Finally, the train whistled. Julesburg was ahead and they hurried back to the car where the women were.

Merina stood and took Emilia's hand. "Emilia needs to go to the bathroom."

Gabe pulled a blanket out of his war bag and handed it to her. "She is going to have to squat by the tracks." He paused a moment and then asked cautiously, "Do you want me to go with you?"

Merina's face turned a dark red. She looked over to where Larry was sleeping and then looked back at Gabe. "Perhaps you could hold the blanket with your back to me?"

Gabe nodded soberly and Rusty turned away to keep from laughing. Merina glared at both of them and hurried off the train to find a spot with a little privacy. There were no trees or bushes anywhere and Merina turned to Gabe. "This will have to do."

He held the blanket up and Merina helped Emilia hold her skirt up. They changed positions and then Merina glared at Gabe until he turned backwards, holding the blanket behind him. She bent his arms to make a semicircle and she had Emilia stand on the open side, spreading her skirt out with her hands. A man started their way and Gabe growled, "Back off, Mister, or you'll be wearing this blanket wrapped around your head." The man turned away and Merina finally stood, shaking out her skirts.

Her face was still red, but she stood up straight and held her head high as they hurried back toward the train. She washed Emilia's and her hands in the horse tank. As Gabe helped her up into the car, she looked up and murmured, "Thank you, Gabe. That was—was—"

"Embarrassing? Yes, I am sure it was, but I was glad to help." He leaned closer and whispered, "But maybe Larry will be awake the next time you need to go!"

Merina looked startled and then began to laugh. They were both smiling as they sat down.

Cappy looked at them and the steady flow of people boarding behind them. "We better take some turns 'fore we leave our seats next stop. We jist might lose 'em otherwise."

Gabe nodded. "We'll have to figure out bathroom breaks too because we need to water the horses at Sidney."

The train started and once again, people settled in for the ride.

Gabe looked over at Merina. "So what did your letter say? From a friend or a job offer?"

She looked at him suspiciously, but he kept his face innocent. She pulled the letter out and handed it to him.

He looked at her in surprise. "This is signed by five different women, all in agreement that you be the next teacher! Molly Rankin, Beth Rankin—they must be related. Sadie Parker, Josie Williams, and Martha McCune." He grinned at her. "Well, I guess you have a job. So much for my hope that you would be available to do some riding."

Merina was quiet for a moment. "Perhaps I can help one day on the weekends."

Gabe studied her face. "Twenty miles is a long way to ride after you have worked all day. I just need to figure out a way to get you to stay."

Merina's face turned red again and Gabe chuckled.

She pointed at the letters peeking out of his pocket. "And who are your letters from? Perhaps from some woman whose heart you broke when you rode away."

It was Gabe's turn to blush. He grinned as he shook his head.

"Sicily Waggoner has been trying to marry me off for years. She wrote to give me the name and address of a gal who is a neighbor of theirs....in case I would like to write to her."

Merina's dark eyes sparkled with laughter. "And?"

"And no. I don't need any more distractions or complications." He looked intensely at Merina and added, "I have more than I can handle right here."

Emotions flashed through Merina's eyes so quickly that Gabe couldn't track all of them. She pointed at the second letter. "And that one?"

Gabe handed it to her. "It is from a girl too. One of the riders who died in the stampede when Cole's cattle ran over us had letters from his girl. I wrote her a note telling her what happened and sent her his wages." He paused and added quietly, "She sent that back, thanking me."

Merina read the letter. Her eyes were soft as she looked up at Gabe. "That would be a very difficult letter to write."

Gabe nodded, "But she deserved to know and as trail boss, it was my responsibility."

Merina studied his face and then said softly, "You are a kind man, Gabe Hawkins. You hide your heart, but it is large." Her eyes sparkled as she added, "Perhaps if you didn't work so hard to hide it, you wouldn't be so grumpy."

Gabe's face registered his surprise and then he laughed. He nodded his head and stated ruefully, "Perhaps. Maybe someday I will work to change that."

Cappy had moved over to talk to Rusty and the woman next to Merina started a conversation.

Gabe leaned back in his seat with a smile. He pulled his hat over his eyes and went to sleep.

CHAPTER 19

THREE ANGRY WOMEN

IT WAS NEARLY 12:30 P.M. WHEN THE TRAIN PULLED INTO THE STATION AT SIDNEY, NEBRASKA. Gabe was up quickly to water the horses. Cappy, Rusty and Nate all followed him out of the car. They ran along beside the train and quickly pulled the doors open to the cars that held the horses. They hooked ropes to the horses and led them to the water tank.

The horses were almost done when a child's voice was heard. She was crying and talking in Spanish. Gabe paused and listened as he looked that direction. When he heard a man laugh, both he and Rusty handed their ropes off and raced back to the train car.

A man was holding Emilia up as she kicked at him. Another had his arms on Merina's shoulders and a third was holding Larry by one arm. She was beating on his face with her free hand.

Rusty grabbed him and jerked him away. He threw him up against the side of the car and smashed him over the head with his gun.

Gabe's face was white as he looked at the two men. "Take your hands off them or I'll drop you where you stand."

The one who was holding Emilia dropped her and Gabe caught her with one arm. He set her down without taking his eyes off the two men in front of them.

The one holding Merina dropped his arms and stepped back. He sneered at Gabe and laughed.

"You cowboys are all alike. You think you are such the gentlemen. We were just havin' a little fun. 'Sides, that one liked it." He pointed at Merina and Gabe hit him. The punch dropped him to the ground and Emilia began to kick him, calling him names in Spanish.

The last man backed up. He held his hands open over his guns and Gabe pointed outside. "No gunplay around this many people. A stray bullet could go right through the side of this car and hit someone. You want to fight, let's take it outside."

The man stared and as Gabe started to turn around, the man reached for his gun. Gabe drew as he turned and slammed his gun down over the man's head. Merina's knife was in her hand. Her face was pale, and she was trembling, but the knife was up and ready. Gabe put his arm around her for a moment and then took the knife. He shoved it under the seat and drug the man to the open doorway. The three men were dropped unceremoniously down the steps. Rusty turned back toward the trembling Larry and Gabe picked up Emilia as he sat down by Merina. Her hands were clenched in front of her and she was trembling. She looked up at Gabe and whispered, "I almost killed him."

Gabe nodded. "I saw that, but it is better that you didn't. Always better to leave broken jaws and cracked heads behind than dead bodies." He squeezed her hands and then looked at Emilia. He made sure that she wasn't hurt and then he hugged her.

"That bad man wanted to sit in your seat. I told him he couldn't. He was a bad man. He pinched my arms, so I kicked him."

Gabe looked over to where Larry and Rusty were talking. Larry's face was white, and she looked angry.

Rusty looked up with a grin. "Ya know, I think these here women could a taken those boys without our help. I don't think I want to tangle with any of 'em when they're mad like this."

The conductor stepped through the door and looked them over. "Problem in here?"

Gabe jerked his head toward the steps. "Those three fellows were bothering our women. We had a discussion, and they lost."

The conductor nodded slowly. He pointed toward the knife that had slid partway out from under Merina's seat. "Might want to put that away, Ma'am. Never know—you might need it again."

He tipped his hat and nodded at them. He leaned out the door and bellered, "Get the sheriff down here. I want these men locked up. All aboard!"

Nate and Cappy made it back just as the train was pulling out. Nate studied Gabe's face and then looked at Merina. Cappy just grinned and pulled Nate into a seat.

Gabe picked up Merina's knife and she slid it into a scabbard under her skirt. He didn't see exactly where it went but it looked like the scabbard was attached to her thigh. He looked at her and laughed as he shook his head.

"Remind me never to make you mad. I don't want that thing stuck in me."

She rolled her eyes and Emilia chattered until she became tired. She stayed on Gabe's lap and he held her while she slept.

"She sure is a sweet little gal." He looked sideways at Merina. "Every feller ought to have a sweet gal, at least one anyway. Maybe several."

When Merina looked up at him, he grinned and winked at her.

Merina laughed and then looked seriously at him. "You don't think about things for long, do you? That fight is just over, and you are olvidar—you are—are moved on."

Gabe shrugged. "Doesn't do any good to dwell on it. It's over. I try to think and plan ahead, but some things just happen and there is no time to think. Just time to react. My first instinct is to shoot but I am trying to be more civilized. Like maybe just break their jaws." His eyes twinkled and he grinned at her.

"See that conductor would have pulled us off this train and taken us in for questioning if someone had died. We would have been able to straighten it out but it sure would have messed up our trip. And what about the horses? We gave him an easy way out. You ladies were obviously upset, and he was willing to ignore the knife. The bad guys went to jail and everything is good."

He added softly, "But that doesn't mean I didn't want to shoot them when I heard Emilia crying and saw that man's hands on you." He paused. "And little Larry too."

Merina's eyes were unreadable as she looked up at him.

Gabe put his arm around her shoulders and pulled her closer to him. She didn't resist and he left his arm there while they both slept.

CHAPTER 20

WISDOM FROM A CHILD

GABE AWOKE ABOUT AN HOUR LATER. Merina's head was tipped against his side. Her black hair lay against his shirt and long lashes curled down over her cheeks. Emilia was starting to stir, and Gabe softly kissed the top of Merina's head before he removed his arm.

She opened her eyes and then sat up.

Gabe pointed at Emilia. "I'm guessing she will need to go to the bathroom again. You need help this stop?"

Merina blushed and then nodded.

Gabe grinned at her, "Well, let's be the first ones off then so we can get the best spot! According to the schedule, this is Bushnell, Nebraska. The next stop will be Pine Bluff and that is in the Wyoming Territory."

Emilia sat up. "I'm hungry, Señor Gabe."

Gabe winked at her. "Well, I just happen to know where some food is. We'll go to the bathroom here and then eat once we're done." He grabbed his blanket again and Emilia skipped down the steps in front of him. Rusty had a blanket in his hand as well and the two men helped both women down. Gabe looked from one to the other. "You want a big circle or two smaller ones?"

Neither woman answered and Rusty grinned. The men found a couple of bushes and stood with their backs to the women, holding the blankets out. Once everyone was finished, the women went to wash their hands.

Gabe looked around. "The country is changing. More brush here and not so much open prairie." He paused as he looked the country over and then turned back to Rusty.

"So is Larry going to be all right staying with three men? Merina won't stay. She is staying in town with the McCunes until she gets a place of her own."

Rusty nodded. "It's different since we's married. I guess it'll depend on the house though. She'll want a little privacy. I should prob'ly start lookin' fer a place though. The baby is goin' to change things. 'Sides, you'll have more men there when Angel an' Miguel get back."

Rusty paused and then looked sideways at Gabe as he added innocently, "Might want to start on a bunkhouse. I mean if y'all get married, that's goin' to change things."

Gabe was quiet and then he grinned. "Never know. Might find me a widow woman out here who's itching to get hitched. I might do it too if she has land."

Rusty's mouth fell open and he turned to look at Gabe. When he saw the grin on Gabe's face, he chuckled. "Ya had me goin' a bit there, Boss." He looked seriously at Gabe. "Merina's a good little gal. I think ya spooked 'er a little in the beginnin'. No gal wants to feel like she's the second choice so ya might have to work a little harder." His blue eyes danced as he added, "But ya seem to be pickin' up yore spurs a little an' lookin' ahead more 'stead of behind."

Gabe studied Rusty and then slowly turned red. "I have sure received a lot of advice on women in the last two months. Shoot, if I could remember all of it, I would pert'neer be an expert—on women for sure and maybe even marriage. And I know nothing about either."

Rusty shoved his hands into his pockets and laughed. "Bein' married is purty nice if ya like the little gal yore hitched up with." He was quiet and then added seriously, "Larry is a sweet woman an' I see more reasons ever' day to love her more. I don't reckon there will ever be a day I regret askin' 'er to be my wife. Oh, there was a few times 'fore we married that I was a little nervous but that was 'cause I didn't know if I could measure up. We're happy an' we cain't wait to meet this little one." He paused and then added, "I do worry 'bout supportin' a family though. Cowboys don't make much an' there will prob'ly be more kids."

Gabe nodded. "You need to get your own place. We'll have to work on that…while we build a bunkhouse." The two men were smiling as they strolled back to the train and loped up the steps.

Merina had passed out the food and everyone was eating.

Gabe sat down by Emilia. "Where is my sandwich? Did you eat all the food and not save me anything?"

Emilia smiled at him. "We saved you one. Merina kept the biggest one for you."

Gabe's face lit up and Merina's neck turned a little darker. "Emilia, you sit over here while you eat. Let Señor Gabe have some peace."

Emilia frowned but slid out of her seat and sulked over to where Merina pointed. She squatted on the floor and used the chair seat as her table.

Gabe slid down next to Merina. "Well then, I'll just sit a little closer to you. That works for me." He winked at her and once again, her dark eyes flashed too many emotions for him to catch. Everyone had a full canteen and the water tasted good even if it was a little warm.

The train was just picking up speed when it ground to a stop. A small herd of buffalo was slowly crossing the tracks. A big bull swung his head and struck the engine. The entire train shuddered as the reverberations moved through the cars. He snorted a couple of time and hit it a second time before he finally crossed the tracks.

Rusty had lifted Emilia up on his lap so she could see out the window and she watched the buffalo in amazement.

"Count them, Rusty. How many of those big buffers are there?"

"Twenty-one so that's jist a little ol' herd. Why there used to be hundreds of 'em in a herd."

"Do people eat them?"

Rusty nodded, "Sometimes they do. I've eaten buffalo steaks 'fore. The hides are mighty heavy. Take a purty big man to pick a hide like that up, but they's sure warm."

Emilia looked at Rusty for a moment and then calmly stated, "Señor Gabe could pick one up. He's a strong man and he's my friend."

Rusty's blue eyes twinkled. "Why I reckon he could. Think he should get married?"

Gabe's face turned a dark red and he choked on his sandwich. He took a big swing of water and almost choked on that when Emilia answered.

"Maybe but I don't know who he would marry. Married folks hug and kiss on each other like you and Larry do. I don't think Señor Gabe likes to do that."

Larry blushed and Rusty chuckled. He was just getting warmed up and this was becoming more fun all the time.

"Well how about Merina? Think he could marry her?"

Emilia stared at Rusty and then shook her head. "No, Nina is my sister."

"You don't want him to marry your sister?"

"No because Señor Gabe is nice and if Nina gets mad at him, he might run away. We don't like it when Nina is mad.

"No, I think he should marry a nice lady, like a grandma."

Rusty was trying hard not to laugh and Gabe's face turned even more red.

"I would like a grandma and Señor Gabe could marry one. Then she would always be nice to me and she would give me candy."

Everyone but Gabe and Merina was laughing. Gabe was trying to drink water and Merina had her face almost buried in her sandwich.

Rusty looked around at the little group as he laughed. "Well there ya go. Ol' Gabe cin marry a grandma an' this here operation will be ridin' high an' smooth. I'll get to work on that fer ya, Boss."

Emilia climbed back up on Gabe's lap. "I want you to be *my* daddy when you get married, Señor Gabe. Then I will have a daddy and a grandma."

Gabe's face was still red, but he pulled the little girl close and kissed the top of her head. "I reckon I would like to be your daddy, Emilia. I hope if I ever have a little girl that she is just like you." He smiled at her and Emilia put her hands on either side of his face. She rubbed her nose against his and laughed before she slid down.

"Nina, can I have a cookie? I know you have some. Please?"

CHAPTER 21

ONE MORE STOP

PINE BLUFF WAS ONLY THIRTY MINUTES PAST BUSHNELL. The stop was a brief one and Gabe could feel the excitement in him.

"One more stop before Cheyenne! Hillsdale is less than an hour from here and Cheyenne is only a half an hour past that. We are almost home!"

Gabe was getting restless and he finally walked out to the gangway again and stood there. The mid-afternoon sun was warm, but he could feel the dryness in the air.

"I almost need to pinch myself. I sure never dreamed I would own a ranch in Wyoming when I started this last drive."

Merina stepped through the door and Gabe moved over to make room for her.

"I think you are too excited to sit much longer."

Gabe chuckled and agreed. "I have wished for this to happen most of my life and I sure didn't see it coming. Cappy loaned me the money to buy my own steers and that was like the beginning. First Cole gave me what was left of his herd and then Gallagher left me his." Gabe was quiet a moment and then added softly, "I am benefitting from their deaths. Doesn't seem right when you think of it that way."

Merina studied his face and then shook her head. "No, I think that when it is our time to go, we just go. It was time for Señor Cole and Señor Gallagher to leave this world. The cattle had to go to someone. You were chosen and you must be grateful."

Gabe rested his eyes on her face and looked at her intently. She returned his gaze for a moment and then looked away.

"Merina, you are a wise woman." His eyes twinkled as he added, "I think I like you almost as much as I like Angel."

Merina looked up in surprise and then she laughed. Once again, Gabe was amazed at the similarities between the sister and brother. The two visited a while longer and when the door opened to show more restless passengers, they gave up their places and walked back inside.

Gabe's eyes were shining when they sat down. "We will be in Cheyenne in fifteen minutes. We will need to get Rowdy's horses to the livery and ours as well. I think maybe we will ride them there. That way, we can all stick together and there will be more help moving the horses. Let's saddle up as quickly as possible. We want to keep them calm so try not to show your excitement."

Merina frowned as she listened. "Señor, we did not wear our riding skirts and we cannot ride astride in a dress."

Gabe looked at the two women. He frowned slightly and then nodded.

"We will lead your horses. Are you all right with walking into town? We can meet you at the hotel since we need to get rooms for the night."

CHAPTER 22

CURLY JOE

MERINA GRIPPED EMILIA'S HAND AND WALKED WITH LARRY TOWARD THE MAIN PART OF TOWN. She saw several hotels. The Rollin's House and the Eagle were fairly close together. The Eagle seemed to be a little smaller and didn't look as fancy.

She pointed as she asked, "How about the smaller one? I think the bigger one will be more expensive maybe."

Larry nodded. Her stomach squeezed a little at the thought of spending money on a hotel. Rusty had given her their money to carry and she knew how little there was.

Merina saw the worry flash across Larry's face.

"Perhaps we could share a room? Maybe Rusty could stay with Señor Gabe and that will save us one room."

Larry nodded and smiled. "We don't have very much money to work with. Rusty is a hard worker but I think I should get a job too. We are going to need a place of our own when the baby comes."

Merina was quiet. If Rowdy hadn't paid her for Cole's horses, she wouldn't have any money either. She also was trying to stretch her money as far as she could.

"Maybe you could teach with me. We can ask Mrs. McCune."

Larry looked away and tears filled her eyes. "No, the baby will come in a few months and they wouldn't want a teacher who would only be there part of the year."

She smiled at Merina. "Rusty told me not to worry. He said we will stay with Gabe for a few months and by then, he will have something for us." Her smile became bigger, "Besides, I can always charge Gabe to cook for his men!"

The two women were smiling as they climbed the steps to the Eagle Hotel.

A tall man chewing on a toothpick stepped out of the doorway. He stared them up and down.

"Well lookie here. The train brought in two more women and just when I was thinking how short on women we are here." He looked from one to the other and stepped closer.

"How about you?" He grinned as he tried to take Merina's arm. "You up for a little fun tonight?" His eyes slid toward Larry. "She looks like she's been partying already, but I bet you could give a man a good time."

Merina jerked her arm loose and slapped the man. Her face was pale and tight as she moved to the side to walk around him.

The man rubbed his face and laughed. "Well now, ain't you a sassy little gal. That's just the way I like 'em." He reached for her arm again and then yelped in surprise at a sharp kick in the knee.

"You leave my sister alone, you bad man! Gabe will come and punch you for being bad!" Emilia shouted as she continued to kick him.

The man jumped back, rubbing his knee and Emilia went after him, kicking for all she was worth.

Merina calmly walked around him and into the hotel. "Come, Emilia. That is enough."

Emilia kicked the man one more time and then glared as she stomped after her sister. She stopped and looked back at him when she was inside as she shook her finger at him. "You are a bad gringo."

The man stared after the small girl in surprise and then chuckled as he rubbed his legs. "I don't recall ever being set on by anyone quite that short." He was still grinning as he went down the steps two at a time and strolled up the street.

Several cowboys were driving a herd of horses toward the livery and Curly watched as they rode by. His eyes narrowed down and as he studied them, he began to form a plan. Another man joined him and nodded toward the horses.

"You thinkin' what I'm thinkin', Joe?"

Joe nodded his head. "Tell the boys to meet me about 7:00 this evening by that line shack outside town. Have them trickle out a few at a time. We'll take that remuda tonight."

The second man drifted away, and Joe sauntered on up the street to the nearest saloon. Curly knew the owner well. He also knew that James McDaniel kept his kegs cold, and Joe was hankering for a cold beer.

Joe's father, William Sturgis, had moved to Cheyenne in 1873 when Joe was sixteen to join the cattle business with William's brother, Thomas. The two men formed the Northwestern Cattle Company and the Union Cattle Company. Now they were among the most prominent cattle ranchers in Wyoming.

Joe's mouth twisted in an ironic smile as he downed his beer. "If I'd stayed and worked with Pa, I'd be a partner now too," he muttered under his breath.

He slammed the glass down on the bar. "Give me another, Jimmy."

James McDaniel filled the glass and handed it to Joe. "Been by to see yore Pa? He sets a store of hope on ya. He'd take ya back today if you'd buck up an' ride straight."

McDaniel paused and added quietly, "Both yore pa an' yore Uncle Tom were some of the big pushers to form the Wyomin' Stock Grower's Association several years ago. That group was started to catch livestock thieves. If ya ain't goin' to see 'im, might be best if ya just moved on. Be a pure shame if a pa had to help hang his own son."

When Joe said nothing, McDaniel looked hard at him. "Word is the sheriff has posters on a Curly Joe. The last one come in from Montana. Seems he shot a couple a cowboys an' one still had the thong hitched over the hammer of his gun." McDaniel paused and added softly, "I don't spose the sheriff will start anything out of respect fer yore pa—unless ya cause some trouble here. An' since ya ain't here to see yore pa, I'm guessin' that's what ya have in mind."

Joe swished the beer around in his glass and stared at the amber circles. When he finally looked up, he was grinning.

"Now Jimmy, I reckon I can come back home if I want to reminisce the good ol' days here. Town seems kinda quiet though—sure not like she was six years ago when old Cheyenne was kickin' and howlin'. Kinda slow 'round here."

McDaniel didn't answer. He was worried for Joe's father. He leveled a hard glance at Joe and started to wash beer mugs. "I think you spent too much time with those thugs you used to hang out with in New York before you came here. Yore pa thought that a fresh start would get ya on the right track, but ya threw all his offers back his face."

Joe slammed his glass down and leaned across the bar the grab the smaller man. He picked him up and shook him before he dropped him back down to fall on his washing pan. He threw some change on the bar and stalked out.

Curly Joe was a tall man, over six foot in his socks. His reddish-brown hair was in tight curls all over his head and he usually had a couple of days growth of red stubble on his face. Large, meaty shoulders tapered down to lean hips and he wore a gun on each side. He laughed a lot and liked to joke around but the smiles didn't seem to show in his eyes. For those who didn't know him, Curly Joe was a charismatic man who just wanted to have a good time.

Those who knew him well would not agree. Joe's violent temper was easily unfettered and killing came easy to him. Maybe if he had quit the outlaw trail three or four years earlier, he could have been redeemed. Now he just didn't care. He scoffed at the law and those who tried to enforce it. His guns were fast, and no one had beaten him yet. The soiled doves found him interesting but Curly liked a challenge, and the little gal who had slapped him stayed on his mind.

Curly Joe strolled down the street and sat down on a barrel by the livery. He propped his feet up and began to whistle as he whittled on a stick he had found.

The cowboys who had been driving the horses walked out of the livery and headed up the street. When they walked up the steps to the Eagle Hotel, he began to grin.

"Yessir, I'm a guessin' those fellows are with the little gals I bumped into. Reckon I am going to have to take things in my own hands if I want to get acquainted." He dropped his feet down and sauntered into the livery.

The wiry little hostler looked hard at him through bright blue eyes and then turned his back. He kept forking dirty hay and Curly had to jump back to keep it from landing on his boots.

He let out a startled cry as he stumbled and reached to grab the smaller man. The hostler spun around with the pitchfork tines inches from Curly Joe's neck. Curly backed up and dropped his hands.

The hostler nodded at him. "Ya jist go 'head an' see if'n ya cin git that gun out 'fore I stick ya with this here dirty fork."

Curly's eyes narrowed and then he laughed a dry laugh. "I just came to check on my horse."

The hostler nodded toward the back. "He's in the same stall ya put 'im in. You's the only one what rubbed yore horse down. The rest a those boys that come in with ya left their hosses in there jist a wet with sweat. Don't think much of a man that treats his horse poorly. An' since yore runnin' with 'em, I don't reckon ya care that much neither."

Curly looked carefully at the bandy-legged old man and then moved his eyes around the barn. *This old man is sure pushin' me hard. He probably has somebody sittin' up somewhere with a gun on me right now, just itchin' to shoot.*

He spread his hands wide and backed up. "I'm just here to check on my horse." Curly picked up a curry comb and a rag. He headed back to where his horse was stabled, looking the penned horses over as he sauntered along, whistling under his breath.

The hostler watched him for a moment and then disappeared.

Curly curried his horse, moving around it and taking quick notice of where all the horses were penned. He talked softly to his horse as he worked. "It's going to take a little time to get all of them out. We are for sure going to have to get rid of that hostler. I'm guessin' he sleeps here from the looks of him." The horse looked around curiously at the man who rode him. The big bay had the lines of a thoroughbred and was built for speed. His horse was the one thing that Curly always treated well.

Curly liked horses. The comb paused for a moment in his hands. "I should have bought me that little ranch several years ago that I looked at. It was all set up to raise horses and I'd be makin' a decent livin' by now." He smiled as he thought of the girl who almost made him an honest man. Her name was Audrey, but he had called her Andy. "Her daddy could tell I was headed down the wrong road, and he ordered me off their ranch. Told me not to come back unless I left the outlaw trail and took an honest job." He patted the horse and it nickered softly at him. "And that is why I call you Andy."

Curly quietly saddled Andy and another horse that he used as a back-up. He led both out of the livery and tied them behind the barn.

CHAPTER 23

A Cheyenne Welcome

ROOSTER SMITH HAD BEEN A HOSTLER FOR A LONG TIME AND BEFORE THAT, he had ridden the outlaw trail himself. He could spot a horse thief walking down the street. He recognized Joe Sturgis and he knew the man was up to no good. He also knew that some of the horses stabled in his livery were already sold to Rowdy Rankin. The Rankins were like family to him, and Rooster was mighty protective of his family.

"Joe Sturgis done went bad. Sad deal too 'cause his ol' man's a fine feller. 'Course Joe was bad 'fore his pop moved 'im out here. He done hung 'round those thugs back east he claimed was his friends fer too long. Ol' Bill tried his best after his wife died but Joe jist turned crooked. Calls hisself Curly Joe now an' thinks he be a tough man. Well I be onto 'im an' he ain't pullin' none a his dirty deals here.

"I believe we'll jist have us a little party. We be a waitin' fer Joe an' his boys ta show up, an' it won't be fer no tea party."

Rooster pulled his hat down hard on his head, hung his pitchfork on the hook and strolled out of the barn with a piece of straw hanging out of his mouth. He tipped his hat to all the ladies and winked at the kids. Cheyenne was his home and had been since its beginnings. No tinhorn outlaws were going to steal his horses.

Lance Rankin's Rocking R hands had moved their business to the Tin Restaurant after Barney Ford, owner of the Ford House, moved back to Denver. The Tin House as it was called, had received its name because they were served on tin table service. The food was good most of the time and there was always plenty.

Rowdy Rankin was especially sad when Barney left. Not only were the two men friends, but Barney always made sure that Rowdy received two plates of food without asking. Barney's food was delicious as he prided himself on being the best, and he was missed.

The town had even given Barney a parade and a party the day that he loaded his belongings in his wagon. One of Cheyenne's own had moved away.

Rooster spotted the men who had stabled the new horses eating at the Tin House. There were two women with them now and one small girl. *Guess a couple a those boys must be married.*

He stopped by their table and nodded at the men. He winked at the little girl and slipped her a piece of hard candy from his pocket. She stared at it a moment, looked sideways at the young woman beside her, and then popped it into her mouth.

"So I see ya brung yore wives an' are treatin' 'em ta a fine meal at this here fancy eatin' house." He looked around the group with a big smile on his face.

The oldest man at the table grinned and nodded, "You's 'bout half right. These here two young folks is married. They's Rusty an' Larry O'Brian. That good lookin' little gal 'cross the table is Merina an' her sister is Emilia. That's Nate an' I'm Cappy. I'm the voice a reason in this here crowd an' the grumpy one on the end there is Gabe." His smile became wider when Gabe looked at him in surprise. The younger man's neck slowly turned red and Cappy chuckled.

Rooster studied Merina and then turned his wise eyes toward Gabe. He did that several times until both Gabe and Merina were blushing.

"I hear marryin' helps that but I cain't say fer sure as I ain't never been married." His bright blue eyes were sparkling with orneriness and Gabe shook his head. He reached for the hostler's hand and grinned back at him.

The old man chuckled. "I'm Rooster. I been 'round this here town since she first came ta be. Not much happens I don't know 'bout. In fact, they's some new fellers here in town who seem ta be powerful interested in hosses. They seem ta have an eye fer quality hoss flesh an' they's a few hosses in that barn, oh say sixty or so, that they like a lot."

Gabe frowned. "Those horses are already sold. Rowdy Rankin should be here tomorrow sometime to take possession."

Cappy's eyes became serious. "Now I didn't say nothin' 'bout *buyin'* hosses. I jist said they was interested."

Gabe's eyes became hard and he stared at the hostler. "You saying we need to keep an eye on those horses tonight?"

Rooster nodded. "I reckon that'd be good thinkin'. Now ya see those loud boys at that back table? Well, they's riders fer the Rockin' R. They brung cattle in today an' loaded 'em on the train ta go east. They happen ta ride fer Lance Rankin, Rowdy's brother. Now they'd be powerful sad if they missed the party ya boys 'ill be havin' tonight."

His eyes sparkled again with laughter as he added, "Sides, Miss Merina here is the best lookin' woman those boys seen in some time. Now since Gabe here ain't marryin' 'er, why how 'bout I bring those fellers over an' kinda inner'duce 'em. Friendly like. An' then I'll ask 'em if they want ta party with ya fellers tonight, ya bein' newcomers an' all."

Gabe was listening closely to Rooster and when the hostler added the marrying part, he almost choked on his food and took a huge gulp of water. Merina's face tinged red under her olive skin and Rusty laughed out loud.

Rusty looked over at Gabe and nodded. "I reckon that'd be fine. The boss jist choked some on his food, so I'll answer fer 'im."

Rooster's grin was huge as he winked at Merina. He tipped his hat again at the smiling Larry. "Ladies, I want ya ta know that ol' Rooster is here ta please, 'specially when it comes ta the ladies." He winked again and moved spryly through the crowded room back to the large table in the back.

CHAPTER 24

JAMES AND GRACE

THE RIDERS AT THE BACK TABLE GRINNED AT ROOSTER AS HE WALKED UP AND THEN THEIR FACES BECAME SOBER AS THEY LISTENED. Suddenly, they were all craning their necks and looking around people to see who all was at the table Rooster was gesturing toward. It was just a few moments before the riders stood and headed toward the side of the table where Merina was seated.

They gathered around with their hats in their hands and grinned shyly at her while Rooster did the introductions.

One of the quieter ones stepped forward. "Ladies, gents—welcome to Cheyenne. I'm Joe Johnson. I'm the foreman at the Rockin' R. We'd sure be pleased to help ya out tonight." Joe had been working for the Rocking R since '72. He was a Kansas hand and had come to Cheyenne with his brother Hicks, and their cousin Smiley. Smiley was killed seven years ago but Joe and Hicks had made a home on the Rocking R.

Joe's life before the Rocking R had been a hard one and he appreciated the chance that Lance had given to both him and Hicks. He rode for the brand and was fiercely loyal to both Rankin brothers.

"We noticed some tough-lookin' fellers in town earlier. They all kinda drifted out a town 'round suppertime but they all headed the same direction. We was just talkin' that they looked like trouble."

A short man in the back spoke up. "I recognized the big one. He's Curly Joe Sturgis an' he's wanted up in the Montana Territory for stealin' cattle an' gunnin' down some cowboys. Curly's gang was makin' off with some Slash B cattle owned by Rock Beckler in the Bitter Root Valley up there. A couple of Rock's hands came up on Curly's gang. Those riders didn't even know the cattle were bein' stolen. They thought Curly had bought 'em.

"Rock told us to gather 'em in close. He said that a buyer would be comin' by later that day or the next. Curly just up an' started shootin'. He killed Pete before he could even get the thong off the hammer of his gun. He shot Dally as he started to reach for his rifle.

"I ride for Rock an' those fellows were my friends. I'd sure like to help catch 'em if that's what you fellows want to do."

Gabe studied the riders and then looked again at the man who had spoken. He stretched his hand toward the man.

"Gabe Hawkins. You said you ride for the Slash B?" When the short man nodded, Gabe asked, "You know a fellow by the name of James Long?"

Merina looked at Gabe in surprise. She leaned forward as the Montana cowboy stared at him.

"I did know him. He was one of the fellows that Curly shot. We called him Dally, Dally Long but he told me that his given name was James."

Merina's breath caught and she looked quickly at Gabe.

Gabe stared at the man. His eyes were bleak as he looked away. Rusty looked from Merina to Gabe with surprise and then he frowned.

Gabe's eyes came back to the short rider and he put out his hand. "Sorry to catch you off guard. I was asked by a friend to try to track

James down. That wasn't the answer I was hoping for. You said you rode with him?"

When the man nodded, Gabe asked, "What's your name? I guess I need to write your boss a second letter. I just sent him one asking about James."

"The name is Stub, Stub Jackson. The boss sent me down here to talk to Rowdy Rankin about horses. The two of them have been correspondin'. I was told to be here by today to look 'em over, so you see, I have double reason to help you tonight." He paused and then added, "I can take your letter with me if you want. I'll be back home before the mail ever gets there an' I can give it to the boss." Stub's blue eyes were hard as he looked at Gabe.

"Tell your friend that Dally was a good man. He always talked about a little gal by the name of Grace. Wrote her several letters but he never heard back from her. He knew she'd moved an' he figured that she never received 'em. He sure thought a lot of her. If your friend knows her or knows where she is, I'd sure like to write her an' tell her about Dally."

Gabe's face turned pale and Merina addressed Stub with a smile. "Stub, I will write that letter for Gabe. I never met Grace, but we know some of the same people. I will be glad to help out. If you don't mind walking me to the dry goods store, I will get some paper and write it for you now." She gave him another smile and added, "In case you leave town before I see you again. It looks like all of you will be busy this evening."

Stub looked surprised and the other cowboys were immediately jealous.

Merina leaned over to Emilia and whispered, "I have to go back to the hotel. Why don't you go sit by Larry?"

Emilia beamed at her sister and slid off her chair. She ran around the table and climbed up on Gabe's lap. He kissed her cheek and then looked back up at the men. His face was tight and he growled, "Let's go on over to the Gold Room Saloon and have a beer. I appreciate you boys offering to help and I am going to accept your offer."

As the men stood up, Gabe handed Emilia to Larry. His eyes were hard and Rusty looked at him in question. Gabe shook his head slightly as he dropped some money on the table. The men all trooped out and headed for the Gold Room.

Cappy's bright eyes were watery and he blew his nose a couple of times as he followed the younger men. Rooster fell in step beside him. They walked in silence and then Rooster commented softly, "I take it that little gal passed away?"

Cappy nodded. "Gabe was soft on her an' it's been hard on 'im." He wiped his eyes again and muttered a curse. "She were a sweet little gal. Like a granddaughter ta me. James was 'er first friend. Guess they's together now."

CHAPTER 25

THE ROCKING R HELPS OUT

STUB OFFERED MERINA HIS ARM AS THEY STEPPED OFF THE BOARDWALK AND INTO THE STREET. She paused and then looked up at him.

"Señor, Grace is dead. She died of diphtheria. Señor Gabe was informed just a month ago." She paused as her dark eyes met his and tears formed in their corners. "He was in love with her and this has been very difficult for him. That is why I offered to write the letter." Merina's voice was soft, and Stub's face tightened as he slowly nodded.

"Señor Gabe was asked by Grace's father to try to contact your friend. Señor James saved Grace's life as a child and her father left all he owned to James when he left this world. First Grace's mother, then Grace and finally her father. The entire family is fallecer—they have all perished."

Stub was quiet for a moment and then he nodded.

"Dally used to talk about her from time to time. He told me once about that wagon train. Terrible thing to leave sick folks like that an' especially little ones. He never dwelt too much on what he did. He just said they rode to the closest town an' Grace was adopted there. He was angry with Grace's Pa for not wanting him in the beginning but as he became older, he understood." Stub paused and then added softly, "He had told the boss that he was quittin' after fall round up. He was headed to Kansas City to see if he could find her. Said he'd saved a little money an' he was leaving." Stub looked down and shook his head.

"Those rustlers just cut down on them. Pete an' Dally were pards. Dally kept Pete out of trouble but the two of them would do anything for the other. Dally was tryin' to pull out his rifle, but Curly Joe would have shot him either way. He always made sure there was no one left to talk."

Merina was silent a moment as she studied his face. "I think perhaps you know this Curly well."

Stub nodded bitterly. "We rode the owlhoot trail together for a time. I was a poor outlaw though. I didn't like stealing an' I didn't like killing." Stub's mouth twisted into a wry grin. "Kind of hard for a feller to make a livin' as an outlaw if that's how he thinks."

Merina laughed softly and they crossed the street quickly. She purchased the paper and then they found a table in the Ogallala House. She quickly wrote out the note and then handed it to Stub to read.

"I think your home is far away, Señor. If the letter is lost, you will know what it says, and you can tell Señor Beckler."

Stub read it slowly and nodded as he put the note in his pocket. He studied her for a moment and then drawled, "Miss Merina, if I thought there was a chance for me with you, I'd quit my job an' move to Cheyenne." He grinned as she blushed." He squeezed her hand and added, "Hawkins is a lucky man an' I hope he knows it. I will make sure nothin' happens to him tonight."

Merina smiled. "Thank you, Señor Stub." Her dark eyes danced as she looked up at him. "I will think of you if I change my mind."

Stub threw back his head and laughed. "Let's go find yore friend an' yore little sister. I think maybe we should get you back to the hotel before this party starts."

Stub and Merina were smiling as they left the Ogallala house. Gabe had just walked out of the saloon and he saw Merina laugh up at the rider. He glared in their direction and then saw Rusty grinning at him.

"Don't wait too long, Boss," the red-haired cowboy drawled as he laughed.

Gabe frowned and shook his head. "We need to focus on those horses. Let's start this ball rolling."

It was decided that the Rocking R riders would all sleep in the livery and would scatter out through the stalls. No one wanted any shooting around the horses, so they would try to take the outlaws quietly as the stalls were opened. Gabe and Rusty would be outside with Cappy and Rooster. Stub offered to keep Nate with him, and they were going to hide in the corrals.

The night was quiet and several of the riders dozed as they waited.

CHAPTER 26

A Challenge at Midnight

AN OWL HOOTED AROUND MIDNIGHT AND THE WAIT-ING MEN WERE INSTANTLY ALERT.

Curly led his men cautiously toward the livery. He had heard the owl too and held up his hand. Just then, an owl swooped off a roof in front of them and flapped its large wings loudly as it flew away. Curly lowered his hand and the group of seven men continued up the quiet street. He gave hand signals and his men ran silently toward the dark barn.

The first outlaw through the door ran all the way to the back. There was the sound of a gate unlocking and a quiet scuffle. The second man followed him and hissed at the sound. He heard a grunt in reply and began to work the latches to the three stalls he was in charge of. Something walloped him over the head, and he dropped soundlessly. His body was pulled back out of sight and a Rocking R rider took his place. In a matter of minutes, the outlaws were out of action, tied, and the Rocking R riders were moving toward the door of the barn.

Curly hissed at his men, "Turn them loose!"

The barn was quiet and then slowly riders appeared, guns drawn. They surrounded Curly who was mounted on his horse, holding the reins of the other six animals. He dropped the reins and swung his horse. Gabe's huge hand grabbed his shirt front and jerked him off his horse.

Curly staggered and then stood to face the silent group of me. He looked around the circle of men and laughed.

"Well, boys, I believe you got one up on me. I've never been bushwhacked quite so slick in all my days of robbin' folks." He looked around the men with careful eyes and then asked calmly, "Mind if I get a smoke?"

Stub's voice came from the corral. "You just go ahead, Curly. I've got you covered, an' I'll put a slug through yore cold heart if you go for yore gun."

Curly looked toward the direction of the voice in surprise. "That you, Black? What are you doin' in Cheyenne? Quit your cushy job as the boss's pet rider, did you?"

Stub's voice was clear and without emotion as he answered, "He sent me down here to look over some horses—the same ones you tried to steal."

Curly carefully took the makings for a smoke from his pocket, rolled his cigarette and lit it. When he was done, he threw it down on the ground and laughed at Gabe.

"Looks like you're the big he-wolf in this outfit. How about you an' me shoot it out? I win, I walk. You win, I'm dead."

Gabe stared at the man and backed up. "I'll give you a fair try but you aren't going to walk free."

Curly's hand flashed for his gun and Gabe shot him. The outlaw looked down at his chest and at the gun falling from his hand. He stared at Gabe with a look of surprise on his face. "You killed me! I've been cut down by a lousy cowboy."

Gabe said nothing as Curly collapsed. Stub walked over and squatted down beside him.

"So long, Curly. Ya haven't always been a good man, but ya died brave."

Curly tried to laugh but he choked as he gripped Stub's shirt. "Tell Andy. Tell her I'm sorry. Tell her I should have...."

A wagon came racing down the street. James McDaniel was driving. The man beside him dropped to the ground while the wagon was still moving. William Sturgis ran to his son. He held Joe's lifeless body as he sobbed silently.

All the men but Gabe drifted away and disappeared into the night like wraiths. Gabe stood silently to the side, holding Curly's horse.

Sturgis looked up at Gabe. His eyes were red and he blinked hard as he stared at the quiet man standing in front of him.

"Are you the man who shot him?"

Gabe nodded. "He gave us no choice, Mr. Sturgis. The boys took the rest of the gang up to the jail but Curly refused be taken alive.

"He died brave though. There was no backwater in your son." He paused and added, "I'm sorry I had to be the one to take him from you." Gabe was quiet a moment and then asked, "Do you know an Andy? Curly mentioned her as he was dying."

William Sturgis stared at Gabe for a moment longer. His face crumpled and he nodded. "I'll talk to her."

Gabe helped Sturgis lift Curly Joe into the back of the wagon. He tied Curly's horse to the side of the wagon. As McDaniel drove the wagon away, Joe's father sat in the back and held the lifeless body of his only child.

Gabe lifted his hat and wiped the sweat from his face. He watched the wagon disappear down the moonlit street and he shook his head. "For all the bad Curly was, he still had a pa who loved him," he muttered bitterly.

Curly Joe Sturgis died that quiet night on the dusty streets of Cheyenne. He died in the town his father had moved him to as a young man to get him away from the life of violence he was living in New York. His tombstone would read:

CURLY JOE STURGIS
OUTLAW, RUSTLER AND KILLER
DIED WITH HIS BOOTS ON
DIED A BRAVE MAN
JUNE 14, 1879

CHAPTER 27

A Meeting with the Lawyer

THE NEXT MORNING CAME EARLY. Merina and Larry had Emilia up and packed by 6:00 a.m. The three went down to breakfast. They were nearly done when the men arrived.

Gabe looked tense and nervous but Rusty's eyes were twinkling as he strolled up to their table.

"Well, good mornin' to the three purtiest gals in this here place!"

Larry laughed as her eyes went around the room. They were the *only* women seated in the dining area.

Rusty's smile became bigger, "Well, south of the Montana Territory then. I ain't never been to Montana, so I ain't familiar with women up there."

He kissed Larry and winked at Emilia.

"Emilia, I think I like cuddling with Larry here better than Gabe. He gets a little grumpy if I try to cuddle with him."

Emilia studied Rusty's face and then she looked at Gabe. "I told that bad man who tried to hug Nina that you would punch him."

Gabe looked at her in surprise and then both men looked from Merina to Larry.

Larry laughed. "Well, he didn't get far. Merina slapped him and then Emilia about kicked his shins in. She is a fierce little protector."

Gabe waited for Merina to respond.

She shrugged her shoulders. "I slept with my pistol and my knife last night, but he didn't come back. I think maybe he is gone."

Gabe studied her face, but she had dropped her eyes to focus on her food.

He looked at Larry again and she laughed. "I like traveling with these two. The men may bother us but not for long." She looked over at Rusty. "I might need to get a knife like Merina has though and strap it to my leg."

Rusty shook his head and grinned. Their food arrived quickly, and they were soon done eating.

"When are we riding out to your ranch?" Merina's excitement showed in her eyes.

Gabe grinned for the first time that morning. "We'll ride over to Badger's house here in town first. If he's there, we will set a time and if he's not, we will head out." He paused and looked at his friends.

"I need to show Gallagher's papers to a lawyer here first. I think I will wander down the street. I saw a sign for one next to the Painted Lady. I don't think it will take me too long. Besides, he may not even be open yet since it is just a little after 7:00 a.m. Maybe you can all go for a ride, check out the town."

Cappy shook his head. "Nate and me are goin' ta look fer fishin' holes. We'll be back in a few hours. We cin find Badger's house."

Merina, Emilia, Rusty and Larry headed toward the livery and Gabe walked down the street to the law office. The sign said, *Levi Parker, Lawyer for the People.*

Gabe tried the door, but it was locked. He slapped his hat on his leg. "Shoot, it's Saturday. I reckon he won't be open until Monday." He was just turning to walk away when a tall man with a big smile strode up the street.

"Something I can help you with? I don't usually open on Saturdays except for appointments. I have a family function this afternoon though and decided to work a couple of hours before."

Gabe hesitated. "I have some legal questions and some papers I would like you to look at if you have time."

The lawyer nodded and put out his hand. "Levi Parker is the name." He was broader through the shoulders and chest than Gabe was and just a little taller. His brown hair was curly, and his eyes were hazel with flecks of blue. The man's face was friendly, and his hands were strong and rough like those of a working man.

He was still smiling as he asked, "And you are?"

Gabe shook his hand. "Gabe Hawkins. I'm a newcomer to Cheyenne."

Levi unlocked the door and gestured for Gabe to go in. The lawyer's office was long and rather narrow with a large stove in the corner. A tall receptionist's desk and some chairs sat against the walls. Levi led Gabe past the desk to his personal office and unlocked that door. The large desk he seated himself at was hand-made and had a brand carved into it. Gabe sat down and then pointed at the desk.

"Y'all make that? You sure are handy with wood if you did."

Levi laughed, "No, I work with mules. My woodworking skills are a little more primitive. Tiny Small is the fellow you need to talk to if you want something made."

He looked at Gabe curiously. "You talk like a Texan."

Gabe grinned. "I am. Grew up down by Bandera. I've been a cowboy most of my life and am finally going to put down some roots."

Levi's eyes opened in surprise. "Bandera? That's the area I grew up in! I think I'm a little older than you though. My folks had a nice little spread south of Bandera. We ran a few cattle and some horses. The folks died when I was nine and I was sent to an orphanage down by San Antone. Did your folks ranch?"

Gabe slowly nodded. "We had a little two by nothing ranch. My Pa lost it after I left home. I was trail boss for Dan Waggoner when I heard Pa was going broke. I quit and went back home to see if I could save the ranch, but I was too late."

Levi nodded. "Growing up was kind of hard on some of us. I rode for Waggoner too. I was with him for four years. Good man. He had just married his second wife. I ran away with my best buddy when I was twelve and Dan Waggoner gave us a herding job because he felt sorry for us." Levi quietly added, "In fact, my wife was married to that old pal before I met her. She was newly widowed when I came to Cheyenne the first time. Life is kind of funny with how it twists around." He leaned forward and reached out his hand, "Now let's see what you have for me to look over."

Gabe pushed the packet of papers across the desk toward Levi. "I brought a herd north from Texas to Dodge City for Joseph Gallagher. He died of diphtheria while I was on the drive. I received this packet of papers in Dodge saying that he left the cattle to me. He asked me in that letter there to try to find a young man by the name of James Long. He was going to turn his business and land holdings over to him. I was told last night the young man died several months ago."

Levi glanced quickly at Gabe's face as he took the packet. The newcomer looked tense. The lawyer spread the papers out in front of him. He quickly glanced through them and then went back to read several pages more closely.

He looked up at Gabe when he was finished. "Mr. Hawkins, it appears here that you have been bequeathed a sizeable amount of land and investments. Mr. Gallagher invested wisely over the years. Manhattan, Kansas is growing, and these properties have increased quite rapidly in value.

"Some of the investments can be managed from here but others should be supervised. It looks to me like you have a decision to make, whether you stay here or move back to Kansas and manage his holdings."

Levi looked down at the papers and then up at Gabe's tense face. Gabe's expression was almost one of sadness instead of excitement.

He asked carefully, "Can you tell me why Mr. Gallagher chose to leave his business to you?"

Gabe's face was tight as he looked past Levi. He looked out the small window and then looked directly at the man across from him. "I was sweet on his daughter. She died before we were able to know each other well but she wrote me a letter when she was dying. I reckon her feelings were the same.

"Grace's mother, Kate, caught diphtheria and brought it back home to the rest of the family.

"Joseph and Grace were to meet the herd in Dodge City but by the time we reached Dodge, both Kate and Grace were dead." Gabe took a deep breath. "Joseph died shortly after and this packet was waiting for me in Dodge."

Gabe's eyes were watery as he added, "I guess Joseph didn't have any relatives to pass things on to. Grace was adopted and he always regretted not adopting the James mentioned in there" Gabe pointed at the papers. "Grace told me that they had lost contact with James when he was fourteen or fifteen. They had tried to find him with no luck."

He looked over Levi's head and then added softly, "Grace and James were part of a wagon train crossing Kansas. The train came down with some kind of sickness and the healthy wagons abandoned the sick ones. Those two little kids were the only survivors out of the sick wagons. Grace was six and James was not much older. He managed to get them both to the closest town which was still over sixty miles away.

"The Gallaghers were passing through that town and wanted to adopt Grace. James begged them to take him too, but they didn't. Grace said her pa always regretted that and he wanted to make things right with James.

"Now they are all dead and Gallagher left his business holdings to me." His face was still as he added quietly, "I don't deserve it though and am benefitting from the death of a fine family." Gabe's voice was bleak, and the sadness showed in his face. He finally leaned back in his chair and gave Levi a twisted smile. "Heck of a thing to have feelings for a woman you barely knew and especially one who is dead."

Levi was quiet. He had watched Sadie work through her grief after Slim's death. *Life can be a tough road to travel.*

Levi stacked the papers and laid them down. "Well, I guess he saw something in you that he trusted. You know, lots of men would have made no effort to find the fellow in front of them if that meant they would inherit more."

Gabe frowned and Levi laughed. "I believe Joseph Gallagher chose you because you were an honest man. He was unable to fix things with James, but he knew you would try. And no matter what happened, an honest man was going to inherit his wealth. I think, Mr. Hawkins, that you are going to be a fine addition to Cheyenne."

Gabe's neck turned a little red under his tan and he squirmed in his chair. He finally met Levi's friendly smile and grinned back. "So, Lawyer Man, what do you recommend that I do?"

"Well, I guess that depends on where you want to focus your interest. Do you want to stay a cattleman, or do you want to be a businessman in Kansas? You know, you could possibly do both if you wanted to move back there. I think it will be harder from this far away."

Gabe leaned forward in his chair with excitement on his face. "Mr. Parker, I am buying a ranch here. I haven't seen it yet, but I am meeting with the seller today. I know cattle and I want to ranch. If I have some extra capital to invest in more land and more cattle, then I will be a happy man. As far as the investments go—if they can be handled from here, maybe we can hang onto them. The rest of them, I think I want to liquidate."

He leaned back in his chair and stretched out his long legs as he studied Levi's face. "I have a hand by the name of Rusty O'Brian. I think a lot of him, and he could use a leg up. What would it take to make him a partner in those investments? Rusty can buy or sell almost anything. Think I could send him out there to liquidate things?"

Levi hid the surprise he felt and then smiled inside. *And this is exactly what Gallagher saw in this man. An honest man with lots of character.*

Twinkles flashed in Levi's eyes as he studied Gabe. "You know, Mr. Hawkins, I am actually headed to Manhattan this next week to take care of some business for another client of mine here. I would be willing to work with Mr. O'Brian and see what we can get done if you want to send him out then." He grinned at Gabe and added, "For a fee of course."

Gabe nodded soberly and then grinned as he agreed, "Of course." The two men shook hands again as they stood.

"Let me work up a partnership agreement. Maybe the two of you can come in and meet with me on Monday. I leave Tuesday morning so you will need to move quickly."

Levi paused and then asked, "Is Rusty married? And if he is, do you want his wife's name on that partnership?"

Gabe looked surprised but nodded. "I guess I just assumed his wife would be part of it. Yes, let's put her name on it too. We call her Larry, but her name is Laurel. Their last name is O'Brian. I have a younger brother too by the name of Nate if you need to add his name."

"If he's under eighteen, his signature is optional so that is up to the two of you."

"Go ahead and put his name on the contract. If he wants to come in, I'll have him sign."

Levi stopped at the tall desk and checked his appointment book. "Let's plan to sign papers at 10:00 on Monday morning, June 16."

Gabe nodded and strode back up the street toward the livery. His friends were stopped in the street talking to a pretty woman in a buggy. He could see the heads of two children and when the woman moved, it was obvious that she was pregnant.

He strolled up to the buggy and Rusty looked down at him with a grin.

"Boss, this is Sadie Parker. She is the wife of the lawyer you been a talkin' to."

Sadie stretched out her hand with a warm smile. "Welcome to Cheyenne, Mr. Hawkins. I hope we will be seeing more of you."

Gabe grinned as he took her hand. "Thank you, Ma'am. I'm sure you will. Cheyenne doesn't look all that big."

Sadie drove on down the street and her two children leaned out of the buggy to wave at them.

Larry's smile was huge. "We have talked to so many people and everyone is so friendly. I think I am going to love it here."

Rusty looked down at Gabe. "I have yore hoss saddled. It doesn't sound like Badger lives too far from here. I'll bring 'im up here if yore ready to head over."

Gabe nodded. Emilia smiled at him and he stepped up beside her. "Well, Hawk looks excited. Think he's ready to go see my new ranch?"

Emilia nodded excitedly. "And I am going to live there too. And Nina and Angel and Miguel. We are all going to live on your ranch."

Gabe grinned and looked up at Merina. "I reckon that would be just fine." He looked back at Emilia. "What about Rusty and Larry or Cappy and Nate? Are they going to live there too?"

Emilia frowned. "Yes, but I think you are going to have to build a bigger house."

Gabe laughed and pinched her cheek.

Rusty was back quickly. He handed Gabe the reins to Buck and the six of them headed across town toward Badger's house.

CHAPTER 28

COMMUNITY OF FRIENDS

BADGER ANSWERED THE DOOR WITH A BIG SMILE AND INVITED ALL OF THEM IN. Gabe recognized Martha and she gave him a hug.

"Mr. Hawkins, it is so nice to formally meet you, especially since you are smiling and not punching someone this time."

Gabe grinned as he returned the hug.

Emilia looked from one to the other soberly. "Señor Gabe punches men when they aren't nice."

Gabe blushed and Martha's eyes twinkled. She whispered to Emilia. "I know he does. I have seen him do that. In fact he punched a man one time who was rude to me!"

Her smile became bigger and she pointed at herself. "My name is Martha. And who might you be?"

Emilia thumped her chest. "I am Emilia and that is my sister Nina. Angel and Miguel are my brothers. They went back to Texas for a while, but they are coming back." She pointed toward the O'Brians.

"Rusty and Larry are married and Larry has a little bitty baby in her tummy. He's been in there a long time and I don't know when he's coming out. And Nate and Cappy went fishing. They are coming later."

Martha was laughing and Badger chuckled as his blue eyes danced.

"Well, I reckon that little gurl jist took care a inner'ductions. Come on over here an' sit down. My Martha made some cinneymon rolls an' we'uns 'ill all have us some coffee."

He winked at Emilia. "How 'bout you'ins, young lady? Ya drink coffee or would ya rather have root beer?"

Emilia's face puckered up in a puzzled frown and Merina spoke.

"Root beer would be fine, Señor Badger. I will have it as well and thank you."

Badger quickly helped Martha fill the glasses and cups. He sat down opposite of Gabe.

"So, ya ready ta make this here deal final? Judge Parker wrote me up a contract an' all we need is yore handle on that bottom line."

While Gabe was looking the contract over, Badger laid down a second sheet. It had livestock listed along with the prices.

500 cows with calves by their sides: $35 = $17,500
60 mules. $150 each for jacks or mares and $50 each for fillies or colts.

"Now if'n ya want anythin' off'n there, we cin add that on ta the contract." Gabe studied the contract and the lists. As they had agreed in Dodge City, Badger offered his six thousand acres of land at $7 per acre.

"I for sure want all of your cattle. I don't know much about mules, but I would like to learn. Let's do four team mules and maybe a couple of colts that I can try to break. Shoot, I might just have Merina handle that. She's a pretty savvy horsewoman."

Merina glanced toward him in surprise. Gabe didn't look up as he continued to study the list.

He looked up from the livestock list with surprise. "You don't own any horses?"

Badger's blue eyes snapped as he shook his head. "Naw, I prefer mules. But I hear Rowdy jist bought a bunch if ya need ta hit 'im up."

Gabe looked startled and Badger winked at him. Gabe studied the older man and then grinned. *Badger doesn't miss much, I'm guessing.*

Badger added the mules and the cattle to the bottom of the land contract and Gabe signed it. The total came to $60,200.

"Do you want a bank draft or cash? I can have either for you this afternoon."

Badger waved his hands. "A bank draft is fine. You'ins cin bring it with ya when ya come out ta the ranch. We'uns done moved off a'ready so you'ins cin move in right away. My Martha left all the food stock. We'uns is too old ta be packin' that stuff.

"An' ya might want ta cull a few a those cows. They's too many fer the land you'ins have. Jist bought me some replacements an' I ain't sold off the first yet."

Badger looked around at the smiling group as he grinned. "Let's meet up after dinner, say 'round 1:00 an' head out. My Martha planned a welcome party fer you'ins an' the folks 'ill start comin' 'round 4:00. Ya don't have ta feed 'im though 'cause ever'body 'ill bring a little somethin'."

The young people looked at the McCunes in surprise and Martha beamed.

"We get together quite often. Our family is growing, and we enjoy all of the little ones."

She turned her eyes toward Merina. "I hope you are considering the teaching position. It will be a one room school not too far from Gabe's ranch."

"Lance, Rowdy's brother, bought his ranch from Old Man McNary and they put up a little house for the Old Man just up the hill. Old Man McNary passed away last year, and the kids decided to add on a room

157

to make it a schoolhouse. You would live in the house and just open a door to be in the schoolhouse. Of course, the house comes with the position and Lance said you can stable your horse at his place.

"We are getting more kids in the neighborhood now and Cheyenne is fifteen to twenty miles for everyone. We decided it was about time to open our own school."

Merina smiled and nodded. "Yes, I am very much looking forward to it. When do you usually start school?"

"The kids have been talking about that. They were thinking of maybe starting a little earlier this year and then taking off a month through roundup. They will talk to you this evening." Martha's smile was broad as she added, "Of course, they just think that we are inviting the new teacher over. They have no idea that we sold our ranch."

Gabe looked from Martha to Badger in surprise and then frowned. "Will they be all right with you selling it to a stranger?"

Martha laughed. "Oh, they know we'd only sell to someone we'd want as a neighbor, Gabe. We want to fill Cheyenne with decent, hard-working people and we are adopting all of you! Welcome to our little community of friends."

CHAPTER 29

THE CONTRACT

BEFORE ANYONE HAD A CHANCE TO RESPOND, Cappy and Nate appeared in the open door. Cappy sniffed the air and licked his lips when he saw the cinnamon rolls. Badger waved him in and Cappy strolled up to the table.

"Well lookie here, Nate. We's jist in time."

Cappy swept off his hat and bowed to Martha. He greeted Badger with, "Hello, ya ol' scallywag." Gabe grinned to himself. *Those two men know more people than I will ever meet.*

Cappy turned back to Martha and she hugged him.

"Mornin', Miss Martha. We shore missed ya 'round Manhattan once ya was gone." He lifted a cinnamon roll out of the pan, "An' I missed yore cookin' most of all."

He grinned around the room at his friends. "I was thinkin' on courtin' Martha when Badger swooped in an' swept 'er off 'er feet. Fine friend he is." He winked at Larry and Merina as he drug Nate forward.

"This here good-lookin' young man is Gabe's baby brother. He's a happier, younger version of that sour feller what jist bought yore ranch."

Nate grinned and Gabe tried not to frown. "I'm not that grumpy, Cappy, and sure not all the time."

Nate started laughing and Rusty grinned. Gabe's neck turned red. "Well, maybe I've been a little grumpy, but drives take a lot of thinking and planning."

Rusty's grin became bigger. "And building a ranch won't?"

Gabe glared at him and Rusty laughed.

Gabe stood and shook Badger's hand. "I'll go get that bank draft and I'll have a second one for your percentage of Gallagher's cattle. I have his records in my tally book so I can give you a statement."

He tipped his hat to Martha. "Martha, it's been a pleasure. I haven't had cinnamon rolls in more years than I can remember."

Martha grabbed Gabe and hugged him again. "Thank you for being such a gentleman, Gabe. I'm looking forward to spending more time with you."

She hugged Nate as well and thrust another roll in his hand. "My goodness, Nate. You are almost skin and bones. We'll have to see if we can put some meat on you."

Gabe laughed as he looked from Nate to the smiling Martha. "Well good luck with that. He eats enough for three men the way it is."

The little group said their goodbyes and followed Gabe to the hitching rail.

Gabe waved down the street. "Let's plan to meet at the Inter Ocean Hotel at 11:30 for dinner. If we eat early, we can be ready to meet the McCunes by 1:00. My treat today and Nate, you come with me."

As the two brothers rode up the street, Gabe pointed out businesses. When they rode by Levi Parker's law office, Gabe nodded with his head. "I met with that lawyer this morning to go over Gallagher's business holdings. Badger called him Judge Parker, but his sign says lawyer. We have another meeting with him on Monday morning at 10:00 to draw up the papers." He paused and added quietly, "I'm bringing in Rusty and Larry as partners on Gallagher's holdings."

Nate was quiet a moment and then asked cautiously, "Was he rich?"

Gabe grinned at his younger brother. "Not sure. He had quite a few investments. I'm going to send Rusty back to Manhattan with the lawyer next week. They will liquidate the holdings that require hands-on management and we'll probably hold onto the rest. Shoot, you might want to move back there someday and take over."

Nate stared over at his brother and then slowly shook his head. "I don't think so. I don't want to live in town and rub elbows with city folks all the time. I want to go fishing, chase cattle, and ride horses."

"And learn to dance?"

Nate's eyes lit up as he nodded, "Yeah, and learn to dance."

Gabe chuckled and the brothers rode in silence for a bit.

"What do you think of calling our ranch the Diamond H? I needed a name when we were charging things and that's what I used. Thought I should ask you before we finalize it though. It would be an easy brand to create though and not that easy to change."

Nate's nodded. "I like it. I have been thinking on a name and couldn't come up with any that I liked better. That would be just fine."

The brothers dismounted in front of the First National Bank of Cheyenne. When Gabe told the perky little receptionist that he wanted to make a deposit as well as get two bank drafts, she went back to get the bank president. She was flirting with Gabe outrageously when Robert Baker rushed out to meet his newest customers. Robert frowned at her and then hurried his newest customers back into his office.

Banker Bob was efficient, and it didn't take the Hawkins brothers long to complete their business.

The receptionist smiled at them and waved prettily as they left. "Do come see us again, Mr. Hawkins. My name is Cora if I can help out or even show you around the town." She fluttered her eyelashes and Nate stared at her in surprise. Gabe ignored her but Nate turned around and looked again.

"What was wrong with her? Why was she acting so silly?"

Gabe swung his arm around his brother's shoulders. "That's called flirting, Nate. Gals do that sometimes to try to get our attention."

Nate frowned. "I've never have seen Larry or Merina act like that."

Gabe laughed out loud as he agreed. "No and you probably won't either. But then, neither Larry nor Merina have to work too hard to get a fellow's attention."

CHAPTER 30

ESTABLISHING THE DIAMOND H

THE BROTHERS STOPPED AT THE LAND OFFICE AND THEY REGISTERED THEIR BRAND. 'Hawkins Brothers, owners, Diamond H Ranch.' Gabe drew their brand out.

The land agent who was also the brand inspector wrote it down in his book with nearly another two thousand registered brands.

Nate leaned over to look at some of them and whistled. "I didn't know there were so many brands out there!"

The land agent laughed as he agreed. "You can get a brand quite easily. Now getting into the Stock Growers' Association is a little harder although I am sure Badger will recommend you. It's a powerful organization and if I was a cattleman, I would try to become a member. They have their requirements though. Acres run and cattle owned are two of the big ones. You don't have enough acres to be considered now but take that up to fifteen or twenty thousand and you might be."

Gabe nodded quietly. *I'll talk to Badger. I have never even thought of belonging to an organization like that.*

He thanked the land agent and the two brothers strolled back outside. Gabe checked his watch and then pointed down the street.

163

"Nate, let's go get a couple of new shirts and then go for a bath. Once we are settled, we can start doing our own laundry but for now, I think new shirts are in order."

They met Rowdy on the street and visited awhile. He handed Gabe payment for the fifty-nine horses.

"Those are sure nice horses, Gabe. Think you can find me some more like that?"

Gabe shook his head slowly. "I'm not sure. Tall Eagle is a friend of mine from down in Oklahoma. He captured and broke those horses. He left us at Ogallala to join up with some of his people. He said he was going to look for a brave named Broken Knife but other than they are Arapahoe, I'm not sure how to get hold of him."

Rowdy laughed out loud. "Well, you should see quite a bit of him then. Broken Knife is a good friend of my brother Lance and his wife Molly. They may even be at Badger's this evening to meet the new teacher."

Gabe's face showed his surprise and Rowdy's grin became bigger.

"I doubt Broken Knife cares if he comes to meet a new teacher but his sister is a good friend of Molly's so they just might come. In fact, Martha mentioned inviting some of their youngsters to attend school. That teacher is going to have her hands full if that happens. She could end up with a passel of kids.

"I hear she's older and quite experienced though. The wives set this all up and haven't told us much."

Gabe stared at Rowdy and then chuckled. "Your wives must be quite the ladies."

"Well, they don't exactly just sit around and take orders, I can tell you that." He grinned as he shook Gabe's hand.

"I guess we'll see you tonight then. Badger said that he had invited you."

Gabe nodded as he grinned. "We'll be there. Maybe that teacher will be young, and I'll decide to stay."

Rowdy laughed again and headed down the street. He wanted to get the horses back home and settled before they left for Badger's that evening.

Nate was quiet until Rowdy was gone and then he looked over at his brother.

"Doesn't Rowdy know we are moving here?"

Gabe grinned at him. "Evidentially not. Old Badger kept this sale under his hat." He paused and rubbed his hand across his face. "And what is the deal with those women and the schoolteacher? This is going to be an interesting community, Nate. I would say that those wives are pretty darn independent." He winked at his brother as he drawled, "Guess it's a good thing I don't have one since I want one who is quiet and submissive."

Nate snorted and the two walked toward the supply house with smiles on their faces.

Nate chose a bright red shirt and Gabe picked a dark red one. They headed to the bath area and were soon soaking in the tub.

"How cold does it get here, Gabe? Think we'll need heavy coats this winter?"

Gabe stared at his cigar and frowned. "I guess I haven't even thought that far. I reckon we will. You will be going to school every day, so we are going to need to figure out a system in our house." He grinned down at his younger brother. "Maybe I will put you in charge of laundry."

Nate thought a moment and then shook his head. "Nope. You can pay Larry to do it." He looked sideways at Gabe as he added with a grin, "Since we're rich now."

Gabe looked over at his little brother and then chuckled. *We both grew up with little money and scrapped just to eat. I'm trying not to count on Gallagher having a lot, but it does make a fellow think.*

Once again, they threw their dirty shirts in their bath water and tried to scrub them. The water was getting cold and other than taking the dust off the outside, it really didn't do much good.

They tied the wet shirts to the back of their saddles and rode down to the Inter Ocean Hotel. Nate was quiet as he looked around.

"I've never been in such a fancy eating house," he whispered.

"I have but never one where I paid myself."

Gabe winked at his brother and they both laughed.

"See anybody you know? If not, let's find a table towards the back that will be big enough for all of seven of us."

Rusty and Larry were the next to arrive. Rusty was grinning and Larry looked beautiful. Her curly hair was a dark red and hung in ringlets from her head. Gabe felt a moment of remorse for making her cut her it off.

The brothers stood and Rusty pulled out Larry's chair.

Gabe grinned at her. "You know, Larry, I think motherhood looks good on you. You keep getting prettier all the time." He was smiling but it was true, and Gabe meant it.

Rusty's smile was proud and Larry blushed as she laughed.

Cappy swept into the room escorting a lovely Merina and Emilia. Merina had on a new riding skirt and Emilia had on a new dress as well.

Gabe's tongue felt like it was stuck to the roof of his mouth. He smiled without speaking and pulled out chairs for both of them.

Emilia looked around and whispered loudly, "This is kind of a fancy place, Señor Gabe. Are we supposed to whisper in here?"

"You can if you want. And you sure look pretty today. Did you get a new dress?"

Emilia nodded excitedly. "Yes! Do you want to see me twirl?" She was off her seat and twirling before anyone could stop her.

Gabe was chuckling as he looked over at Merina. He drawled, "You look beautiful too, Merina. Would you like to twirl for us as well?"

Merina's eyes opened in surprise and she laughed. "Not right now but gracias."

Gabe was still grinning as he spoke. "Found out some interesting information today. Those ladies who signed your teaching letter let their husbands think that you are quite old and have lots of experience. Guess those fellows are in for a surprise." His eyes sparkled as he added, "But a good surprise. And, they are thinking of opening up the school to some Arapahoe children too."

Larry leaned forward with excitement all over her face. "How exciting. I know a little Arapahoe. Not too much but a few words. My father liked to trade with the Indians, and we had several groups that sought us out every year."

Merina studied her friend. "You are going to help me at least part of the day until the baby comes. I'm not sure I can do this alone."

Gabe had rarely seen Merina worried, but she seemed tense. He leaned toward her and patted her hand.

"Hey, I didn't say that to worry you. I think you will be an awesome surprise. Besides, the women are the ones who pay the most attention to the education of their children. Obviously, they are confident that you can handle it. Otherwise, they wouldn't have all agreed to offer you the job."

Merina gave Gabe a slight smile and settled back in her chair.

He looked around the little group. "Also, no one knows that Badger sold us his place. They all think we are just visiting. Badger and Martha must have some kind of plan so let's go along with them and see what happens this evening." He sat back in his chair and grinned, "Now enough business. Let's eat and enjoy!"

CHAPTER 31

A Fine Day for a Ride

EMILIA AND MERINA WERE QUIET DURING THE MEAL. The little girl was doing her best to make no messes. Nate was nervous as well. He finally looked at Gabe in frustration.

"Next time, let's just eat some place normal. I can't figure out what fork to use and my elbows are sliding this cloth around. Then it gets caught on my belt buckle."

Merina began to laugh and soon all of them were laughing.

Gabe shook his head. "So much for trying to give this crowd a little culture."

The rest of the meal was more relaxed. Many of the patrons were cattlemen and no one seemed to notice that they were new to the area.

When the meal was completed and they moved back outside, everyone took a deep breath.

Rusty bumped Gabe as he grinned.

"Thanks, Boss, but y'all don't need to bring me here again. Makes me kinda miss biscuits an' beans."

Larry rolled her eyes. "Well, I actually enjoyed it. Thank you, Gabe."

Cappy winked at him and Merina agreed with Larry. "It was very nice, but I think I prefer to eat at home. I think there is more talking when it is not so fancy."

They were mounting their horses when Badger appeared driving a buggy.

"Ready ta go see you'ins new home? Jist fall in here an' we'll mosey on out."

Gabe rode beside the buggy and listened as Badger pointed out ranches and shared information along the way.

"We come here in '68. I met my Martha that year an' we was married in Julesburg. Lance an' Molly was married 'for they headed west. They picked up Sadie in Julesburg. That's where she met Slim, her first husband. He were gunned down a year an' a half later. Tough time fer Sadie an' then the Judge come along. They's a happy couple now.

"'Course Rowdy be Lance's brother. We all thought he done died in The War, but he made it out. Met little Beth back in Georgia when he were a lookin' at his own tombstone. Turned out that was Beth's brother buried there." Badger was quiet a moment and then he chuckled. "Rowdy brung that stone back here a couple years back when they put up one fer Beth's brother. Beth warn't much in favor of it but ol' Rowdy insisted. Said if'n it warn't fer that tombstone, he'd a never found Beth an' moved ta Cheyenne. Reckon he was right too. Now it sits at their place in Beth's flower garden. Rowdy built 'er a bench an' she likes ta sit out there some.

"Doc Williams 'ill be comin' out too. He married 'bout six-seven years ago an' they jist had their first little one. Now his wife, Josie, she be Slim's sister. That makes 'er Sadie's sister-in-law an' Doc is Beth's brother. Beth an' him moved out here from Georgia not long after Beth met Rowdy at the cemetery.

"We have us a fine community out here, so we was real picky 'bout who we brung in." Badger grinned up at Gabe. "Been keepin' an eye on ya fer some time. We decided after last winter that we was ready ta move ta town full-time. My Martha has her a clothin' store an' Sadie works there as a seamstress.

"I been a writin' back n forth with ol' Dan Waggoner. We'd done decided we wanted ta sell ta you'ins so I went on down ta Dodge with Rowdy, hopin' ta catch up with ya.

"When I got ta Dodge, I had a wire from ol' Dan tellin' me what you'ins done fer 'im what with gittin' their cattle back. We'uns is jist real pleased that ya accepted our offer." Badger's bright eyes were sincere as he looked at Gabe.

The younger man was quiet. Finally, he asked, "Why do you call Levi Parker 'Judge.' I didn't see judge on his sign."

Badger laughed and his bright eyes sparkled. "Ol' Levi, he likes ta argue. He's a durn good lawyer too. Sneaks up an' hits from the side. I want 'im on my side if they's gonna be a problem. Some a Lance's hired hands started callin' 'im that an' it stuck. I reckon he be a judge someday but right now, he's purty happy bein' a lawyer an' messin' with his mules. An' playin' with little Sadie too. He's a good daddy."

The rest of Gabe's party listened as Badger talked. Martha just smiled and nodded from time to time.

Larry was amazed that they had only been married eleven years. *They act like they've been together for years.*

Merina was quiet as she tried to process all the family connections. She hoped that the women would be pleased with their decision to offer her the teaching job. She was startled from her contemplation by Gabe's question.

"So why didn't you tell your kids you were selling your ranch? I sure don't want a bunch of family upset that I bought something they were counting on."

Martha laughed. "We didn't really plan it that way. They are so busy that they didn't notice all the trips back and forth that we were making as we moved. We just figured that since they didn't notice, they could all find out together. Oh, they'll be a little surprised, but we have been talking about moving to town for several years.

"Molly's father was a widower when he moved here, and he remarried just a few years ago. We see him and his wife quite a bit. And of course, Badger goes out to see Lance or Rowdy whenever he gets too bored. They are more than happy to put him to work."

"How many children do the rest of them have? I was wondering how many would be in school?" Merina was hoping to get an idea of who all the kids were so she could begin to make family connections.

Martha pursed her lips and began to count on her fingers. "Well let's see.

"Lance and Molly have five. Sam is the oldest. They adopted him on their trip back here from Georgia and he's fifteen. Paul Broken Knife is next and he's eleven. Abigail is a little sweetheart and she's eight. She was named after Lance's mother. Henry is six. He was named after Badger. Of course, he thinks they should call him Badger and not Henry. The baby is three and one-half and her name is Olivia Blue Feather after Molly's mother and Molly's friend Blue Feather. And what a little scamp that Livvy is!

"Lance and Molly met Broken Knife and Blue Feather in '68. Blue Feather is Broken Knife's sister and they are Arapahoe. Broken Knife is a big man around here. He saved Molly's life during Paul's birth. Paul's life too for that matter. Lance and Broken Knife are brothers now so of course Rowdy is as well.

"Rowdy and Beth have six children. He and Beth adopted Rudy and Mari when those little ones lost their family. They are eighteen and eleven. Rudy is in St. Louis studying law. Levi saw his interest and took him in as an intern for several years. Now Rudy is on his way to becoming a lawyer too.

"Mari is a sweet little girl. She will want to be your helper. The twins are nine. They are Ellie Elizabeth and Eli August. Of course Ellie is named after Beth and Eli is named after Beth's brother who died in the War Between the States. They are scamps and you will *not* want them to sit together. The next is a little girl of three named Pauline. Rowdy's given name is Paul, and Pauline is just precious. The baby is Emmaline and she is one.

"Now you won't have Levi and Sadie's children as they live just outside Cheyenne, but they will be here this evening. Little Levi is nearly seven and they call him Slim. He probably won't answer to Levi. He knows the story of his name and is pretty proud of it. Sadie was pregnant with him when Slim, her first husband, was killed. That was a hard time for Sadie and for us too. We all loved Slim. And then Levi came along." Martha smiled and was quiet a moment before she continued. "Their little girl is almost three and her name is Rose. She is just as sweet as Sadie.

"They are expecting in just a few months too so we will have another baby. Badger and I get so excited when another little one is born.

"Doc and Josie just had a little girl. She was named Charlene after Josie's brother. His given name was Charlie and he hated it. We only knew him as Slim." Martha paused and wiped her face. "Goodness. I think I just talked for a full five miles.

"Now tell me a little about yourself, Merina. How did you come to be part of this friendly group?'

Merina looked startled and then smiled. "My brothers are both riders. We actually all worked for Señor Cole down by Buffalo Gap in Texas. Angel came north with Señor Cole's herd and Miguel took a riding job in Oklahoma. After Señor Cole died on the trail, Señor Gabe offered both Angel and Miguel riding jobs." Merina lifted one shoulder and shrugged.

"There was nothing for Emilia and me after Señor Cole died since our parents are both gone so we came north to join our brothers." She smiled over at Gabe as her dark eyes sparkled. "Señor Gabe gave me the wrangler job on the drive from Dodge City to Ogallala. I guess he didn't want me following along behind the herd doing nothing."

Badger looked over at Gabe and winked as he laughed evilly. Gabe's neck slowly turned red, but he said nothing.

Martha looked back at Nate.

"And how about you, young man? How old are you? I am guessing you will be in school as well."

"I'm fourteen but I'll be fifteen in a few weeks. My birthday is June 28." He paused and then slowly nodded. "I don't like school. Ma made me go some, but Pa didn't think it was necessary. Gabe says I have to go here though." He smiled shyly at Merina and added, "I am glad Miss Merina will be my teacher. She is going to teach me to dance."

Badger interrupted, "Well, you'ins better git started. They's a big dance in town on the 28th an' with that bein' yur birthday an' all, you'ins probably 'ill want ta go."

"How 'bout you'ins, Gabe? Ya want ta learn ta dance too?"

Gabe laughed and shook his head. "Naw, it's too late for me. I have two left feet and girls get tired of me tromping on them. I just sit on the side and watch...and eat. I used to fight some but I'm more peaceable now."

Rusty started laughing and Larry joined him.

"Compared to what? I only seen ya walk away from one fight. Usually, it's over 'fore the other feller even knowed it started." Rusty was grinning and Gabe finally grinned back.

"Well, I am a little sudden but I'm peaceable at heart."

This time Merina laughed, and Gabe turned red.

"Why don't all of you pick on someone else? First you call me grumpy and now you say I fight all the time. You are going to give me a just plain bad name before I even get to know folks."

"Well, we know ya ain't much of a lady's man. I stepped in an' charmed Larry right from under yore nose." Rusty winked at Larry and she rolled her eyes.

Nate was grinning and Gabe looked over at him. "You join this party and I'll box your ears."

"An' that's what I'm a talkin' 'bout. Peaceful? I don't think so!" Rusty grinned at his boss and pulled his horse around as Gabe swung Buck toward him.

"Maybe we should talk about how a one-legged cowboy planned to spend the back half of a drive riding in the wagon with Larry there. Shoot, you took every advantage of that accident as you could." Gabe's voice was sarcastic as he looked over at Rusty.

Rusty laughed and winked again at Larry. "I'd be plumb ashamed of myself if I hadn't. Worked out purty good fer both of us, didn't it, Sweetheart?"

Larry was laughing and Merina joined them. Emilia had become quiet and Gabe lifted her off Hawk.

"How about you ride in the wagon for a while and give Hawk a rest?"

She shook her head furiously, "No, I want to ride with you!"

Gabe put her in the saddle in front of him and Emilia snuggled in. She was soon asleep.

He grinned at Badger. "My rules for cattle drives have always included no women. Somehow, I managed to end up with three women on this last one and it worked just fine. Still, this little girl is my favorite. She is always glad to see me, never argues and thinks I'm just wonderful." He winked at Merina and put one big arm around Emilia to keep her from falling off just as Badger pointed to the right.

"That there is the lane what runs up ta Lance an' Molly's spread. They's about fifteen miles from town an' you'ins ranch is about five more."

Gabe studied the land and then asked, "Badger, how about you and Martha spend the night? Maybe we can ride out and look the ranch over

175

tomorrow. You said there are two bedrooms so the two of you can take one and the women can sleep in the second one. The men can sleep in the barn."

Badger looked over at Martha and she smiled.

"I reckon that 'ill work. Now let's pick up the pace. Lance's place is quiet, so I reckon the party is a'ready started."

CHAPTER 32

THE NEWCOMERS' WELCOME

WHEN THE LITTLE TROUPE RODE INTO THE RANCH YARD, THEY SAW PEOPLE EVERYWHERE. Women were running between the house and the yard with food while the men were setting up boards on barrels. Gabe recognized Rowdy and some of the riders from the night before. A second man appeared who looked like Rowdy's twin, so he assumed that was Lance.

The kids came running to greet Badger and Martha. "Pappy! Grammy! Did you bring us any candy?"

Two women immediately scolded them. "Ellie and Eli! Don't ask for candy. You have to wait until it is offered."

"Henry and Livvy—you know the rules too."

Both women hurried to the greet the riders.

"I'm Beth, Rowdy's wife. Welcome to Cheyenne! This is Molly, Lance's wife, and all of these wild children belong to us."

She reached for Merina's hand. "Merina, it is so nice to meet you. Everyone was so excited to come this afternoon to welcome you." Beth gave a happy giggle. "Of course, the men think you are much older. We didn't tell them—they just assumed so we didn't correct them."

Molly rolled her eyes. "We thought about correcting them, but our men think they know everything. Please, get down and make yourselves comfortable. Sam and Paul—come get these horses and put them in the barn. Be sure to water them first and fork them some hay."

Levi and Sadie drove into the yard with their family followed by another buggy with a small blond woman and a smiling man.

Beth hurried to greet them.

"Josie, let me hold Charlene while Reub helps you down. And then come in the house. We have food on the stove." Beth raced toward the house kissing the baby.

The small blond woman was beautiful, and she was laughing as she stretched out her hand.

"My name is Josie, and this is my husband, Reuben. Most people here will call him Doc. He answers to both so either is fine." She waved as Levi helped Sadie down.

"Have you met Sadie and Levi yet?" When they all nodded, Josie linked arms with Merina and Larry. "Come with me to the house. We are almost ready to eat so you can both rest a bit before you talk all night. Sadie and Martha, come on to the house."

Merina looked around at the women in amazement. They were a flurry of activity, and they worked together like cogs in a wheel.

Larry sat down gratefully, and Sadie sat beside her.

"Sometimes it is nice to take advantage of being pregnant," Sadie whispered. Her smile was friendly, and Larry laughed as she agreed.

"Is this your first?"

Larry nodded. "Yes, I'm so big and I still have nearly two months to go."

Sadie's face lit up. "I'm close too. Levi had to deliver little Levi. That must have scarred him because he passed out during Rose's birth too. This time we are just going to make sure the room is cleared so he doesn't break anything when he goes down."

Larry stared at her for a moment and her eyes opened wide. Sadie laughed.

"Oh, don't worry. Lance and Rowdy are fine. None of us can figure out why Levi faints but he does. I think it is ridiculous since he has birthed hundreds of mules and horses, but he tells me it is not the same."

Molly looked over at Sadie and laughed dryly. "Well, maybe if you hadn't traumatized the poor man so on the first one, he would be able to handle it now."

Sadie blushed and giggled. "I was a widow when I met Levi. Our oldest son is from my first marriage. Slim had passed away before little Levi was born. Doc wasn't in his office and Levi ended up delivering him. Yes, I'm sure it was a bit traumatizing for a bachelor!"

Martha hurried in surrounded by lots of little ones. She had a sack of candy and proceeded to give each child two pieces as she shooed them back outside.

"Be sure to wash your hands in the tank when you are done," she called as they raced out of the house.

Martha looked around at the buzzing kitchen with a smile on her face. "I see that you have all met. We are so excited to have Merina as a teacher here. We can all go up tomorrow and show her the school."

Gabe stepped through the door with a happy Emilia. "See? There is Nina. And I think Martha has candy for you."

Emilia reached for the candy and looked up at Martha. "Are you a grandma?"

Martha smiled. "I sure am."

"I want Señor Gabe to marry a grandma so I can have one too." The little girl was sincere as she stared up at Martha.

Martha lifted her up. "Why Sweetheart, Gabe doesn't have to marry a grandma. I would be glad to be your grandma."

Emilia's smile was huge as she looked over at Merina. "Did you hear that, Nina? I have a grandma!"

Merina smiled and her dark eyes sparkled.

Martha handed Emilia some candy and pointed at the door. "There are a lot of kids out there. I bet you can make some new friends if you want to play."

Emilia looked at Merina and then grabbed Gabe's hand as she drug him outside. "Come with me, Señor Gabe. Let's go play."

Gabe tipped his hat at the women and grinned. "Excuse me, I have to introduce my best gal around." Emilia was chattering as she pulled him out the door.

The women were quiet a moment and then as a group, they looked over at Merina. Her face blushed a deep red and the women began laughing.

Beth whispered, "We are here to help!"

Merina's face became even redder and then she laughed. "You ladies seem to be encargo—you are the bosses of your husbands?"

The women all laughed, and Molly rolled her eyes. "Oh, they think they are in charge and we just let them think that. Then we do what we want.

"So tell us about yourself, Merina. Emilia is your little sister. Do you have brothers?"

The women were soon peppering Merina with questions about her family and her life in Texas.

CHAPTER 33

NEW OWNERS AT THE DIAMOND H

BADGER INTRODUCED GABE AND RUSTY TO THE MEN.
Emilia had slid down his leg when Olivia and Pauline came to ask her to play.

Lance shook Gabe's hand and commented, "Badger said that you were hoping to settle up here. Do you have a location in mind? I hadn't heard of anything for sale lately."

Gabe grinned and looked over at Badger.

"Why I done sold Gabe this here spread. He's packed an' movin' in after today. My Martha an' me moved out last week. No one noticed so we figgered you'ins could hear it today!"

There was a stunned silence as the men looked from Badger to Gabe and then ripples of laughter spread through the group of men.

Lance slapped Gabe on the back and grinned. "Well then, welcome to the neighborhood. We wondered when Martha and Badger were moving to town."

He looked at Badger and added dryly, "It will be nice to have a neighbor again since you have hardly been here in the last year."

Rowdy laughed as he shook Gabe's hand. "I kind of wondered when you had your meeting in Ogallala, but Badger here was mum on the way back home."

Lance's Rocking R hands and Rowdy's R4 hands came over to introduce themselves. Joe especially was pleased with the new neighbor.

"I was hopin' you was goin' to be settlin' here. It will be a pleasure to have ya as a neighbor."

Gabe gripped Joe's hand. "I sure appreciate you boys helping out last night. You turned the tide in our favor when you took care of all those fellows in the barn."

Lance looked toward the house and then put his finger over his lips. "If we are quiet, maybe we can get food before we are run over by that herd of kids," he whispered. "Their folks ought to work harder to keep them under control." He winked at Gabe and led the way to the house.

Molly met them at the door. "Oh no you don't. You call those kids and then Doc can lead the grace."

Lance turned around and whistled loudly. The kids came on the run making as much noise as a herd of thundering cattle.

"Fold your hands and pray. Then you can eat or go play."

The children gathered in a loose group. Gabe almost started laughing at the bumping and scratching that took place as they bowed their heads. As soon as the grace was finished, they were off again. Gabe scanned the ranch yard as he looked for Nate.

"If you are looking for Nate, he is already fishing with Sam and Paul." Rowdy laughed and pointed toward the creek. "Those two boys would live in the creek if they could so Nate will have some dedicated fishing buddies here." He paused and added with a grin, "But you notice they didn't take Abigail or our twins. Those three younger ones just want to play in the water, so the big boys are always trying to ditch them."

Gabe chuckled in agreement. When Rowdy and he stepped through the door, Lance had his arm around Molly and was teasing her. She finally waved a spoon at him and he ducked as he laughed.

Levi looked around the loud room and then shook his head. "Gabe, you just don't know what kind of outfit you have hitched your wagon to." He grinned at the man. "I had no idea that you were buying Badger's place when I talked to you this morning. Badger had me write up that contract several months ago but he didn't tell me a name. Of course, Sadie had it all figured out by the time I made it home." His eyes twinkled and he chuckled. "I have a hard time tracking with that woman, but she sure makes me happy."

Gabe laughed as he agreed. "I don't know much about women. What I do know confuses me so I reckon that tracking part would be right."

Sadie looked over where the two men stood and smiled at Levi. He started toward her as he spoke over his shoulder, "See? Just one little look and my old heart is tingling." He winked at Gabe and quickly pulled the chair back for Sadie to stand.

Merina slipped through the crowd until she stood by Gabe. She whispered, "They are very loud."

"But they are friendly. Surely your family functions were loud too."

Merina's dark eyes danced as she laughed up at him, "Si, but it was all in Spanish, so outsiders didn't know so much what we were talking about."

Beth rushed over and handed them each a plate. "You go through the line first. These men eat a lot, so it is best to be toward the front."

Lance reached over and squeezed his sister-in-law. "Now that is all Rowdy." He glanced over at the laughing Reuben and added, "and Doc over there. They are the hungry ones."

Doc looked up in surprise and then shook his head. "Not me but make sure you are in front of Levi."

The women had left the hot food in the house. The fresh produce and the desserts were outside on the make-shift tables.

Gabe took his plate and then wandered down to the barn. The kids were in the loft and were throwing hay down.

"You kids better come down from there. I am going to need that feed for this winter."

The barn became silent and then five children climbed slowly down the ladder. Abigail looked up at him with large blue eyes and asked, "Are you going to live here with Pappy and Granny?"

Gabe laughed and shook his head. "No, your grandpappy and grandma are going to live in Cheyenne. I am going to live here with my brother."

The kids gathered around and studied Gabe curiously. "Can we still come and play?"

"You sure can, whenever you want. Now if you are hungry, maybe you should go wash and head on up to the house." Gabe chucked Abigail under the chin and she smiled up at him.

As they raced out of the barn, Gabe strolled in and looked around.

The kids had made a mess of the stacks of hay, but the barn was solid. He was surprised at the amount of tack that was still hanging on hooks. "I don't think Badger took hardly anything with him."

Lance followed Gabe into the barn. He muttered under his breath as he looked around. "Let's pull these doors shut and I'll help you fork that hay back up later. Those kids and their hay forts."

Gabe pointed at the tack. "We didn't really talk about anything but land, cattle and mules. I guess I'll have to ask Badger what he wants me to do with all this."

Lance shook his head, "Naw, if you already signed papers and it was left here, he meant to do it. Badger and Martha are good folks. They are always helping someone. I'm not sure how the two of you met but he likes you. Otherwise you couldn't have *forced* him to sell his place." Lance chuckled. "He's almost as cantankerous as his big jack mule he rode out here from Kansas City."

"I wonder if Badger was ever in Manhattan, Kansas with that big jack. Some of those bartenders there are still talking about a mule and an old man who helped to clean up the town." Gabe glanced at Lance's face as he commented.

"That was Mule. Badger, Molly and I were passing through on our way here in '68. Old Mule helped clean up a few bad memories from Mollie's past." He looked over at the younger man. "You riding out to look things over tomorrow morning? I might come with you if you can wait till 7:00. We border Badger's—this place—and I need to check the fences. We share a couple of ponds as well."

The two men pulled the barn doors shut. When they wandered back up to the house, Merina was surrounded by cowboys. Lance grinned at Gabe.

"I don't know if you have any plans for that little gal, but if you do, you might want to move a little faster."

Gabe watched the riders and pushed down the irritation he felt but he said nothing.

Rowdy strolled over to where they were and nodded his head toward the barn. "The kids tear up a bunch of hay making forts?"

Gabe chuckled and Rowdy shook his head. "Well, they know not to open the barn doors so we can help you fork it back up."

Rowdy watched the riders surrounding Merina and then laughed. "My foreman is going to be sorry he didn't come. He told me that he didn't need to get all dressed up to meet an old school marm. He fancies himself as a ladies' man though and he won't be happy that the boys have one up on him."

Nate and the two older boys walked up the lane. They were in deep conversation and carried a large string of fish. Nate's eyes were shining as he showed Gabe.

"You wait till you see that fishing hole, Gabe. It's deep enough to swim in too. The water is cool and clear as can be."

The taller of the two boys put out his hand. "My name is Sam Rankin, and this is my little brother, Paul."

Gabe shook both of their hands. He nodded at the fish. "What are you going to do with those?"

Sam pointed toward one of the sheds. "Badger keeps salt in there. We'll salt them down and maybe Martha can cook them for dinner tomorrow." He looked over at Gabe and grinned. "Nate told me you bought this place. It will be nice to have another fellow to fish with." Sam's eyes were bright blue and sparkled with orneriness. Blond hair fell out of his hat and his shoulders were already wide. His boots were scuffed, and his hands were as calloused as Nate's were.

As the three boys walked away, Gabe heard Sam ask, "So how well do you know this teacher? Ma says I have to go to school, and I don't like school much."

Lance nodded toward the boys. "We adopted Sammy when he was just a little tyke. Of course, he wants to be called Sam now. We had a hard time keeping him in school last year. I hope Miss Merina can spark a little more interest."

Gabe laughed. "Well, she has already offered to teach Nate to dance." His eyes glinted with humor as he added dryly, "He wanted to learn in the dance halls in Ogallala and I refused. That's when Merina offered to teach him."

Lance's eyebrows shot up and he chuckled. "Dance halls, huh? I guess you've been up the trail enough times to know that wasn't a good idea."

He waved across the wide stretches of grass. "So do you have any riders or do you and Nate plan to run things?"

Gabe frowned as he studied the cattle grazing in the distance. "Merina has two brothers and they should be here in several weeks. They headed back down to Texas to take care of some family business. Rusty is a good hand too. I just hope I have enough work to keep them all on. Badger only has around five hundred head of cattle and some of them are cull cows. I need to run more to make things work." He grinned at the man next to him. "So I guess I'll have to bid against you when the next parcel of land comes up for sale."

"Yep, I would pretty much buy up any land that sells but Molly whoas me down. She's the brains behind this outfit." Lance's face was serious, but his eyes glinted as he added, "Of course, Beth is the brains at Rowdy's place too." He elbowed his brother and Rowdy grunted.

"Yeah, Beth pretty much runs circles around me." His face was bland as he added, "You'll have to come over sometime and see my tombstone. I have it in Beth's flower garden."

The three men began laughing, and Rowdy headed back into the house to get more food.

Lance nodded at Levi. "So, have you met Levi here? He's the best lawyer in Cheyenne. Wait till you see him in action. Shoot, we just pack up the kids and make it a picnic, it's that entertaining."

Levi laughed. "You need to keep an eye on Lance. He has a real short line from reasonable to crazy when he's mad. Add Rowdy to the mix and you should just walk away." Levi grinned and bumped the man beside him.

Lance's blue eyes sparkled as he shrugged. Then he drawled, "The boys told me about the party you had down by the livery last night. I believe the word they used to describe Gabe here was 'sudden.'"

His eyes were more serious as he added, "Jonesy told me that Curly tried to harass your women yesterday afternoon. He said Merina shut Curly down. That and her little sister kicked him until he backed up."

Gabe's face showed his surprise. "Larry and Merina wouldn't talk about it, so I didn't know what had happened." He grinned at the three men, "Merina can take care of herself though. She keeps a big knife strapped to her leg and she isn't too shy about using it if someone she loves is in danger. I think your kids will be safe with her. Men, I'm not so sure about."

Levi turned to study Merina. She was still surrounded by riders and he walked over to take her arm. "Now you fellas have hogged this lady long enough." He led her back into the kitchen where the women were gathered.

"I just rescued Miss Merina from a whole passel of cowboys. You need to keep her busy here so they can't try to drag her away again." He winked at Merina and sauntered back outside.

The kids began to trickle into the house to eat. Sam and Nate were the last to arrive. Nate stopped by Merina.

"Miss Merina, when do you think we can have a dance lesson? June 28th isn't very far away and there is a dance in Cheyenne."

Merina smiled at the serious young man.

"How about tomorrow night? I am going to move tomorrow morning so we can use the school for your lessons. I don't have any way to play music though so we will just work on foot movements."

"Gabe can play the harmonica. I will ask him if he'll help out," Nate replied excitedly. He rushed outside to ask his brother while Merina stared after him in surprise.

Sam turned his hat in his hands and slowly walked up to Merina.

"Miss Merina, I'm Sam Rankin. I reckon I'll be the oldest kid at school, and I don't like school much.

"What do you like, Sam?"

"Well, I like to break horses, work cattle, ride, and fish."

Merina studied his face and then she smiled. "Well we will see if we can't work some of that into your learning. Breaking horses is all about science and handling cattle is about strategy. I think you might like school this year, Sam."

Sam wasn't convinced but he nodded and walked slowly outside to where Nate was talking excitedly to Gabe.

"Gabe, can you play your harmonica tomorrow night so Miss Merina can start my dance lessons? She said I can come over."

The cowboys who were close enough to hear perked up. "That lady teacher is gonna offer dance lessons? Shoot, boys. I want to learn to dance!" It wasn't long before all the riders for both brands were talking about the dance party at the schoolhouse the next night.

Gabe shook his head and chuckled. He stepped through the door of the house and laughed as he pointed behind him.

"Well, Merina, you have been in Cheyenne for less than twenty-four hours and you already have all the cowboys from two ranches all stirred up."

Merina stared at Gabe and her neck slowly turned red.

"So this dance party tomorrow night. I reckon I will have to bring my harmonica since you will now have every single man within a hundred miles wanting to learn to dance." He was still laughing as he backed out of the door.

Merina stared after him and then looked around at the women. "But I only offered to help Nate!"

The women all laughed. "Maybe we will go too and help you. We'll see very quickly how serious they all are!" Beth's bright eyes were dancing as she laughed.

Molly looked at Merina. "How wonderful that Gabe plays the harmonica. I am sure you enjoyed that around the campfire on the trail drive."

"We did not know. He never played it for us." As the women stared at Merina in surprise, she added, "Perhaps because he is very bad." Merina's bright eyes sparkled in merriment, but her face was still. All the women stared at her for a moment. Then they began to laugh and make plans for another party.

CHAPTER 34

MUSIC AT SUNSET

THE WELCOME PARTY BROKE OFF AROUND 8:00 P.M. and the neighbors headed back home. Once everything was put back together, Rusty took Larry for a walk. Badger and Martha retired for the night while Cappy and Nate headed to the creek to look for night crawlers.

The sun was just starting to go down and Gabe sat down on the edge of the porch. The air was cooling off for the evening and he smiled as he looked over his ranch. He pulled the harmonica out of his pocket. He always had it with him but most of the time, he kept it wrapped carefully in his saddle bags.

He stared at it for a moment and then put it to his mouth and began to play. The song was called *Home on the Range*. One of the riders had sung it on a drive he bossed several years ago. That rider sang it every night around the campfire and all the men knew it by the time they reached Dodge City.

Gabe leaned back against a corner post on the porch. He pushed and pulled the notes out of the small instrument and didn't hear Merina come out of the house to stand behind him. When he was done, he silently tapped it to remove any moisture and then leaned back again. He almost jumped when Merina spoke.

"That was beautiful, Gabe. What is that song about?"

"It's called 'Home on the Range,' and I guess the fellow who wrote it was just reminiscing on how pretty the plains are. I hear he wrote it in Kansas somewhere but lots of drovers sing it now when they are riding nightguard." He grinned up at Merina and began to play a Mexican Hat Dance. She began laughing and he stopped as he grinned. "Maybe you can teach Nate that dance. I think I would like to see you dance to that."

Merina's eyes were dark and unreadable. Gabe put the harmonica back to his lips and began to play "Camptown Races." The beat was fast and loud. Merina moved closer and Gabe tried not to smile at her as she laughed. He slowed it down and began to play a slow ballad. Merina sat down on the porch beside him and listened. As the last notes drifted away, she looked over at him.

"Why did you not play for us on the trail? Your music is beautiful."

Gabe was quiet a moment and then tapped his harmonica on his leg. He thought for a moment as he looked over at her.

"I play when I'm happy, I guess. Drives take a lot of planning and I am constantly thinking about what needs to be done or where the next water is. I never relax and enjoy myself." He paused and then added softly, "This ranch is like the gold at the end of the rainbow. I have wanted this for so long and now here it is. We are sitting on the porch of my own house. Nate is digging for worms in our own creek." He looked over at Merina. "I'm happy. For the first time in a long time, I am contented."

Merina's eyes were dark and unreadable. Gabe whispered, "But since that song brought you closer, I'll play another one to keep you here just a little longer." The next ballad was a love song. He couldn't remember the name of the song, but the music swelled and dropped adding emotion to the notes.

As the last note died away, Gabe looked over at Merina. She had leaned forward and held her knees as she rested her chin on them. She turned her head to study the man beside her.

"Are you trying to court me, Gabe?"

Gabe stared down at the harmonica and tapped it gently again. When he looked at her, his eyes were dark.

"Would you let me court you?"

Merina was quiet a moment. "Perhaps. But only if I knew that it was me you wanted to court."

Gabe looked out into the shadows left by the setting sun before he looked at Merina again. "I'm sorry I called you Grace. I really din't mean to do that. I was apologizing to you—I don't even know why I said her name."

Merina hugged her knees so he couldn't see her heart beating and she worked to keep her voice even. "You said it because Grace is still in your heart. When your heart is free, you may court me…if my heart is free."

Gabe's chest squeezed tightly at her words, but he turned to look at her keeping his face free of emotion. "Have you ever been in love, Merina?"

She smiled and pulled her knees tighter. "Once I thought I was. I was sixteen and he was a rider at a neighboring ranch. He said he was from New Orleans. He was very dashing, with a large bigote—a—I think you say mustache. He laughed a lot and loved to dance. He was a very fast dancer and we danced the Hat Dance often. And then one day, he just rode away. He never said goodbye—he was just—poof. He was gone. I was very sad, but I did not cry. Instead, I became mucho angry. I told myself no more men. They take your heart and break it up in little pieces, but they never give you back all the parts." She paused as she stared into the evening shadows. "I think I am not so mad anymore."

"But you won't tell me his name."

"No, Señor Gabe. You know many men and he might be your friend." Merina's bright eyes sparkled as she looked over at him. She stared off into the evening again and then looked over at Gabe as she smiled softly.

"So you have your memories of Grace and I have my memories of him. Both are dead to us and still, we remember. Perhaps that is good, perhaps it is bad. I think that memories can be good if you don't live so long in the past. Life is very fast. It is important to smile and rejoice each day. You must not miss special moments because you are living for yesterday."

Gabe stared at Merina and then shook his head as he looked away. "You are very wise for someone who is so young."

Merina laughed softly. "Nineteen is not so young where I come from and I will be twenty in October." She looked over at Gabe and her eyes were full of laughter. "Play me another song and perhaps I will think of you as I try to sleep."

Gabe chuckled and put the harmonica to his mouth. The ballad he played was softer and slower than before. Merina was quiet when he finished. They both sat in silence and watched the sun go down. Then she stood and smiled down at him. "That was a beautiful song for a beautiful evening, Señor Gabe. I believe I will think of you as I sleep." She smiled softly at Gabe and then she was gone.

Gabe smiled into the darkness. He tapped the harmonica lightly on his britches and then carefully wrapped it back up. He smiled again as he dropped it into his pocket.

He had found the harmonica in the bunkhouse at Dan Waggoner's the first year he rode for Dan. A previous rider had left it there. No one could remember who that rider was so young Gabe acquired it and began to practice. He usually played when no one was around although sometimes the riders convinced him to play a song or two. When he rode for the King Ranch, he played some on Saturday nights with a local band. Sometimes on those nights, he would cut loose and play a song on his own. Mostly though, he played it alone. He had never played a girl a song before and he could still smell Merina's scent even after she was gone.

Gabe smiled again. "I think my heart is breaking free, Merina," he murmured to himself as he stood and strolled down to the barn. Lance or Rowdy had gone in and restacked all the hay because the barn was once again neat and tidy.

He lay down on his blanket and put his hands behind his head. He didn't hear any of the men come in and slept until early morning.

CHAPTER 35

A Morning Ride

GABE WAS UP EARLY. He had horses for Cappy and himself saddled by 6:30. He hesitated and then saddled a horse for Merina as well. Rusty looked over at him and grinned.

"Don't say anything. This is starting out as a pleasant day and I want it to stay that way. Besides, Merina has been looking forward to seeing this ranch almost as long as I have." Gabe pulled the girth strap tight before he looked up at his friend.

Rusty's grin became bigger and he chuckled as he walked away. "Maybe she dreamed about you last night," he called over his shoulder.

Gabe looked up in surprise. He grabbed a stirrup off a hook on the side of the barn and threw it at the ornery cowboy. Rusty ducked it easily and was still laughing as he led his horse out of the barn.

Nate walked through the door of the barn just in time to see Rusty duck the stirrup. He picked it up and held it out to Gabe. "Not like you to throw tack around," he commented with a grin.

Gabe snorted and led the horses out of the barn. "We are leaving by 7:00 if you want to go along with us to look the range over." As he led the horses to the hitching rail, a large mule let itself out of a pen and ambled up to the house. Gabe gave it a wide berth as he walked around it and into the house.

Badger was sitting at the table and Gabe pointed behind him. "That your mule that just let himself out of the pen?"

The old man grinned and nodded. "He's been known to do that a time or two. I'll be a takin' 'im back with me so you'ins don't need to worry none 'bout 'im."

The three women were busy in the kitchen. Gabe noticed that Merina wore her riding skirt. He grinned. *Guess we were both thinking alike.* He sauntered over to the chair beside Badger and sat down.

"So is this how it works when you're married?" he asked the two men who were already eating. "You just sit down, and your wife brings you food."

Larry laughed as she set a plate in front of Gabe.

"Why yes, Boss, that's how it works. Unless of course you aren't married—then, you pay the person who is cooking."

Gabe was taking a bite and he almost choked. He looked up and she smiled sweetly at him. "Cooks' helpers get $25 a month. Of course, if I stay, I will be the head cook and that will cost you more. And, if you want me to do your laundry too, that price will go up again."

Gabe looked over at Rusty and shook his head.

"What happened to that sweet, quiet gal you married? The one who barely talked? I think I almost liked her better."

Larry rolled her eyes and Gabe looked over as Merina sat down. "Want to ride out with us this morning? Lance is coming over at 7:00 and we'll leave as soon as he gets here."

Merina paused as she looked back toward the bedroom where Emilia was sleeping in a little pile on the floor.

Martha waved her hands at Merina.

"You just go ahead. Emilia and I are going to make bear sign this morning. I think the riders would enjoy a little treat tonight at your dance lessons—since you will probably have every single man within a hundred miles there." Martha's wise eyes were dancing as she laughed.

Merina stared at her for a moment and then shook her head.

"I don't think so. Only the riders for the Rankins know about this and that will be enough. Next time, I am going to limit it to young men fifteen years old and under."

Gabe grinned around his food and said nothing. He agreed with Martha. *Merina has no idea what she has taken on.*

Lance banged on the door and then strolled in. He looked at the full plates and then pulled up a chair without being asked.

"Martha, you know I am always happy when I am in time for one of your meals." He grinned over at Gabe. "Better hire you a cook or you fellows are going to starve. I doubt Badger will let Martha stay so you had better treat Larry right." He winked at the young woman and she laughed as she filled another plate.

The men ate quickly. Badger had finished first and quickly saddled Mule. Both Nate and he were waiting when Gabe, Merina and Lance left the house.

"Badger, I don't know why you haven't taught old Mule to saddle himself. He seems to know every other order with or without you saying it," Lance commented.

Badger grinned at his friends and winked at Merina.

"Now Mule is what I call notional. He only does things what he wants ta do. He could saddle hisself but he don't figger he needs ta waste time doin' that when I cin do it fer 'im."

Lance laughed and nodded, "Kind of like his owner."

Badger grinned and then led the way out of the yard at a trot. They rode around the land that Gabe had purchased all morning. The fences were in good shape. Badger hadn't let anything get run down. Gabe was amazed that a man as old as Badger could maintain so much fence.

"Badger and I work together a lot. My hands have maintained all the fences in the past and Badger paid me. I am guessing you will maintain them yourself." Lance looked in question toward Gabe who nodded.

"How do you decide whose fence is whose?"

"We can do it however you want. Some fellows do it by the section and others by the pasture. We share the entire west side and part of the fence on the south. That gulley there would be a good divider. You tell me what part you want, and I will take the other."

Gabe chose the southern part and the men studied the ponds.

"If it gets too dry, we open some fences and share more water. We haven't had to do that much. Of course, before '66, we hardly fenced anything. Once they started bringing the herds up after the war, we had to preserve our water and our grass." Lance shook his head. "The time will come when over-grazing is going to catch up with us. Some of these new investors don't have a clue how dry or how cold it can get up here."

Gabe studied Lance's face as he thought about that comment.

"Lots of new outfits moving in here?"

Lance snorted as he waved his arms around. "Shoot, everyone wants to make money on cattle right now. We haven't had a bust for some time. Investors from back east and even across the pond think they can come here and get rich." He shrugged before he continued. "Right now that is happening for lots of cattlemen. By next year, we'll have more moneyed men in Cheyenne than some of the big cities, and our population is less than three thousand. There is even talk of putting up streetlights!" He shook his head and then grinned at Gabe.

"That's why Molly won't let me buy more land. She says we have to pay cash—no borrowing. That way if things go belly-up, we can still survive. If you are leveraged too tight, it's harder to hang on through the lean times." He chuckled again as he looked at Gabe, "So hang on for the ride and spend wisely!"

"You ever bring any Angus or Hereford cattle in here, Lance?"

"I have a few. It's a little harder to get them here but once they are established, they do well. Good idea to take delivery in the spring if you can so they can acclimate to the weather all summer. The ones I have seen that were brought here in the fall didn't do as well."

Merina was quiet as she listened to the men. She didn't know as much about cattle breeds as she did about horses. Still, she enjoyed the discussion and the exchange of ideas. She glanced over at Gabe and he was staring out at the land beyond the fence line.

"See more land you think you need, Gabe?" she teased. He glanced over at her with a quick grin and then chuckled.

"Sure am. I kind of like the way Lance thinks when it comes to land."

Badger pointed in the direction that Gabe was staring. "That there's the parcel what's a comin' up fer sale this fall here. Good water most years but she's a little rough. A man 'ould want ta ride it 'fore he offered any cash. 'Course, if'n he were a prudent feller, he'd ride over there right 'way." Badger grinned over at Gabe.

"You aren't interested, Lance?"

"Nope, Molly said no more land this year," Lance stated mournfully. "Hate to pass it up but I love my wife more than a piece of ground," he added with a wink at Merina.

Gabe didn't say any more. Merina knew the owner would be paid a visit soon and she smiled.

They arrived back at the ranch just in time for dinner and once again, the women had it waiting for them.

"Sure wouldn't take too many meals like this to spoil me completely on my cooking," Gabe commented as he looked at the spread. "Guess Rusty knew what he was doing,"

Larry rolled her eyes and Rusty squeezed his wife before he sat down.

Emilia bounced over to Gabe and twirled in front of him. She had on a long apron and was covered in flour.

"I helped Granny Martha cook. We made bear paws. Do you like bear paws, Señor Gabe?"

"Well I reckon I do but I can't say as I have ever tasted them. Do you have any left?"

Emilia grabbed a bowl off the table and almost dropped it. Gabe caught it and Emilia never missed a beat.

"There they are. I don't think they look like bear paws. They are little cakes with holes in them." She popped one in her mouth and smiled at Gabe around it.

He ate one and then opened his eyes wide.

"And you helped make these? Boy, are they tasty. Better share some with Rusty and Badger. Nate and Cappy too. Here, let me have another one in case they try to eat them all. Maybe Merina should give me hers as well."

Merina looked over at him coolly and helped herself to two.

"I don't think Señor Gabe knows how much we like donas, does he?"

Emilia smiled happily and climbed up on a chair beside Gabe to eat.

CHAPTER 36

A PROPOSITION FOR RUSTY

ONCE THE MEAL WAS OVER, THE WOMEN CLEANED UP QUICKLY. The kitchen was sparkling in no time and Badger hustled Martha to the waiting buggy. Mule was turned loose to follow behind.

"We's a gonna take Miss Merina ta 'er new house so's she cin settle in a bit 'fore the dance lessons tonight." He grinned at Gabe and added, "I reckon she's a gonna need her a nap today an' tomorrow too 'fore this here deal is done."

"What time does this shindig start tonight? I can come a little early to help you set up for it." Gabe looked over at Rusty. "Larry going too?"

Rusty shook his head. "Naw. She said she's stayin' home. She's a goin' to help Merina settle in today though.

"I'll come over fer a time. I won't take no lessons, but I'll come fer the food."

Merina and Emilia were on horseback. Emilia waved at Gabe as they rode out of the yard. "Goodbye, Señor Gabe!" Merina smiled over her shoulder and the buggy rattled out of the driveway.

Nate and Cappy were fishing again and wouldn't be back until the afternoon sometime.

The ranch was suddenly quiet, and Gabe pointed toward a small building. "Let's go get us a root beer. Badger built an icehouse and I saw a jug of it in there last night."

The men were soon seated on the porch steps. Gabe stretched out his legs and looked over at Rusty.

"How would you like to be my partner on those investments that Gallagher left me? I need a fellow to go to Kansas with Levi on Tuesday to look them over. Maybe negotiate the sale of some of them."

Rusty stared at Gabe in surprise and then shook his head. "Don't have the money to buy into somethin' like that. I'll help ya sell or whatever ya need but I cain't do it as a partner."

Gabe leaned forward and picked up a stick off the ground. His face was serious as he looked at Rusty.

"I didn't ask if you wanted to buy in. I asked if you wanted to be a partner. I visited about it some with Levi when I talked to him yesterday and he is drawing up papers. We meet with him on Monday--you, me, and Larry. He is leaving for Manhattan, Kansas on Tuesday and he offered to take you with him. That's why we need to speed things up." Gabe looked away and was quiet a moment before he continued.

"You and Larry along with Merina's family are my family now. Besides Nate and Cappy, I don't have any relatives. Gallagher left quite a bit of land and holdings, and it sounds like it is enough for two families. I want you to make a go of it. A fellow should be able to give his wife and baby a home." Gabe broke the stick in half and added, "I didn't buy in or deserve any of this so I guess I can share it with whoever I want."

Rusty was quiet for a moment and then shook his head. "Boss…"

Gabe laughed, "Just Gabe now. We are partners so there is no boss." He paused and then added, "Of course, you can still call me that if you want. I do like the way it sounds."

Rusty laughed and relaxed as he chuckled.

"Levi was checking around to see if there were any small ranches that you might be able to pick up around here. I'd like you to still work here if you want, but if you can get your own place, that would be good too."

Rusty stared at this man he considered his best friend and then roughly wiped his eyes. "Durn, must have somethin' in my eyes. They seem to be a waterin'."

"I don't know much about what Gallagher owns in Kansas, but you are the best dickering man I have ever met," Gabe stated quietly. "Levi will show you what holdings and land we have. I told him to liquidate what we couldn't manage from here and then hang onto the rest." Gabe paused and added, "Of course, if you think you would rather live by Manhattan and manage from there, that would be fine as well. There is some really nice grass around there in what they call the Flint Hills."

Rusty was quiet as he looked at Gabe and then stared out over Gabe's ranch. His blue eyes were full of excitement. "I reckon Larry would be closer to her folks if we moved there. Can I look things over an' then decide? I want to talk it over with Larry too."

Gabe nodded. "Our appointment with Levi is at 10:00 tomorrow morning. Once we finalize things with the partnership, you can buy your ticket. Larry can go with you if she wants or she can stay here." He paused, "Well, she can stay with Merina while you are gone. You can make that decision. You and Levi talk things over back there, and I am good with what you decide. I would hate to have you leave but you do what's best for your little family."

Gabe chuckled as he looked at his friend. "I just had a vision of you in your fancy boots with your britches tucked in and tails on your coat."

Rusty laughed dryly and agreed.

"I reckon I'm a little too much of a cowboy to be much of a fancy feller even if I cin dicker." He looked over at Gabe.

"I don't know how to thank ya, Gabe. I never had nothin' growin' up. I been a worryin' how I was goin' to make this family thing work, but I shore never thought a this."

Gabe grinned and slapped Rusty on the back.

"You just work your magic and make us both some money. Anybody who can sell wagons, mules, and horses like you did these last two months should be able to turn a profit on things that are supposed to make money.

"Now let's go through that barn and see what we need you to sell and what we are going to keep. I guess building that bunkhouse will have to wait until I can hire some men to help me." He added dryly, "The way I'm losing hands though I might not even need a bunkhouse!"

CHAPTER 37

Dance Lessons!

RUSTY AND GABE WORKED WELL TOGETHER, and they soon had the walls of the barn stripped of items they didn't need. Gabe wanted to focus on cattle where Badger's business had been mostly mules. By 4:00 p.m., they had gone through most of the buildings. An old wagon was sitting behind the barn and Rusty walked around it.

"Shoot, that's in better shape than the one I growed up with. I cin fix that up an' we'll have us a good wagon in no time."

They pulled the wagon out of the tall grass and rolled it into the barn.

"Y'all need ya some chickens, Gabe. Batchin' it like yore gonna be, it would shore be nice to have some fer breakfast."

Gabe nodded and the two of them soon decided where the coop should be built. They turned all the horses but Buck out in the pasture behind the barn. Buck was let loose to graze on the grass in the yard. "You'll be taking me to dance lessons tonight, old fellow, so be on your best behavior."

They quit at 5:00 and headed for the creek to clean up. Cappy and Nate were just coming up and they had more fish.

"We'll get these here fish started bakin'. I'm a gonna show Nate how ta cover 'em in mud and bake 'em in the coals."

When Gabe and Rusty came up from the creek, the smell of baked fish filled their noses. Gabe roughed up his little brother's hair. "I might have to give you more time off to fish if you can catch them like this. These are darn good. Now you get cleaned up as soon as you are done. We need to be over at the schoolhouse by 6:30."

They arrived at the schoolhouse just a little after 6:30. The yard was full of rigs of all kinds as well as lots of horses. Men loafed everywhere.

Gabe pointed at the crowd. "When a pretty woman offers to give dance lessons, the word gets out!" He knocked and a worried Merina answered, quickly shutting the door behind him.

"What am I going to do? There are too many to even fit in the schoolhouse!"

"I reckon you will have to take them in shifts. Molly and Beth mentioned coming over to help. If they come, you can have people outside and in." He chuckled as he studied her face. "Of course, the majority of them are not here to *learn* to dance—they are here to dance with *you*."

Merina blushed and stared out the window. "How did they all find out? We only planned this yesterday."

True to their word, Molly and Beth arrived about 6:45 with food and Martha's doughnuts. They set the food out in the back of Molly's wagon. The men were almost as excited about the bear sign as they were about dancing with the new teacher.

The large teacher's desk was pushed to the side of the room. There was a water barrel in the room for the students to use and some of the cowboys offered to fill it. Molly laid the water dipper on top of it and they were ready.

Merina gathered everyone outside and explained how the lessons would work.

"I want to thank all of you for coming. Molly and Beth will help those of you outside and I will work with those inside. We will rotate one group out and the next group of ten back in. We will go until 7:30, take a fifteen-minute break and then go again until 8:15. Mr. Hawkins has volunteered to play his harmonica so we will have music."

She paused and then added, "If you hear that I am giving additional lessons, please be aware that those lessons will be for the school students only and will be by appointment.

"Also, Martha McCune as well as Molly and Beth Rankin provided the food for you. Please thank them."

Gabe followed her back inside and they began. The first group was mostly students and Merina showed them some faster dances. He slowed it down to a Texas two-step as cowboys filled the room and he tried not to laugh when they were more interested in smiling at Merina than in learning to dance. Several times he started laughing and missed some notes as Merina glared at him from behind a cowboy's back.

At last it was 7:30. Gabe tapped out the harmonica and stood to stretch his legs. Merina took off her boots and rubbed her toes as he grinned at her.

She shook her finger at him. "I do not want to hear anything from you." She massaged her toes and whispered, "My feet have never been stomped so many times."

Gabe strolled outside just in time to see a cowboy ride up. The man looked confused as he spoke to some of the riders lounging around the school yard. One handed him some bear sign and he ate it as he looked toward the schoolhouse.

Gabe sauntered up to him with a grin on his face and put out his hand. "Howdy, Spur. Fancy meeting you all the way up here."

The mounted cowboy chuckled and then pointed at the cowhands grouped all over the yard.

"Howdy, Gabe. You ridin' up here or did ya buy ya a place?" The cowboy's face split into a smile as he shook Gabe's hand.

"Just bought Badger's ranch. How about you?"

"I ride for Rowdy. I've worked for him two different times since he bought his ranch. Good boss and I like my job." He pointed around at the cowboys standing around in groups and talking.

"Feller said there were dance lessons here tonight. Who's teachin'? I heard the school marm was an older gal."

Gabe laughed. "You heard wrong unless you think twenty is old." He chuckled and added, "She offered to teach some of the kids, but the word got out and her class size expanded!"

Just then, Merina came to the door and clapped her hands.

Spur was staring at her in surprise and Gabe chuckled. "Good to see you, Spur. I am the volunteer music, so I'd better get inside."

Merina barely noticed the mounted cowboy before she walked back into the schoolhouse. He stared toward the school for a time and then slowly rode to the west looking back several times.

The second set of lessons went even faster. Gabe winced for Merina a couple of times when awkward men stepped completely down on her feet.

When it was over, each cowboy came and thanked Merina, one at a time. They thanked Molly and Beth as well and helped them load the empty bowls and pans into Molly's wagon. Gabe was going to dump the water barrel, but Merina stopped him. "I will use that water for baths so just leave it for now."

Gabe nodded. He grabbed Nate. "You and Sam top off that water barrel. Merina needs it to be filled."

He drug the big teacher's desk back into place. They all pulled the student's desks back into rows. The little building was cleaned up and back to normal in no time. As the riders drifted back to their ranches, Merina invited her helpers in for some coffee.

Emilia had fallen asleep after playing hard with the other kids. Merina pulled off her shoes and laid her in bed with her clothes on.

Molly and Beth sank into chairs and both began to rub their feet.

"I appreciate Rowdy's dancing even more after this evening," Beth stated as she giggled. "Although I think they were almost disappointed to see Molly and me. Most of those cowboys came for the dance and not for the lessons."

Merina blushed and Gabe laughed out loud. "That's what I told her. Thanks for letting me be right once tonight, Beth."

All three women had worn boots and their feet were still bruised.

Molly looked over at Merina. "If you ever decide to do this again, don't expect me to help. I am going to stick with Lance, although Rowdy and Levi are excellent dancers too."

Merina handed each of the women a cup of coffee. They drank theirs quickly and hurried back outside.

Gabe followed them and helped Molly up into the wagon. He gave Beth a foot up and then the yard was empty. Rusty had only come for the bear sign. He left early and Nate had gone home with Sam. Gabe was to pick him up when he rode by the Rocking R.

He leaned against the door jamb and looked over the yard. From the doorway, Molly and Lance's ranch was less than a quarter mile to the east. He couldn't see Rowdy's ranch headquarters, but he knew it was to the west. A small creek wound around between the two ranches. It was a nice location for a little house and the school as well.

"Who did Martha say lived here before?"

"Old Man McNary. Lance bought the Rocking R from him the year he married Molly. He was like a grandfather to all the children and died several years ago. Slippery slide, merry go round and swings too. He made and put all of them up himself. Molly said he was like a father to Lance." Merina paused as she looked at the playground. "She said Lance took Old Man McNary's death hard." A smile flitted across her face. "Now his yard is a playground."

Gabe looked over at her and smiled. "Did you dream about me last night?" he asked as devils danced in his eyes.

Merina tried to look at him coolly and then laughed.

She held up her fingers and pinched them together. "Maybe a little." Her dark eyes were laughing back at him.

"I'd play you a song, but I think my lips are numb." He pushed on them as he looked at her seriously and then added, "I don't recall ever having a woman make my lips go numb before."

Merina stared at him and then she blushed a dark red. "Don't say that! Someone might hear you and think the wrong thing."

Gabe laughed and dropped down to sit on the porch. "How about one last song."

Merina sat down beside him, and Gabe began to play a soft ballad. The music swelled and then became soft as the music sifted through the evening air.

When the song was over, Gabe tapped out his harmonica and looked over at Merina's profile.

"I am going to miss seeing you every day, " he said softly.

Her body was still for a moment and then she looked at him as lights danced in her eyes.

"I think maybe I am too handy. Like pockets. They are only missed when one does not have them."

Gabe chuckled. "Maybe but I do like pockets. Can't think of a time I wouldn't want them around."

Merina laughed softly. "Gabe, I believe you are trying to flirt with me."

Gabe laughed out loud. "Well trying is probably accurate. That is not something I have done often so I wouldn't know where to start. I just know that I like it when you smile. I like your laugh and when you sit beside me looking up like that, my heart sings."

Merina went completely still, and Gabe almost kissed her. He started to lean toward her and then he faced forward.

Instead, he stood and offered her his hand. He pulled her up, but Merina didn't let him pull her close. He stared at her for a moment and then smiled.

"Yes, Angel was right. You are a difficult woman, Merina."

Gabe whistled for Buck and the horse came trotting up to him. He laughed softly as he looked down at Merina one more time and shook his head.

As he trotted his horse toward Lance's ranch, he called back, "I'm riding into Cheyenne tomorrow morning with Rusty and Larry. We'll leave around 8:30. We want to be in town a little before 10:00 if you'd like to ride along." He paused and then added, "I'll know you want to go if Mascota is tied at the hitching rail."

He raised his hand and turned Buck again toward the Rocking R.

Merina stood in the doorway for a moment and then walked back into the house. She leaned against the door after she closed it and smiled.

"You make my heart sing too, Gabe."

CHAPTER 38

THE NEW NEIGHBORS

GABE WAS UP EARLY. He checked all his supplies and then made a list of the things he needed in Cheyenne. He put a pack saddle on one of the mules and tied it to the hitching rack in front of the house.

Nate and Cappie came out of the barn wiping their eyes. Gabe pointed toward the house.

'Rusty, Larry and I are headed into Cheyenne to sign papers this morning. Maybe you can help Cappy start on a chicken coop. I saw a bunch of chicken wire rolled up in the back of the barn. There is some lumber behind there too. I'd like it big enough to hold at least twenty hens."

Larry was just coming into the kitchen and began to hurry when she saw Gabe.

"No hurrying on my account. I am going to ride over to the south side and look at that fence again. I think I am going to buy some black cattle to cross with these longhorns and I don't want any bulls getting mixed up. I'll be back by 8:00 and I'd like to leave by 8:30."

Rusty tucked his shirt in as he rushed for the barn. "Hold up a minute, Boss, an' I'll ride with ya."

The two men rode at an easy lope for the first half mile and then slowed down to a time-eating trot.

"Larry said she'd stay here 'stead of goin' to Kansas with me. She'd like to go but she's feared that we'll be busy an' she'll be on her own all the time." He added, "She said she's up fer movin' if it's the last time. Said I'd better make sure that's what I want to do 'fore she hikes back 'cross country again." He grinned at Gabe. "So I guess we'll see."

Gabe nodded and then pointed at the ranch across the fence. The top of the house could just barely be seen over the crest of the hill.

"That piece is going to be coming up for sale. I think I'll ride over there tomorrow and talk to that feller about buying his ranch. It lays right next to mine. It would be nice to have more land and especially some that butts up to me." He paused as he studied the layout. "Might even be a good place for Angel and Miguel. If I had that, I might not need a bunkhouse."

Rusty nodded in agreement and then added innocently, "Probably need to add on to the house though. Looks like ya'll 'ill need more room 'fore long." He kept his eyes straight ahead and when Gabe snorted, he started laughing.

Gabe stared at him. "You go snooping around folks at night or do you just do lots of assuming?"

"Lucky guessin', Boss. That's all…but I do think that harmonica is helpin' yore cause."

Gabe snorted and pushed Watie into a run. Rusty's horse leapt to keep up and almost unseated the ornery cowboy. Both men were laughing when they stopped at the fence line.

A man was riding toward them. He stopped at the fence.

"You the fellers who bought Badger's spread?"

Gabe nodded. "Gabe Hawkins from down in Texas. This is Rusty O'Brian."

"Chester Reith. I spose Badger told you I was sellin' this place."

Gabe grinned and chuckled. "He did and I was hoping I could maybe come over tomorrow morning and talk to you about it—maybe ride around it some and look it over."

Chester stared from Gabe to Rusty and then spoke to the younger man. "Yore boss know his hind end from an apple barrel?"

Rusty laughed and nodded seriously. "I've known Gabe here fer nigh on ten years. Been on four drives north from Texas with 'im. He was the best trail boss I ever worked with. The boss knows cows an' he knows grass. He'll have to learn stockin' rates up here an' cold weather too, but he's a true cowman."

He turned to Gabe and added, "An' y'all cin throw a nice little bonus my way fer that there spiel." His eyes were twinkling, and Gabe choked as he turned red.

Chester looked hard at the two of them and then chuckled. "I like you boys. Come on over tomorrow mornin' around 8:00. Plan to stay for dinner. I'll have my Missus fix us somethin' to eat after we get back from ridin' around the land."

He waved his hand as he rode away and Gabe wacked Rusty.

"I almost fell off my horse. What if he hadn't thought that was funny?"

Rusty laughed wickedly as he ducked. "Ya have to read folks, Boss. That's why ya put me in charge of the sellin', ain't it? I knew that ol' boy wouldn't go fer no baloney an' what was the truth shore sounded like it. I jist said what he may a been a thinkin'." Rusty was still laughing when they rode up to the house.

Nate was standing by the door fidgeting. "I'd like to go along with you, Gabe. Afterall, I'm a partner too. I might need to sign something."

Gabe laughed and swung his arm around his brother's shoulders. "All right, we'll make it a family deal." As they walked into the kitchen, Gabe asked dryly, "You want to come too Cappy?"

Cappy scratched his scruffy head and then shook it. "Naw. I'll start on that coop an' I'll stop when I'm tard. Might even take me a nap. 'Member, I come up here ta take it easy, not ta work all the durn time."

Gabe grinned and they all sat down to eat.

Larry paused a moment and looked over at Rusty. She hesitated and then asked, "Gabe, would you mind if Rusty led us in a prayer before we eat?"

Gabe dropped his fork and blushed slightly. "I reckon that would be a good thing. Go ahead, Rusty."

"Lord, we thank ya fer this here food an' fer the friends 'round this table. We thank ya fer bringin' us together an' fer makin' us a family. Amen."

Gabe was quiet a moment and then he looked at Rusty. "That was a fine prayer. Amen to that."

They helped Larry clean up quickly and they were all on their way by 8:30. As they rode by the Rocking R, Gabe looked hopefully for Mascota but there were no horses tied to the hitching rail.

Rusty caught Gabe's eye and winked. Gabe glared at him. "I think you're a durn snoop is what I think."

Nate looked from one to the other in confusion and Larry laughed.

"Don't ask me how he does it, Gabe, but he just knows."

Rusty pushed his horse closer to Larry's and squeezed his wife. "I shore am goin' to miss ya whilst I'm gone. An' ya better not have that little ol' baby early 'cause I want to be there fer the birthin'."

Larry smiled up at him and Gabe laughed. "She'll be with Merina, so she'll be in good hands."

CHAPTER 39

Let's finalize This Deal!

A BRIGHT-EYED YOUNG WOMAN WAS SEATED AT THE TALL RECEPTION DESK WHEN THEY WALKED INTO LEVI'S OFFICE. She smiled at Gabe and asked, "Are you Mr. Hawkins?"

When Gabe nodded, she slipped off her chair and knocked softly on Levi's door.

"Mr. Hawkins is here to see you, Mr. Parker."

Levi opened the door and waved them in. He pointed toward the young woman. "This is Annie Small. Her husband is the one who built my desk if you want to talk to her later."

Annie smiled brightly at all of them and then quickly went back to work.

The men seated Larry and then pulled chairs up to be close to Levi's desk. Levi shook hands with all of them and then slid a packet of papers across his desk and stacked them in front of him.

"Any questions before we start?" He paused and then added, "You are all in agreement to this partnership?"

As they nodded, he smiled. "Good. Let's get started."

"These papers outline the partnership and all four of you need to sign them. This paper, Gabe, gives me permission to talk to the bank about Gallagher's investments on your behalf. It also allows me to file a copy of your partnership with them. The way I have it set up, any one of you can make decisions in the event the other partners should die. Otherwise, those investments or sales must be agreed by all four of you *unless* you give me as your lawyer permission to act in your absence. This paper gives me that right as long as one partner agrees. I added this sheet because it will allow Rusty and me to buy or sell while we are in Manhattan. Now, I am going to step out while you read these over and discuss them. I will be back in about ten minutes. If you finish earlier, just let Annie know."

They all read through the contracts and Gabe picked up his pen. He grinned at Rusty and Larry.

"Well, you ready to do this?"

Rusty stared at the paper and Larry waited for him with her pen held upright. He finally looked up at Gabe.

"I don't think I cin do this. I feel like a durn freeloader. I got nothin' to offer in return."

Gabe pushed the paper toward his friend.

"Sign it, Rusty. I didn't work for this money either. We can be two freeloaders working with another man's capital to build secure futures for our families. If we lose it all, then shame on us. But what if we grow it? What if we build it into something that only Gallagher could have dreamed of creating? Sign the papers and let's start putting your talents to work. We all know this venture requires skills that Nate and I don't have."

Rusty studied Gabe's face and then he grinned. "Well, when y'all put it that way." He signed his name with a flourish and Larry signed hers beside his. Nate opened the door.

"We're done, Miss Annie."

Annie stood and went to the bottom of the stairs that were at the back of the office.

"Mr. Parker, we are ready for you."

Levi was back quickly. He looked at the four excited faces in front of him and he laughed. He shook each person's hand.

"Congratulations to each of you. Rusty, we are on the 9:00 train tomorrow morning and we will be gone for a week. Don't buy your return ticket yet but get your ticket to Manhattan, Kansas right away.

"We'll be rubbing elbows with some moneyed men. You and I will never match up to them but make sure your shirts don't have any holes." His smile became bigger as he added, "Don't worry about the socks. No one will see those. See you in the morning!"

Annie smiled at them as they left. "If you need to see Tiny, he works out of a shop by our house on the west end of town, north of the tracks. He should be there all day."

Once they were outside, Gabe handed Rusty $200. "See what Martha has at her store. We just as well give her business if we can. I hear that Levi's wife is quite the seamstress. She might have some shirts that would fit you. Pick up two or three and a couple of pairs of britches." His eyes twinkled as he added, "I know you used to be quite the dandy so here is your chance to live it up. The rest of the money is for the trip."

Rusty stared from the money to Larry and he blushed. "Don't quite seem right fer a man to buy a new outfit when his wife ain't had a new dress since 'fore they was married."

Larry laughed. "Well then, you had better make some money because you are going to buy me at least one new dress when you get home."

Rusty squeezed his wife and whispered in her ear. Larry smiled up at him and he helped her up on her horse. He looked over at Gabe.

"We'll see you back at the ranch. I am going to try to get that wagon fixed up before I leave."

Gabe nodded and waved as the O'Brians headed south out of town.

"What are we going to do?" Nate asked as he looked at his brother.

"We are going to find Tiny. I want to order a desk for the ranch and a crib for Larry. Let's go see if we can find his shop."

CHAPTER 40

THE BROTHERS

THE TWO BROTHERS RODE SLOWLY THROUGH TOWN. Gabe smiled as he looked around. *This is my town, my home.*

"So what do you think, Nate? Think Rusty will be back or will he decide to stay around Manhattan?"

Nate pondered a moment and studied Gabe's face from the side.

"I think he will stay in Kanas."

Gabe looked over at his brother in surprise. "Now why would you say that?"

"Well, Rusty likes to wheel and deal and I think he will get to do a lot of that this week. He is going to have fun. Plus, you said there is good grass outside Manhattan. Combine that with Larry being from Dodge City and the way the trains run…he is going to move back to Kansas."

Gabe chuckled as he nodded. "I think you might be right. You know, we planned to drive north from Dodge with nine riders plus Cookie and two women. One rider stayed in Dodge, four stayed in Ogallala, Cookie went on north to Montana, Tall Eagle joined up with his band, Angel and Miguel are in Texas and Rusty may take Larry and move to

Kansas. Now here we are buying more land and I am going to be short on help. I sure hope that Angel and Miguel come back."

Nate's eyes crinkled at the corners as he tried to look serious.

"Maybe you should marry Merina. Then you would be guaranteed that one hand would always be around."

Gabe stared at his little brother and sputtered a couple of times. He muttered under his breath and finally laughed.

"Don't you start on me too. I am already getting more advice that I can handle."

They wandered through a few side streets. They finally found Tiny's small house and the shed next to it. Saws and hammers could be heard along with men talking and laughing. Gabe dismounted and stuck his head in the door.

"I'm looking for Tiny Small."

A large man stood up in the back of the room. "Ya found 'im. What ya want 'im fer?"

Gabe walked in with a smile on his face followed by Nate. "I'm Gabe Hawkins and this is my brother, Nate. We bought Badger McCune's ranch.

"I saw the desk that you made for Levi Parker and I wondered if you would make me one too. And a crib for one of my hands."

Tiny studied the man in front of him and then walked over to a table where an order book was laying open. He sized Gabe up with his eyes and wrote down some figures.

"Ya want a mix a wood like Levi's? An' yore brand in it?"

Gabe thought a moment. "I'm not that familiar with the wood that is available here so you can use your judgement. I do want my brand in it on a top corner like you did his. It is the Diamond H Ranch. I'd like Hawkins Brothers 1879 on the front panel."

Tiny made some notes and drew a rough sketch. He shoved the book toward Gabe. "That kind a what yore thinkin'?"

Gabe studied it and then looked at Tiny in surprise. "That's exactly what I want." He looked around the shop. "I want a crib for one of my hands too."

Tiny lifted a small crib up and set it on the counter. "Like this?" When Gabe nodded, he asked, "Want anythin' on the ends?"

Gabe grinned as he studied the crib. "Think you could put a cattle drive on there? That's where they met. They were married in Dodge at the end of that drive from Texas."

"I cin purty much make whatever ya want but the fancier she gets, the more it'll cost ya." Tiny drew out a man on horseback and a woman riding in front of him with cattle between them. The cattle trailed around the side of the crib until the two people came together on the opposite end and were riding side by side, holding hands with cattle grazing around them.

Gabe stared at the drawing and then looked up at Tiny in amazement. "How long have you been doing this? I don't think I have ever seen anything like that anywhere."

Tiny's big face split into a grin. "I used to ride fer Lance. I was a Rockin' R hand through an' through. Then the Judge come along an' had me make his furniture. That's when I figgered out I could make a whole lot more money off ya fellers than I ever made ridin' with ya."

"I'm sure you can. What do I owe you? I'll go ahead and pay you now."

Tiny did some calculations. "$65 fer the desk an' $18 fer the crib. I added some extry on the crib fer all the carvin'. If ya want a chair with that desk, make it an even $100."

Gabe handed him $100 and shook his hand. "How will I know when you are done?"

"Ya cin pick it up in two weeks. We's a little backed up right now. Bring a wagon 'cause I don't deliver."

Gabe shook his hand and then moved out of the shop quickly. He stepped around the corner and bumped into Merina, nearly knocking her down. He caught her as she staggered.

"Merina! Are you okay? I sure am sorry."

She nodded as she straightened herself up. As she stepped around him, Gabe commented quietly, "I was hoping to see Mascota tied to the hitching rail this morning."

Merina blushed and hurried inside the building.

Gabe fiddled with Watie's reins for a moment and Nate asked casually, "Want me to go on back to Martha's store and look at shirts?"

Gabe looked up quickly to see his little brother grinning at him. He shoved him and laughed. "Get out of here, you ornery kid. I'll wait for her and see if she'll eat dinner with us."

Merina wasn't inside long and came out with a smile on her face. It changed to surprise when she saw Gabe waiting by her horse.

His eyes twinkled as he looked down at her. "I guess I don't really care *what* hitching rail your horse is tied to if that means you'll ride with me."

Merina stared up at him and then laughed. "You are a persistent man, Gabe Hawkins."

Gabe nodded soberly. "I don't know much about women but persistent I can do." He grinned as he helped her up on her horse.

"So what brings you to Cheyenne?"

Merina looked down at him and smiled. "Do you really care what brought me here or are you just working up to inviting me to eat with you?"

Gabe chuckled and nodded. "You have me all figured out. I need to buy Nate a couple of shirts. That kid is growing faster than he wears them out and that's fast. After that, I would like to invite you to eat with us."

Merina's dark eyes sparkled as she laughed. "Since Nate is along, it will be like three friends sharing a meal so I guess that will be fine."

"When are you going to let me court you, Merina?" Gabe's eyes were intense as he looked up at her.

Emotions flashed through Merina's dark eyes as she studied his face.

"It seems like to me that you already are." Her voice was soft, and the blush traveled up to her cheeks.

Gabe's face lit up in a smile and Merina laughed.

"You look just like Nate when you smile like that. Carefree, happy and excited."

"Well maybe you should hang around me more and you might see more of that smile."

Merina rolled her eyes and they rode back toward Martha's store laughing and talking.

Nate had a couple of shirts in his hands when they walked in and Gabe looked at them. "Did you try them on? Your arms have gotten long this summer."

Sadie walked out of the back and laughed when she heard his question.

"Good morning, Mr. Hawkins. Yes, he tried them on. I have some that might fit you as well if you are interested."

Gabe paused and then nodded. "I only need one though."

Sadie held up two shirts and Gabe stared at them. He finally chose the dark blue one. He held it up to himself and nodded. "This will work."

Merina picked up a few sewing supplies and some soft pink fabric.

"For Emilia?" Gabe asked. Merina nodded and he added some pink ribbon to his pile along with some candy.

"I have to make sure she doesn't find another favorite cowboy," he commented as he laughed.

"I don't think there is much chance of that. She liked you the first day you caught her on the stairs," Merina answered dryly. "You are her Señor Gabe."

"Unlike her big sister who thought I was a bothersome gringo and a ladies' man."

Merina ignored him.

"Any suggestions where I should take a lady for dinner, Sadie? I know a little gal who is real picky about who she is seen with."

Nate started laughing and Merina turned her head away as a slow blush climbed up her neck.

Sadie's looked at the three of them and then back at Merina as she shook her head. "They are all alike, Merina. And wait until his friends become involved. Ask me about our wedding someday!"

"Take her to the Rollin's house. It isn't as noisy as the Tin House and the food is good every day. You might want to send Nate ahead to get a table though."

Merina looked at her suspiciously and Sadie giggled as her brown eyes danced. "Just being neighborly, Merina." A little boy of seven or so appeared behind Sadie. His eyes were bright blue, and he had blond curls poking out all over his head. He grinned at them and then tried to dash outside. Sadie caught him and sent him back into the room behind her. "I'm almost ready to go, Levi. You keep an eye on your sister and we will pick up your father in just a bit."

Gabe took Merina's packages and put them on his pack mule. They walked across the street to the dry goods store and he handed the clerk his list.

"I can pick that up after dinner."

"Are you Gabe Hawkins?" When Gabe nodded, the man continued, "I'm Isaac Herman. Badger told me that he sold you his ranch. Welcome to Cheyenne, Mr. Hawkins." He held out his hand and Gabe shook it.

"This is Merina Montero. Her brothers work for me. You may have met my younger brother, Nate. I think he was going to stop in here for something."

Herman laughed and laid two pairs of socks up on the counter. "Yes, he said to add this to your stack."

Gabe grinned and paid the man.

"If you want to leave your pack mule, I'll load your supplies when I have time." Herman nodded to Merina, "Ma'am. Welcome to Cheyenne. We are always excited to see women move to our town."

Merina smiled a thank you.

"Folks are sure friendly here," Gabe commented as he tied the mule more securely. "And where is your little sister? I thought maybe you left her with Martha, but I didn't see her."

"No, Molly offered to keep her. Livvy and Emilia are just a year apart in age and are becoming fast friends." She looked up at Gabe. "Kind of like Nate and Sam."

"Friends are good for Nate. He never really had many friends down where we grew up. He worked for food from when he was small. Amazing he is such a happy kid. He is making up for being hungry for years now with the provisions he goes through. He can pack away more food at one sitting than two hungry men." Gabe paused and added softly, "He's sure excited to have a friend who likes to fish as much as he does."

Nate waved at them from a back table and Gabe guided Merina through the crowded room to where his brother was sitting.

"Good thing Sadie told me to go ahead. This place was nearly empty just ten minutes ago."

They ordered and Merina visited easily with Nate. The young man laughed easily, and Gabe wished he could be a little more relaxed like his brother. *Maybe it is age. That and responsibility. Probably experience too.* Slowly, he began to loosen up. He enjoyed Merina's laugh. It was soft and he liked the way her eyes sparkled when she smiled.

"Do you want any more dance lessons, Nate? June 28th is just a few days away if you do."

Nate looked at Gabe and his older brother shrugged. "Pick a time and we'll come over."

"How about Friday night around 6:00? I will cook you supper and then we'll practice for a little while after that."

Nate nodded excitedly. Finally, their food arrived, and he focused on eating.

Merina watched him for a while and then laughed. "I grew up with brothers, Nate, but they didn't eat nearly as much as you. You are a hungry young man."

Nate finished faster than the two of them. He stood and looked at Gabe. A smile lurked around his mouth and in his eyes as he commented casually, "I'm going to head home. Rusty was going to work on the wagon and he is going to need help if he is going to get that done before he leaves tomorrow. I'll take the mule with me." He was out of the room before either Gabe or Merina could tell him about Merina's supplies in the saddle bags.

Gabe leaned back in his chair and stretched out his legs. "Well, I guess I will just have to bring them over to you one day this week." He paused and then added hopefully, "Or maybe you could come over?"

Merina laughed at him. "You are so obvio—so—so--you do not try to hide your words."

Gabe thought about that and nodded. "I'm not much on games and I guess that makes me a little short on words." He looked at her and almost added something but stood instead. "Ready to go? I need to get something done today even though I am enjoying spending it with the prettiest girl in Cheyenne." He grinned when Merina blushed and was still laughing as he guided her outside.

CHAPTER 41

A SLOW RIDE HOME

AS THEY RODE SLOWLY TOWARD THEIR HOMES, Gabe told Merina about his meeting with their neighbor, Chester Reith.

"I'm going over tomorrow morning to meet with him and look his place over if you want to come along."

Merina hesitated. "I'm not sure if I should."

"Would you like to?"

Merina's eyes shined. "I would love to, but I don't want to start any rumors."

Gabe studied her face and then looked down the road. "Reith seems to be a solid fellow and I doubt he is prone to gossip. I'll introduce you as the sister of two of my hands. You can bring Emilia if you want." His eyes were serious when he looked over at her. "Rusty is leaving on the train tomorrow for Kansas and I would really like someone unbiased to look at Reith's place with me.

"He offered to feed us dinner but if Cappy and Nate come along, that is a lot of extra mouths."

"Why is Rusty going to Kansas? Is Larry going with him?"

Gabe was quiet for a moment. "Rusty is going to partner with me on Gallagher's investments. He is a master at buying and selling things. He is taking the train with Levi Parker at 9:00 tomorrow morning but Larry decided to stay here. Rusty will be gone a week or maybe more." Gabe looked out over the grassy prairie before he looked at Merina. "I was hoping Larry could stay with you since she can't stay with three single men." He paused and then added, "Nate thinks they will move to Kansas when this all shakes out."

Merina watched the emotions wash across Gabe's face, and she was quiet for a moment.

"I think it was a good thing for you to help them. They had nothing and now they will have something to build with. You have a big heart, Gabe, but you hide it much. And now you will miss them because they are like your family."

Gabe stared ahead and then finally looked over at Merina with a twisted grin.

"You just summed it all up in a few sentences. I reckon that is right. And if Angel and Miguel decide to stay in Texas, I will be short-handed." He looked intensely at her a moment and then looked away. When he looked back, he added simply, "And if you leave, I'll put my harmonica away."

Merina's heart beat heavy in her chest, but she forced herself to keep her voice even. "I am going nowhere, Gabe." Her eyes sparkled as she added, "Remember, I am a wanted woman in Texas, and I have no desire to go to jail."

Gabe's face slowly broke into a grin and then he laughed. "You are a difficult woman to understand, Merina. Still, I'm glad that you decided to hitch a ride north in a livestock car to join your brothers."

It wasn't long before they arrived at Lance's house. Nate had tied the pack mule to the hitching rail and Emilia came running out of the barn with Livvy by her side.

"Señor Gabe! Are you coming to visit too? I had so much fun today!"

232

Livvy had blond hair and bright blue eyes that sparkled when she smiled. Gabe looked down at the two little girls and shook his head. Lance was walking up from the barn and Gabe waved toward the little girls.

"Kinda look like double-trouble to me."

"Girls are always trouble." When Molly poked her head out the door, he winked at Gabe and added loudly, "but I sure do love having them around." He grabbed his wife and swung her around. They were both laughing when he put her down.

"Have time to come in?"

"No, but I'll come by one day this next week. I am going to meet with Reith tomorrow morning and look his ranch over."

Lance's eyebrows raised and he chuckled as he looked down at Molly.

"Look at that, Molly. Another man who loves land! If I wasn't tied up tomorrow, I'd offer to go along."

Gabe laughed. "Merina is going to go with me and be my unbiased third party." He looked down at Emilia. "How about you, Emilia? You want to go for a ride with Nina and me tomorrow morning?"

Emilia looked from Gabe to Livvy and frowned. "If I don't go, can I stay here and play with Livvy?"

"I have just been thrown aside for a pint-sized girl!"

Molly laughed at the look of surprise on Gabe's face. "Men always get so full of themselves and then one tiny little girl lets the air out of you!" She looked up at Merina. "If you want to drop off Emilia here when you go by, that will be fine." Her eyes sparkled with laughter as she added, "Then I can leave *all* of ours with you some evening in return."

Merina laughed and agreed. Emilia was running off to play and Merina called to her. "Come, Emilia. We need to go home. You are going to come back in the morning, and I want you in bed early."

Emilia walked sulkily back to Merina, stopped in front of her and folded her arms with her lip stuck out. "I don't want to go with you. I want to live here. This is a fun house."

Gabe grinned and reached down his hand. "How about you run towards me as fast as you can, and I'll see if I can catch you with one hand?"

Emilia's face lit up and she charged his arm. Gabe grabbed her and rolled her up as he tickled her. He finally settled her down in front of him, grabbed the lead rope to the mule and waved to the Rankins as he turned toward Merina's house.

Molly watched them go and sighed. "I so enjoy watching young couples court."

Lance snorted. "Young? Gabe's not that much younger than you or me. And besides—"

Molly squealed and Lance chased her into the house.

Merina slid off her horse as soon as they arrived at her little house and Gabe handed Emilia down. He carried her purchases to the house and then took Mascota's reins from her.

"I can drop him off at the barn, so you don't have to take the time."

Merina nodded gratefully. Gabe stood hesitantly for a moment and then kissed Emilia. The little girl was almost asleep. He winked at Merina as he mounted his horse and drawled, "I'd like to kiss her big sister too, but I'd better wait until we are courting."

Merina's face blushed slightly as she turned to go into the house and Gabe rode away whistling. He looked back and tipped his hat once. He couldn't see Merina, but her kitchen had a window and just maybe she was watching.

He led Mascota into the barn, rubbed him down and gave him a bait of oats. "Now you take good care of her, boy. She's a pretty special little gal."

CHAPTER 42

A TERRIBLE COOK

RUSTY WAS UNDER THE OLD WAGON WITH NATE SQUATTED BESIDE HIM WHEN GABE RODE INTO THE YARD. He unloaded the supplies and then led Watie and the mule to the barn.

"How does it look? Fixable?"

Rusty's face had a streak of grease on it and his hands were covered in the black gooey substance.

"She's almost ready to go. Not much was wrong. Needed a good greasin' but I shore have driven worse ones than this." His face drew into a worried frown. "Larry up? She was crampin' a little when we come home."

Gabe looked toward the house in surprise as he shook his head. "I didn't hear anyone so maybe she is resting. She can stay here tomorrow after you leave. I'll take her over to Merina's tomorrow afternoon or evening in the wagon. Merina is going to go with me in the morning to look at Reith's ranch."

Rusty studied the tall man beside him and Gabe turned red. The ornery cowboy began laughing and Gabe walked away. "We aren't courting," he growled over his back.

"Sure, Boss. Whatever you say."

Nate watched and listened but didn't say anything. When Gabe glared back at him, he shook his head. "I said nothing."

"But you thought it." Gabe was still growling as he rubbed his horse down. Soon he started to smile. "Tomorrow is going to be a fine day, Watie. A horseback ride with the prettiest gal around and maybe buying another ranch. Life is good." He slapped Watie as he turned him loose and then strode toward the house.

He slowed when he saw the chicken coop. Cappy had completed it. He looked around for the little man and Rusty pointed south.

"Cappy rode off several hours ago. Took a couple a mules an' some cages that he found but never said where he was headed or when he'd be back."

The men peered in the house. It was still quiet, so they all went down to the creek to cool off and take a bath. Gabe nodded at Rusty's black fingernails.

"I suppose by the time you get back, your hands will be as lily white as a girl's. You'll decide you like prancing around with the big dogs and won't even want to come home. Good thing Larry is staying, or you might not come back to even say goodbye."

Rusty grinned and splashed Gabe as he dove under the water. The next few minutes were loud and noisy as the men splashed and played like kids.

Larry was just coming out of the bedroom when they walked into the house. Her face was pale, and she quickly moved her hand away from her stomach.

"Ya doin' all right, sweetheart? Still crampin' some?"

Larry smiled up at her husband as he pulled out a chair. "It think I am just tired…and maybe a little worried about you leaving."

Gabe watched them for a moment. When Larry started to get up to help with supper, he shook his head and pointed at the chair.

"Nate and I bought batching supplies today. You just sit there, and I'll make some of the worst biscuits you have ever eaten. Nate, open those beans and dump them in this bowl." Gabe sliced off some bacon and began to mix up the biscuits.

Larry started to laugh. "You forgot the baking powder, Gabe. You have to use baking powder!"

Gabe stared at her in surprise and then dug in the cabinet. He found a can of baking powder and started to turn it up to shake some in. Rusty grabbed the can from him as he stared at Gabe in surprise.

"Ain't ya never made biscuits 'fore, Boss?"

Gabe grinned as he nodded, "Sure have and they are always terrible."

Larry looked over at Gabe. "Two small spoonfuls, Boss. And cut a little fat into that flour mixture."

Rusty snorted and pushed Gabe out of the way. "Let me show ya how to make the durn biscuits." He soon had them made and dropped onto a pan to cook.

Gabe winked and sat down by Larry. "Works every time," he whispered with a grin. She stared at him a moment and then began to laugh.

CHAPTER 43

GOOD COMPANY

RUSTY WAS UP EARLY. The men had slept in the barn since they had given Rusty and Larry the house for the night. Larry's eyes were red and Rusty's emotions wobbled back and forth from worried to excited.

He was leaving at 7:00 a.m. Larry had packed and repacked his bag three times. He finally took her by the shoulders. "Larry Sweetheart, I'll only be gone a week, mebbie ten days. Now everybody 'ill be gone today an' I want ya to rest up. Gabe 'ill take ya over to Merina's when they git back from lookin' at that ranch to the south." He squeezed her shoulders and kissed the top of her head. "Put a smile on that purty little face. I 'spect a happy wife an' a healthy baby when I git back." He kissed her again and then strolled outside to saddle his horse.

"Ya want me to jist leave 'im at the livery? I'm guessin' y'all be in town this week sometime."

Gabe nodded and then shook Rusty's hand. "Good luck and make us proud." He grabbed Rusty's hand and slapped his back before he wrapped him up in a bear hug.

"Now durn it, Boss. I jist calmed Larry down. Don't ya go a makin' too big a deal a this here trip."

Rusty walked back to the house leading his horse. He picked up Larry to swing her around as he hugged her. He chucked her under the chin and whispered, "I'll bring ya somethin' purty back."

He mounted his horse, waved, and headed north at a lope.

Gabe watched him go and then looked at Larry as he asked, "Rusty already eat?"

"He was too nervous. He said he couldn't keep it down if he did eat so he skipped breakfast and just took a jar of coffee."

Gabe put his arm around Larry's shoulder as he led her back into the house.

"If you aren't up to cooking, I can make some biscuits."

"You know, Gabe, I don't know how much of that was put on and I am too hungry to take a chance. You sit down and I'll make some griddlecakes."

A commotion sounded in the yard and chickens started clucking. A rooster crowed and Gabe looked up in surprise. He stepped to the door in time to see Cappy dump the last of the chickens in the coop.

Cappy was grinning as he washed his hands in the tank. "Should have a few eggs by this evenin'."

Gabe studied the chickens and then looked at the ginning old man. "Are we ever going to know where they came from?"

Cappy laughed wickedly and shook his head. He looked over at Larry.

"I think I'll stay here today and keep Larry company. I had a durn hard day of it yesterday." He looked toward the barn where Nate was yawning as he walked into the daylight. "Nate goin' with ya?"

"Going where?" he asked as he looked at Gabe.

"I am going to talk to a neighbor about buying his place just to the south of us. You are a partner so you can sure come along if you want to. Merina will be over in a bit so it will be the three of us."

"Or he cin stay here. We cin start buildin' some gates an' then go fishin' after dinner. Which 'ill it be, Nate?"

Gabe looked at Cappy and the wily old man winked. "Jist helpin' ya out. Ya don't seem ta be movin' too fast an' another feller is a goin' ta slip in an' cut ya out. Now let's go eat. I cin smell those griddlecakes all the way out here."

Nate grinned. "I'll stay here. Luck, big brother!" He slapped Gabe on the back and followed Cappy into the house.

Gabe was following them when he heard a horse. He walked toward Merina with a smile on his face. He offered her a hand down and hung onto her hand for a moment before he released it.

"Had breakfast yet? Larry made griddlecakes." Without waiting for an answer, he led Merina into the house and pulled out a chair.

Larry filled their plates. Both she and Merina looked at Gabe as they waited to eat. He stuttered and then dropped his hat onto the floor.

"Boys, let's say a quick prayer."

Cappy pulled off his old hat and Nate bowed his head.

"Lord, we thank you for this food and for the folks here at this table. Watch over us today as we go about our work and guide us on our journey." Gabe squeezed Merina's hand when he finished. She smiled at him and everyone began to eat. When they were done, Cappy shooed Gabe and Merina out the door.

"We cin help Larry clean up. Git on over ta Reith's. Look his fences over. He's an old feller an' he can't get down in those holes ta fix fences if they's in places they's hard ta git at. An' look at the ponds. She's been a dry spring so look ta see how far they's dropped.

"An' watch out fer an' old brindle bull. He's a mean one an' he'll take ya fer no reason other than he feels like it." Cappy shook his head. "That bull's gonna kill somebody. He throws good calves, but he'll take a man if he's off'n his hoss. He's a killer bull, that's what he is."

241

The only gate between the two ranches was in the southeast corner of Gabe's land and the ride across the pasture in the early morning was an enjoyable one. Birds swooped low in their pursuit of bugs and the cattle they rode through were in good condition. They had lost most of their winter hair and were sleek and shiny.

Gabe looked over at the woman riding beside him and smiled. *This is just about as nice of a day as you could ask for.*

CHAPTER 44

An Old Friend

CHESTER REITH'S RANCH HEADQUARTERS WERE DOWN IN A LITTLE COULEE. The lane to the house ran north around the house and wound through the sloping hills toward Cheyenne. The buildings were solid, and the ranch was tidy. There were no broken fences or trash to be seen anywhere.

Chester waved at them as he walked up from the barn. He spotted Merina and his step caught a moment before he continued toward them.

"Get on down an' we'll go talk over there at that picnic table. The missus made some cookies an' lemonade. I reckon you already ate breakfast."

He peered at them from under his beat-up cowboy hat and Gabe nodded. He gave Merina a hand down, led their horses to the hitching rack and looped the reins over the pole.

Chester looked from one to the other.

"You two courtin'?"

Merina immediately blushed and Gabe grinned. He looked over at Merina and then shook his head. "Naw. She won't let me court her. This is Merina Montero. Her brothers, Angel and Miguel work for me."

Chester shook both of their hands and then smiled at Merina. "You look just like your mama. You know, I tried to court her once, but she only had eyes for your pa. He was the best horseman I ever did meet, an' he cut a fine figure of a man on horseback or on foot." He paused and grinned at Merina. "You kids used to come in my store when I had that little tradin' post down on the Brazos."

"Uncle Chet!" Merina's eyes went wide, and she hugged the older man. She looked over at Gabe with a huge smile. "We knew him when we were small!"

Chet's face lit up in a pile of happy wrinkles as he nodded. "I was married to my Sarah then. She had come over from Ireland with her pa. I was ridin' with an outfit south of the Brazos when her wagon went through my little town. I just pulled up my stakes an' followed them.

"Sarah's pa was true Irish. That man could sell anything. He set up that tradin' post an' I found a ridin' job close by. When Sarah's pa died, we married, an' I helped her run it for about six years."

The old man's eyes became sad as he added softly, "My Sarah died in childbirth. I sold the tradin' post, packed my horse an' headed north. I wandered around for a couple of years an' stopped when I hit Cheyenne. Old Man McNary already had most of the land to the south an' west of Cheyenne tied up, so I started to look around toward the east of him for a ranch. I didn't know McNary until I moved here but he became my first friend in the territory."

A buxom woman was hurrying out of the house carrying a tray of lemonade and cookies. Her face was pleasant and the smile wrinkles around her eyes were deep.

"Now Chet, don't you be bothering these kids with your old stories." She looked at Merina and smiled. "I suppose he was telling you how he met me on the street in Cheyenne, me on my fine horse with my boots and my britches. Oh, I know women didn't wear pants much back then, but I did. I helped my pa on the ranch and a dress just didn't work."

Chester laughed as he stood up and put his arm around his wife. "I was just gettin' to that part. This is my Nancy." His blue eyes twinkled as he smiled down at her. "I had never seen a woman in britches, an' she filled them out just real nice. I about fell off my horse which was embarrassin', me bein' a cowboy an' all. I found out where she lived, an' I went callin' the next day.

"Her pa said I couldn't court her until I owned my own ranch. I bought this here place the followin' mornin' an' showed up that night at their house with the deed in my hand."

Nancy beamed at her husband. "That was twelve years ago. I was forty when we met, and Chet was fifty-one. I told him that we still have some good years left and he either needed to hire some help or sell this place. I'm tired of working so hard." She looked from Gabe to Merina and laughed. "Looks like we are selling."

Merina smiled at the two people in front of her as she put out her hand to Nancy. "I knew your husband down in Texas when I was small. We always called him Uncle Chet. He used to slip us candy when we came into his trading post. I'm sure Sarah weighed out more than we bought because Mamá said we always had more than we paid for."

Chester waved at the table. "Sit down, kids, and let's talk about this place."

They visited about the ranch with Chester and Nancy for nearly two hours. When they finally rode out to look it over, it was nearly 9:30 a.m. Nancy didn't ride with them.

"A horse went over on her last year and she is still painin' a little from that. I wanted to take her to the doctor, but she refused. I reckon she broke somethin' because she had a hard time of it for several months. She's better now but still a little stiff.

"So when you kids gettin' married?"

Gabe choked and turned a bright red while Merina looked straight ahead without answering.

Chet looked from one to the other and chuckled. "Well, when you get that worked out, be sure to send us an invite. I'd sure like to be there."

Merina turned her head to look at him and then started laughing. "I think it is a good thing you moved away before I grew up. You would have had me married off by the time I was sixteen."

Chet shook his head and looked at her seriously. "Nope, I would have been choosy. Not just any old feller would have been good enough for my little Nina."

Gabe's face had been returning to it normal tan and he blushed again.

Merina looked from Chet to Gabe before she looked away. She faced forward again and was quiet.

Chet pointed ahead of them at a brindle bull pawing the dirt. "That there is old Brindie. He's a mean son of a gun but he throws good calves.

"Nancy won't let me shoot him. I keep telling her that he is going to kill somebody. He don't bother either of us but, he'll sure go after a stranger on foot. Longhorns are a funny critter. They ain't afraid of a man at all on the ground, but put him on a horse, and they get respect."

Gabe could feel his neck hairs raise and Buck snorted as they rode by. The bull kept his distance but watched them until they were nearly a quarter of a mile away. Then he turned and walked back to the cows.

For the most part, the fences were good. Cappy was right about the gullies and the areas with brush. The fence was weak there. Gabe studied the grass and the ponds. Even though the spring had been dry, the pastures were not overgrazed, and the ponds were still in good condition.

"I have this place fenced into five big pastures, about three thousand acres each. More fences could be added and that would help the cattle graze it more evenly, but I'm an old feller an' I'm done buildin' fence.

"There are fifteen thousand acres in here, give or take a little and I'm asking $8 an acre. I usually run about seven hundred or eight hundred head of cattle. There are seven hundred head in here now and that would be another $21,000 at $30 a head. "Most of the cows have calves by their sides but I just figured a flat $30 for both singles and pairs.

"We'll ride over to the North Pasture now to look at the horse herd. I like Arabians and I sell a few of those. I used to break my own horses but now I hire it done." He studied Merina a moment.

"As I recall, you used to have your daddy's way with horses. You still work with them?"

"Si, I love horses." Merina's eyes were shining as she answered. She petted Mascota's neck. "Mascota is the first horse that I raised from a colt and broke. My brothers and I worked for a rancher down in Texas and when he saw my love for horses, he turned the horse breaking over to me. His name was Charles Cole.

"The señor took a herd north this past spring, but he died on the way to Dodge City in a stampede. I did all his bookwork. I knew that Rowdy Rankin of Cheyenne had purchased a stallion and some mares from him. Señor Rankin was to take delivery in Dodge City in Kansas. I rode with them to Dodge City, gave Señor Rankin the bill of sale, and met my brothers who were trailing a herd north." She smiled slightly at Gabe as she added, "Señor Gabe was the trail boss and that is how I met him."

Chet looked from one to the other and grinned. He started to speak and then just laughed as he shook his head. He pointed ahead toward the horses.

"There they are. There are some in there that should be worked with now. I have been working on the blood lines and I like the results. I was going to offer them to Rowdy for $80 - $250 a head but I decided to wait and see what you wanted to do."

Gabe studied the horses while Merina guided her horse forward. One of the stallions snorted at her but Mascota kept his distance. She slowly rode through the herd and stopped her horse as she studied each animal.

Chester watched her and then looked over at Gabe. "If you don't snatch up that little gal, you are going to make one of the worst mistakes of your life."

Gabe went still and then looked at the old man with clear eyes. "I'm working on it, Chet. I was hung up on a gal who died when I met Merina and she's a little leery yet." He patted his pocket and added with a grin, "But I have a harmonica and the serenading at night seems to soften her up."

Chet's old eyes sparkled, and he chuckled. He was quiet for a moment and then looked down at his horse. He slapped the reins against his leg.

"Merina comes from fine stock. Her family was hard up, and Sarah did give them extras when they came in. Her mama's name was Consuelo and Merina is just as pretty as her mama was. She has her pa's eyes though. Carlos was her pa's name. He always looked like he had a secret joke and was laughing about it." Chet looked out over the horses for a moment before he continued.

"Carlos made a living for the family moving herds and people across the Brazos. He stayed busy and life was all right. Then he went down during a crossing. He was working with a bunch of greenhorns who didn't do what he told them, and they ran a herd of cattle over the top of his horse. Angel was somewhere around fourteen. He roped his father and drug him out, but Carlos was hurt bad. The family struggled to make ends meet after that, but Consuelo was proud and wouldn't accept help.

"My Sarah died shortly after that happened, and I moved away. I heard their pa healed up and went back to work. Then some years later Carlos was helping a big cattleman from over by Dallas cross some cattle. Not sure what went wrong but Carlos went down again and that time, he didn't make it.

"A friend down there wrote and told me that they all went to work for a wealthy rancher. It wasn't long after that their mama died. I just received another letter from my friend this week saying that Cole had died, and the kids had scattered. I am plumb tickled to know that they are here and working with you."

Gabe spoke quietly as he watched Merina. "Cole left his place to them. That is why Angel and Miguel are not here. They received word in Ogallala and headed back down to Buffalo Gap to finalize the sale. I haven't heard anything from them, but I think it could be a little rough. Squatters and rustlers were moving in. Angel wasn't worried. He said they have plenty of friends."

"Angel is a fine man. He's a good friend and I'm lucky to have him as a rider. I don't know what all Cole left them, and we don't know how long it will take to finalize everything. Miguel....Miguel is a little wild. He has some growing up to do. He likes his guns and he likes to play. I hope he stays around and settles down, but he might just take off too." He grinned at Chet and added, "Both of those brothers are tough though. I was mighty pleased to have them on the trail with me."

Chet didn't answer. His friend had told him that Cole was wealthy and had a lot of business holdings in Chicago. Still, there was no guarantee that everything would go to the Montero's. If they had the ranch and the cattle, that would be a good start.

"Think they'll come back? They might decide to stay and run things down there."

Gabe chuckled and pointed toward Merina. "She is a sassy one. Some fellow tried to force his way into the house after Cole left. Merina keeps a knife strapped to her leg and she used it on him. She won't go back because she is afraid they will arrest her."

Merina rode back toward them. Her face was excited even though she tried to keep in bland.

"Uncle Chet, you have some wonderful horses, both good breeding stock and working horses."

Gabe nodded his head toward the herd.

"Well, let's make a list and see what the total comes to. Merina, can you remember enough about the horses to be able to identify specific ones on paper?"

When she nodded, Gabe turned to Chet. "Let's figure out the horses and then give me a total. I would like to talk to my lawyer before we finalize things. I want to make sure I have enough capital to swing this. He'll be gone for about a week or so."

CHAPTER 45

PUT IT ON PAPER

NANCY HAD DINNER READY WHEN THEY ARRIVED AT THE HOUSE. The meal was delicious, and the talking relaxed. Once the meal was completed, Chet pulled out a paper and showed them the figures. He had all the horses listed along with descriptions and prices. Merina circled the ones that she thought would benefit Gabe. She studied an Arabian filly listed for $120, hesitated, and then skipped over it.

"May I help you with dishes, Señora Reith?"

The two women cleared the table and Chet brought out his ledger book so that Gabe could see his calving records. The two men studied and discussed the numbers and then Gabe studied the list of horses that Merina had checked. He circled the Arabian filly Merina had liked before he handed the paper over.

Merina had circled eight mares, four fillies, and one stallion as well as twelve stock horses for the ranch remuda. With the filly Gabe had added, that was twenty-six horses.

Chet chuckled as he looked Merina's list over. "That girl knows her horses. She skimmed the cream right off the top." He pushed the completed list over to Gabe...$143,650. Gabe stared at the amount and his stomach almost clutched. He nodded and folded the paper before he tucked it into his pocket.

"I will talk to my lawyer and my partner as soon as they get back in town. I can let you know by the end of next week at the latest."

Chet nodded as he studied Gabe's face. "Well, since it won't technically be offered for sale until this fall, I reckon we have some time."

Nancy hugged Merina. "You come back any time, and Gabe, you too. I hope you kids buy this place."

Gabe laughed. "I'll be in contact next week. Thank you for showing us around and for dinner too."

Merina was quiet as they rode away. Gabe waited for her to comment and finally asked, "Well?"

"Oh Gabe, they are such friendly people. It was just wonderful to see Uncle Chet after all these years. And Nancy is so-so welcoming."

Gabe stared at her for a moment and then laughed.

"And the ranch? What do you think of the ranch?"

"Si, the ranch is beautiful. The ponds still have water after so little spring rain and the grass makes the cattle fat. And the horses. I so wanted to circle that little Arabian filly, but she did not benefit your herd. I wanted her for my own. Yes, you should buy the ranch if you have the dinero." She paused and added quietly, "That is a lot of dollars though. I don't think you should borrow if you don't have the dinero in your hands."

"Well, we will have to wait and see what Levi and Rusty come up with. I have no idea what Gallagher had in assets or what is available to sell. Plus, half of everything we sell or take in is Rusty's."

The two visited the rest of the way back to Gabe's ranch. Gabe finally pulled Buck to a stop. Mascota stopped so suddenly that Merina lurched in the saddle. She looked sideways at Gabe.

"Merina, when are you going to let me court you? Shoot, everyone we meet thinks we are courting already."

Merina's cheeks tinged pink and her eyes sparkled as she laughed. "We will talk about it on the 28th when you dance with me in Cheyenne."

"I can take you to the dance?"

"No, but if we are courting by the time the dance is over, you may ride home with me." Merina's dark eyes were full of laughter.

Gabe stared at her a moment and then muttered under his breath. "You sure are making this hard for a fellow."

"Si, we will see how important it is to you to have pockets around you, or if you will give up easily."

Gabe laughed and put out his hand. "Shake on it!" When Merina put her small hand in his, Gabe squeezed it.

"Deal," he stated with a grin, and he didn't let go of her hand for the last mile home.

CHAPTER 46

A Busy Week

THE NEXT WEEK WAS BUSY. Gabe wanted to cut hay in several of the meadows and stack it in the barn.

"Most fellows here let the cattle graze on the dried grass over the winter. Why can't we do that?" Nate complained. He often worked without a shirt because he didn't like to do laundry. Now that they were batching, each man was responsible for his own clothes.

The hay cutting was a slow job. They used long, curved scythes to cut the hay off six to ten inches from the ground. Once it dried which only took a day or two, they raked it into piles and used a pitchfork to pile it into the wagon. When the wagon was full, they drove it to the barn. The hay was pitched onto the lift and then hoisted up to the loft. By the end of the day, they were tired, sweaty, and itchy….and someone still had to cook supper.

The first few days, Cappy had offered to take over the cooking. The eggs for breakfast were a nice change but after the third day of biscuits and beans for dinner *and* supper, Gabe and Nate offered to take their turns with cooking too. Nate only knew how to cook fish and that meant that he was able to fish every time it was his turn to cook.

Sunday was their fifth day of cutting hay and Nate looked up at Gabe hopefully as he pushed the beans around on his plate when they quit at 2:00 that afternoon. "You remember we were supposed to go to Merina's tonight for supper and dance lessons?"

Gabe frowned as he nodded. "I know but I told Cappy to let her know we wouldn't make it, that we would still be haying.

"You can fish for supper though. We will want to eat around 6:00 p.m. to get everything cleaned up and in bed by 7:30. We have two more full days of cutting and then we should be done with that little patch."

They cut hay for three more hours and then quit for the day. Nate was just heading to the creek with his fishing pole when Merina and Emilia rode into the yard. They were both dressed up and Emilia had prairie flowers in her hair.

Gabe strolled out to meet them as he buttoned his shirt. He had hay stuck to his britches and Merina laughed as she looked at him.

"How many more days of haying?"

"Two more days and then we are quitting. The loft is completely full, and the back of the barn is as well. It has been a long five days and since it is Nate's turn to cook tonight, he is going fishing." He waved at his little brother as Nate disappeared down the lane.

"Can you stay for a bit? I was just going to rinse off in the creek if you can give me five minutes."

Merina nodded and Gabe grabbed some clean clothes and headed for the creek. She could hear the brothers talking but she couldn't decipher the words.

"Can I go swimming too, Nina? This dress is itchy."

"Señor Gabe is not swimming, Emilia. He is taking a bath."

Emilia's eyes opened wide. "In the creek? Can we do that, Nina? Then we wouldn't have to pack the water so far."

Nina shook her head and Emilia was fidgeting when Gabe walked back to the house. He had several nicks on his face from shaving quickly and using the water as a mirror.

"So where are you ladies headed, looking so pretty?"

Emilia's eyes lit up as she twirled. "We went to church and look at my dress! Nina made it for me."

Gabe looked at Merina in surprise. "What time was your service?"

"It was at 10:00 this morning. We went to Mass at the new brick church, Saint John the Baptist. We have not been to Mass in so long and I have missed it. The church is huge. The priest said there was seating for nearly three hundred people and the church was almost full."

Gabe scratched his head. "The last time I was in a church was at Rusty's wedding and before that, why I was younger than Nate. Ma took us some when we were small but there wasn't much chance when we were cowboying." He studied her face and then grinned. "Maybe we will just come over to your house next Sunday and go to church with you."

Merina laughed and her dark eyes sparkled. She took Emilia's hand and stood.

"We must go. Tomorrow we are helping Molly make soap and she is going to give me a few chickens for helping." Her smile became bigger. "Perhaps if we are courting by next Sunday, I will fry chicken for you after church."

"I would like that." His eyes were intense as he smiled at her. "Both ways.

"Cappy offered to do the cooking here but he only knows how to cook biscuits and beans. Nate cooks fish and I try to shoot a rabbit or a grouse now and then. I will be glad when Cookie gets back so we can have some decent meals. It's hard to cook when you are working away from the house all day. And when Cookie comes back, I hope he stays."

Merina had wondered how they were doing the meals. She was tempted to offer to help but she only smiled.

"I will see you Saturday then."

"Saturday it is and Sunday too—and maybe more often after that."

Merina blushed and hurried out the door. Gabe gave her a foot up and stood close to her horse as he smiled up at her.

"You are a picture of pretty, Merina."

Merina could feel her heart beating quickly but she only smiled. "Thank you, Señor Hawkins."

She turned her horse back up the drive followed by Emilia, and Gabe watched them go. Emilia turned around in her saddle and waved happily. Gabe raised his hat in reply. Merina didn't turn around and Gabe was a little disappointed. Then he smiled. "I'll see her at the dance on Saturday and just maybe we can start courting."

CHAPTER 47

RUSTY'S NEWS

GABE, NATE AND CAPPY HAYED STEADILY FOR TWO MORE DAYS and then on Wednesday, June 25th, Rusty rode into the yard with a glowing Larry by his side.

"Whatcha doin', sittin' 'round on yore laurels whilst I been off workin' hard fer eight days?"

Gabe and Nate had just forked the last of the hay into the barn and Cappy was putting the wagon away. The two brothers were sitting at the little picnic table, sipping root beer, and munching on hard biscuits. Both were hot, sweaty, and itchy. They glared at him in unison and Rusty grinned.

"Dang, Nate. Y'all hang 'round with yore grumpy brother much longer, yore gonna act jist like 'im." He helped Larry off her horse and then stepped toward Gabe with a big smile and an outstretched hand. "Howdy, Boss. Sure is good to be back."

Gabe slowly smiled. "I guess you have some good news to share?"

"Shore do. I'm thinkin' we need to celebrate!"

"And will I be losing my best man to Kansas?"

Rusty scratched his head as he looked at Larry. "We ain't talked much 'bout that. Levi wants to see us in his office today though. He said 5:00 if y'all cin make it 'cause he's booked up the rest a the week." Rusty gave Gabe a sincere look.

"I like ol' Levi. He's the genuine deal. Smart, savvy an' a good sense a humor too. Said I reminded him a Sadie's first husband, his ol' pal Slim. I sure am glad he was with me 'cause I was in way over my head. Those boys throwed so much legal talk an' big words 'round that I almost took off my boots. In fact, I told one feller that. He was a blusterin' around. I put my leg up an' started to pull my fancy boot off. I told that feller that it was gettin' so deep that I didn't want his hooey to go over the tops a my good boots." He winked at Nate and added, "Kinda glad I didn't though. My ol' socks was full a holes." Rusty's ornery face lit up in a big grin and the brothers laughed.

Cappy came out of the barn and slapped Rusty on the back. He kissed Larry's cheek and said gruffly, "Good ta have ya back." He winked at Larry. "I'm tard a workin' so hard."

He chuckled when Nate stared at him with an open mouth.

"Working! You drove the wagon and didn't even get out of it!"

"Now, Nate, I done told yore cranky brother that I'm here ta rest a little. I'm an old feller an' I cain't be workin' so hard as ya durn boys." Cappy laughed again wickedly.

"An' now that Rusty is back, he cin take my place. I'll spend my days nappin' an' takin' care a chickens—unless ya want me ta go back ta cookin'."

Gabe and Nate both gave a big "No!" in unison and Cappy strolled toward the house laughing. He looked back and waved at Larry. "Come on up ta the house, Larry. I'll give ya a soft chair an' git ya some root beer. Them durn boys done fergot ya is even 'round."

Larry laughed. "That does sound good. We have been helping Molly put up her garden and my back is sore today."

Rusty helped his wife up and kissed her cheek. He whispered, "I always know when yore close, Larry, 'cause my ol' heart tingles." She laughed up at him and then followed Cappy to the house.

"Today at 5:00, huh? Well, that might work." Gabe looked over at Nate and grinned. "I want to get some fencing supplies. I am going to add a couple more gates between Reith's and our south boundary. Nate and Cappy cut some posts so we can start on that tomorrow."

Nate groaned. "I am going to be too tired to even dance on Saturday at this rate. Can't we just take a day off?"

Gabe studied his little brother's frustrated face. "Well, I reckon you can have the rest of today off but clean up before you go in the house. And be ready to leave here by 3:00 this afternoon."

Nate brushed himself off as he rushed to the house calling, "Cappy! Want to go fishing?" He looked over his shoulder and grinned at Gabe. "I'll take a bath while I'm fishing."

Cappy poked his grizzled head out the door and grinned as Nate rushed by him. Before long, the two were headed to the creek.

Gabe walked with Rusty as he led their horses to the barn. Rusty whistled as he looked around.

"You fellers been busy. This off that one little meadow out east?"

"Yep, and next week, I want to put up some on Reith's. I'm a little worried about the winters up here. The old timers talk about how it used to be but the new ranchers scoff at them. They say cattle can chew on the dry grass. I just want to be a little prudent in case the old timers are even close to right.

"Didn't see or hear anything from Angel, did you? I thought he would be back by now."

Rusty slapped his pocket. "I 'most forgot. The express agent handed this to me as I left town today."

Gabe scanned the telegram and then looked up with a smile.

"Angel said they are on their way home. They left Dennison on the 24th. That should put them in town tomorrow." He frowned. "I sure hope everything went well."

Rusty studied his friend with ornery eyes and asked casually, "How's Merina?"

Gabe's neck turned red. Then he looked up and grinned. "Guess we'll know after Saturday. I'll see her at the dance."

Rusty looked over at his friend. "Say, you know a feller by the name a Spur? George Spurlock. Tall good-lookin' feller from down around New Orleans. Sports a big mustache."

"Sure do. Good man. I knew him down in Texas. We rode for several of the same outfits and were pards for a time." Gabe glanced over at Rusty. "He rides for Rowdy Rankin here and has for several years. Why?"

"Jist wondered. Thought he looked familiar."

Gabe nodded.

"I ran into him during a break in Merina's dance lessons. He was on his way back to the ranch from shipping horses and thought he had missed a party. His buddies let him go on thinking that the new school marm was an older gal and he was a little surprised to find out she was young."

His eyes probed Rusty's face. The cowboy was working to keep it free of expression and Gabe frowned. "You have something else to say?"

Rusty shrugged. "Not really. He was talkin' with Merina when I stopped to get Larry an' they seemed to be old friends. He was a teasin' her 'bout dancin' with 'im."

Gabe's body went still, and he looked away from Rusty. *Merina— sixteen years old—Cajun cowboy.* He replied casually, "I think they knew each other down in Texas. He rode for a ranch not far from where she lived about four years ago.

"Say, how do you like the shirt that Sadie made you? I was thinking of ordering one today while I'm in town. I can't find any with long enough arms."

Rusty studied his friend. "Gabe, I didn't mean to—"

Gabe shrugged. "They knew each other four years ago. If the feelings are still there, then that's how it is. Spur is a good man." He looked over his shoulder. "I'm taking a bath."

CHAPTER 48

SMALL TALK

GABE GRABBED A CLEAN SHIRT AND SOCKS. He slammed his hand into the doorway as he left the house and woke Larry up. She was just getting out of bed when Rusty walked in with a frown on his face. He shook his head.

"Durn it." When Larry looked at him in question, Rusty's frown became deeper. "Oh, I told Gabe that Merina was talkin' to that Spur feller. They was jist talkin' but it seems that Merina was sweet on him some time ago. I should a jist kept my mouth shut an' let things play out.

"Gabe knows the man an' likes 'im. An' I know the boss well enough to know that he won't make a play fer a gal who's sweet on a buddy. If she chooses Spur, Gabe's heart 'ill break again an' maybe this time fer good."

Larry was quiet. Spur had been at Merina's house twice. He just "happened to be riding by" when he stopped in the first time. It was obvious that they knew each other from the past and shared memories. Larry touched her husband's arm.

"Just let it go. If they are meant to be together, love will find a way. If not, well…then you can't do anything about it anyway. At least Spur is a decent man."

Larry frowned as she thought of the first time Spur had stopped in. Merina had been angry. She couldn't understand what was said but Spur evidentially deserved the tongue lashing he received because he just kept his head low and took it. When Merina had finished spitting at him in Spanish, she had stomped back into the house and Spur had ridden away. He had come back several days later with wildflowers. Whatever he said made her laugh as she took them.

Larry took Rusty's arm and squeezed it as she smiled up at him. "I'm glad we are past the courting stage. It can be exhausting. Now tell me about the land around Manhattan."

Larry was sitting on Rusty's lap and the two of them were laughing when Gabe came in. He looked at them and his tense face relaxed as he chuckled. "I guess I wasn't the only one who missed this fellow." He stuck his head back out the door and bellowed, "Nate! Time to go!"

"Larry, did you ride one of Lance's horses or is it from the livery?"

"It's Lance's horse. I think Rusty rode one from the livery. Why?"

"Larry can ride in the wagon. No point in using another man's horse if you don't have to. We can drop it off there on the way by. As soon as we have horses saddled and the wagon hitched, let's head out."

Gabe headed for the barn and Rusty followed him as he looked back at Larry. "All business. That's how he hides his heart. Durn knucklehead."

Cappy followed Nate slowly up to the house. Nate was carrying a big string of fish and Cappy took them.

"You boys—an' Larry—go on. I don't feel like no long ride tonight ta eat when I cin have baked fish right here." He grinned over at Larry and then nodded toward the barn. "Guess I'll be back in the barn tonight."

Gabe was quiet for the first mile. Rusty and Larry were in the wagon and he looked over at them. "We need to start on a bunkhouse. Cappy shouldn't have to sleep in the barn. He's too old to be doing that."

"Ya know, I seen some rocks piled up out in one a the pastures. Mebbie we cin haul them in fer a foundation. Gonna need some wood though. There's a little in the barn or there was 'fore ya stacked the hay. Not 'nough fer a buildin' though."

Gabe nodded as he thought. "We can pick up some tonight. That will get us started anyway."

Rusty looked over at his friend but Gabe said nothing else as he looked ahead at the road.

Nate began to talk about the dance and told Rusty that Merina had given him a private lesson. Gabe looked surprised but said nothing.

"So what all did y'all learn to do? Waltz'? Two-step? Polka? Mexican Hat Dance?" Rusty was grinning as he questioned Nate.

Nate grinned as he answered, "All but the polka. I kind of have the two-step down but I stepped on Merina's toes when we waltzed. She drug me through the hat dance. It was a lot of fun, but I need more practice. Her feet move really fast for that one." He looked over at his brother. "Ever do the Hat Dance, Gabe?"

Gabe was quiet a moment and then nodded before he answered. "I used to do it a lot. Always enjoyed that dance.

"I can't waltz either. I've been told that my feet are too big, but the two-step is a good one to know."

Rusty looked at him in surprise. "Thought y'all didn't know how to dance."

"I said I didn't dance. Didn't say I didn't know how. I don't much like dancing unless I have a partner who can keep her feet out of my way." Gabe chuckled as he looked at his brother. "And not very many of them can."

CHAPTER 49

RIDING HIGH

SADIE MEASURED GABE AND HAD HIM PICK OUT THE COLOR OF SHIRT THAT HE WANTED. He hesitated and then chose purple as he grinned at her.

"I've never had a custom shirt or a purple one, so we'll just ride high this time."

"It will be ready by Friday but if you want it for the dance, I can send it home with Martha. You can go by her house before to change if you want to wear it."

Gabe nodded distractedly and then strolled down the street to where Rusty was loading boards and barb wire in the back of the wagon.

"We have everythin' on yore list, Boss. Good thing y'all are ridin' a horse as that pile is a little wobbly an' the wire would be downright painful."

Gabe nodded and the little party turned their horses down the street. They were at Levi's office a little before 5:00 and Annie greeted them with a smile.

"Mr. Parker will be out in a moment. Just take a seat and he will see you as soon as he's free."

The door to Levi's office burst open and an angry woman flounced out followed by a grim man. She jerked the door open and got up in the wagon with no help.

Levi appeared in his door. He grinned and shrugged his shoulders. "Sometimes I tell folks what they don't want to hear. Come on in."

He nodded his head at the departing wagon. "Unlike that one, I think this meeting is going to make all of you happy." He leaned through the doorway to talk to Annie.

"Go on home and take care of that big man of yours. I'll see you in the morning." He sat down behind his desk and smiled at them.

"Well, did Rusty tell you about his trip?"

"Didn't say much at all. Didn't want to tangle up the details so I figgered I'd leave that to the judge," Rusty replied.

Levi spread the papers out in front of them and went over them one by one.

"Joseph Gallagher owned property in Kansas City and in Manhattan." He pointed to the papers. "These show the Kansas City investments. Rusty opted to sell those." He looked over at the cowboy and laughed. "His sales techniques are quite unusual, but they seem to work." Rusty's face was bland but his eyes sparkled as Levi talked.

"The long and the short of it is, Gallagher owned property in Kansas City that a bank wanted and Rusty made them pay. He was also an early investor in the bank that was sold, so you won twice."

Gabe looked over at Rusty and started to laugh. "Now I wish I had been there."

"Here are the figures for what the property brought. He sold the stock in the bank and this number is the total for that sale."

Levi let them stare at the numbers for a moment. Gabe blinked and Nate picked the paper up. He whistled and then took a pad out of his pocket and started making a list.

Levi paused and looked over at him. "Do you have some questions, Nate?"

The boy shook his head and pointed at the sheet. "No sir. I am just making a list of the things I'm going to buy with my share of that number."

Gabe picked up the list and read it out loud. "Fancy boots like Rusty's, saddle with silver conchos, new bed, Sharps .45-110 rifle, twin colt revolvers with ivory stocks, and new socks."

Everyone began to laugh, and Gabe chuckled. "You might get two things off that list but you sure aren't getting all of them. I can live with the bed and the socks though."

Nate's face fell. "We are rich, and I still can't have nice things!"

Gabe signaled for Levi to continue.

"Gallagher also invested in properties in Manhattan. His most recent purchase was a ranch south of Manhattan in what they call the Flint Hills. That area is known for its rich grasses. The topsoil is thin and flint rock is close to the surface so much of it will never be good for tilling. It is great grassland though." He stopped a moment as he looked at Rusty. When the man said nothing, Levi continued.

"Some of the lots that Gallagher owns in Manhattan are still increasing in value. He also invested in a bank there. Rusty opted to keep those properties." Levi paused. "Anything you want to add, Rusty?"

"I rode out an' looked that ranch over. Nice place. Has an old house on it but it's a nice piece a grass an' a purty ranch. Larry would be closer to 'er folks an' we decided to move back there."

Gabe knew that was coming and he still felt like he had been kicked in the stomach. He looked over at the happy cowboy and shook his hand. "Good for you, Rusty. Shoot, you'll probably own half of Manhattan by the time you have ten or eleven little ones trailing after you."

Rusty choked and Larry started to laugh. She pointed at her stomach. "Well, he has a head start because Doc Williams said this one will be twins."

Rusty choked again and everyone began to laugh.

Gabe's eyes opened wide and Rusty grinned. "No point in wastin' 'round. Jist as well git the party started."

Levi reached across his desk to shake hands with Gabe. "Gabe, you have the capabilities to become one of the bigger cattlemen around Cheyenne if you invest your capital in cattle. Of course, you don't have to do that. This town is growing and there are investment opportunities outside the livestock industry if you want to diversify." He grinned as he added, "A rancher south of you who was to sell this fall was in to see me today. He took his ranch off the market so I'm guessing your ball is already rolling."

Levi showed everyone where to sign. "I suggest that you open a joint account for the partnership but you should each have a personal account as well so we can transfer the funds across. That will take a couple of days."

He laid down a last sheet of paper. "That is an accounting of my expenses and charges. My fee will come out of the partnership before the money is dispersed." He smiled around at the group. "Any other questions?"

Larry's face was pale as she studied the sheets in front of her. Finally, she looked up at Levi. "Any chance this is a mistake?" she whispered.

Levi's face was serious, but his eyes twinkled as he shook his head. "Nope. These numbers have been checked and rechecked." His face broke into a smile as he added, "I wouldn't be much of a lawyer if I made mistakes like that."

The papers were signed, and the four partners stood. They walked outside, looked at each other and then started laughing.

Gabe rubbed his stomach. "Let's get something to eat. Nate and I had hard biscuits for dinner, and we are both ready for some real food." He looked at his companions. "Tin House or Rollins's House?"

Nate turned toward the Tin House. "I'm saving my money for that rifle," he stated with a grin and the rest followed him down the street.

CHAPTER 50

ANGEL COMES HOME

GABE TOOK THE BANK DRAFT OVER TO CHET AND NANCY REITH on Friday morning, June 27th. Nancy stared at it and then her eyes filled with tears.

"I remember when this was our new dream. Twelve years seems so long ago but it's not really." She smiled up at Gabe. "My father is still on the home place. When we told him we were thinking about selling, he asked us to move in and take over." Her eyes filled with laughter as she added, "I guess we aren't quite done with ranching, but then, I did tell Chet that we had a few good years left."

Chet shook Gabe's hand. "We'll let you know when Pop is ready to sell. Maybe you will be ready to buy more land." His wise eyes were sparkling a bright blue and Gabe laughed.

Chet looked around Gabe to peer outside. "Where is my little Merina? I thought maybe you'd bring her by when you came today."

Gabe was quiet and then shook his head. "No, we've been busy haying and I haven't seen much of her this week. She did stop by last Sunday and said she had gone to Mass, so she is settling in the community."

Chet nodded. "Well, come visit us sometime and tell us what your plans are here. We'll just be north of Cheyenne on the Z Bar Ranch. Pop settled there in the 1830's. He made treaties with the Indians and traded with them. He has no intention of leaving so we'll probably carry him off the ranch when he passes."

Gabe marked where he wanted his gates on the way home. Since he was skipping the dance the next evening, he could work all day Saturday and just might have them done by evening.

When he rode in the ranch yard, he saw Angel's horse tied to the hitching rail and his face lit up. He strode into the house and wrapped the smaller man up in a bear hug.

"Señor, I think if you do not put me down, I will have to use my small knife on you."

Gabe dropped down in a chair. "Well? Tell us about your trip. Any trouble?"

Angel's face was sad as he looked at Gabe, but his eyes sparkled. "Si, my sister is wanted by the law for killing a hombre. I told them it could not be her because she was on a cattle drive from Texas to Ogallala. The lawman said he would talk to you."

Gabe choked on his coffee and then laughed. "We'll worry about that when it happens. What else?"

"We sold the ranch to the Hashknife. They were pleased to add more land to their range. They offered to help us clear out the bandits who had squatted there. It happened so quickly that I did not get to use my small knife and only one man died. They ran their horses very quickly to the south when the cowboys chased them with their ropes. I think maybe no one has ever crossed the Brazos so quickly.

"Señor Waggoner said to tell you hello. He was mucho helpful and Señor Ridgway seemed to know him well. We have many papers for Merina to read and then we need to meet with el letrado—the lawyer—to go over them before they are signed. We rounded up five hundred head of Hereford cows. Miguel and I pushed them north to the 6666 Ranch. They will trail them north to Ogallala with their cattle in the spring. Perhaps Miguel can go down to help them on the drive." He added softly, "I think maybe Señor Cole was a wealthy man, but he was not so good with cows."

Angel took $200 out of his pocket and handed it back to Gabe. "I thank you for your help. Maybe soon, we will buy our own ranch. Or perhaps we will go into business with you. Perhaps our families will someday be one, yes?"

Gabe looked away and then back at his friend. He tried to laugh but could only manage a tight smile. He shrugged. "Perhaps." He looked around for Miguel and didn't see him.

"Did Miguel come back with you?"

"I think our brother is not so much interested in working. He is more interested in drinking and women. He is in Cheyenne and will meet us when we talk with the—the lawyer.

"I will go now to see Merina. Do you want to come with me? Maybe help us to read the turkey tracks on this paper?"

Gabe slowly shook his head. "No, I want to build some gates. I am going to haul some stone in here too while the wagon is free so we can start on the bunkhouse."

Angel studied the big man beside him. "And tomorrow? Do you go to the dance?"

"No, I will be putting in those gates." He turned his back before Angel could see his face and called over his shoulder, "It's good to have you back, my friend. See you this evening."

Gabe headed back outside and led his horse into the barn. Angel could see him rubbing the horse down and he looked at Rusty."

"Something happened while I was gone?"

Rusty frowned and shook his head slightly. "Spur came back."

Angel's eyes narrowed down and Rusty growled, "Gabe's friends with 'im. Says he's a good man an' he won't cut in on a buddy. Gabe's walkin' away. An' don't talk to Merina if that's what yore thinkin'. Gabe wants 'er to be happy."

Angel slowly nodded. "I think I will not go to the dance. I think I will work with my friend."

Rusty nodded and then stood. "Let's go unload that wagon. Gabe needs it empty to haul that rock."

Angel went to see his sister that evening. He came in late and slipped into the barn. Gabe had given Cappy his bed while Rusty and Larry had the second bedroom. Angel rolled out his blanket by Gabe and went to sleep.

Gabe glanced over at the lithe cowboy and smiled. *He looks so much like Merina.* It was nearly two hours before his mind shut down and he was able to go to sleep. When he did, there were no dreams.

The four men worked on the south fence until noon. Larry fixed them dinner and then Angel and Gabe went back out while the rest cleaned up. Nate left early and went over to Lance's to pick up Sam. Larry and Rusty were going to go in later.

Cappy was nowhere to be found. He kept disappearing in the morning and showing up at night with a smile on his face.

Gabe just grinned. Cappy had officially retired.

CHAPTER 51

A Bad Accident

ANGEL INSISTED THAT THEY TAKE THEIR HORSES WITH THEM TO INSTALL THE GATES.

"Señor, we may need to leave the wagon and it would not look dashing for me to ride a mule, especially one with no saddle."

Gabe laughed and Angel saddled horses for both men. He led Buck while Gabe drove the wagon with the gates, the barb wire, and the fencing tools. They had built two gates the day before and this was the last one that Gabe had marked out. He jumped out of the wagon and cut the wire.

"It's quite the feeling, Angel, to cut the wire between two ranches that you own when a year ago, I wouldn't have dreamed of buying one."

Angel started to tie Buck to the wagon, but Gabe waved at him. "Let him graze. He'll come when I call."

The afternoon was hot. Gabe took his shirt off and laid it over the wagon to dry. He had just finished the gate and was turning to pull it into place when Brindie charged. Gabe leaped to the side, but the bull hooked him with his horns and tossed him into the air. Gabe landed heavily and staggered to his feet. The bull charged again but was met by an angry stallion.

Buck charged the bull with his mouth open as he screamed. His front feet came down on the bull and he swerved away as Brindie changed directions and charged the horse. Brindie raked his horn along the stallion's side as Buck swerved to get out of the way.

Angel grabbed Gabe's shirt from the wagon and raced his horse toward the bull, waving the shirt. The bull stopped. It swung around to face this new threat and Buck lunged at him from behind. He bit the angry bull, taking a huge bite of flesh. The bull tried to turn again but Angel slapped him in the face with the shirt. "Get in the wagon, Gabe! I will lead him away." Gabe staggered toward the wagon and climbed up over the side. He stared grimly at the hole in his side. He was bleeding but not as heavily as he thought he would be. Buck was circling the wagon and snorting. Gabe called to him and petted him.

"Easy, Buck. It's all right." He pulled the rifle out of the scabbard and checked the loads. Then he climbed out of the wagon and looked Buck over. The horn had cut Buck's side as slick as a knife. The skin was severed at an angle, and the two pieces would need to be stitched back together. It didn't look like there was any penetration in Buck's side or stomach and Gabe breathed a sigh of relief. He talked softly to his horse and the animal calmed down.

Gabe looked up as he heard Angel yelling. The cowboy was headed back with the bull in pursuit.

"Shoot him! Shoot this diablo!"

Angel swerved to the side and Gabe shot the bull. It took four bullets to bring him down. The huge animal skidded to a stop as his left horn dug a deep furrow in the ground. Angel cursed him in Spanish and Buck tried to get loose to charge him again.

Gabe waved at Angel. "We need to get Buck back to the house. He needs stitches." Gabe collapsed on the ground and Angel stared at him.

He cursed as he dropped from his horse and rushed toward his friend. He squatted beside Gabe and carefully moved the man's left arm aside. When he saw the oozing hole in Gabe's side, he cursed again.

"Gabe, you will have to help me. I cannot lift you into the wagon. Stand and we will get you help."

Buck nuzzled Gabe's neck and nickered softly. Gabe opened his eyes. "Take care of my horse."

Angel grabbed his arm. "Stand up, Señor. You must take care of your own horse. He will not let us touch him."

Gabe stared at Angel vacantly and Buck nickered again. Gabe struggled to his feet and took hold of Buck's reins. Angel gently took them from his hands and looped them over the saddle horn. He led Gabe to the back of the wagon and then gently pushed his friend backwards until he was sitting on the open end.

"Lay down, Gabe. We need to get help."

Angel jumped up on the wagon, and they raced back to the house with the two horses running beside them.

Rusty and Larry were just getting ready to leave. The red-haired cowboy took one look at Gabe. He grabbed the reins to Angel's horse and spurred him toward Cheyenne. He had heard that Doc Williams was an excellent surgeon and they were going to need one.

Gabe grabbed Larry's arm. "Stitch up Buck. I don't want that cut to get infection."

Larry's face was pale. "We need to take care of you first, Gabe."

He shook his head. "Buck won't go down for anyone but me. You have to do it while I'm conscious."

Gabe tried to sit up and Angel helped him carefully.

"Take his saddle off. Buck, Stand."

The horse stood trembling while Angel took off his saddle. "And bridle."

Gabe struggled to stand. "Buck, Down. Down," and he pointed toward the ground. Buck went down on his side and lay there breathing heavily.

Larry came out with her needle and thread. Her hands were shaking.

"Clean it first. Horns are dirty and he could get infection."

Larry washed the wound while Gabe talked to his horse. He slowly lowered himself down and knelt across the horse's neck. He put his hand around Buck's mouth and lifted the horse's head up about four inches. "Still, Buck. Still." The horse went still and barely moved as Gabe continued to talk to him.

"Larry, you need to be quick. I may give out and when that happens, he will try to get up."

Gabe petted and whispered to the horse while Larry began to stitch. Buck tried to kick and tried to throw his head, but Gabe held on and talked until he was calmed down. Each time the needle went in, Buck would tremble. She was almost done when Gabe began to slide sideways. His hand slipped off Buck's muzzle and the horse lunged to his feet. He nuzzled Gabe and nickered softly.

Larry talked softly to him as she applied echinacea and clipped off the extra thread. He laid back his ears once and snapped at her. Larry jumped back and Angel put a halter on him. "Easy, Buck. Pay attention to your boss."

When Larry was done, the two of them lifted Gabe up and almost drug him into the house. They laid him across his bed and Larry began to clean around the wound. Her lips trembled as she looked at the holes—a large one in the front and a second toward the back in his side. Angel had laid a cloth across the wound. It was seeping blood, and he put a blanket under Gabe.

"I should try to find Nate," Angel whispered.

Gabe stirred and shook his head. "It's his birth…day. Let…him play." He tried to grin up at Angel. "Not bleeding…bad enough…to be…bad."

Larry looked at him skeptically. "Gabe, you were gored."

"Been shot before and it bled worse than this." He took a couple of ragged breaths and then opened his eyes to look at Angel. "Should butcher that bull. Lots of meat."

Angel looked at his boss and started to laugh. "Si, and I will take the horns so you can hang them in your house as a memory." Gabe grinned weakly and passed out.

Buck was trying to come in the house. Angel attempted to keep him out, but the horse pushed his way in. The vaquero finally shrugged and backed out of the doorway. Buck walked cautiously through the house and into the bedroom. He sniffed Gabe and nickered at him. Gabe was still unconscious, and the horse refused to move. He kept his nose close to the man's face and nickered from time to time.

Nearly an hour and a half later, Angel heard horses running up the lane. Rusty dropped to the ground and grabbed the reins to both winded horses. He led them to the barn and quickly rubbed them down before he raced back to the house.

Larry had hot water boiling and Doc was studying the wound.

He looked up at the two men. "Let's move him out on the table. I need a flat surface to work. I need to make sure no organs were damaged. Larry, scrub that table first, and then you wash up to help me."

When the table was clean, the men carried Gabe out followed closely by the horse. The surgeon looked at the animal. "He can't stay in here."

Angel touched Gabe's shoulder. "Gabe, send your horse outside. The doc needs some room."

Gabe's eyes were unfocused. Angel pointed at the horse. "Send him out. He's in the way."

Gabe lifted his hand weakly and pointed at the door. "Out, Buck. Go."

Buck snorted and Gabe gasped, "Go."

The horse snorted again and walked out the door. When he was out, he turned around and put his head and front feet inside. He stood there and stared at the man lying on the table.

Angel pointed at the horse and then at Gabe as he chuckled. "Better not mess this up, Doc. You're being watched."

Doc Williams looked up in surprise and then waved Angel back. "Stay back. We need to keep him as clean as possible. And don't let that horse back in here."

He quickly cleaned and examined the entry and exit wounds. The flow of blood was light coming out of the wound; it was more of a trickle. Doc checked Gabe's gums and fingernails. Both had good color. "His gums and fingernails tell me that he isn't losing a lot of blood so that is a good sign. We shouldn't have any internal bleeding."

Doc studied the color of the blood and breathed easier. "No dark blood either so no liver damage," he muttered quietly. He probed the wound carefully and then breathed a sigh of relief. He looked up at the people in the room. "I don't see any organ damage. Now we just need to clean him up and keep the infection out."

Doc Williams continued to work on Gabe for over an hour. When his patient started to come to, the doctor gave him chloroform and Gabe passed out again. Finally, Doc Williams was satisfied that the wound was clean. He applied poultices to both openings of the wound. Larry handed him some clean strips of rags and the surgeon bound the poultices in place. He stepped back and washed his hands as he looked down at his patient. "You are one lucky man, Gabe."

Larry stared down at the man lying on the table and her lips trembled. She looked up at Doc Williams. "I don't mean to question you but are you sure no organs were damaged? It is hard to believe that a horn could go in like that and not hit anything vital."

Doc Williams smiled. "The human body is an amazing thing, Larry. When an object penetrates someone's body, their intestines pull back. It's a natural protection that the body has. They pull away. A bullet moves too fast but something like this gives the body time even though it looks fast to us. In addition, the location was important. If the horn had turned the other way or penetrated higher, it would most likely have been lethal. Regardless, infection in both Gabe and his horse are something to be concerned about.

"I want those bandages changed every day and the poultices twice a day. Smear honey over the open wounds and then sprinkle echinacea powder over that. Make sure to keep it covered and clean. He also needs to lay on his stomach. Five days would be best but for sure, three days to help that wound to drain and heal.

"I will be back out Monday evening to check on him. He is most likely going to run a fever. If it gets high before Monday and you can't get it down, send someone in for me."

CHAPTER 52

A WORRIED BROTHER

THE DANCE WAS A LIVELY ONE AND MERINA DIDN'T SIT DOWN UNLESS SHE HID. Spur made sure that he had plenty of turns and he was every bit as smooth of a dancer as she remembered. Still, she kept her eye on the door. It was after 10:00 p.m. when Nate finally received his turn. He held out his hand and they danced an easy two-step.

"You are learning quickly, Nate. Moving with the music and keeping the beat—you are doing a fine job."

Nate grinned as he focused on the dancing. Merina's eyes searched his face. "Where is Gabe tonight? I thought he was coming."

Nate's smile faded and he missed a step. "I don't know what happened, but he changed his mind yesterday. No one tells me anything, but Gabe has been mad ever since Rusty got back."

Merina was quiet. She had not expected to see Spur so far from Texas. The first time he came by, she had yelled at him. *I didn't expect him to come back.* But he did come back and the next time he brought wildflowers for her. Nate was talking and she almost missed what he said.

"…have a fight? Is that why he didn't come tonight?"

"No. I saw him on Sunday, and we talked about this evening. I haven't seen him since. Maybe he is just busy."

Nate groaned as he nodded. "We have been working like crazy. We cut off a bunch of hay and stacked it in the barn. Gabe was going to build gates today between our ranch and the Reith Ranch since we bought it."

"You did buy it?" Merina's eyes were shining. "I am so excited for both of you. I know Gabe wants to grow your land and cattle holdings."

The song came to an end and Nate bowed. "Thank you, Miss Merina, for the dance lessons and for the dance."

Doc Williams came to the dance late and Nate saw him talking to Lance. They looked his way a couple of times and Nate frowned as he muttered to himself, "I wander if something is wrong. Maybe I should go home tonight instead of staying with Sam."

Sam walked in just then. "Finally dance with the teacher? She's been purty popular tonight."

Nate watched as Spur spun Merina around the floor. She was laughing up at him and Nate frowned. Gabe had loaned him his pocket watch so he wouldn't be late, and Nate checked it. 11:00 p.m.

"I think I am going to go home. Doc Williams was late getting here, and something is going on. Your folks look worried and I want to make sure Gabe is all right. If everything is okay, I will come over tomorrow and we can go fishing."

Sam nodded and then watched him go with a puzzled look on his face. He wandered over by his parents. "Nate left early. Said he was goin' home, an' he might be over tomorrow to fish. Sure funny he'd leave a dance early after bein' so excited to come."

Molly looked over at Lance and frowned. Lance pointed toward the door where Nate was disappearing. "Why don't you ride home with Nate and make sure he gets there all right. He's new to the area and that road can be confusing in the dark. You can spend the night if you want."

Sam looked at his friend's departing back and then around the dance floor. The girl he wanted to dance with had disappeared and he dashed after Nate.

"Wait up, Nate. I'll ride home with you. That road's no fun in the dark by yourself."

Nate grinned in appreciation and the two friends rode off in the dark for home.

"So is Gabe courting Merina?"

Nate shrugged. "Not that I know of. I thought he was sweet on her, but I don't know what's going on. He decided not to go to the dance yesterday. He's been mad and grumpy ever since."

Sam listened quietly. "I wonder what kind of teacher she will be. I don't like school, but she told me she was going to try to teach me some things I would like to learn about." Sam frowned and muttered, "I can't think of a thing I would like to sit around and think or write about. Or read about for that matter." He looked over at his friend. "You go to school much?"

Nate paused and then slowly shook his head. "Naw. Ma taught me to read and do my sums. Our old man wasn't around much. We never had any money and he left Ma and me with nothing to eat most of the time. I worked jobs here and there to buy food. Ma was sickly most of the time, so it was up to me to provide."

Sam stared across at his friend. The moon was coming out and he could see Nate's face in the moonlight. "A pa who don't take care of his family? What kind of a pa is that?"

Nate grinned at him. "A lousy one. Gabe left home when he was fourteen and he sent most of his money back home. He didn't know that Pa was gambling with it until several years ago. Pa finally died. Gabe quit his foreman job and tried to save our little place, but it was too far gone. He took a riding job closer and then Ma died. I moved into the bunkhouse on the ranch where Gabe was working. He was foreman by then and his boss gave me a swamper's job. Last April, Gabe took that Dodge City trail boss job with a fellow out of Manhattan, Kansas by the name of Gallagher. He made me wrangler and we headed north. We had nothing to take with us but Gabe's horse, Buck, and our saddle rolls." He grinned across at Sam again and added, "Gabe said we didn't have a pot to pee in. I told him we didn't need one 'cause we usually peed outside anyway."

The two friends laughed. They rode in silence for a while and then Nate asked, "You want to sleep at our place tonight? We can go fishing all day tomorrow. Cappy found a spot that is clear full of fish. I catch three or four every time I go. Cappy showed me how to pack them in mud and bake them. We eat fish a lot."

Sam nodded and was quiet as he thought about all that Nate had told him. He knew that he was adopted but he had never experienced a lack of love. *My first parents were killed by outlaws. I don't remember much about them, but I knew I was loved. Sissy loved me too before she died. I don't remember her much either, but she always hugged me. Lance and Molly have been the only parents I really remember. I guess I never thought much about what it would be like to grow up hungry and without a Pa.*

Nate shifted in his saddle and began talking again.

"Lots of folks think that Gabe is cranky and sometimes he is. Mostly though, he's just always trying to figure things out. After we sold the cattle in Dodge City, he smiled a lot. I don't think I have ever seen him so happy. Most of the time, he acts more like a pa to me than a brother. That day though, he acted like my big brother and I liked it."

The two boys rode in silence for a while and then Nate asked, "You ever been poor?"

Sam shrugged. "I don't really know. We ain't poor now but we ain't rich either. My first folks was killed by outlaws when I was real small. I don't remember much about them. We might have been poor. Sissy hid me in the potato barrel an' the outlaws didn't find me. They took her with them when they left. Lance an' Badger found her. Then they came back an' got me.

"I remember bein' really scared. I had to go to pee, so I climbed out of the barrel an' then hid in the tack shed. I stacked the saddles an' blankets all around me, but it was scary for a little tyke. The coyotes howled really close an' I remember animals sniffin' around the shed." Sam's voice was quiet as he added, "I was alone for almost two days an' I cried a lot. After Sissy died in a rockslide, Molly offered to be my momma an' since they was married, Lance became my pa. Ma was already pregnant with Paul an' I was excited to have a brother."

Nate was quiet as Sam talked. *Pa had left but Ma was always around to take care of me. When she died, Gabe took care of me. I reckon being poor is easier than losing your family.*

He looked over at Sam and grinned as he punched his shoulder. "We'll have to sleep outside tonight or else in the barn with the men. Cappy gets to sleep in the house along with Rusty and Larry. Gabe is going to build a bunkhouse, but he hasn't started on it yet." He thought about the last two days.

"Boy, do I hate putting up hay."

Sam nodded in agreement. "My favorite thing to do is ride an' rope. I really like roundup. We bring all the cattle in, brand 'em, an' castrate the bull calves. The cattle that are ready to sell are sorted off an' trailed to town to go out on the train." He looked over at his friend. "I want to go on a real trail drive, but Pa says I'm too young."

Nate nodded. "Gabe says he's not going on any more cattle drives but I had fun. On the drive to Dodge City, I was the wrangler. I took care of all the horses. By the time we hit Dodge, we had over eighty of them. Every time Gabe and Angel killed outlaws, we took their horses.

"The rivers were the scariest part. I didn't like crossing them. Gabe was the trail boss and it was his job to find the good crossing spots. John Kirkham bought our steers in Dodge and we helped him move them on to Ogallala, Nebraska. He said Gabe was the best trail boss he had ever worked with."

Nate looked slyly over at Sam. "Mr. Kirkham wants to take another herd north. Gabe said he wouldn't go but I offered to. We can go together if you want."

Sam's eyes lit up. "I'll almost be sixteen by next summer an' then I can take off on my own. Let's go on a trail drive next summer!"

The two friends planned excitedly for the next ten miles and were at Nate's home just before midnight.

CHAPTER 53

Amigos

CAPPY'S OLD VOICE SPOKE OUT OF THE DARKNESS. "Ya two fellers jist hold up. Don't be tryin' ta sneak up on me in my sleep."

Nate grinned toward the voice and waved his hat. "It's me, Cappy, and Sam Rankin. I came home from the dance early." He stopped his horse and frowned. "Why aren't you in the house? And where is Gabe?"

Cappy stepped out from behind the barn and limped toward the young men. He was stiff most of the time anymore but when he was awakened in the middle of the night, he could hardly bend his legs.

"Nate, give me yore hoss. Then ya go on an' look in on Gabe. That durned ol' bull a Reith's gored 'im this afternoon an' he's laid up. Doc says he'll be all right but he's a hurtin'. He might be a fightin' a fever too so if he ain't quite right, that's why.

"Sam, ya come with me. Once we take care a these here hosses, we'll mosey on in there."

Nate raced into the house and slammed the door to Gabe's bedroom open. He heard Rusty curse in the next room as bare feet hit the floor on the run. He was just bending over Gabe when Rusty shoved through the door with his gun drawn.

The moon lit the room, shining in through the window.

"Dadgummit, Nate! What are ya doin' crashin' in here at midnight? I might a shot ya if I hadn't stubbed my durn toe."

"Gabe! You all right? Why didn't you send for me?" He shook his brother's arm until Gabe opened his eyes.

"Don't touch my side there, Nate. I'm a little banged up. And I didn't send for you because it was your birthday and you have been talking about this dance for weeks.

"Now clear those tears out of your eyes. I'll be fine. That bull didn't catch anything important." Gabe groaned as he shifted position. "I'm more worried about Buck so check on him before you go to sleep."

Gabe spotted Rusty bent over in the doorway, rubbing his toe and tried to laugh. It hurt too bad and he gasped. When Cappy and Sam pushed through the door, he shook his head.

"You managed to wake up the whole durn house. Next thing, Larry will be in here."

Larry's curly head appeared behind Rusty. She had a blanket wrapped around her and she laughed. "Well, Rusty made so much noise when he stubbed his toe that the Rankin's probably heard him."

Gabe looked around at the small group of people. He was about to speak when Angel appeared at the window.

"I think, Señor, that there is no more space in your small room for a tired vaquero. I will just stay out here and speak to you through the window."

Gabe tried to snort and then groaned. "You all go back to bed and no one bother me until daylight. Then Larry can check my side and see if my poultices need changed. Now all of you, get out of here." He pulled Nate down and hugged him as he whispered, "Love you, little brother."

Larry paused and moved toward the bed. "Doc Williams said that you need to lay on your stomach to help the wound drain. Can you turn over or do you need us to help you?"

Gabe tried to turn but fell back with a groan. Nate and Rusty helped him turn over and Larry adjusted his pillow .

"Now all of you get out and quit worrying about me. And thank you." Gabe's voice was muffled as he talked through the pillow.

Everyone traipsed out of Gabe's room and Rusty pulled the door shut. He looked around at the wide-awake group of people.

"How 'bout some coffee or root beer? Badger had that stuff stashed all over this ranch and we have moved it to the icehouse."

As everyone nodded, Rusty pointed toward Nate and Sam. "You two still have yore boots on. Go git a jug an' bring it in here."

Angel fell in beside the two boys and Nate looked over at him. "Gabe sounds all right. Was he hurt bad?"

Angel nodded, "It was bad. Doc Williams worked on him quickly. He will heal, but we have to watch for infection." Angel looked toward the house. "The horns of bulls are very dirty, and he will get the fever today or tomorrow. We will have to watch him and Buck too. Infections can come on quickly." Angel put his arm around Nate's shoulders. "Your brother was lucky. The bull threw him, but the horn did little damage. I think maybe the angels watch over him."

Nate stared at Angel. He could feel the fear surge through him. Angel squeezed his shoulder.

"Come, let us drink some of this fine root beer and tell some stories since we are awake."

Sam grabbed the jug and Nate hooked the door to the icehouse as the friends headed to the house for a late-night visit.

Larry had put on a dress and was serving some cookies she had made. Cappy filled the glasses and Angel raised his glass to the room. "May we always be amigos!"

Everyone raised their glasses and the stories started. Gabe listened from his bed and went to sleep with a smile on his face.

CHAPTER 54

A Common Friend

MERINA WAS THE LAST ONE TO LEAVE CHURCH ON SUNDAY MORNING. Spur had offered to ride home with her after the dance, but Martha had already invited her to spend the night in Cheyenne. Merina had accepted Martha's offer gratefully.

She enjoyed Mass and without a fifteen-mile ride to town, it was an easy morning. Her little sister spent Saturday night with the Rankins. Merina rolled her eyes. "Soon, Emilia will not want to live with me at all. They are much more fun than I am."

The late breakfast at the McCunes' was delicious. She helped the older woman clean up and was on her way to the livery when Badger caught up with her.

"You'ins goin' by Gabe's place? I was goin' ta ride out that way an' check in on 'im."

When Merina didn't respond, "Unless ya'd rather ride alone."

Merina's face colored and she shook her head. "You are welcome to ride with me. I just hadn't planned on stopping by."

Badger looked over at her. "Wahl, seein's how he be hurt an' all, I thought I'd take a little of my potion by, jist in case the fever comes on."

Merina stopped and stared at Badger as her face went pale.

"He was hurt?"

"Bull gored 'im yesterday. Doc was out there last night an' checked 'im over. Said he be all right. I'm worried 'bout the fever though an' thought I'd check in."

Merina was almost running when Badger finished talking. He grabbed her arm to slow her down.

"Now don't ya be a worryin'. Ol' Gabe's been hurt worser than this an' made it. 'Sides, this time he has a durn good doc lookin' in on 'im." He grinned at her, "But I know he'd shore appreciate a gal who loves horses ta look in on Buck. Mebbie ya should take 'im home with ya. Ol' Buck ain't too fond a strangers a messin' with 'im an' he needs ta be looked after." His ornery eyes danced. "Or, you'ins could jist go on over ever' day an' work on that horse….an' check on Gabe."

Merina turned a deep red and then she laughed.

"Badger, you are a—a—I don't know what you are, but you are something."

The little man grinned at her and took her arm. "I reckon that jist about sums it up, Miss Merina. Now let's get on out to that ranch an' check on yore feller."

Merina wanted to race her horse, but Badger kept their pace easy. He grinned when he saw how impatient she was.

"Where is that little sister? I have candy fer 'er but I ain't seen 'er since the dance last night."

"Molly and Lance took her home. Livvy and Emilia have become fast friends and are together whenever possible. Pauline was spending the night too so their house should be full of little girl screams and giggles by now."

"Well, ol' Gabe sure has 'im some fine neighbors. I reckon I should point out that he's been a sleepin' in the barn an' see if we'uns can't get us a barn raisin' a goin'. 'Course, it'd be a bunkhouse an' not a barn but we'uns could do it the same way. Yessir, I'll get ta work on that."

Merina was quiet as she glanced over at Badger. He was looking off on the distance and squinted his eyes.

"Looks like ta me that they's some extry hosses ta Gabe's place. Reckon the word's a gittin' out 'bout his accident."

Merina stared at him and then squinted her eyes. She couldn't make out any details of the ranch this far out.

"You must have very good eyes, Señor Badger."

"I reckon I cin see what I want ta see," he replied with a grin and a wink.

Merina laughed. The ornery little man beside her was old but he was full of life. "You have lived around Cheyenne for many years?"

"Naw, my Martha an' me come here with Lance an' Molly in '68. Then Rowdy showed up after we all thought he was dead an' our family grew. Little Sadie lost her first husband an' we added more ta the family. Now Gabe's here. We done added him an' Nate too. An' since we added ya two gurls, we'll take yer brothers. My Martha has 'nough love ta go plumb around."

Merina was quiet. She gazed intently at Badger.

"I think, Señor Badger, you have a very big heart that you hide beneath your laughs."

Badger winked at her and chuckled. "I reckon we's close 'nough if'n ya want ta take the last half mile a little faster."

As Merina raced her horse into the yard, Spur walked out of the house. He tipped his hat and grinned at her. "Mornin', Miss Merina. Ya shore are a picture to look at on a Sunday mornin'."

Merina stared at him and then quickly dismounted. "I need to see Gabe."

Cappy grabbed Mascota's reins as she ran toward the house.

Angel was sauntering out of the kitchen door when Merina ran into him. She punched his shoulder and began to scold him in Spanish, talking rapidly and shaking her finger at him.

"Why did you not tell me that Gabe was hurt? Must I hear it from Badger this morning? You should have told me as soon as it happened or at least by last night. I am angry with you, Brother."

Rusty touched her shoulder and then jumped back when she whirled toward him. "Jist a minute, Miss Merina. There wasn't much time to tell folks. Nate jist found out last night when he come home. Doc was here over two hours an' it was late by then. Angel here saved Gabe's life so ya should be a thankin' 'im an' not a yellin' at 'im like that."

Merina's face crumpled and Angel put his arms around her. He whispered to her and then pointed at Gabe's room. She wiped her eyes and then quietly knocked on the door. She closed it after she entered and quickly crossed the room to his side.

"Gabe? I just heard. You will be all right?"

Gabe rolled slowly to his back. His face was pale, and he gasped from the pain, but he tried to smile up at her. "Hello, Merina. I was hoping you would come by. Now sit down here and let's have a talk."

Gabe's eyes were a deep blue as he studied her face. She thought they looked sad, but she couldn't tell for sure.

"We have a common friend."

Merina's eyebrows raised. "Señor?"

"My friend Spur just stopped by."

Merina's face went still. "Si, he was leaving when I arrived."

Gabe winced as he shifted his legs.

"Spur was my first pard. We rode together for Dan Waggoner for nearly four years after I left home. When I was made trail boss in '72, Spur left there. I heard he took a trail boss job in south Texas. I was on a drive for Waggoner when he headed north the first time. He helped trail some cattle to Wyoming and just didn't come back to Texas. He worked up here at the Rocking R for several years before he headed south again. He came over to Waggoners' one evening and that was the first that I knew he was back. Said he'd hired on with the Milletts but was thinking of quitting. He was a little leery of what some of those boys were doing."

Gabe frowned and winced as he tried to shift positions. "Those Millett boys were a wild crew. Word was that only a rustler or a fellow who was good with a gun could get a riding job there. Spur's fast with his gun and he knows how to handle rough men. That's probably why the Millett brothers hired him.

"We talked some then about Wyoming and maybe going together. He liked it up here and wanted to come back someday. I was content with my job though. Then he just pulled out.

"I'd heard that he'd headed back north, but I didn't know where he was—until the dance lessons. When Rusty got home, he talked about a man named Spur talking with you like an old friend." Gabe paused and added softly, "I knew then that my old pard Spur was the man who left you at sixteen. That's when I decided not to go to the dance."

Merina's face was pale as she listened. When she thought of her conversation with Gabe about the man she had loved at sixteen, her face became even more pale.

"Gabe—"

Gabe shook his head. "No, let me finish. Now you and me never courted so I reckon that gives Spur an inside edge. And I won't fight with a pard for a woman, even though I want to for you."

Tears ran out of Merina's eyes. "Gabe, I don't want to hurt anyone," she whispered.

He patted her hand. "You follow your heart, Merina. If Spur wins it--well, I admit I will be sad, but he is a good man and he will make you happy. Besides, I'm not sure I ever made you laugh like you said he did, and laughing is good for the soul." Gabe tried to smile but the smile didn't reach his eyes.

Merina was quiet as she looked at Gabe. She pinched off the sobs that were starting in her chest.

"One more thing. Would you take Buck home and keep an eye on him? He tried to bite Larry and she doesn't need to take any chances like that. Angel does all right but Rusty is just plain leery of him. I don't want him to get infection—lockjaw will kill him. And keep the flies off that cut. I don't know if screwworms are a problem here, but you know what to look for.

"Now you go. I'll have Nate let you know if I get worse, but I don't want you here when the fever takes over. Who knows what I'll say." He tried to grin at her but winced instead. "The next two days will be my worst." Gabe's eyes were full of pain when he looked at her.

"Be happy, Merina. And take care of my horse."

CHAPTER 55

STAY OUT OF THEIR BUSINESS!

NO ONE WAS IN THE KITCHEN WHEN MERINA LEFT GABE'S ROOM. She went to the barn and hooked a rope to Buck's halter. Mounting Mascota, she rode back toward the Rocking R leading Buck.

The little girls were nowhere to be seen when Merina arrived, and Molly stuck her head out the door to call to them. When she saw Merina, she waved at her to come in.

Molly studied her face and then asked quietly, "How's Gabe?"

Merina's eyes filled with tears. "I'm not sure. He said not to worry, and Doc is coming back out tomorrow night. Badger rode out with me from town. He said he has some kind of potion for Gabe to drink."

"Badger's potion can work miracles," Molly laughed. "It tastes as terrible as it smells but it cuts a fever." She hugged the younger woman.

"Don't you worry. He will be fine. Doc Williams is a fine surgeon and if he said Gabe will get well, he will.

"Why don't you go home and take a nap. Come back this evening and pick up Emilia. The girls are playing well together. Rowdy and Beth are coming for supper. You just as well come down too. Emilia can go home with you afterwards.

"And put Gabe's horse in the barn. I'm guessing that he asked you to take care of him. There is a big jug of petroleum jelly in the tack house. Cover that incision and it will keep the flies off. If it looks like they are still bothering it, we can put a bandage on it for now. We'll ask Rowdy tonight about what else you should do."

Merina led Buck into the barn. She tied him in the stall and then found the tub of petroleum jelly. She rubbed the thick, sticky jell onto Buck's incision talking to him quietly. He looked around at her several times and shook his skin, but he stood calmly.

She hugged his neck when she was done. "You get well, Buck. Gabe is counting on me to make sure you heal, and I don't want to fail him."

The big stallion nickered softly, and Merina untied him. She brushed Mascota down and gave them both some oats and hay. She petted them as she left the barn and walked toward her house.

When she awoke, it was nearly 5:00. She slapped some water on her face and rushed the quarter mile to Molly's house. Beth and Rowdy were already there, and Merina hurried to help Molly.

"I guess I must have been tired because I just woke up," she whispered.

Molly laughed and Emilia launched herself at her sister.

"Nina, I have had so much fun. This is Pauline and she is my friend too! And we played with dolls and we dug in the dirt and now we are going to play in the barn!"

Lance and Rowdy both hollered at the same time, "Stay out of the hay!"

The three little girls went running outside and Beth handed Merina the baby. "If you'll hold Emmaline, I will help Molly."

Merina looked down at the little blond girl and smiled at the bright green eyes. "Well aren't you just the prettiest little sweetheart. Let's go take a walk." She lifted the little girl to her hip and walked outside pointing at things as she talked to her.

"So what is going on with Merina and Gabe?" Molly asked as she watched Merina walk across the yard

Lance rolled his eyes. "Why don't you women stay out of their business? Maybe they don't need your help."

Molly sniffed. "Men rarely get it right in the beginning. They can always use some help."

Rowdy chuckled as he squeezed his wife.

Beth puckered her brow. "I was just thinking about Spur. I'm not sure if he knows Merina. I just know that he has been down this way several times since she moved in and he whistles a lot lately." She smiled up at Rowdy and added as she giggled, "He can be surly, kind of like someone else I know, but my someone smiles more than he used to. I just wondered if Spur had met someone."

Lance put up his hands. "Don't even think of getting involved. Spur is a top hand. Rowdy doesn't want to lose him and Gabe is a fine neighbor. Let them work it out."

Molly frowned, "But—"

"But nothing, Molly. Matchmaking can only go so far. Leave them alone." He chuckled as he added, "Look at it this way—if it works for either of them, you can help with the wedding."

Molly swung her spoon towards him, but Lance ducked and caught her. "My sassy Molly. I do love you, Molly girl."

Rowdy added quietly, "To make this more complicated, the two men are old friends. They knew each other down in Texas and rode as partners for some time."

No one said any more and Merina was soon back in the house with a sleeping baby on her shoulder. Molly pointed toward a bedroom and Merina laid Emmaline down in a small crib. She shut the door softly and walked out to the kitchen to see what needed to be done.

CHAPTER 56

BADGER'S ADVICE

LANCE STOOD AND LOOKED OUT THE DOOR. He glanced around at Molly as he commented, "Better put on two more plates. Badger and Martha are here. They must have come separately since she's in the buggy and he's on Mule."

Martha entered the house in a rush and hugged everyone. "I miss all of you so much. I told Badger we needed to come out and see the kids tonight. Here are some fresh rolls and cookies to add to supper since we are inviting ourselves."

Badger was in the house quickly. He stopped by Merina. His bright eyes twinkled as he winked at her.

"Merina, how's 'bout you'ins 'n me go check on Gabe's horse. I brung some salve with me that I made up. Think it might help that thar cut heal without leavin' no scar." He took her arm and guided her out the door quickly.

"So many people overwhelm me," she whispered.

Badger chuckled as he nodded. "We's a noisy bunch fer sure." He looked at her seriously as he added, "Don't mind Molly 'n Beth. They's good folks. Jist like ta match folks up. Why if it was up ta those two, there wouldn't be a single feller in the territory. 'Course, they's happy married an' they jist want that fer ever' body else.

"Now tell me how yer neighbor is."

Tears glinted in the corners of Merina's eyes as she shrugged. "He told me to go home. He doesn't want me around if the fever comes on." She laughed dryly. "He's more concerned about his horse than he is about himself."

"Shore now, that's the way it would be. Ol' Gabe never did own much an' Buck here took 'im lots a miles. A feller's horse gets ta be a friend an' ya fergets he's a durn horse."

Merina attached a rope to Buck's halter and tied him before Badger entered the stall. The old man studied the cut that went diagonal across the horse's ribs. He whistled softly.

"That be a bad cut, but she could be worse. That durn bull shore wanted ta prong 'im. I'm a guessin' ol' Buck was a tryin' ta keep 'im off Gabe." He wiped the petroleum jelly off the wound and handed her the tin can he had in his pocket.

"That there stuff has some o' the same things you's a usin' but I mixed it up an' made a cream. Leave the jelly off at night an' only use it of the day. That jelly 'ill keep those thar stitches wet an' they'll take longer ta heal.

"Now spread that thar cream over it an' then wipe it off in the mornin' when ya clean it."

Merina applied the cream liberally to the cut. She could smell some of the dried herbs that Badger had used, and the smell was pleasant.

Buck nickered at her and pushed his head into her arm. She whispered to him and he nuzzled her.

"That ol' boy likes ya. I hear tell he don't take ta no one but Gabe. Shoot, he might not want ta go home after bein' here fer three weeks er so."

Badger grinned at her and then shut the stall door after they left. He pointed at a barrel and then sat down on a stool.

"Now tell me what's a troublin' ya."

Merina looked in surprise at the old man. Her blush couldn't be seen in the barn, but she could feel her face become warm. She paused a moment, then spoke softly.

"I knew Spur in Texas. He courted me when I was sixteen and then left without saying goodbye.

"Gabe and I were sharing stories one evening, and I told him about the cowboy who had broken my heart down in Texas. I didn't tell him Spur's name. I just said he was a cowboy from New Orleans.

"I didn't know where Spur had gone. He just left without saying goodbye. Now he's here four years later, ready to take up where we left off." She shrugged.

"I was angry, and I shouted at him. Gabe heard about that from Rusty and figured out that Spur was the cowboy who had broken my heart." Tears filled her eyes as she added, "They rode as partners for four years and are still good friends. Gabe thinks I'm Spur's girl."

Badger listened silently and then looked over at the horses before he answered.

"Ya know, ol' Gabe got his nickname a Preacher a defendin' my Martha. That boy's an ol' Texas gentleman when it comes ta the ladies. I reckon he won't fight a friend fer a gurl, 'specially if'n he thinks the other feller were first."

Tears filled Merina's eyes as she nodded.

Badger stood and pulled Merina up. "I reckon, Miss Merina, that only you'ins an' God cin figger this here deal out. Jist foller yer heart an' don't be a tryin' ta tell it.

"Now let's go eat some good food 'an don't you'ins worry none 'bout folks a teasin' ya." He grinned at her and chuckled. "When they figger out who's what an' what's who, they won't know what ta do nohow since both a those fellers is friends. Why it's durn near a conundrum."

CHAPTER 57

ADD ONE MORE PLATE

THEY WERE JUST STARTING TO EAT WHEN SOMEONE **KNOCKED ON THE DOOR.** Spur stood there with hat in hand, smiling as Molly opened the door.

"Evening, Mrs. Rankin. I spotted some of Lance's cows out on the trail coming from Cheyenne. I brought them home and they are penned in the corral."

Lance stood and looked out the door. He growled as he recognized the cows. "Those two old girls haven't seen a fence they can't jump.

"Come on in, Spur. I sure appreciate that and the least we can do is feed you supper."

Spur accepted and walked in with a smile. His smile became bigger when he saw Merina.

"Evenin', Miss Merina. I would have hurried those cows a little faster if I had known you were here."

Merina blushed and dropped her eyes while everyone laughed.

Spur looked the same to her as he had four years ago. A big black mustache drooped on either side of his upper lip. His dark eyes were almost black, and he laughed easily. Thick black hair curled from under his hat. She wasn't sure how tall he was, but her head was in the middle of his chest when she danced with him. *And my, can he dance. Yes, Spur is just as handsome as I remember.* His smile had always gotten to her. When she first met him, that smile made her melt. *But that was then. Now I am older and wiser. I won't let his charm take over this time.*

Beth filled plates for the kids, and they were all having a picnic outside. Their happy chatter and laughing trickled in through the windows and Merina smiled. Spur caught her eye and winked at her. He started to say something and then grinned instead.

Molly set a full plate in front of him. Spur studied it for a moment and then drawled, "I'm not sure which of you lady's is the best cook but I sure am glad that I'm close enough to eat food from all of your tables."

Lance led the grace and the conversation picked up. The meal was a noisy, happy affair. When they were done, the women cleared the table and Merina stood to help. She heard Lance say, "Spur, I hear you and Gabe knew each other down in Texas." Merina hurried to the wash basin and kept her back to the men as Spur answered.

"Sure did. Gabe was my first friend after I left New Orleans. We rode as partners for four years before we split an' went on our own. I am tickled pink to know he is up here. I had no idea until I saw him at the dance lessons." Spur's eyes moved to where Merina was washing dishes. He studied her for a moment before he added, "He's a fine man an' a good friend."

Badger leaned forward. "Say, ya know those boys been a sleepin' in the barn? They been a haulin' some rock up ta put up the foundation fer a bunkhouse but now Gabe's laid up. The rest of 'em is busy cuttin' hay."

"I'm a thinkin' we should throw us a barn raisin' party an' put up a bunkhouse. Could be done in a day if'n we'uns all helped."

Beth leaned forward excitedly. "That is a great idea, Badger! We haven't really done anything to welcome all of them to the neighborhood.

Let's plan it for next Friday. That is Independence Day so we can make it a party!"

Molly nodded her head in agreement. "I need to go into Cheyenne this week to pick up some things. Maybe Beth and I could each bring home some lumber."

Merina had turned around to listen and they both looked over at her.

"I will be glad to watch the kids. Just tell me what day," Merina replied with a laugh. "Although, I don't know how I am going to keep that many kids busy all day."

Lance stared from one woman to the other and then shook his head as he looked over at Rowdy. "I don't think we have much say in this, but if we are going to do it, pick up that lumber on Monday or Tuesday. That way if they don't have it, we will have some time to change to a new date." He grinned as he looked around the room. "Charge it to Gabe's ranch. We will help him build it, but we aren't going to help him pay for it."

The room was soon abuzz as the men made lists of the supplies that would be needed, and the women made plans for the party to go along with it.

"Have you ever been to a barn-raising, Merina?" Beth's eyes were bright with excitement.

Merina shook her head. "No, Señor Cole built a new barn before we worked for him, but he hired it done. It took many more days than one."

Molly laughed as she pulled Merina into the circle of women. "Oh, believe me, it will only take one day." She whispered in Merina's ear, "Besides, we have the prettiest teacher in the territory. Those men will have more volunteers than they will have work for."

Merina stared from one woman to the other and her eyes opened wide. "But I didn't know that women attended this barn building."

"Oh, everyone will be there. The men do the work, the kids run wild and the women provide the food and refreshments. It is like an all-day party with just a little work along with it. When the day is over, the barn is built."

Lance nodded as he laughingly agreed with his wife. "Well, the men might not agree with all that, but it is a fun day. A nice way to introduce Gabe's crew to the neighborhood too." He looked from Spur to Badger.

"Either one of you want to make a visit to see what building materials they already have? Might not hurt to include his hands in this so they can be close on Friday."

Badger offered to get the information and Spur nodded.

"I will offer to help them get the foundation up. That way, the mortar can be dried by Friday when you start putting up the walls." He slid his eyes over toward Rowdy as he grinned.

Rowdy waved his hand. "Go on. You have two days and then I need you back at the R4."

"I'll send a couple of men over too. I saw those rocks that were stacked out in the pasture. They are almost a two-man job just to move around." Lance looked over at Badger.

"Where did they come from anyway?"

The old man shrugged his shoulders. "Don't know. They was there when I bought the place. Another feller must a hauled 'em in 'cause I ain't seen' no rocks like 'em nowhere else. I seen a pile of 'em up by the barn when I was there yesterday so Gabe's hands been a tryin' ta move 'em in."

Badger stood up and Martha immediately began hustling around to gather her pans.

"We'uns 'ill jist mosey on over there now an' make a visit. Don't be a goin' ta bed 'til we'uns get back now.

"Come on, Mule. You'ins cin foller along here whilst I ride with my wife."

Badger rushed outside and was soon in front of the house with the buggy. He helped Martha in and hustled the team out of the yard followed by Mule.

Lance shook his head as he watched them go. "Hard to believe that he is as old as he is. That man just never runs out of energy."

They could hear Badger singing to Martha as he drove down the lane.

The dishes were done, and Merina called for Emilia. She smiled at the two women. "Thank you for the wonderful meal and for watching Emilia. Let me know what day you want me to watch your children." As she took Emilia's hand and started for the door, Spur stood.

"I'd like to thank you too. I will walk Miss Merina home—if she'll allow me."

He followed Merina out the door. She didn't disagree so he fell in step beside her as he led his horse.

"Emilia, you want to ride my horse instead of walking?"

Emilia's dirty little face peered up at him. "Señor Gabe would ride me on his shoulders."

Spur's eyebrows went up and then he scooped up the little girl and plopped her on his wide shoulders. "Like this?"

She squealed in delight as he began to run around, swooping and bending as she hung on."

Finally, he slowed down and waited for Merina to catch up. He had both of his hands around Emilia's legs as he smiled down at Merina.

"My hands are full, but I will offer you my arm if you want to take it."

Merina paused as she looked up at him and then she laughed. Her eyes became serious as she spoke softly, "I missed you when you left. You should have said goodbye."

Spur frowned and he nodded. "I have regretted that for over four years now. If you will let me stay for a bit tonight, I will explain the whole thing."

Merina studied his face and then slowly nodded. "Si, but I have to give Emilia a bath so you will have to wait."

Spur's eyes were serious as he agreed. "You are worth waiting for, Merina."

Merina met his eyes and then looked away from the intensity she saw in them. She could feel the old feeling in her stomach that she used to get when he looked at her and she frowned. She muttered in Spanish, "Why must you bring back memories? They are best left where they died."

Spur chuckled. "You forget that I am fluent in Spanish, Merina, but go ahead and mutter at me. I like how it sounds."

Merina almost stopped and then laughed. "You always made me laugh, Spur. I think maybe I mistook my enjoyment of your company for something else."

Spur was quiet for a moment. "Then I hope you will give me a second chance to see if I can change that."

Emilia was sliding off to one side and he slipped her down to carry her. "Your mother must have born Emilia shortly before your father died."

"Si, she was very small. Mamá was so sad. I helped her much, but she became sick and she never did get completely well. We all went to work for Señor Cole and when he offered part of his big house to us, Mamá seemed to be getting better. Then one day, she became very ill and she died.

"Miguel took a riding job in the Indian Territory and Señor Cole decided to go north with a herd. Angel did not want him to go but Señor Cole thought it would be simple." Merina was quiet for a moment and then added softly. "Angel knew that Señor Cole could not make it without him, but he did not want to leave. I told him to go but it was very difficult for me after they left. Not all of the men were so nice."

Spur's mouth drew down in a hard line and he cursed softly under his breath. "I should never have left you."

Merina laughed as she looked up at him, "But Señor, you gave me your big knife. I wear it always and it saved me.

"I took the horses that Señor Cole had sold to Señor Rowdy and loaded them on the train. Emilia and I rode with them to Dodge to meet our brothers. And now I am here."

Spur put his arm around Merina and pulled her close. "Ah, Merina. I have missed you."

CHAPTER 58

OLD FRIENDS

MERINA HEATED WATER FROM THE DRUM. She gave Emilia a quick bath scrubbing her fingernails and feet as she sang to her. Emilia's head was already bobbing when Merina put her in her nightgown and placed her in bed. Emilia didn't open her eyes and her sister quietly closed the door.

"Come, sit with me on the porch and tell me why you left." She waited until Spur sat down and then she seated herself a little ways away from him.

Spur frowned as he leaned back against the support post. "I took a trail boss job with an outfit headed north when Dan Waggoner hired Gabe as trail boss on the Waggoner Ranch. His son, WT, was a good cowman too and old Dan didn't need another trail boss.

"We took that herd all the way to Cheyenne and I just stayed. I liked it up here. After the third winter, I headed back south. I decided that I'd had enough snow and cold.

"I rode for several outfits kind of drifting around. In '74, the Millett brothers moved in on Miller Creek and they were hiring. They offered me a foreman job and I took it.

"There were three brothers: Eugene, Alonzo and Hiram. They were tough boys, but they worked together well most of the time. I had heard the stories about how wild of an outfit they ran, and they were every bit as rough as I'd heard. Of course, so was I back then. Besides, that area was wide open in those days and you had to be tough to hold it." He broke the stick that he was fiddling with and threw it down on the ground.

"The first year wasn't bad. The boys raised a little cane when they could and shot out windows of any town we went through. We were one of the first outfits to trail herds north on that route you took to Dodge City. Some folks give that trail a name, but you know there isn't any real trail. You just move cattle north and trail them according to water and water crossings.

"Then settlers started moving in. The Milletts owned lots of grass but they used a lot of open range as well. No cowboy likes settlers tearing up the sod and the settlers didn't like us cowboys. Before long, we were cutting fences that the settlers put up. We'd run our cattle right through their homesteads. I gave orders not to shoot any of them, but it was still a darn reckless thing to do. I met you that second year and I thought life was pretty good.

"One night, some of the boys took a herd of long horns and ran them through a family gathering. Cut the fence and charged a whole herd down on those folks. One man died trying to save his family and that blew the cork off.

"I didn't know anything about it until one of the hands woke me up around 2:00 a.m. and said we needed to clear out. The sheriff was coming with a posse. Since I was foremen, everyone assumed that I had given the order.

"I saddled my horse and we headed west. We turned north around daylight and caught a herd headed for Wyoming. Some of the boys split off along the way. I don't know who all was involved or even who gave the order, but I was in the cross hairs of the good citizens." He looked over at Merina.

"I wanted to go by your place, but the sheriff was between you and me. I thought about writing you lots of times but every time I started, I couldn't find the words." He sifted some dirt through his hands and then leaned back.

"I heard the widow to that man who died had five little kids. I had a little bit of money saved and I sent it to her. A fellow I knew here was headed to Nebraska. I had him mail it there so they wouldn't come here looking for me—in case she tried to sic the law on me. I told her who I was and that I hadn't given the order. I said I was sure sorry about her man."

Merina was quiet as Spur talked. When he finished, she said simply, "You found the words for the widow. You should have found the words for me."

Spur scooted closer to her. "Merina, you were sixteen and I was a man grown. I had never had strong feelings for a woman before and it scared me. I knew I couldn't support you with the wages I was earning but if I had gone back, I would have asked you to marry me." He turned her face toward him. "Now how do you say that in a letter?"

Merina looked at him. Emotions flashed through her dark eyes before she looked away. "I would have run away with you if you had asked," she replied softly. "You had four years, Spur." She was silent a moment before she added, "But then what would have become of Emilia when Mamá died? It is better this way."

Spur kissed her and then held her face. "And what about now? Would you still run away with me?"

Merina turned her head and Spur dropped his hand around her back. She looked out over the black night and shook her head. "No, much has changed. I am not so much persuaded by a dashing vaquero who charms me with his smiles."

Spur chuckled and pulled her closer. "Well then, I guess I will just have to keep charming you." He leaned back on his hands and studied her profile. "So tell me, Miss Merina, how did you get this school marm job?"

They visited like the old friends that they were, and Spur left around midnight. It was going to be a short night and a long day tomorrow, but he was smiling as he rode east.

Merina watched him until the night took him away and then she stepped back into the house. She touched her lips and frowned as she climbed into bed beside Emilia.

CHAPTER 59

A Fast Night Ride

GABE'S FEVER SPIKED AROUND MIDNIGHT AND THE ENTIRE RANCH WAS TRYING TO KEEP HIM IN BED. Rusty finally grabbed Miguel.

"Go get Merina! Stay with Emilia until she wakes up and then come back."

Miguel had a big black thoroughbred that liked to run, and Miguel let him run that night. He beat on Merina's door and called softly for his sister.

Merina jerked the door open. She had a blanket wrapped around her nightgown and a shotgun in her hands. Miguel's face was grim as he stepped inside.

"Gabe's fever is up, and we can't keep him in bed. You need to come. He is too strong. We are going to have to tie him down."

Merina dressed quickly and Miguel gave her a leg up onto the large gelding. "Give him his head and let him pick his speed. I will stay with Emilia. Go, little sister." As Merina rushed into the night, Miguel added softly, "Go to your man."

The night was cool, and Miguel's horse loved to run. He galloped easily most of the way and then ran the last half mile. He was blowing when they arrived. Cappy grabbed the horse as Merina jumped off. He squeezed her shoulder as she rushed into the house.

Gabe was standing up. He was trying to pull off his bandages and was yelling for everyone to get out of his way. He was leaving and leaving now.

Merina pushed her way through his friends blocking the door and stopped in front of him. She pointed her finger at him and then at the bed.

"Gabe, you get back in bed now. You are sick and I will not have you disrupting this house. Now go!"

Gabe stared at her for a moment. He frowned and tugged on the bandage.

Merina slapped his hand away. "Put your arm over my shoulder and I will help you to bed. Shame on you for behaving so badly."

Gabe staggered and Merina slipped her shoulder under his arm. She guided him back to his bed and helped him to sit down. As he laid back, he smiled at her. "I missed you, Merina. I was coming to see you." He put his hand up to her face and cupped her cheek.

Tears filled Merina's eyes. "Gabe, don't talk. You are very sick, and I need to change your bandages."

He stared up at her with feverish eyes as she moved his hand and began to untie the bandages.

Merina looked behind her toward Nate and Sam. "Do you think you can find some moss down by the creek? I want to pack his wounds and I need several handfuls."

Nate nodded and the two of them left quickly.

She looked at Rusty. "How about some root beer for Gabe? I think it will make him feel better." She looked hard at Angel. "Be sure to get the jug that Badger brought today."

Cappy heard Merina's request and brought in a new jug of root beer from the icehouse. Rusty uncapped the potion Badger brought and

322

started to gag. "I think this here stuff's seen its better days. I reckon we better throw it out."

Angel grabbed it. "No, Señor. It always smells bad. We give this to Señor Gabe, and we drink with him." His dark eyes twinkled as he added, "My sister knows he will not drink it alone, so she wishes to trick him."

Rusty began to chuckle. He filled glasses of root beer for everyone but Gabe. He poured Badger's potion into another large glass, filling it half full for Gabe.

Angel studied the glass and then looked toward the bedroom where Merina was talking softly to the big man. "I think we should give him a full glass. Maybe he will sleep the rest of the night and we will all have some rest, yes?"

Rusty held his nose and started gagging again.

Larry grabbed the jar and dumped more into the glass. "Good grief, Rusty. *You* don't have to drink it. After all the things you have had on you and in your mouth, I don't know why this bothers you."

Rusty pointed at the seeds floating in the mixture. "I know where them thar seeds started an' I know what they come out of. That sets my mind to thinkin' on where the rest a that mixture come from an' my mind's a reelin' at the possibilities."

Larry rolled her eyes and handed each man a glass of root beer. She gave an extra glass to Rusty to carry for her. She carried a glass in each hand and gave them both to Merina. "Here you are. We could all use a little drink of something tonight so we will join you."

Merina adjusted Gabe's pillow so he could drink. "We will all have some root beer with you, Gabe." She took the glasses from Larry and handed one to Gabe. "Now drink it up. It will help bring your fever down."

Gabe lifted the glass to his mouth and sniffed it. He frowned and tried to hand it back to Merina. "I think it went bad. There's something wrong with this batch."

Merina's face was calm as she sniffed it and pretended to take a drink. It took all she had to keep from choking, but she calmly handed it back to him. "No, it is fine. Perhaps your nose isn't working so well tonight."

Rusty staggered into the kitchen and ran for the outside door as his gags became more violent. Angel chuckled and lifted his glass.

"To you, my amigo. May you have many years on this ranch and many small vaqueros as well."

Gabe grinned at Merina and tapped her glass with his. He drank nearly half of the glass, stared at it a moment, and then drained the rest. His eyes were glassy as he looked up at Merina. He smiled loosely.

"I reckon that was the best batch yet. It really tingled going down."

Merina took a small drink of hers and then finished unwrapping his wound. Gabe tried to take her hand.

"Marry me, Merina. Make my heart sing again." His eyes were dark and intense for a moment and then they glassed over as he passed out.

Merina's hands went still as she tried not to cry. Larry moved quickly to help. She hugged Merina and then the two of them unwrapped the tight bandage.

Merina gasped when she saw the gaping hole. The wound was red and inflamed. Larry studied it for a moment and then stated quietly, "I will bring you some hot water. I hear the boys coming now."

Nate and Sam burst through the door. They had filled a can with moss and Merina took it from them. She carefully washed both openings and then packed the moss inside. She applied Badger's paste to the outside of the wound and then smeared it with the honey that Larry held. She smelled the wound several times but didn't smell any rot. *Our Dios has been with you, Gabe.*

When she was satisfied, she rebound the wound. Gabe's face was flushed, and she bathed it with cool water. He wore no shirt and she bathed his chest was well. The two women rolled him over on his stomach. When they were done, Merina stood.

"He should sleep the rest of the night. I will be back first thing in the morning." Her hands were shaking, and she tripped as she walked toward the door. Angel grabbed her and whispered in Spanish.

"Stay with him, Merina. Miguel is with Emilia. He will bring her here in the morning. Stay with my friend and help him to heal. It will do Gabe's heart good to see you in the morning."

Merina held Angel and cried into his shoulder. Rusty handed her a blanket and she walked back over to the bed. Cappy brought in an old rocker and Merina whispered a thank you before she sat down. She touched Gabe's head. Then she wrapped the blanket around herself and leaned back in the chair. Rusty quietly closed the door and everyone drifted back to their beds.

Sam and Nate were the only ones who were still awake. They took the jug of root beer down to the creek and threw rocks in as they talked for several more hours.

"Your brother is a powerful big man," Sam remarked as he took a drink.

Nate tossed a rock and then nodded. "He's always been strong. I have never seen anyone be able to calm him down like Merina did though. I thought we were going to have to tie him to the bed."

Eventually, the night chill took over and the two friends went back to the barn. Cappy heard them climb into their blankets and he smiled. *Nate found 'im a friend. Those two 'ill be lifetime buddies, shore 'nough.*

CHAPTER 60

A Change in Plans

LANCE WATCHED MIGUEL RIDE BY THE NEXT MORNING WITH EMILIA BEHIND HIM ON MERINA'S HORSE. He looked back at Molly.

"I think you ladies had better move to Plan B. Looks like maybe Gabe took a turn for the worse."

Molly hurried to the window.

Lance pointed at the disappearing rider. "Miguel just rode by with Emilia behind him. I heard a horse go by here twice last night running hard and I wondered. I'm guessing Miguel was sent to get Merina. That means that she won't be in any shape to watch a bunch of wild kids. Maybe you should turn them loose on Martha and Samuel."

Molly frowned and slowly nodded. "Think we should wait a day to go to Cheyenne?"

"That might be a good idea. I'll ride over this morning with two of the boys and see what's going on. Spur should be here before long and we can all go together."

"Can you send one of the hands to tell Beth so she doesn't make the trip unnecessarily?"

"I'll send Jonesy. He'll be glad to help out."

Lance strolled out of the house and Jonesy was soon riding out of the yard, headed west toward Rowdy's.

Molly was smiling when Lance came back in. "We certainly have a good crew of men. I am going to bake today. Do you want cookies or doughnuts? I think the men could use a treat."

Lance circled his hands around Molly's waist as he drawled, "The men? What about me? I think I deserve a treat." He buried his face in Molly's hair as he whispered, "My wife has been neglecting me lately."

Molly started to giggle. They were both laughing as the kids began to trickle in for breakfast. She looked around in surprise when Sam didn't appear.

"Is Sam still with Nate? Did you tell him he could stay a second night?"

Lance grinned. "Well, I didn't tell him he couldn't. Guess we are going to have to be more specific now that he has a fishing buddy. Do you want me to send him home or let him help today? You know he will want to be part of building that bunkhouse."

Molly studied Lance and then sighed. "Where did our little Sammy go? It won't be long before he wants to leave home for good."

Lance nodded and then his eyes twinkled as he whispered. "Guess we need to make another one, huh?"

Molly turned a deep red as she shushed him. She hurried to finish breakfast and the table was soon loud with children laughing and talking.

Lance picked up Livvy and kissed her. "What do you think, Livvy? Should Mommy have another baby?"

Livvy's blue eyes sparkled with excitement. "Two, Papa. She should have two. Larry has two babies in her tummy, and I think Mommy should have two!"

Lance's smile became bigger and Molly shook her head. She kissed Livvy's blond head as she hurried by. "Well, maybe Papa and I will talk about it. Now you eat your breakfast."

Lance's grin turned to a chuckle and he winked at Molly. "We sure will. Now who is going to help me this morning? I want to ride to Gabe's, and you will need to have your chore's done before 7:00 if you want to go along."

Paul was quiet for a moment and then looked at Lance seriously. "I'd like to ride over to Gabe's with you this morning. Nate is my friend too."

Lance studied Paul's serious face. The young boy was now eleven and was much quieter than Sam had ever been. He had taken Old Man McNary's death the hardest of all the grandchildren as well. Paul had never been told that he was the result of his mother's rape by some of Quantrill's raiders, and they had no intention of telling him. Only a select few family members knew he wasn't Lance's own blood—and Lance loved him every bit as much as the rest of the children.

He tousled Paul's hair. "You get your cow milked and you can go along." He grinned as Paul shoveled his food in and rushed to the barn.

Molly watched him go with a smile on her face. "Every mother should have at least one sweet boy," she whispered. She turned back to the table just in time to see Henry pull Abigail's pig tail. It jerked her head and she spilled her milk. The table was in chaos as Henry laughed and Abigail cried.

Lance grinned at Molly as he kissed her cheek. "We'll have that talk tonight." He was laughing as he sauntered out the door.

Molly glared at him and then began to straighten the children out. "Every meal is apologies and messes. Not once can we eat without someone crying or spilling something," she muttered as she handed Henry the rag to wipe up the floor. She finally sat down and stared at her cold eggs.

Livvy climbed up on Molly's lap and whispered, "I love you, Mommy." Molly's heart melted and she wrapped the little girl up. "I love you too, Livvy. And Abigail. And Henry." Paul was hurrying through the door slopping milk on the floor. "And Paul too," she added with a laugh.

Paul grinned at his mother and kissed her cheek before he dashed back outside to find his father.

CHAPTER 61

BEING NEIGHBORLY

SPUR ARRIVED AT THE ROCKING R BEFORE 7:00 A.M. and four riders headed south toward Gabe's ranch.

Paul rode beside his father and listened to the men talk. He loved to be included and unlike Sam, he listened more than he talked. He knew that the hands respected and liked his father. He was pleased to be part of the crew that was riding over to check on a neighbor.

One of the riders looked over at Lance and asked, "Who was riding that big black that went tearing by twice last night? I heard it the first time and then about five minutes later, it went by again headed back the other way."

Spur looked at Lance in surprise and then glanced over at Merina's house with a frown on his face.

Lance shrugged. "I heard that too but didn't get up to look."

The rider's name was Paul Short, but everyone called him Shorty. He snorted, "Well, he didn't go far past here an' that about put him at the teacher's house."

Spur was quiet a moment and then looked at Lance. "Think Gabe took a turn for the worse?"

Lance shrugged again. "I hope not. I reckon we'll find out soon enough." He grinned at the concerned faces and added, "Badger dropped off some of his potion there yesterday, so we know he'll be all right."

All the men laughed except Spur. He raised an eyebrow. "Potion?"

Shorty snorted. "Don't ask no more. You don't want to know what's in it in case they ever give it to you! Whatever it is, it's good stuff. I don't know of anyone who died after they was treated with it."

Spur frowned and looked toward Gabe's ranch. *Sounds like someone came to get Merina. Why would they get Merina? Larry was there and she knows some about medicine.*

The men were dragging out of the house as Lance's crew rode up. Rusty looked at them in surprise and then walked toward them with a grin on his face.

"You boys out for an early mornin' ride or jist lookin' fer breakfast?"

Lance chuckled and then nodded toward the house. "We came by to check on Gabe. I thought I'd leave some of these boys and see if they could help you get that foundation laid. Those rocks you are using are a darn big for such small fellows as yourselves."

Rusty and Angel laughed and then Rusty's face became serious. "The boss's fever spiked last night, an' we couldn't calm 'im. Miguel went fer Merina an' she managed to git 'im back in bed." He grinned as he added, "We gave 'im a big glass a Badger's potion an' he slept like a baby. 'Fore that, he intended to leave. We thought we was goin' to have to tie 'im down."

Spur studied Rusty's face and then looked toward the house. "I reckon I'll go look in on him."

Sam and Nate walked out of the barn rubbing their eyes. Lance looked them over and then asked dryly, "How late did the two of you stay up talking last night?"

Sam grinned as he looked over at Nate. "Well, Gabe woke everyone up with all his roaring around. When Merina finally got him settled down, we were wide awake. We went down to the creek. We drank the rest of the root beer and talked awhile."

Nate stifled a yawn and nodded in agreement. "It was late, Mr. Rankin, but I was sure glad Sam was here."

Lance nodded and hid his smile as he looked at both boys. He waved toward the pile of rocks. "Sam, you can help here today until suppertime and then you come on home. You be sure you are working and not cutting out to fish."

Sam looked irritated but Nate grinned. He poked his friend. "Let's go get some breakfast. Larry makes the best griddlecakes and I can smell them."

Spur knocked lightly on the bedroom door and poked his head in. A sleepy Merina looked at him in surprise.

"Spur! What are you doing here?"

"Some of us came by to help put the foundation up, remember? How's the patient?"

Merina leaned forward and felt Gabe's forehead. "He's much cooler than last night. He slept well. He is supposed to lay on his stomach so the wounds drain, but he keeps rolling over."

Spur walked over to where Gabe lay and stared down at his friend. He studied Merina's face for a moment and she slowly blushed.

"Why don't you go eat some breakfast. I can sit here for a little bit and give you a break."

Merina stood and wobbled a little as she dropped the blanket on the chair. Spur grabbed her and she sobbed into his shoulder. "I was so afraid last night. I thought he was going to die."

Spur patted her back and said nothing. His best friend was lying in bed with two holes in his stomach and it looked like maybe they were both sweet on the same girl. He looked over the top of Merina's head to Gabe and then back down at her. His heart pinched at the thought. He led her toward the kitchen and sat her down as he smiled at Larry.

"Better get some food in her and make her get some rest. I'll sit with Gabe for a bit."

Spur shut the door behind him and sat down next to his friend.

"Well, buddy, you didn't tell me we were both sweet on the same girl."

Gabe stirred a little and then opened his eyes. He stared at Spur a moment and slowly grinned.

"That is not the face I was hoping to see when I woke up. What are you doing here?"

"Just checking on you. When horses go running by at midnight, people get concerned."

Gabe frowned. "I remember getting out of bed and then Merina came. I don't remember much after that." He pushed on his temple and added, "I do have a headache though. Almost feels like a hangover and I haven't had one of those in years. My fever must have come up. Sure hope I didn't talk."

Spur laughed and agreed. "You lose your muzzle when you have a fever. Whatever you said, you meant so I hope it was nice."

Gabe laughed and the two visited until Larry came in. "Time to change your poultices. I made Merina lie down so I will change them this time." She smiled at the tall man sitting in the rocking chair. "A rocking chair suits you, Spur."

Spur chuckled as he stood. "I'll check in on you later, Gabe. We are going to work on your bunkhouse foundation today." Angel poked his head in the open door and Spur added loudly, "Some of those rocks are almost too much for your scrawny cowboys."

Angel spread his hands wide. "Si, Señor. These hands were made for caressing women and horses. Not so much for lifting large rocks and rolls of wire. My days here have been difficult."

Gabe tried to laugh and winced. He gripped the hand that Spur offered him. "Thanks for coming by. You're a good friend."

Emilia came racing into the room and Spur grabbed her before she could jump on Gabe. She kissed Gabe's cheek and put her little hands around his face. "Nina told me that you were sick, Señor Gabe. I don't want you to be sick."

Gabe kissed her little hand and smiled at her. "I am going to be just fine, Emilia. Now you go play."

Spur took her hand and she skipped out of the room beside him. "That is my Señor Gabe. He is my friend."

Spur nodded and answered slowly, "Yes, he is my friend too."

CHAPTER 62

THE TRUTH COMES OUT

THE HOUSE WAS QUIET WHEN MERINA AWOKE. She could hear men's voices outside and she peered out the window. They were moving rocks and stacking them onto the foundation for Gabe's bunkhouse. She found a pan and poured some water in it. She sponged herself off and then stared at the mirror as she shook her head. The pretty face that looked back at her looked tired. Her eyes were red, and her hair was a mess. Merina found Larry's hairbrush and brushed out her long hair. She rebraided it and straightened her clothes before she knocked softly on Gabe's door. No one answered and she went in quietly.

Gabe was sleeping and she put her hand on his forehead. He was warmer than before.

"This time, we will not wait so long with the potion." She looked in the can that held the moss and it was nearly gone.

"Gabe, I am going to get moss and then we will change your bandages."

The man never responded, and Merina hurried out of the house. The creek wasn't far away, and the boys had told her last night that there was plenty of moss.

Spur straightened up and watched Merina hurry back into the house. Angel stopped and watched as well.

"Looks like Gabe's fever might have come back up."

"Sí, Señor, but my sister, she is a difficult woman and she will not give up until he is better."

Spur said nothing as they lifted the rock into place. Then he paused and looked directly at Angel. "Gabe sweet on Merina?"

Angel paused and looked away. He finally turned his dark eyes on Spur. "I think, Señor, that is for you to discuss with your amigo. It is not for me to say. You ask me about my sister and two men who are my friends. I do not think I will discuss this with you. Now come, we have more rocks."

Merina appeared in the doorway. "Spur, can you come in here please and bring some root beer? Gabe would like to see you."

Angel pointed toward the icehouse and Spur lifted a jug off the shelf. He carried it inside. Merina had a large glass of something sitting on the table beside two empty glasses. He set the root beer down and sniffed the air. "What is that terrible smell?"

Merina shushed him and spoke quietly. "That is Badger's potion. Gabe thinks we are all drinking root beer. Come and have a drink with your friend."

Gabe was awake and was trying to get out of bed. He glared at Merina and then motioned toward Spur. "Help me out of this bed. Nature is calling and Merina is not going to help me."

Merina fled to the other bedroom and Spur helped Gabe to the door. He looked around as he finished. "Is that root beer? Badger must have liked that stuff. He had jugs of it everywhere." He staggered as he tried to walk through the kitchen and Spur caught him.

"Easy, Partner. I don't want you going down on me. I'm not sure I am man enough to hold you up."

Merina appeared and helped Spur to ease him onto the bed. She handed him the glass of Badger's potion and then gave Spur a glass of root beer.

Gabe smelled it and wrinkled his nose. "This stuff doesn't smell right."

Spur held up his glass. "Here's to you, Gabe, and to new beginnings." He took a big drink and Gabe grinned as he tipped up his glass. He drank it halfway down and smacked his lips.

"That is sure good stuff even if it doesn't smell quite right." He drained the rest of the glass and tried to lay back on the bed.

Merina grabbed his legs and swung them up on the bed while Spur eased his shoulders down.

Gabe grinned loosely at Spur and winked at Merina. "Isn't she just the prettiest little gal you've ever seen?"

Spur studied his friend and then looked over at Merina. He slowly nodded, "I reckon she sure is."

"Merina, when I get out of this bed, I am going to come courting and this time, I'm not waiting." His eyes were getting glassy as he looked up at Spur.

He winked at Merina again and whispered loudly to Spur, "I'm going to ask her to marry me. I'll take my harmonica. She makes my heart sing." His eyes rolled back in his head and once again, he passed out.

Merina blushed a deep red and Spur said nothing. He drank the rest of his root beer, picked up the glasses and quietly left the room.

Tears were leaking from Merina's eyes. "Gabe, why do you have to talk that way? Don't be saying things like that." She sponged off his face and his chest and then kissed his cheek. "Oh, Gabe. Please get well." She said a silent prayer and then sat back in the rocking chair. When Larry came in with dinner, both Gabe and Merina were asleep.

CHAPTER 63

NO SECRETS LEFT

WHEN GABE AWOKE, MERINA WAS SLEEPING IN THE ROCKER. He studied her face and frowned at the tear tracks. Her riding skirt and blouse looked like she had slept in them. His frown became deeper. "She spent the night here. I must have gotten worse. And who knows what I said," he growled softly to himself. *Beautiful Merina.* Gabe closed his eyes and drifted off into a peaceful sleep.

When he awoke again, Merina was gone, and it was dark outside. Larry came hurrying in with a plate of food.

"Are you hungry? Doc said you could eat once your fever broke and it broke this afternoon." She helped him to sit up and then sat down beside him with a big smile.

"It is good to see you awake, Gabe. You had all of us worried. Your fever came up Sunday around midnight and we couldn't get it down. You were trying to leave and finally, Angel sent Miguel for Merina. She talked you back into bed and stayed here until late this afternoon. Spur took Emilia and her back home after we all ate supper."

Her smile widened as she added, "Wait until you see what they all did today. Your rock foundation is up and ready for you to start on the bunkhouse!"

Gabe looked at her in surprise. "I vaguely remember Spur being here. Who else helped?"

"Shorty and another of Lance's hands. I think his name was Chancy. Lance's boys, Paul and Sam helped too. They are both little workers. Lance thought it might take two days, but they finished before supper and everyone has gone home."

Gabe nodded as he chewed. "Larry, I am glad you stayed around for a while. I'm not sure what we would have done without you and Rusty. I just know that I am going to miss you when you leave."

Larry smiled and leaned forward to kiss his cheek. "Well, Rusty and I talked it over. We are going to stay if you will let us live in Chet's house. We hadn't signed the papers yet to buy that little ranch in Kansas and after the last two days, we decided that our family is here. We aren't going anywhere."

Rusty's face appeared in the doorway. "Now don't be a tellin' 'im all our plans. I won't have nothin' to negotiate with." He walked on into the bedroom and grinned at Gabe. "Welcome back, Boss. You had us a little worried."

"High fever?"

"Yep. Merina brung it down."

"I talked?"

"Shore did. To her an' to Spur."

Gabe was quiet. He looked at Rusty and shook his head. "No secrets left, are there?"

"Nope, but I reckon its best this way. An' it come from y'all so we ain't responsible.

"Now let's talk about what y'all want done this week. We cin start hayin' that little patch a grass yonder by Chet's pond. Ya talked a cuttin' that off an' stackin' it in his barn. Or we cin start on the bunkhouse."

Gabe chewed a while and then pointed with his fork. "Let's get the haying done. The bunkhouse can wait but that hay needs to be in the barn. Besides, that mortar will be best if it sits for a while before the walls are put up." He tried to move and groaned. "I hate being laid up with so much work to do."

Rusty chuckled, "Well, ya better figger on somethin' to do 'cause Doc says no work fer two weeks. And y'all's s'posed to be sleepin' on yore durn stomach fer five days. Ya ain't been a doin' that so ya better start. Doc wants those holes to drain."

Gabe's face drew down in a frown and Rusty began laughing. "What's the matter, Boss?

"Ain't ya got nothin' ya like to do in yore spare time?"

"Never had any spare time. Just work and sleep, and I'm about done with sleeping."

Rusty chuckled and shook Badger's jar of potion. "Reckon y'all could drink more a this. It knocked ya out fer 'most six hours. 'Course ya had a headache when ya waked up."

"I remember drinking root beer with some of you, but nothing after that."

"Naw, *we* drank root beer. Y'all drank this. Merina tricked ya into drinkin' it." Rusty's blue eyes were full of laughter. "Y'all was a roarin' around an' Angel sent Miguel to get Merina 'bout midnight on Sunday. She settled ya right down. That gal's a bossy little woman, fer sure." He grinned as he added, "An' ya took orders from 'er meek as a puppy. Plumb whipped, ya was."

Gabe growled around his food but when his friends started laughing, he grinned.

"I don't think I can be held responsible for what I did or said when I was out of my head."

Larry patted his hand and stood. "I don't know, Boss. You said some things that might mean something to someone. Come on, Rusty. Let's go to bed. No one in this house has gotten much sleep for two nights."

CHAPTER 64

WINNERS AND LOSERS

SPUR AND MERINA WERE BOTH QUIET ON THEIR RIDE HOME. Spur looked over at her several times and then frowned as he looked forward again. When they arrived at Lance's barn, Merina stopped but Spur shook his head.

"I'll bring the horse back down--unless you want to walk up."

Libby was waving at Emilia from the doorway and the little girl slid off Merina's horse.

"Can I stay and play awhile, Nina? Please?"

Molly waved from behind her daughter. "Why don't you let Emilia spend the night and you can come down tomorrow when you wake up. I'm guessing you could use some rest."

Merina paused and then nodded. "Thank you, Molly. It has been a long two days."

She stepped off her horse. "I think I will walk to the house." She paused as she looked up at Spur. "You can join me if you want."

Spur pulled the saddle off Merina's horse and helped her to rub him down. She laughed as the horse tried to nibble on her. "We could probably turn him loose and he would find his way home, but I will take him back tomorrow. This is Amigo. He's another horse we raised from a colt. He's Angel's horse."

When they were done, they turned toward Merina's house. Spur cleared his throat. "Merina—"

"Spur, I'm sorry. A lot of things have changed in four years."

"Including my old friend being in love with you. Did you know that?"

Merina paused and looked away. "Gabe was in love with another woman when I met him. She died while he was on the trail to Dodge City. He hadn't known her long so maybe it was more of a dream of what could have been that he was in love with. Either way, it was difficult for him." She looked over at Spur and softly added, "Gabe had me read her last letter to him and I saw him through her eyes. In a way, it was Grace who helped me to see Gabe as the man he is. And then, I fell in love with him. I didn't tell him because I wanted it to be me he saw, not Grace. I wouldn't let him court me until I was sure.

"Then you showed up. Gabe was sure that I still loved you because of a talk we had the night of the dance lessons. Both of our hearts had been broken, and we shared some stories. I told him about you, but I wouldn't tell him your name. I certainly had no idea that you lived here or that you and Gabe were friends." Tears filled her eyes.

"Gabe was hurt because he stayed home from the dance. He told me that you had the inside lane since you and I had courted, and I had been in love with you at one time." Her eyes were dark as she whispered, "He stepped aside because you were his partner, but he has never said anything to me like he did yesterday when his fever was high.

"I needed to see if my feelings for you were still there." She smiled up at Spur and tears sparkled in the corners of her dark eyes.

"You are just as fun as I remembered. You make me laugh and I enjoy myself when I am with you." She stopped and took his arm, "But it is Gabe who makes my heart sing. I'm sorry, Spur."

Spur was surprised at the prick of pain that went through his heart, but he forced himself to relax. He slowly chuckled and Merina looked at him in surprise.

"You know, Gabe was never the lady's man that I was. I usually took whatever girl he showed interest in, sometimes on purpose and sometimes by accident. He was too intense for women back then. Of course, the women that we met in the saloons just wanted to have a good time. Still, I sure never expected old Gabe to win a girl I was sweet on." He looped the horse's reins over his arm and shoved his hands in his pockets.

"Merina, we have been friends for some time. I reckon if I had really wanted to, I would have found the words to say to you. I didn't, you moved on, and that's that. I'd like to stay friends with Gabe and to do that, you and I need to be able to get along with each other. Do you suppose that we can still be friends if I promise to behave and act like a friend?" He grinned down at her. "Shoot, maybe you can name your firstborn after me."

Merina was silent a moment before she answered quietly. "You are Gabe's campañero and you will always be my friend…but I do not think I will name a girl child Spur." Her dark eyes were sparkling with humor and Spur laughed.

"No, I don't reckon you should do that."

Spur left Merina at her door and rode away into the evening light. He looked back once, and she waved at him before she went inside. He frowned as he thought about that night four years ago when he had left Texas on the run.

"Why didn't I write her? Was I so afraid of settling down that I left her behind?" He shook his head.

"That would be a mighty cowardly thing to do but it sure looks like that's what I did. Well, Gabe, you're the winner, and we both know that you will treat that little gal right."

A Visit from the Sheriff

MERINA SADDLED MASCOTA AND HAWK. She led them and Amigo toward the Rankin's house. Emilia was eating breakfast when she tied the horses to the hitching rail.

Molly looked up with a smile and waved her arm at Merina. "Come in and sit down. You just as well eat with us."

Merina sat down with a smile and kissed Emilia's cheek. "Are you ready to go see Señor Gabe today? I need to take Amigo back to Angel."

Excitement spread over Emilia's face. "Yes! I want to see Señor Gabe. I hope he isn't sick anymore. I love my Señor Gabe."

Merina laughed and kissed her sister's cheek again. "And he loves you. You and Livvy can play for just a few minutes and then we are leaving."

Molly studied Merina's face and the younger woman looked away as a blush rose from her neck to her cheeks. Molly laughed and shook her head. "Well, I guess Spur came in second after all. Beth and I weren't sure which you were going to choose." She whispered, "We like both men and we are glad we didn't have to decide!"

Merina laughed as she looked out the door. "The heart does not listen to the mind, but I am glad too. If Señor Spur had asked me to run away with him four years ago, I might have, and I am thankful that I didn't do that either.

"I don't plan to stay at Gabe's long. Do you need any help today with your canning? I have some free time today if you don't mind Emilia running underfoot."

"That would be great. The green beans are coming on and I want to get them out before the grasshoppers eat holes in all of them." She looked at Merina over her shoulder as she stacked up the dishes. "Do you think you can tell Gabe's men about Friday? I know they have been cutting hay and building fence. It would be nice if they knew what we are planning. Tell Larry we will take care of the food. She can maybe have something for us to set food on."

Merina slowly nodded. "Chet had a nice picnic table at his place. Maybe we could bring that over to use. I will talk to Rusty and Angel." She finished clearing the table and the two women visited as they washed up the dishes.

Emilia was excited to see Gabe and came quickly when Merina called. They waved at the Rankins and Merina led the way toward Gabe's house.

Rusty was loading the wagon with haying equipment when they rode into the yard and he walked over to Merina with a grin on his face.

"Y'all is jist the gal I wanted to see. Gabe's gettin' bored an' threatened to foller us today. Mebbie y'all cin talk to 'im fer a time till he gets tired."

Gabe's voice growled at them from the doorway.

"Don't you go making plans on my part. Besides, I am about all rested up. I din't know a fellow could get so tired of laying around."

Emilia slid off Hawk and rushed toward Gabe. She grabbed his legs and smiled up at him. "Señor Gabe, you aren't sick anymore?"

Gabe smiled down at her and then looked over at Merina. "No, I am almost healed, thanks to your sister."

Nate was leading the horses from the barn. He tied them at the hitching rail and tipped his hat to Merina. "Morning, Miss Merina.

I hope you can keep Gabe occupied for a while. And don't help him saddle a horse. He can't do it himself yet." Nate's grin was huge as he glanced at his big brother.

Gabe glared at him. "Don't be getting too cocky. Another couple of days and I intend to be back on a horse."

Merina snorted. "Your horse still has stitches. I think you don't need to ride until Buck is ready. That is a fair rule."

Cappy was walking from the chicken house and pointed toward the road. "We expectin' the sheriff this mornin'?"

The men turned to watch Sheriff Boswell as he rode up. Merina's face paled and Gabe stepped off the porch to stand next to her.

Sheriff Nathaniel Boswell was a man of few words. He had little love for tax collecting or serving warrants on drummed up charges. The wire he had received that morning was from Texas and asked him to follow up on a lead that a murder suspect might be hiding out around Cheyenne. The woman, the wire claimed, had knifed an unarmed man, stolen some horses, and headed north on the train where the stolen horses were sold in Dodge City. Witnesses had seen her in the presence of some men who were headed north with a herd.

The sheriff chewed on the end of his long mustache and snorted. He had received that wanted poster nearly a month ago. He hung it on the wall inside the sheriff's office, but it could have been one of twenty women in Cheyenne let alone in Wyoming. He thought about taking it down, but the picture was of a pretty woman, and men sometimes stopped by his office to talk just so they could look at the poster.

He sized up the group of men watching him as he rode into the yard of Gabe Hawkins's Diamond H ranch. Two tough-looking men and a tall boy leaned against a wagon full of fencing supplies. An older man who looked as tough as old rawhide stood by the corner of the house. One of his hands was hidden, and the sheriff was sure a gun was within reach of it. In addition, there was a pretty young pregnant woman and a beautiful woman of Spanish heritage. His eyes rested on her and then moved to the small girl who stood close to Gabe.

He pulled up his horse and smiled at Gabe as he raised his hand to the group.

"Howdy, Boys." The sheriff tipped his hat and nodded as he added, "Ladies."

Gabe reached up his hand. "Morning, Sheriff. You are late for breakfast, but we might be able to find you a little something if you want to get down."

Sheriff Boswell studied the big man in front of him and shook his head. "Nope, I heard about your accident and thought I would stop by to see how you were getting along."

When there was no answer, the sheriff added, "And to show you this." He handed Gabe a wanted poster picturing a woman.

Gabe studied it and then handed it back to the sheriff. "We only have two women here, Sheriff, and they are both prettier than that." The men grinned and Gabe added, "This poster is from Texas. What makes you think she is here?"

Sheriff Boswell shrugged. "Just following leads. She killed some fellow down on the Brazos and somebody claimed to have picked up her trail in Cheyenne. Thought I'd better check it out."

Gabe nodded slowly. "Heard about that. Word was the fellow was trying to force his way into her house. No men folks around. Dangerous for a woman alone when that happens."

The sheriff's eyes drifted from Gabe to the hard-looking men who stood casually watching him.

"Doesn't look like there would be much of a case. She must have killed a big man's kin for someone to work to track her this far." Gabe's eyes looked like cold pieces of glass as he stared at the sheriff.

Sheriff Boswell chewed on his mustache and frowned as he nodded. "Yep, the son of a big man down around Dallas. The fellow who died was riding for the Millett brothers when this happened."

The sheriff looked over at Merina and asked casually, "Just how did you get to Cheyenne?"

Gabe's face went still as he stepped forward. "Sheriff, you go ahead and check those rail records. We were in Dodge City with that herd on May 3rd. We were at a wedding that evening. Some of the hands left that day and started part of the herd toward Ogallala with John Kirkham. The rest of us left on Sunday. Witnesses including Badger McCune will put Miss Montero with us in Dodge and Ogallala."

Gabe stared at the sheriff as he added softly. "I think, Sheriff, that this deal has a whole lot more to do with who died than with what happened. Now if you feel inclined to take this further, why every man here and Larry too, will be glad to testify as to who was on that trail and how long they were there." He added grimly, "And we can probably find another fifty men who would testify the same even though they were nowhere close to us or our cattle."

Sheriff Boswell's blue eyes drilled into Gabe and the tall cowboy stared back. Slowly, the sheriff relaxed and chuckled. He sat back in his saddle, wadded up the poster and dropped it to the ground.

"I reckon you could at that. Well, like I said, I needed to check it out. I'll send back my report that the women here didn't fit in with their timeline." He turned his horse around and called over his shoulder, "I'll take you up on that meal another day. Ladies." He tipped his hat again and rode back up the road.

Merina was shaking and Gabe put his right arm around her. "It's over. He knew he didn't have a case anyway," he whispered as he pulled her close to him. He staggered as he started to turn around and Rusty grabbed for him.

"I think ya been hero 'nough fer one day, Boss. Y'all keep gettin' up like this an' them holes 'ill take twice as long to heal. Merina, ya git him back to the house an' in that bed."

Gabe didn't argue as Merina helped him into the house. She eased him down onto the bed and swung his feet up. She grabbed the can that had some moss in it and headed for the door.

"I am going to get some moss and change your bandage."

CHAPTER 66

Planning a Surprise

ERINA'S CHEST WAS TIGHT WHEN SHE WALKED BACK OUTSIDE. Rusty was climbing up on the wagon and she stopped by him.

"Do you think you could bring that picnic table at Chet's back here when you come home today? Gabe could sit at that and at least be outside. And the Rankins as well as other neighbors will all be here on Friday for Independence Day. They are going to help build the bunkhouse and finish it in one day. Molly called it a barn-raising." She looked over at Larry who was staring in surprise.

"It is a surprise for Gabe. Molly said to tell you they will all take care of the food—you just need to have some boards and barrels set up to put everything on." She paused and pointed at a flat spot under a large tree. "Maybe we could put the picnic table there and it could be used for food as well as for sitting?"

Rusty nodded in agreement and Merina headed for the creek. Larry hurried to catch up.

"Merina, those things that Gabe said—they were true for all of us." She put her arm through Merina's and smiled at her. "That's what family is."

Merina shivered. "I'm glad that Gabe talked. I was terrified."

Larry whispered, "And he did it without lying. Now come on, I'll help you find some moss."

Gabe was resting when Merina slipped into his room. He woke up when she began to untie the bandage. He put his hand over hers and smiled at her. Merina went still and then smiled back at him.

"Thank you for talking to the sheriff. I was afraid he would arrest me."

"Boswell is a good man. He's a tough sheriff and he was just doing his job. He had to come out, but he knew he didn't have a case. No jury would convict a woman for trying to protect herself." He grinned at her. "But that didn't stop him from trying to trick you into answering his question. He already knew there was no record of you taking the train, and I think he was more than happy to throw out that poster."

Emilia came running into the room. "Look, Señor Gabe! I found a picture of Nina on the ground!"

Gabe flattened out the crumpled poster and studied it. He looked at Merina closely and then shook his head. "No, Nina is much prettier than this. Still, I think I will hang this on my wall so I can look at it every day." He winked at Merina and she laughed.

He was quiet as Merina cleaned the wound and repacked the moss. When she was done, she pulled the bandage tight and sat back.

Gabe studied her face and smiled. "I like having you here. You make this house a home."

Merina's heart beat heavy in her chest and she put her finger over his lips. "Shush, Gabe. You need to rest. Sleeping will make you heal faster."

He took her fingers and kissed them. "How is my horse?"

Merina laughed. "He is almost as impatient as you are to get outside. He is healing well. Badger gave me some salve to put on him. I will take the stitches out next week. Then I will bring him back here. I think the salve is making the scar smaller." She pulled a small can out of her pocket.

"I don't know what's in it, but he made it. Unlike his potion, this smells quite nice."

Gabe sniffed it. "I smell lilacs and sage. The rest of the smells I don't recognize." His eyes were dark as he stared up at her. "Like you. You always smell like lilacs."

Merina blushed. "I help Molly make soap and she adds dried lilacs to her soap mixture before it sets up." She stood and smiled down at him.

"I must go. I need to get Emilia home. She has been running wild for three days and she needs a nap."

"Thank you, Merina. You have kind hands. Perhaps I will see you tomorrow?"

"Perhaps."

She was gone quickly, and the faint scent of lilacs lingered in the air. Gabe smiled as he drifted off to sleep.

CHAPTER 67

TOO MUCH TIME

THE NEXT TWO DAYS WENT QUICKLY. The parents had voted to start school on August 1 and then take the month of September off since that month was roundup time for all the ranches. Most of the older children would be helping to gather and sort cattle.

Merina had much work to do before school started. She was still working on projects for the older students. "I want Sam and Nate to love school as much as the younger children."

Most mornings she helped Molly. Then she worked on the classroom or on lesson plans while Emilia took a nap.

"Beth is coming over this afternoon and we are baking if you want to come down," Molly told her when she arrived Thursday morning. "Why don't you go check on Gabe this morning? Leave Emilia here and then just stop in on your way back home.

"And see if there is anything special that he likes. Lance loves pie and Rowdy's favorite is chocolate cake. We can add one more thing to our baking list if Gabe has a favorite."

Merina's face flushed with excitement as she nodded. She ran to the barn and saddled Mascota. Buck was pawing at the door. She hesitated and then hooked a rope on him.

"You could use a little exercise," she told the big stallion as he nickered excitedly. Merina carefully checked his stitches. The stitches were holding, and the cut was healing. As she led him down the lane, he jerked and tugged on his rope.

"You want to run don't you, boy. I'm not sure that is such a good idea but maybe the last little way. We'll see." She held him back as long as she could. Finally, when the ranch was directly in front of them, she dropped his rope.

Buck snorted and threw up his head. He raced down the road and into the yard, nickering loudly.

Gabe appeared in the doorway just as Buck galloped up, and his smile became wider when he saw Merina.

She laughed softly. "I'm not sure, Gabe, but it almost looks like you are happier to see your horse than me."

Gabe grinned as he petted Buck. The stallion dropped his head over Gabe's shoulder and nuzzled him. Gabe's eyes twinkled as he studied her. "Maybe if you cuddled up to me like he does, I'd change my mind on that."

Merina's cheeks turned a deep red and she muttered in Spanish. Gabe laughed. He pointed at the picnic table under the tree. "Thanks for having the fellows bring that up. It sure beats staying in the house all day. Want to get down and stay a spell? Or did you just come to bring Buck back?"

"Maybe for a little bit. I am helping Molly today. I will take Buck back with me though. I want to take his stitches out next week and then he can come home for good. I just thought you might like to see him."

Gabe was quiet as he looked out over his ranch.

"This is a fine place to sit, Merina. Nate and I own everything you can see in three directions. That's a mighty fine feeling." He added quietly, "I sure didn't think that would ever happen." He studied her face for a moment before he continued.

"Spur came by. He was on his way up to Montana to pick up some horses from the Nez Perce. We had a nice visit."

Merina's neck slowly turned pink and Gabe chuckled.

"Seems the two of you came to an understanding."

"Spur is a fine man and a good friend to both of us."

Gabe nodded. "So now what?"

Merina stared at him a moment and then she looked away.

Gabe chuckled and patted the seat beside him. "How about you come over here and sit next to me so we can talk about this. I'd come to you, but I move so slow that you could be gone by the time I made it over there."

Merina hesitated and then slid up next to Gabe. He put his arm around her and pulled her closer. "Now this is just about perfect."

She smiled up at him and Gabe kissed her. He leaned in for another kiss and then gasped with pain as it stretched his side.

Merina laughed softly. "I think perhaps it is a good thing that you can't move so quickly or bend so far."

"I'll just have to settle with some cuddling for now. So what are we going to do, Merina?"

She smiled up at him. "You haven't even courted me yet. I think that should be the next thing and then we will go from there."

Gabe grinned as he looked down at her and drawled, "So what does a fellow do when he courts a woman? I'm not sure I have ever stuck around long enough to know."

Merina shook her head. "Where did that shy man go who has been hanging around for the last two months?"

"I kicked him out. He moved too slow and my girl almost left me for another fellow. I'm picking up the pace."

Merina laughed as she scooted away from him. "I am not going to sit here and spoon with you. What if the men come back?"

Gabe's eyes were dancing as he asked, "So Emilia was right? You only spoon in the dark? Remember, she announced that at Rusty's wedding."

Merina blushed a dark red and she scooted further away. "I do remember and that isn't exactly what I told her." She went around the table and sat down across from him. "I think a little distance is a good thing."

Gabe's face was serious as he looked across the table at her. "What do you want, Merina? What is the next step in your life—past teaching, I mean."

Merina was quiet for a moment before she answered. "Angel showed me the papers that he signed in Texas. We need to go over them with your lawyer friend, but we were hoping you could go with us. Perhaps when you can ride again, we will go to Cheyenne. Angel wants to buy a ranch and then I will go to live with him. Miguel does not care so much. He wants to be free to come and to go, but Angel and I want a home."

"Maybe we should become ranching partners and pool our money," Gabe suggested. "We'd have to buy another ranch right away though because Rusty and Larry are moving over to Chet's once I get back on my feet." His eyes were intense as he studied her face.

"Or you could just marry me and then our families would be partners anyway."

Merina's eyes sparkled with humor. "You already asked me to marry you several days ago. Of course, you were delirious so maybe you didn't mean it."

"I reckon I meant it." He chuckled as he put his hand over hers. "And how did you answer?"

Merina rolled her eyes. "I didn't have to answer because you passed out."

Gabe shook his head. "Well, that was romantic, wasn't it? I guess I'll have to do that over again. Maybe I'll just spring it on you when you're not expecting it and you might say yes without thinking."

Merina laughed and stood up. "I am going to go. Please call your horse so I can take him back with me."

Gabe stood and followed her over to Mascota. He stiffly helped her up on her horse and handed her Buck's lead rope.

Merina smiled down at him as her eyes sparkled with humor. "I think, Señor Hawkins, that you have too much time on your hands right now. Too much time to plan and scheme. Perhaps I should bring Emilia with me next time so I know you will behave."

Gabe grinned and agreed. "Well that would be just fine. You bring her along. I love little Emilia almost as much as I love you."

Merina laughed softly. "I do have a question for you though. We are baking at Molly's this afternoon and she asked me to find out what your favorite treat was. Lance likes pie and Rowdy loves chocolate cake. She wondered if you had a favorite."

Gabe looked out over the ranch and smiled. "When I was just a little fellow, my ma used to make cookies. She made some with spices in them and sometimes, she'd put little pieces of dried apples in them. Those were my favorite. Sicily Wagner used to make them for me that way too. I've had them once since I left Waggoners. Hardly anyone makes them and for sure not with apples in them." He chuckled as he winked at her, "I'm a simple fellow but I like most anything with apples in it. If we had plenty of apples, Ma would make baked apples with crumbles on top. That was a rare thing though, as we usually couldn't afford the sugar.

"How about you? What do you like?"

"Have you ever eaten sopapillas? My mamá used to make them. They are little like a little pillow of bread. We eat them warm with honey. They become hollow inside when you fry them."

"So they could be filled with apples?"

Merina studied his face and began to laugh. "I suppose they could. I have never eaten them that way."

She started to turn her horse and Gabe held Mascota's head. "Will you be back tomorrow?"

Merina was quiet as Gabe released Mascota. She clucked to Buck and turned back up the lane. She called over her shoulder, "Perhaps Emilia and I will come tomorrow to look in on you....Perhaps." She waved at him and rode out of the yard.

CHAPTER 68

PARTY PLANS

RUSTY HAD MADE A TRIP TO TOWN THAT DAY TO PICK UP SUPPLIES AND HE CAME HOME WITH A DIFFERENT WAGON. It was certainly not an old wagon, and Gabe laughed.

"What poor sucker did you steal that from?"

Rusty pretended to be horrified. "Feller brought a herd up from Texas an' was selling it fer his boss. He didn't know nothin' 'bout wagons or that it was a Studebaker. I said I needed one fer my little wife." He pointed over at Larry who rolled her eyes. "That feller sold it fer $50 an' now Larry an' me have us a nice wagon. Too bad it goes with us when we leave."

"And the chuck box?"

"Rooster in at the livery let me stash it there. Said he might know a feller who wanted one." He pointed toward the back of the wagon.

"I picked up some roofin' supplies an' Badger 'ill bring out yore wagon in the mornin' with more. We jist as well start on that bunkhouse tomorrow since we finished hayin'."

Gabe studied the wagon and slowly nodded. "That should get us started. Did you charge it to the ranch?"

Rusty nodded. "Since we was gettin' so much, I told J.P. Holliday at the lumber yard to take the bill to Levi. The judge would settle it up."

Gabe frowned and Rusty grinned at him. "An' yeah, that 'ill cost ya a little, but I don't trust that Banker Bob as much as I trust Levi so pay it an' be done with it. I ain't on yore ranch account an' ya won't be ridin' fer a time."

Rusty didn't add that two more wagons of supplies would be coming over with the Rankins on Friday or that Samuel was also bringing a load of wood from Cheyenne. Gabe had no idea all the places his business partner had been in town. Rusty had had a productive morning.

The women baked all afternoon. Merina made sopapillas and filled them with some apples that Molly had canned. The women all tried them and decided they were quite tasty.

"Gabe is feeling better?" Molly asked casually.

Merina nodded. "Yes, and he has too much time on his hands."

Molly paused in her stirring to look up at Merina and Beth started giggling. "I know how Rowdy acts when he has too much free time."

Merina stared from one woman to the other in surprise and then slowly blushed.

Molly laughed at her. "Just say yes, Merina, and be done with it. You know he won you over long ago."

Merina ducked her head and muttered in Spanish, "I didn't know I was quite so obvious."

Beth replied in Spanish, "Oh I think we are all aware of how you feel." She hugged Merina and laughed again. "Just let us know when you need help planning the wedding."

Lance stepped through the door, sniffing at the smell of pie. He looked around the room and his eyes settled on Merina. "Wedding? What wedding? Guess Gabe must have kicked his game up a notch since he's been laid up."

Molly and Beth were laughing, and Merina tried to keep the red from showing in her face. She coolly passed the pan of sopapillas to Lance. "Perhaps you would like to try one of these, Señor Lance. It is a food we make often in Texas. We added apples today."

Lance forgot all about the teasing as he ate the new treat. "That is almost like a piece of pie you can eat while you walk." He strolled back outside munching contentedly, and Molly laughed.

"Very smooth, Merina. That will work on the men, but it won't work on Beth or me. Of course, we will see for ourselves tomorrow!"

Merina laughed along with them. "I think that the two of you miss very little that happens around here."

Merina bathed Emilia and put her to bed early since they would have a long day on Friday.

"But I'm not tired yet and it is still daylight," Emilia pouted.

"We have a party tomorrow at Señor Gabe's and you need to be rested up. There will be lots of kids to play with, including Livvy and Pauline. Now close your eyes while I sing to you."

Emilia was soon asleep, and Merina sat down on the porch to enjoy the evening. The night was cool, and the sky was bright with stars.

"What do I want? I do want a home, but I don't want it with Angel. I want it with you, Gabe," she murmured into the night. "When you ask me without joking, I will say yes."

CHAPTER 69

A New Bunkhouse

MERINA HAD HER HORSE SADDLED AND READY BY 6:00 A.M. ON FRIDAY, JULY 4TH. Everyone was meeting at Lance and Molly's so the wagons and workers would leave from there.

Wagons and horses just kept coming. Merina stared at the crowd in surprise.

"I do not think that we fixed enough food for all of these people."

"Oh, we'll be fine. All the women will bring plenty of food. It will be like a giant picnic. We will set it all out and by the time everyone shares what they brought, there will be leftovers." Molly laughed.

"We have potlucks often, but this looks like it might be a little bigger than usual. Word is out that Gabe is laid up and this is what neighbors do. Of course, some of these cowboys came because they are hoping to see single women while others heard that there might be bear sign. Martha always brings that."

Merina was going to saddle Hawk, but Emilia wanted to ride in Rowdy's wagon with Livvy and Pauline. The older children were on horseback, but Beth squeezed the two little girls into the wagon beside her. Rowdy put one-year old Emmaline in front of him and the parade of wagons and riders was ready to move out.

Some of the cowboys were jostling each other to ride next to Merina. She kept her horse close to Beth's wagon and Rowdy laughed as the riders tried to look nonchalant.

Levi and Sadie joined them on the road. Levi's wagon was full of supplies as well. Doc and Josie were the last to join the happy group as they headed south to Gabe's ranch.

Gabe was in the doorway of his house and walked out into the yard when the first wagon pulled in. When he saw the large group of riders and the full wagons, he stared at them in surprise.

Badger was the first to arrive and he pulled Gabe's wagon right up to the foundation of the bunkhouse.

"Now don't ya be a standin' there. Call yer boys out here ta help me unload these here supplies or we's a goin' ta have wagons backed up all the way ta the Rankins'."

Angel, Miguel, Rusty, and Nate appeared with grins on their faces.

"Jist stand back, Boss, an' let us git this here wagon unloaded. Ya cain't lift nothin' so don't be a gittin' in our way." Rusty winked at Nate as he grabbed planks from the wagon. "Take the end a that, Nate. I ain't as young as y'all an' I cin use the help."

Gabe backed up and then stared as more wagons pulled up behind Badger's wagon. The old man looked over at him and grinned.

"Ever been ta a barn-raisin', boy? That's what we's a gonna do today. Those young fellers is a goin' ta do the work an' I'm a goin' ta supervise."

Gabe's voice was quiet as he asked, "You set this up, Badger?"

Badger's bright blue eyes twinkled as he shook his head. "I jist made a suggestion. Rusty there did all the heavy liftin'. That there boy cin talk a jack rabbit out a his ears."

Gabe chuckled as he watched his partner joke while he swung the heavy planks. "I knew he was gone longer than he needed to be yesterday, but I don't know how he managed to set all this up."

"Those women folks was in on it, too. Ya throw an idea out there an' they jist plumb run away with it. 'Fore the words left my mouth, they was a plannin' food an' makin' schedules.

"Merina, ya come on over here an' keep this here cowboy company so he stays outa the way. Ya cin do that, cain't ya?"

Gabe smiled as he walked to Merina's horse and held out his hand to help her down. "Making food, huh? Any chance you have some of those apple pillows you were talking about?"

Merina laughed up at him and looped her arm through his. "You sit down and maybe I'll let you try one. We usually eat them warm, but I had a cool one earlier and they were pretty tasty."

Just as the last empty wagon was pulling away from the foundation, Cappy drove up in a fancy buckboard with a smiling older woman next to him. He jumped down and offered her his hand as he presented her to his friends.

"Boys, this here lady is Margaret Endicott but in jist a few days, she'll be Mrs. Cappy Winters. We is a goin' ta get hitched."

As everyone stared at him in surprise, Nate snorted. "Now we know what you have been doing every day when you disappeared." He looked over at the smiling Margaret. "Say, is that where the chickens came from? We sure are liking those eggs!"

Margaret walked toward the women. She was a small, round woman with a thick bun of white hair. Her face held a constant smile and she was beaming today.

"Anything I can do to help?" she asked Molly who was rushing out of the house. Molly set her food down and hugged her.

"Margaret, I am so glad you came today. Did you come by yourself? We can have one of the riders take you home when you are ready if you'd like."

Margaret's smile turned to a laugh. "No, I came with Cappy. I knew him fifty years ago. In fact, I was sweet on him, but he only talked of his Mary back home in Texas. He looked me up when he arrived in Cheyenne and we have spent nearly every day together since. We are marrying next Sunday, and we'd love to have all of you come."

Molly stared at Margaret for a moment and then hugged her again. "That is wonderful! I know these last five years have been lonely for you.

"Margaret, these are my friends." Molly introduced the women and then grabbed Margaret's arm. "Come with me into the house. Martha will be so excited to hear your news."

Beth watched them go and then looked at Merina with tears in her eyes. "I am so happy for Margaret. She lost her husband in a blizzard five years ago. He almost made it home, but it was snowing so hard he couldn't see. He became disoriented and froze to death just a few feet from their house. Margaret was devastated. They had been married nearly forty-five years."

Merina watched as a happy Cappy joked with the men. She smiled as she looked back at Beth. "That is wonderful. Cappy mentioned a Mary to me one time but I knew he never married. It is wonderful for him to find love again after so many years.

"Does Margaret live by herself?"

"She has a daughter who lives in Laramie. Very pretty girl with bright red hair. She comes home from time to time, but she's not interested in living on the ranch. Her name is Rachel.

"You will probably meet her. Rowdy said Gabe is going to stand up with Cappy at his wedding." Beth paused as Margaret appeared in the doorway with a huge bowl of doughnuts.

"Martha and Margaret have been good friends for nearly as long as Badger and Martha have lived here. In fact, Martha stayed with Margaret for a time after they buried John. Margaret didn't want to move to town.

"She has spent the last two winters in Cheyenne though. She bought a little house not far from Martha and the two of them spend time together. She's a delightful woman."

Molly appeared beside them. She rolled her eyes as she looked toward where the men were working. "Lance always has to be in charge. Look at him giving orders."

Beth was laughing as she looked over at Molly. She murmured, "Kind of like his wife."

Molly looked surprised and as the other women laughed, she did too. "Well…maybe we both do. Come, let's get the rest of the breakfast food out here." She clapped her hands as she hurried back into the house.

Beth laughed. "See what I mean?" Josie and she followed Molly back into the house. Gabe was sitting at the picnic table and Merina walked over to sit across from him.

"Were you surprised?"

Gabe chuckled dryly. "I still am. I can't figure out how this all came together so fast and how all of these people found out about it." He grinned at her and his eyes sparkled with laughter as he added, "Staying on that side of the table today, are you?"

Merina laughed and nodded, "Yes, I am. I know you will try to embarrass me in front of everyone if I get too close to you.

"How is your side? Are you still packing it with moss or is the hole filling in?"

"The hole in the back is scabbed over. The one in the front is smaller but it's slower to heal. Larry changes it for me morning and night." He smiled at her and put his big hand over hers.

"Did I tell you that they are going to stay here? Larry said this is where their family is and they are going to stay."

Merina squeezed Gabe's hand as she smiled. "That is wonderful. They are such a fun couple. I was going to miss them both terribly. They will live at Chet's then?"

Gabe nodded. "Yes, they don't have much to move so it will be fairly easy to move them over there." He frowned suddenly. "I almost forgot that they are going to have twins. I need to order another crib."

"Well, Tiny just pulled in. I guess you can tell him today."

Gabe started to stand and then winced. He sank back down on the bench.

Tiny helped Annie down and then sauntered over to where Gabe was sitting. "Kinda nice ta sit back an' watch other fellers do all the work now, ain't it?" he asked with a grin.

Gabe growled a response and Tiny chuckled. "Say, I have that crib in the back a my buggy. Ya want me ta leave it here?"

Gabe nodded. "That would be just fine. I'd like to give it to them when they are both here so maybe leave it in the buggy for now." He paused and grinned as he added, 'I need a second one. They are having twins."

Tiny's eyes lit up. "I reckon I cin knock that out fairly fast." He nodded toward Larry. "If that's who it's fer, I probably need to do it right away. She looks like she'll drop those kids any day now."

Gabe looked over at Larry in surprise. "She told me she wasn't due for over a month yet."

Tiny studied her and shook his head. "She might not be due fer a spell, but those little ones is comin' soon." He grinned at Gabe. "My ol' granny had the gift a knowin' when a woman was goin' to drop 'er kid an' I reckon I got it too. I ain't wrong too often.

"Mebbie instead of another little rocker crib, ya should git a bigger crib made. They cin sleep together fer a time in that little one but then a bigger bed 'ould be nice. Mebbie one big enough fer both of 'em."

Gabe nodded and Tiny shook his hand. "Heal up fast, Gabe. Now I better get ta work 'fore I get called a freeloader too."

Gabe watched Larry as she walked back toward the house. She was rubbing her back with one hand and had her other hand on her stomach.

Before long, Molly had her by the arm and was leading her over to the picnic table. "You sit there with Gabe and rest awhile. We don't need those babies to come today."

Larry sighed as she sat down, and Gabe looked over at her with a grin. "Those babies dancing inside of you again? I saw your dress bouncing around at breakfast."

Larry smiled as she nodded tiredly. "They have and my back aches today." Her face went white and she gasped as she held her stomach.

Merina stared at her a moment and then quietly stood. She sought out Doc in the crowd of men and hurried toward him. Doc looked toward the picnic table in surprise as Merina talked and then followed her back toward where Larry was sitting.

Gabe chuckled. "Looks like you are going to get checked out today. Doc is on his way over here."

Larry's face went white again and she grabbed the table as Doc arrived. He paused a moment and then rushed to the house. Josie soon appeared. She handed her baby to Merina and the two of them helped Larry to stand. They moved her quickly to the house. The buzz of women's voices increased in volume and then became quiet.

Gabe leaned on the table to get up. "I'd better get Rusty." He looked over at Merina. "Want to give me your arm? You can catch me if I stumble."

She studied him for a moment and then laughed. "I will walk with you, but I have Doc's baby and I don't want to drop her. Sorry, cowboy. If you go down, you go down alone."

Rusty looked up when he saw Gabe and Merina. He paused and looked toward the house. He dropped the board he was holding and hurried toward them.

"Everything okay? Where's Larry?"

Gabe pointed toward the house. "Doc—" He didn't get any more out of his mouth before Rusty was rushing for the house.

Tiny looked up with a grin. He caught Gabe's eye and shrugged. "I ain't wrong very often."

Gabe laughed and they turned back toward the house. Merina looked at Gabe's side and then pulled his shirt up. There was blood on the bandage. She looked up at him. "Put your right arm over my shoulder. I am going to change that bandage. Larry didn't get it done before we all came this morning, did she?"

Gabe started to argue, and Merina began to mutter in Spanish. He looked at her in surprise. "I think you are calling me bad names in Spanish!"

Merina ignored him but stopped muttering as they entered the house. Beth stepped out of the door just then and Merina handed her baby Charlene. "Gabe is bleeding and I am going to change his bandage."

Beth looked from Merina to Gabe and then towards the closed door to Larry's bedroom. She began to giggle. "Well, at least Reub won't have to travel far to see two patients today." She took the baby and Merina helped Gabe over to his bed. He sat down heavily, and Molly popped her head in.

"Need some hot water?" Merina nodded and Molly was back quickly. They unwrapped the bandage and Merina gently lifted Gabe's bandage. The wound was still draining, and the edges were inflamed.

Merina glared at Gabe. "You have been up too much. Doc told you to stay in bed for five days and you didn't do it."

Molly rolled her eyes. "They never do, Merina. Don't bother to lecture him. It will do no good. Let's repack that wound and bind him up. If he's as tough as Lance—and I think he is—he'll be back on a horse in three or four days anyway. You wash that up and I will send some of the kids for some moss."

She left the room in a flurry of skirts and Merina could hear her calling for one of her children. Merina pulled Badger's lotion from her pocket and began to smear it around the raw opening."

Gabe stared at her for a moment and then commented quietly, "I thought that was horse ointment."

"It is. Ointment for animal wounds but it works on el asnos as well. You are very stubborn, Gabe, much like a donkey."

Gabe grinned up at her and then chuckled. "I don't think the name you called me was very nice, but it sounds so much sweeter in Spanish."

Merina's eyes had tears in them as she worked the salve around the wound.

"If you had come to the dance, this wouldn't have happened." she whispered. "This is my fault."

Gabe's eyes were soft as he kissed her hand and then he grinned. "This certainly wasn't your fault...but if you want to spend more time with me to ease your conscience, that would be fine."

Molly was back quickly with moss and Merina packed it gently in Gabe's wound. Molly leaned over to look and then shook her head. "I think you must have an angel watching out for you, Gabe. I'd say you are an exceptionally lucky man."

Gabe grinned up at her and then looked at Merina as he winked. "Lucky twice. I'm still alive and I have the prettiest nurses around Cheyenne."

Molly laughed and the two women tied a new rag around his stomach. He slowly pulled himself upright in bed as he tried not to wince. "If one of you could put your shoulder under mine, I want to get out of here. It's not right to have all this help and not be outside."

CHAPTER 70

THE FIRST BIRTH ON THE DIAMOND H

GABE WAS NEARLY TO THE DOOR WHEN RUSTY SLAMMED THE OTHER BEDROOM DOOR OPEN AND HOLLERED, "One a y'all git on in here. We need another set a hands!"

Gabe almost ran out the door and Molly started laughing. "You want to help, or do you want me to go?"

Merina looked toward the bedroom door. "I have helped before. I will go if you don't mind."

Molly pointed her toward a basin of water and some soap as she hugged her. "Call if you need something."

When Merina opened the door, Rusty looked at her in horror. "She's gonna bust wide open. There ain't 'nough room there fer a head to come out."

Merina took his hand and pulled him up by Larry's face. She pulled the chair closer and said, "Stay by Larry and talk to her." She was trying not to smile, and she kissed Larry's cheek. "You are doing great, Larry. It's so quiet back here that I wouldn't have known there was a birthing."

Larry grunted and then grabbed Rusty's arm. She hung on as another contraction came. He almost fell out of his chair as her fingers dug into his arm. His face was white, and he stared at the small woman gritting her teeth beside him.

Doc was moving quietly back and forth as he checked Larry over. He smiled at her as he patted her shoulder. "Larry, it is time to push. Do you want to stay lying down or would you like to squat on the floor? I think for your size, squatting would be an easier delivery for you."

Rusty stared from the doctor to Larry. "Squat on the floor? Won't that hurt the baby when it falls out?"

Doc grinned at the stressed father. "Not if you catch it. You want to catch the first one or the second one?"

Rusty's face went pale. "I reckon I don't want to catch either one. I might drop it on its head." He paused and then stared at the doctor as he added carefully, "I hope you done this 'fore 'cause I ain't so sure those babies ain't stuck in there. Why a kid's head is big an---"

Doc Williams interrupted him and looked at Merina. "You?"

Merina nodded, "Si, I will catch the first one."

Doc took one of Larry's arms and pointed for Rusty take the other as they helped her out of bed. Rusty stared at his wife's stomach.

"She's gonna bust wide open. Doc, ain't there any other way?"

Larry was panting and groaned as she stood up. She snapped at her husband.

"Rusty, help me to the floor and hold my arm. And stop talking."

Merina knelt on the floor and held her hands under Larry. The young mother pushed hard, and a little head appeared. Merina moved her hands up to catch it and then Josie dropped beside her as the little wet body slid out. A few more pushes and the little boy was quickly followed by the second baby. The two women lifted the wiggling little ones up to the parents and Larry started to cry. Rusty gaped and said nothing. A tear leaked from his eye as he kissed his wife. Both babies had strong lungs and as they protested their new world loudly, the women in the kitchen smiled.

Josie and Merina laid the babies in Larry's arms and she cried some more as she held them. Rusty carefully touched each of the tiny babies lying on his wife.

"Ya did fine, sweetheart. Those are the most beautiful little babies I ever seen." When he felt her body contract again, he looked at Doc Williams in shock. "There's more in there?"

Doc laughed as he patted Rusty's shoulder. "No, just the afterbirth. Let's let the ladies hold them for a moment and we'll get that delivered. Then we can clip the cords and clean the babies up."

Once the afterbirth was delivered, Josie expertly clipped the cords. She and Merina wiped off the babies, swaddled them and handed them back to their mother. Both were attempting to nurse, and Merina slipped out of the room.

She was smiling and then laughed as she looked around the kitchen at the expectant women. "You are going to have to wait for Rusty to tell you what they had. Both babies do look healthy and they are nursing. That is all I will tell you."

Before long, Doc and Josie appeared. Doc was smiling happily, and Josie laughed. "Reub is always excited when he gets to try something new. Since Tiny built us the birthing bed in our office, Reub was afraid he would never be able to experience a birth like this. I'm sure he has some adjustments to make on that bed now."

Doc laughed as he headed outside to clean up. Several of the men stopped to watch him and soon, all the hammering stopped as they waited to see what was going on. Doc shook his head as the men turned. "You are all going to have to wait. I have nothing to say."

Before long, a proud Rusty appeared and carried his new babies through the yard for all his friends to see. Most of the men were surprised as they had no idea that a birthing had taken place.

Rusty grinned at Gabe. "Mebbie someday, y'all 'ill have some a these yore own self."

Gabe laughed as he patted Rusty on the back.

"Meet Lorena Mae an' Oscar James. We wasn't expectin' 'em 'til next month but they was ready, an' Doc says they's fine."

Doc Williams peeked at each of them and nodded as he responded, "Twins usually come a little early. They are healthy so all is good." He looked around at the group of men. "Let's all take a break and toast to Larry and Rusty."

CHAPTER 71

MULE FINDS A HOME

GABE FOLLOWED THE MEN OVER TO THE ROW OF BOARDS SET UP ON BARRELS. The women had been busy. He grabbed some of Merina's pillow bread and a handful of cookies. He stopped after the first bite of the bread and stared at it. Merina was refilling the doughnut bowl and he caught her eye.

"I don't know what they taste like without apples, but they taste mighty good with them."

Merina laughed at him. "I have made them for many years, but apples were a first for me. We made them for you, but the women liked them as well."

A mule gave his strange call and they both turned to watch as a large mule wandered into the yard. The mule meandered over to Badger and shoved him with his head. It stopped and almost seemed to study the group of people gathered around the food. Some of the men became quiet while others turned to see what had stopped the conversation. The mule spotted Merina and snorted. He trotted towards her and the crowd split around him, with several of the men pushing as far away as they could.

Gabe watched the men and then turned to watch the mule as it came towards Merina. It stopped to nuzzle her shirt and she put her arm around its neck.

"Well hello, Mule. I wondered where you were today. How about a doughnut?"

Mule pushed past her and tried to put his nose in the bowl of sopapillas. Merina laughed and lifted one out. Mule took it carefully from her hand, rubbed his head against her one more time and wandered over to the barn. He lifted the latch on the corral gate and let himself in. He pulled the gate shut with his teeth and was soon grazing in the small pasture behind the barn.

Gabe watched in amazement and Badger began to laugh evilly. "Now boys, I always say that a mule is a durn good judge a character. He's takin' a likin' ta Miss Merina there an' ain't no one in his right mind is a goin' ta argue with ol' Mule."

Badger looked over at the gaping Levi and winked. "Mule's a notional feller an' some things he jist decides ta do. But don't you'ins worry none, Judge. Mule's like me. He's more peaceable now that he's an old feller."

Levi carefully studied the mule and then looked over at Badger. He shook his head as he laughed. "I agree he acts like his owner, but I think that both of you bear watching, regardless of how old you are."

Rowdy, Levi and Lance were three of the men who had pushed as far away from Mule as they could get. They knew what he was capable of and they wanted nothing to do with him.

"Looks like ya jist acquired a mule, Gabe. 'Course, this here ranch is been Mule's home fer so long as he's been ta Wyomin'. Once my Martha an' me moved ta Cheyenne, he's started a gallivantin' 'round an' he ain't stayed with us much. Now he likes my Martha but he ain't taked ta no one like he taked ta her since we married." Badger kissed Merina's cheek.

"Looks like he done fallen in love with the same little gal you'ins like, Gabe. An' you'ins best treat 'er right or ol' Mule 'ill have a talkin' with ya.

"Now come on, boys—let's git back ta work. I'm an old feller an' I'm a gonna wear out real soon here."

Some of the men had only heard of Badger and they stared at him. Those who knew him well began to laugh.

"Badger, I don't think you ever wear out and quite frankly, Mule is a pill. I have seen him all over Cheyenne. He's been visiting at my place and was even over at Rowdy's trying to breed some of his mares. I'm glad he decided to come back home." Lance paused and looked over the group of people staring after Mule and added seriously, "And that mule is dangerous. Don't any of you try to befriend him. He isn't exactly accommodating when it comes to making friends…but he's a killing tornado if you mess with folks he claims as his own. Now let's get this bunkhouse finished."

Gabe frowned as he listened to Lance. "I'm not sure I want that mule around here. He could get a notion and hurt one of the men or even Emilia."

Merina shook her head. "Mules are very loyal. He will only attack if he senses danger. He has ridden with me on several of my trips to or from Cheyenne, and I feel safer when he is around." She smiled up at Gabe as her eyes glinted with humor. "Mule isn't so busy building a ranch and he has time to ride with me."

Gabe stared down at her for a moment and then snorted. His face slowly broke into a grin. "How about I hire you on as a cook until Larry gets back on her feet. We about starved to death before she moved back in."

Merina frowned at him and her neck turned pink. "You only have two bedrooms, Gabe, and you need to be in a bed. No, I think I will not stay here and help you."

Gabe's eyes twinkled and Merina turned a deep red. She rattled off a torrent of words in Spanish as she glared at him and then rushed toward the house.

Gabe was laughing as he strolled toward the bunkhouse. Angel fell in beside him. He looked over at his friend as he grinned.

"So my friend, when will you tell my sister that you speak Spanish and that you comprehend all of the names that she calls you?"

Gabe laughed out loud and thumped the smaller man on the back. "When I can get back up on my horse, Angel, I am going to tell her a lot of things. And then hopefully, you won't just be my friend—you will be my brother."

Angel's dark eyes glinted as he chuckled, and he rushed forward quickly to grab a roof beam that one of the men was struggling to carry.

Tiny swore at them when they swung the beam too close to where he was working on six beds. "Ya fellers pay attention ta what yore doin'. I don't aim ta get my head caved in over a durn bunkhouse."

CHAPTER 72

ADVICE FOR GABE

THE MEN FINISHED THE BUNKHOUSE THAT NIGHT ABOUT 6:00. Most of them ate quickly and left. Gabe thanked each man and woman. He shook hands with all of them and visited with them for a moment before they left. Soon, the ranch yard only held five rigs and those belonged to Badger, both Rankins, Doc, and Levi.

Badger pulled a surrey over to the bunkhouse. Six tick mattresses were tied in the back and those were quickly unrolled on top of the bed frames.

He winked at Gabe as he clucked to his team. He called over his shoulder. "Boy, ya better git back on yer feet soon. Half a Cheyenne's been a chargin' on yer accounts." He pulled his team up to the house and bounced down off the wagon, whistling as he hurried up the steps. He was back out in a moment with a smiling Martha on his arm. She waved at everyone as Badger wheeled the two-seated buggy around.

"Why don't you 'ins come in fer supper next Friday, Gabe? You' ins an' yer men." Badger winked at Lance as he spoke, and Lance chuckled.

Martha beamed at Merina and added, "And of course you and Emilia as well. We will have a little family gathering." She waved again and Badger drove his team out of the yard.

Lance watched them go and shook his head. "I don't know how they do that. Martha just seems to know when he is ready to leave." His eyes were dancing with humor as he glanced toward Molly. "I sure wish Molly would treat me that way. I have to *ask* her if she's ready and then wait another half an hour."

Molly rolled her eyes at him and then giggled as Lance grabbed her. He put his arm around his wife, and they walked toward the house laughing.

Rowdy grinned at Gabe. "Better step things up, Gabe. Badger and Martha pulled a party like that on me and it turned out to be an engagement party. They are giving you a week. Beth and I barely had a days' notice."

Gabe stared after the wagon and then looked at Rowdy in surprise. Levi slapped him on the back and Doc shook his head.

"Just get it done, Gabe. Someday, I'll tell you how Josie and I met. This is a loud and ornery family. They are good people though. And now you, like me, have been adopted." Doc laughed again and headed for the house.

Levi was still in the yard. He looked several times toward the pasture where mule was grazing and then after Badger's departing wagon.

"I sure am glad that I didn't know about that mule when Jimmy Baker died. It would have made that whole mess a little bit stickier."

When Gabe stared at him in confusion, Levi frowned. "It was quite a mess. Jimmy and another man were in jail for molesting a woman. They broke out somehow and a mule killed them in the alley. No one but a little orphan boy was around. He was digging in the trash for food and saw the entire thing. He said nobody gave any orders. The mule just attacked them and disappeared. The sheriff thought it was Mule but when he came out here, the old devil was locked in that pasture. I was a little suspicious too, but Badger had been with me the entire time."

Gabe listened quietly and as he watched Mule. The big jack looked up and seemed to stare at him for a moment before it returned to eating. Gabe could feel his neck hairs raise.

"Think I should shoot him? I don't want that mule to hurt anyone here."

Levi shook his head slowly before he answered. "That's just the thing. Mule only attacks the bad element. I know in some cases, Badger has directed him but other times, it is almost like he does it on his own.

"No, I think I would keep him around. You have a very deadly attack mule who will keep his eye on things. That can be a good thing when you work so far from the house."

He grinned at Gabe and elbowed him. "Let's go see what else there is to eat in the house. I have almost worked enough today to eat a second supper. And you can be sure Rowdy has already started."

The kitchen was a noisy place when Gabe and Levi walked through the door. Levi was right—Rowdy had a full plate in front of him and was eating like he was starving.

"You know, the best thing about these deals is the food. All kinds and lots of it."

"Rowdy, Beth feeds you well. You have absolutely nothing to complain about." Molly put her hands on her hips as she stared at him.

Rowdy grinned and pulled Beth onto his lap. "She sure does. She gave me a new start on life when I met her." He paused and added as he kissed her cheek, "And I have a tombstone to prove it."

Levi had his arm around Sadie, and he kissed her as she laughed.

Merina looked at the couples in surprise and Levi winked at her. "Merina, this family is the most huggingest and kissingest family I have ever seen.

"I like it though. I do believe that any time a man can squeeze his wife, he should do it. There aren't always more tomorrows."

Gabe grinned. "I reckon the part about tomorrows is true. About the wife part, I can't say. I don't have any experience in that area....yet." He winked at Merina.

Merina blushed and rushed toward the spare bedroom. "I am going to check on Larry."

CHAPTER 73

MULE TO THE RESCUE

THE FIRST HALF OF THE WEEK WENT QUIETLY. Merina took out Buck's stitches on Thursday morning and took him back to Gabe's ranch. The yard was quiet, and she knocked on the door. No one answered when she called. Merina walked down to the bunkhouse and stepped inside. The men had moved in and five of the bunks showed use. She smiled at the scent of fresh wood. She waited about five minutes before she mounted Mascota and turned him back toward Molly's house. Buck nickered as she rode away, and Mule rushed up to the fence bucking. His call started as a whinny and then ended up as more of a snorting sound. Merina laughed and turned her horse toward the fence.

"I don't have any treats for you, Mule, but if you want to come over tonight, I will have something special for you."

She was smiling when she left the ranch yard and the smile was still on her face when she arrived at the Rocking R.

Emilia ran by without stopping. Merina laughed and walked back to where Molly was making soap.

"I'm thinking about trying a new scent, Merina. Are you tired of lilac or shall we keep it the same?

Merina looked toward Gabe's ranch and paused. "I like lilac, but we can change if you want to."

Molly's eyes followed Merina's and she was laughing when the younger woman looked at her again.

"So Gabe was gone? I'm guessing he will be over later today then. That means he is back on a horse." She stirred the mixture and looked up at Merina seriously. "He was a lucky man. Most wounds like he had do not end with smiles."

Tears filled Merina's eyes. "Si, I thought he would die the night I went over there. Then he drank some of Badger's potion and he seemed to improve. I can't really explain it. He doesn't remember much but it was bad."

Molly's eyes searched Merina's face and then she laughed. "That potion has saved several of us. It is good to keep around for bad fevers although the smell of it is enough to make you gag. Thank heavens you don't remember because they say the taste is worse." Her eyes were serious as she added, "They gave it to me when I was pregnant with Paul. Lance too, when he was shot.

"Help me pour this soap onto that pan and you can take some home. Just leave Emilia here. The girls are playing well like they always do. If Gabe doesn't come by, you can come down this evening and pick her up. Otherwise, you can get her in the morning."

The two women finished the soap and Merina went home. She was hoping that Gabe would come by and went to the window several times as she baked to look for his horse. She started supper around 6:00 and was singing when she heard a voice in the doorway. She turned around with a smile on her face. It faded when she recognized the man who had entered her house.

Rance Thume stood in the doorway with a sneer on his face. He was the twin brother to the man Merina had killed in Texas. Both rode for the Millett brothers whose ranch was close to Cole's Circle C. They

392

often hung around Cole's ranch. Both had tried to walk out with Merina and their intentions had been far from honorable.

Jack Thume was wild and even meaner when he drank. He had tried to force his way into Cole's house shortly after the men left on their drive north, and there was no one to help Merina stop him.

The knife Spur had given Merina was a large one and as Jack rushed her, she shoved it into his chest. Jack's eyes registered shock as he stared down at the knife. "My brother will get you for this," he snarled as he staggered and fell to the floor.

Merina stared at Jack for a moment and then pulled the knife from his chest. She wiped it on his shirt. Her breath was coming quickly as she rushed to pack a bag. She woke Emilia and the two of them slipped away from the ranch with Diablo and ten of the best mares. Merina knew Cole had sold the horses to a Rowdy Rankin with delivery for May 3 in Dodge City, Kansas. She intended to have the horses in Dodge when Señor Rankin arrived. The one hundred ninety-five-mile trip to Dallas was long, and Merina feared for both of their lives. The Thume family was wealthy and even though both Jack and Rance were known outlaws, their father doted on his twin sons.

When Merina finally reached the shipping pens in Dallas, she presented the freight agent with a bank draft to ship the horses north to Dodge City. She often signed correspondence for Cole as well as handled his bookkeeping, and was able to forge his signature with ease. Once the paperwork was completed, Merina pretended to leave but instead slipped into the car with Diablo. The stallion would let no one touch him but Merina, and the two sisters rode north in the livestock car to Dodge City.

Now Jack's brother was here to claim revenge for his twin and Merina's breath caught in her chest.

Rance leaned against the doorjamb as he stared Merina up and down boldly. "I knew that sheriff was lyin'. That $500 reward Pop put on yore head had lots a fellows lookin' fer ya. A couple a drifters was in Cheyenne when ya rode this way after church last week an' they wired us. Pop sent me up on the next train an' here ya are." He smirked again. "Ya always was one to go to church. Always thought ya was too good fer Jack an' me. Well, I'm here to show ya that ya ain't. Ya come from trash an' trash is all y'all ever be.

"Jack didn't know ya carried a knife, but I do an' I'm ready fer ya." Rance pulled a knife from inside his shirt. He slid his finger close to the edge and leered at Merina. "Y'all an' me are gonna have us some fun, an' then I'm a gonna cut ya up bad. Ya won't be so purty when ya cross over to the other side. That mean ol' pa a yours won't even recognize his purty little daughter." Rance laughed at her and added, "It give me pleasure to run my horse over the top a him. He was tough to kill but we got it done."

Merina's face was pale, and her breath was coming quickly. However, she was quiet as Rance moved away from the door and started for her. She put the table between the man and herself. He lunged and then stopped when he heard a strange sound behind him.

Mule stood in the doorway of Merina's house. He snorted and then charged the man in front of him. Rance screamed as Mule's mouth closed over his shoulder. The knife dropped from his hand and the big mule drug him outside. Rance was tossed in the air and that was the last thing he would remember before the mule stomped him to death.

Gabe was just riding by Lance's house when he heard the scream. He spurred Buck and the horse broke into a run. He was still several hundred yards from Merina's when Mule tossed the man up in the air and began to stomp him. Gabe slid from his horse and rushed into the house. Merina was on the floor. She had her knees pulled up to her chin and was sobbing quietly.

She looked up in terror when Gabe burst through the door. Her sobs shook her body as he reached for her.

"Merina! You all right?" Gabe pulled her close and Merina shook as she hugged him.

"His name was Rance Thume. It was his brother I killed in Texas. He was going to cut me, but Mule stopped him."

Gabe heard a snort and slowly looked over his shoulder. Mule once again stood in the doorway. He stared at Gabe and snorted again.

Merina looked at the mule and almost laughed. "I told Mule to come over this evening and I would have a treat for him. I had better get him one."

She loosened herself from Gabe's arms and took two of the apple sopapillas she had made. She walked over to the mule and gave them to him. Merina hugged his neck as Mule ate them contentedly.

"Mule, thank you for saving me. You are a wonderful friend," she whispered into his hair.

Mule nuzzled her neck and wobbled his lips on her arm. He stared at Gabe for a moment. Then he backed out the door and disappeared.

CHAPTER 74

GABE MAKES HIS MOVE

GABE COULD FEEL HIS NECK HAIRS RAISE. He picked up the knife laying on the floor and stared at it for a moment. "That belong to Thume?" he asked as he laid it on the table.

Merina nodded and Gabe pulled her close. "Merina, marry me. Come and live with me on my ranch. It's not home without you." He stared into her dark eyes and then added with a grin, "I'll even let Mule live with us…but he can't come in the house."

He pulled her tighter and kissed the top of her head. Merina let herself melt against him and when Gabe kissed her, she returned his kiss.

He sat down on a chair and pulled her onto his lap. "So about this wedding."

Merina laughed softly. "I think, Gabe, that maybe you just want a cook."

Gabe grinned at her and nodded. "Well, there is that. I kind of like Rusty's babies though too. I think I might want some of those if I could find a woman who was willing."

Merina's dark eyes danced with humor. "I think finding a woman would not be so hard. Finding a wife seems to be difficult for you."

Gabe chuckled as he smiled at her. "So how about you, Merina? Will you be my wife? Will you help me fill that house with little feet?"

Merina smiled at him. "Maybe we should wait. Perhaps next year."

Gabe stared at her in surprise and then he frowned.

Merina giggled as she kissed his cheek. "I will talk to the priest on Sunday after Mass. I am sure he will want to meet with both of us before he agrees to marry us though."

Gabe grinned. "Now, I am all about efficiency. I'll just come with you to Mass. Then we can set a date on Sunday for next week sometime."

Merina laughed and Gabe kissed her again. She pulled away and slipped off his lap. She stared at him and then murmured in Spanish, "I think it is not so good for us to be alone together. You are very exciting, and I am tempted be more friendly than I should be."

Gabe laughed out loud as he stood up. He replied in Spanish, "Merina, you are a truly beautiful woman. You are very tempting to me as well, but I will be a gentleman...until we are married."

Merina's eyes opened wide and she stared at him as she blushed. "You speak Español?"

Gabe's eyes were twinkling as he replied in Spanish. "Si, Señorita Montero. I grew up in south Texas. Many of my friends spoke Spanish and our conversations mixed both languages. Yes, I speak it well...and I have understood every name you have called me since we first met."

Merina glared at him and a torrent of words flooded from her mouth.

Gabe pulled her close again and laughed as he looked down at her. "That wasn't very nice, but it sounds so pretty when you say it that I guess I just don't care." His face grew serious.

"How about you finish whatever it is that you are cooking while I bury Thume. Then we can ride back to Lance's and tell Emilia that I will be her pa. I think that will make her happy."

Merina's chest tightened as she looked toward the door and Gabe kissed her. "It's over, Merina. I'm sure no more men will be sent but I will report this to the sheriff when we go into Cheyenne just to play it safe."

He whispered, "I won't let anything happen to you and neither will Mule."

Merina studied Gabe's face and then she touched his cheek. "Mi amor," she whispered.

"Yes, mi amor, my beautiful Merina." Gabe's chest tightened as he pulled her close again and kissed her. He limped out of the house and stared at the man lying on the ground for a moment.

Gabe found a shovel in the woodshed and buried the outlaw by the creek. His wound was healing but the digging pulled. He stopped several times to hold his side. When he was finished, he didn't carve a marker. He stood over the grave for a moment and stared down.

"I reckon by now you have had your meeting with the Maker. I'm not going to put up a marker or tell Merina where you are buried. You are gone from this life and you will never bother her again." He kicked some brush over the fresh dirt and when he walked away, nothing indicated a fresh grave had been dug or that a man was buried there.

Gabe ate Merina's cooking for the first time that night. He enjoyed the flavors and the spices she used. They brought back memories of the foods that he had grown up with.

"That was a fine meal, Merina. I will try to survive for a few more days since I have this to look forward to." He winked at her as he leaned back in his chair.

Merina laughed softly. "I think we should get Emilia. It will soon be dark, and Molly may already have her in bed if we don't hurry."

Gabe nodded. "I'll scrape plates while you wash dishes." He managed to bump into her many times and Merina finally shook her finger at him.

"I think, Gabe, that you are not such an awkward man as you pretend. You sit down and leave me alone or I will never finish these dishes."

Gabe chuckled as he agreed. He wandered outside and stared at the ground where Rance had died. He threw some fresh dirt over the ground and tightened the cinch on Buck. The filly grazing beside Buck was the one Merina had wanted to buy. He had dropped her reins when he raced toward Merina's house, but she had followed. He tightened her cinch as well while he talked to her.

"Bonita, you behave this evening. You are a pretty girl but an ornery one. No crowhopping and bucking around when Merina rides you."

Merina soon appeared in the doorway and looked at the filly in surprise. She walked toward the horse talking to her. Bonita watched Merina with her velvety eyes and then nickered softly. Merina mounted her and the horse stood quietly.

Gabe shook his head. "I call her Bonita and she crowhops every time I try to ride her. Pretty little filly but temperamental as can be."

Merina laughed as she patted the filly. "Bonita means pretty, and you are a pretty girl. You will have fine colts with Mascota." She looked over at Gabe. "Thank you, Gabe. She is beautiful. Perhaps when it is daylight, we will see if she can beat Buck. Maybe when we ride to church." Merina was smiling as she led the way to Lance's. They were both laughing by the time they arrived.

Lance opened the door at the sound of horses and stared at the smiling couple. His face broke into a slow grin and he hollered over his shoulder. "Start planning that wedding party, Molly. We are going to have another one in the neighborhood."

Molly appeared quickly and then rushed outside. Merina slid off her horse and Molly hugged her. "I am so happy for both of you." She looked over at Gabe. "And it took you long enough to make your move."

Gabe grinned as he climbed down. "All in the timing, Molly. Now, where is Emilia. I want to talk to her."

Molly frowned as she looked toward the house. "I just put them down. They had a long day. Maybe you should---"

Emilia burst out of the bedroom and raced toward Gabe. She threw herself at him and he caught her up. She took his face in her hands and rubbed her nose on his while she laughed.

Gabe kissed the little girl. "Emilia, I am going to marry Nina," he whispered softly, "and then I'd like to be your papá if that is okay with you."

Emilia looked seriously from Gabe to Merina. "Well, I wanted you to marry a grandma but since I have Grandma Martha, I guess that will be okay." She whispered loudly in his ear, "She isn't always so nice though."

Gabe laughed and hugged the little girl. "We'll see if we can change that because I like her a lot."

Emilia beamed at him and slid down. She ran to her sister. "Señor Gabe is going to be my papá!"

Merina picked her up and nodded as she laughed. "Yes, he is. Now you go back to bed quietly, so you don't wake Livvy up. I will come and get you in the morning."

Emilia slid down her sister's legs. She hugged Gabe again as she smiled up at him and then skipped back to the bedroom and shut the door. They could hear her whispering loudly, "Señor Gabe is going to be my papá!"

Molly laughed as she looked back at Gabe. "She adores you. Just know that parenting has its challenges and don't be surprised when that changes from time to time.

"I guess Badger and Martha knew what they were doing when they planned that party for tomorrow, didn't they? Do you want to come in?"

Gabe shook his head. "No, we just wanted to tell Emilia. I don't want to keep you up or wake up the rest of the kids. I'll see you tomorrow afternoon."

He gave Merina a leg up and they walked their horses back to her house. The quarter of a mile ride went quickly, and Gabe stared at Merina for a moment when they arrived. He cleared his throat and then said huskily, "I think I will head on home. You look too pretty in the moonlight and I am not going to want to leave if I get down." He helped Merina off and then backed Buck away. "I'm not even going to kiss you."

Merina laughed as he turned away. He lifted his hat and then urged the horses to a lope.

CHAPTER 75

SPANISH LACE

GABE ARRIVED AT MERINA'S EARLY WITH A SMILE ON HIS FACE, LEADING BONITA.

Merina looked at him in surprise. "I'm not ready yet. We don't have to be there until 5:30 and it won't take us three hours to get to town."

Gabe's eyes were twinkling as he looked down at her. "Thought you might want to talk to Sadie about a wedding dress. I hear she has made quite a few around Cheyenne."

Merina stared up at him a moment and then shook her head. "No, I have Mamá's dress. I had hidden it in a trunk in Cole's barn. Angel shipped it to Cheyenne while he was in Texas. Badger told me last week that it had arrived at the freight office. He picked it up for me, so my dress is at their house."

Gabe looked at Merina intently and she slowly blushed. "Don't look at me like that, Gabe."

He laughed. "I am just visualizing you in Spanish lace and I like what I am seeing. We can take the wagon to church on Sunday and bring your trunk back then."

"I want Sadie to make me a shirt and vest though so let's go in early today."

Emilia was playing with dolls and she smiled up at Gabe. "Would you like to play dolls with me, Señor Gabe?"

Gabe squatted down beside her. "Not today but you can take one with you if you want. We are going into Grandma Martha's for a party. It will be late when we come home so you can ride with Nina or with me. We won't take Hawk."

Emilia rushed into the bedroom calling behind her, "I will ride with you. And you can brush my hair. Nina chases the rats and they bite me."

When Merina walked out of the bedroom, Gabe and Emilia were both on the floor. He was brushing her hair carefully and she was chattering to him." Merina watched them for a moment and smiled. Gabe still favored his left side, but he was moving more easily. He looked up when she appeared and winked at her.

"And when I am done brushing your hair, maybe I will brush Merina's hair too."

Emilia turned around and frowned at him. "Nina is a grownup. Grownups fix their own hair."

Gabe chuckled and they were soon on their way to Cheyenne. Emilia talked non-stop for nearly a half hour and then fell asleep.

Merina was quiet for a bit and then looked over at Gabe. "Molly would like to have a party at her house after the wedding. She called it a reception. She said the people will all bring food like they did for the barn-raising. Their cook can make us a cake if you want. She wondered if there was any certain meat or food that you would like."

Gabe looked at her in surprise and then shook his head. "I don't much care about the details." He reached over and took Merina's hand. "All I care about is my bride. The rest is just extras. Party or no party, I don't care." He studied Merina's profile and then asked, "What about you? Anything special that you want?"

Merina studied his face and then slowly shook her head. "I want us to be married at my church in Cheyenne. It is Saint John the Baptist Catholic Church and Father Cummiskey is the pastor. I don't care about anything else though. I can't eat when I'm nervous, so I don't care about the food at all."

Gabe chuckled and squeezed her hand. "Well then, let's just have fun and let Molly run the show. She can tell us what we need to do, and you don't have to be nervous. How does that sound?

"Of course, tonight might be a challenge. Badger's family is darned ornery so we will be joshed a lot tonight. I'm guessing they are all expecting us to be engaged so we won't even have to announce that." He frowned and looked down at her hand. "I don't even have a ring. Pa sold the one he gave Ma when they married so she never wore one. Maybe someone tonight can tell me where to find one in a hurry."

Merina smiled at him. "I don't have to have a ring, Gabe. It doesn't matter."

Gabe shook his head and his eyes were intense as he studied Merina's face. "It's important to me. There is little my Pa did that I want to copy. He wasn't much of a man and was even less of a husband. Ring or no ring, I want my wife to know how special she is to me." He squeezed her hand and Merina smiled.

"You are a fine man, Gabe Hawkins. My father would have approved of you."

CHAPTER 76

LOTS OF MEMORIES

GABE WAS RIGHT ABOUT THE JOSHING. All the family was gathered at Martha and Badger's when they arrived. They were primed and ready to tease the newest members of the clan. Of course, Badger had planned this from the time that he met both Merina and Gabe. Still, he was pleased his conniving had worked.

He lifted his glass of root beer high and hollered, "Here's ta the newest neighbor an' a fine man. Took Gabe a long time but he finally worked up the nerve ta ask Miss Merina ta be his bride. I hope Merina here makes that durn cranky cowboy more pleasant an' agreeable, an' I hope they done fill that house ta the brim with little ones."

Everyone raised their glasses and talked over each other. Beth's eyes were bright as she asked, "Do you have a dress, Merina? Sadie can help you make one if you need to." She smiled over at Sadie and added, "Actually we all can."

Martha hustled all the women into a back bedroom and pointed at the chest sitting in the corner. "Badger picked that up from the freight office last week and it is supposed to have Merina's mother's wedding dress in it." She clasped her hands in excitement as she added, "Quick! Open it and let's have a look."

Merina walked over to the chest. She quietly ran her hands over the ornate carving on the front of it. She was just about to open it when Larry rushed into the room carrying her twins. Molly and Beth each took a baby from her and tried to divide their attention between the babies and what Larry was saying.

Larry hugged Merina. "We just heard. Gabe helped us to move over to Chet's house the day you dropped off Buck. He came over and told Rusty and me this morning. We are so happy for both of you!" She looked at the chest. "Is this the chest Angel had shipped back? He told us he had shipped it from Texas. Quick, open it and let's see."

Merina took a key from around her neck and slipped it into the lock. The old brass padlock ground as the key turned. The lock bore the initials of WB. Merina's eyes were misty as she smiled up at the women. She pointed at the lock. "The WB stands for the lock maker, W. Bohannan, but Papá told Mamá that if you read it upside-down, it looked like two C's on top of each other followed by an M. Mamá's name was Consuela and Papá was Carlos. Carlos and Consuela Montero."

Beth's pretty eyes filled with tears and she kissed the baby she was holding. Her tender heart felt the emotion that Merina was feeling. "What a lovely memory, Merina. Did your father make the trunk?"

Merina nodded. "It was a wedding gift to Mamá. I was so afraid that it would be destroyed after we left." She lifted the cover to the trunk and stared down at the contents. She carefully lifted out some old tintypes that were wrapped in muslin and then brought up the wedding dress. It was a beautiful Spanish gown with lots of hand-tatted lace. The waist was small, and the skirt dropped delicately, alternating large rows of lace with embroidered cotton. The sleeves were a sheer lace and the neckline was scooped with lace rising almost to the neck. The veil was long and was made of almost the same lace as the insets in the dress. Merina smiled as she held it carefully.

"Grandmamá made this for Mamá. She tatted all the lace by hand. Mamá said that she would tat rows and rows of lace every day. She did so from the time Mamá was small. She put them away and then when Mamá was to marry, she brought out all the rows of lace and made the dress. My great-grandmamá made the veil. She wore it in her wedding as did my grandmamá. Then my mother wore it in hers." A tear leaked from Merina's eye as she smelled the dress.

"I can almost smell my mamá when I hold this."

The women were quiet for a moment and then they surrounded Merina. Sadie asked softly, "Do you want to try it on to see if it fits?"

Merina shook her head. "I tried it on four years ago and it fit loosely so I'm sure it will fit. I will try it on at home. I can adjust it if necessary, but I don't think that I will need to." She smiled at the women. "I am so happy it was not lost or destroyed." She held the dress for a moment and then folded it carefully. She started to put it back into the trunk and then paused.

Martha watched her and then hurried to the back of the room and pulled out a valise. "You can put it in here if you don't want to take the trunk home with you tonight, Merina. We can wrap it up in a sheet so it stays clean."

Once the dress was wrapped and stowed in the valise, each woman hugged Merina. She was going to be a beautiful bride. As they filed out of the room, Merina smiled at Larry. "Would you like to stand up with me at our wedding? You are the first friend I made after we left Texas and I would love to have you beside me."

Larry smiled and her eyes sparkled. "I would love to. Gabe asked Rusty yesterday so we will both be up front with you. Hopefully, some of the women will watch the babies." She laughed softly. "Gabe asked Angel as well even though he will already have Nate and Rusty beside him. Angel told him that he and Miguel would both walk you up the aisle. That means that you might want to ask two more women." She squeezed Merina's hands and then hugged her. "It is going to be a wonderful wedding and you will be a beautiful bride."

CHAPTER 77

HER MOTHER'S DRESS

GABE WAS WATCHING THE DOOR AND HE SMILED AT MERINA WHEN SHE CAME OUT OF THE BEDROOM. He studied her face closely and then walked across the room to put his arm around her. "Everything good?"

Merina nodded. "Yes, it is just emotional to see my mother's wedding dress and know that I will be wearing it." She smiled up at him and Gabe almost kissed her.

He caught himself and looked around the room. Several of the men were grinning at him. He glared at them and muttered under his breath.

Lance laughed. "Don't stop on our account. We all enjoy a little cuddling with our wives."

The men who were listening laughed and Gabe grinned. He looked down at Merina and she backed away from him shaking her finger. He laughed out loud and nodded. "I'll keep that in mind."

Nate watched his brother and smiled. *Gabe is really happy. I am too. I like Merina.*

Cappy showed up just before supper with his wife-to-be and invited everyone to his wedding on Sunday. "The weddin' 'ill be at 1:00 an' Margaret an' me would be honored fer all of ya's ta come."

The pretty red head with them looked at Levi in surprise and then smiled. She put out her hand to Sadie. "You must be Sadie. Mr. Parker talked about you after he was shot in Laramie several years ago. I knew you had to be someone special. My name is Rachel."

Sadie looked at Rachel in surprise and Levi grinned. "I was out of my head and I apologize for anything I might have said. Thank you for sitting with me though. And if there is ever a need for someone to sing, you just volunteer. I do remember your singing."

Angel and Miguel were walking through the door and Levi grinned as he pointed around the room.

"This smooth hombre sliding up here is Angel. At least that is what he calls himself. Miguel is behind him. That's Nate. Gabe over there is the groom. You know Martha and Badger and all the Rankins. Rusty and Larry O'Brian have the twins. They live on Chet Reith's place. Merina there is the bride."

"Are you here for your mother's wedding or are you moving to Cheyenne?" Lance's face was curious as he watched Rachel.

Rachel laughed and shook her head. "No, I am just here for the wedding. I will be returning to Laramie on Tuesday. I have applied for a teaching position there and hope to hear back his week."

The room became quiet as everyone looked from Merina to Gabe. Gabe shrugged his shoulders. "That's all up to Merina. We haven't talked about it."

Merina looked cautiously from one face to the next. "I can maybe teach the older boys in the mornings. I would rather work with Gabe on the ranch than teach all day though." Gabe's face lit into a huge smile and Lance frowned.

"Durn it. Just when we thought we had a teacher, she had to go and get married." Lance's eyes settled on Rachel and he grinned. "How about you, Rach? We have a teaching position right here and the house is attached to the school. Merina will be moving out in a week or so to get married. You won't even have to wait to hear back from the school board since we are all here."

Rachel stuttered a little as she looked around the room. "I—well, I will think about it. You have all caught me off guard."

Soon the room was full of happy suggestions and pleadings for her to stay.

Rachel laughed. "I will give it some thought. Let me get through Mother's wedding first. And thank you all for the offer."

Tiny had made Martha a table that rolled out to expand with extra leaves. He had also made extra chairs and several benches. The little ones ate outside, and Martha was able to seat all the adults around her new table.

The food was delicious as always and the laughing was plentiful. Gabe was one of the first ones to leave.

"Martha and Badger, I want to thank you for the nice evening. We need to get Emilia home. I guess we'll see everyone at Cappy's wedding." He nodded at Rachel. "It was nice to meet you, Rachel. I do hope you will take that teaching job so I can have my wife around all the time. After all, she promised that she would cook for me." He grinned over at Merina and she laughed.

Merina stood and then paused. "I can help clean up before we leave."

Molly shook her head. "Nonsense. We are spending the night in Cheyenne. Rowdy and Beth are as well. We will clean up. You both go on home. You aren't as familiar with that road at night as we all are anyway."

Rusty and Larry bundled up the babies and soon everyone in Gabe's party was outside. Angel followed them out and Gabe grinned.

"I figured you'd be inside trying to talk that redheaded teacher to stay. You always have had a thing for red-haired women.

"Si, this is true. But tonight with the moon so bright and the air so warm, I think of past loves. I think I will ride home with you. Miguel can talk to the teacher."

Gabe stared at his friend in surprise. He couldn't remember a time when Angel had ever missed an opportunity to flirt with a woman, especially a pretty redhead.

Emilia was already falling asleep. Gabe bundled her into the back of Rusty's wagon and the little group headed for home. Rusty, Larry and Angel rode on south when Merina turned off while Gabe held Emilia on his horse. He carried her into Merina's house and placed her in bed. He paused by the outside door.

Merina smiled up at him. "I am not going to invite you in because it is late. Don't forget church on Sunday and Cappy's wedding at 1:00."

Gabe grinned and gave her a quick kiss. He leaned in for a second and Merina backed up.

"Good night, Gabe. I will see you Sunday morning at 8:00."

Gabe rode away chuckling and then remembered the knife. "I had better take that with me. I might need to show it to the sheriff. I will just take care of that tomorrow." He turned his horse around and loped back to Merina's. He could hear her singing and he listened for a moment before he knocked on the door. There was a gasp inside and he quickly spoke.

"It's me. I want to take that knife with me to give to the sheriff. I don't want it around here, especially with Emilia here."

Merina opened the door a crack and peered at him. He could hear her coming back to the door and when she handed him the knife, he saw her lace sleeve.

"Trying on your wedding dress? Just can't wait to marry me, huh?" He laughed and Merina laughed back through the crack in the door.

"You have a way of being where you should not be, Gabe."

Gabe was quiet a moment. "Can I see you in it? I'd like to see you first before everyone else does."

Merina was quiet a moment and then she whispered, "I will open the door, but you cannot come in and you cannot try to kiss me."

She waited until he agreed and then she opened the door. She looked so beautiful that Gabe almost lost his breath. Before he could move, Merina pushed the door partway closed.

Gabe's voice was soft when he spoke. "I can hardly breathe now. I will probably pass out when I see you walking up the aisle."

Merina studied his face and then murmured softly, "Mi amor. I have loved you since Grace showed me your heart. Please go home before I open the door again."

Gabe backed slowly away. He smiled at Merina and tapped his heart. "You put music in my heart, Merina. You make it sing."

He mounted his horse and led Bonita toward the east. He pulled out his harmonica and was playing a ballad as he rode away.

Merina leaned against the door and smiled. She touched her dress and then looked up. "I found mi amor, Mamá. I will wear your dress and Grandmamá's veil. I will try to make you proud of the wife and mother I will be. And you too, Papá. You would like this man."

She put her hand over her heart and smiled as she looked out the window. She couldn't see Gabe, but she could hear his harmonica as its music trickled back through the night.

"You make my heart sing as well, Gabe." Merina smiled as she looked over at the attached school. "I would have liked to teach but I will love to ride horses and work on our ranch with my husband. My heart is happy." She carefully slipped the wedding dress off and pulled on her nightgown before climbing into bed beside her sister. The little house was quiet, and Merina was still smiling when she fell asleep.

Printed in the USA
CPSIA information can be obtained
at www.ICGtesting.com
LVHW051504080224
771185LV00052B/1231